A MATTER
OF
LIFE AND SEX

OSCAR MOORE

A MATTER
OF
LIFE AND SEX

A DUTTON BOOK

DUTTON
Published by the Penguin Group
Penguin Books USA Inc., 375 Hudson Street, New York, New York 10014, U.S.A.
Penguin Books Ltd, 27 Wrights Lane, London W8 5TZ, England
Penguin Books Australia Ltd, Ringwood, Victoria, Australia
Penguin Books Canada Ltd, 10 Alcorn Avenue, Toronto, Ontario, Canada M4V 3B2
Penguin Books (N.Z.) Ltd, 182-190 Wairau Road, Auckland 10, New Zealand

Penguin Books Ltd, Registered Offices: Harmondsworth, Middlesex, England

Published in the United States by Dutton, an imprint of New American Library, a division
of Penguin Books USA Inc. First published in Great Britain in a hardcover edition by Paper
Drum and in paperback by Penguin Books Limited, under the pseudonym Alec F. Moran.

First U.S. Printing, July, 1992
10 9 8 7 6 5 4 3 2 1

 REGISTERED TRADEMARK—MARCA REGISTRADA

LIBRARY OF CONGRESS CATALOGING-IN-PUBLICATION DATA
Oscar Moore, 1960–
    A matter of life and sex / Oscar Moore.
        p.   cm.
    ISBN 0-525-93484-7
    I. Title.
PR6063.06718M38   1992
823'.914—dc20   91–44639
                                          CIP

Printed in the United States of America

PUBLISHER'S NOTE
This is a work of fiction. Names, characters, places, and incidents either are the product
of the author's imagination or are used fictitiously, and any resemblance to actual persons,
living or dead, events, or locales is entirely coincidental.

To James,
for all his help,
and
Patrick, for all
his love.

CONTENTS

Dear Mrs Harvey,

I have known I would have to write this letter for
two years. It has taken me that long to finish the
manuscript you will find enclosed.

Hugo and I argued long and hard as to whether I
should send it to you in advance of its publication. I
don't think we ever completely resolved the debate as to
what sending it to you would achieve, for you or for us
or for the book. However, we both felt you had the right
to see it before it was published.

You must be wondering who I am. We did meet,
briefly, at Hugo's funeral, two years ago. I don't expect
that you remember. Although I was not one of Hugo's
oldest friends – indeed, when he died we had known each
other maybe only six months – I came to know him
extremely well. I spent most of the day with him for the
last two months of his life. That wasn't difficult. We
were both in the same hospital ward. That was where we
met and so often coincided. Sometimes as visitors. Later
as patients. Both there for longer and longer stretches.

Hospital could have been a miserable place, a kind
of ante-room to the tomb. Indeed, with Hugo gone it has
become that and thankfully I spend less time there. But
while we shared our lunch hours and afternoons, I was
transfixed and happy listening to his stories, feeding him
his pills and his high-protein mush, arguing with him
when he became sullen and laughing with him as he
relived the more absurd moments from an unusual past.
But to me it was not so much the life that was unusual as

the candour with which Hugo shared his experiences. I suppose that was what attracted me to Hugo and the idea of writing this book in the first place.

As you must know, Hugo was an excellent storyteller. He could give the most fleeting anecdote its own sense of drama. They were the cautionary tales in which he, the hero, was the ridiculous, but also the naive, protagonist. He told them not from a desire to shock and surprise but in the belief that the same things had happened to other people everywhere in different ways in different arrangements and combinations. For Hugo sex was both an addiction and an absurdity. He used to describe his life as one long battle between his head, his heart and his hips. He never doubted that the hips would win.

Hugo once said to me that he could not regret anything that had happened to him because in every instance it had been his choice and in every instance he had been aware that he had no choice. He relished his mischievous adventures among the lowlife. He saw himself as having sneaked out the back door while no-one was looking, just to take a peek, and like the little boy with his nose squashed against the sweet-shop window, he couldn't tear himself away. He was his own victim. All along he knew the sweets behind the glass were poisoned, but he enjoyed them too much to put them down. But Hugo never blamed himself for the way his life ended, and he never blamed anyone else either.

He certainly didn't blame you or any of his family for anything that happened to him. He was very worried that you might interpret this book as some act of revenge by proxy. Hugo was as candid in his opinions of the rest of his family as he was in those of himself. He used to say to me, as we argued about how I should broach this whole issue with you, that you and his sisters and your husband had the misfortune to be his most easily accessible material. You were the people he looked at first and studied longest. You were also the people he loved and knew best. This book is not some poisoned dart fired from the safety of the grave. You are his victims only in so far as he made use of your stories to help tell his own. It was very important for Hugo that I explained this to you.

Hugo's greatest sadness was that he died before you and your husband, and that he had to inflict that wound, the worst wound of all, the loss of a child. As Freud said, it is only after the death of one's parents that one is free to die. Hugo died without permission.

I think I have said enough. And very probably much too much. The rest should speak for itself.

Yours sincerely,

Oscar Moore

I

TWO WHEELS TO PARADISE

Hugo was a liar. Of course, he lied to escape punishment and ended up being punished for lying, but he was also a fantasist whose lies invented a world where everything was extraordinary. At primary school while toying with the rose-hip syrup slopped in the middle of his semolina, he would entertain the girls with stories of his youth in India (the large pink place on the classroom map) and explain how the vestigial third ear joined to his real left ear was the swelling of a poison bee sting.

Everyone lied at primary school. Rosemary's father was Batman and her brother was Robin. Mandy's father had a stable of horses (in addition to the polite pony she trotted around Hadley on Saturday mornings), and Jonathan's father was always about to move up the ladder of the monopoly board and buy a house in Mayfair. Hugo soon countered that with the lie that his father had bought a house in Curzon Street, and when a new boy arrived late at St Monica's C. of E. Primary School for girls and boys, Hugo and his little sister together lied about the two houses their parents owned in Hadley. One large and one small. They always seemed to go back to the small one but that was explained by their father's constant absence in foreign parts. Somehow he was always back in time for PTA meetings and the school play.

At this stage Hugo still had a rough idea what was true and what wasn't and his classmates also had a rough idea that everything he said was untrue. He was already an odd fish, always skipping with the girls and never playing football with the boys. Quick-witted and smart-lipped he had no real friends and no real worries. Except for money. He had no real money either and that worried him. It worried him even more that his parents didn't seem to share his concern.

Hugo had always been convinced that he was born to greatness. But at seven years old Hugo's idea of greatness had little to do with the world arena and much more to do with social

5

notch-counting on the Hadley yardstick. A lot of things counted as notches in Hadley, and each one was etched on Hugo's mind: a big house with more than four bedrooms and a long garden with an optional pool (indoor was beyond comprehension, outdoor was useful only to show off with), model cars with pedals, roller skates with fibreglass wheels, two cars (one Jag) and a two-car garage, holidays in Gibraltar or Majorca and a pony for the eldest daughter. Later of course the eldest son would get a moped then a motorcycle and, if he was still alive by seventeen, driving lessons. Several sons of Hadley never made it to the driving lessons. That was the down side of the notch-counting. But Hugo was too young to understand about teenage death and parental irresponsibility. He just wanted his father in a bigger car and the family in a bigger house.

Some might balk at a child so precocious, so aware of the accoutrements of wealth before his pocket money had reached double shillings, but Hadley was in large part to blame.

The daily walk to school was enough to instil in Hugo a keen sense of social lacking. Hadley was a hill and the Harveys lived at the bottom of the hill. As Hugo walked up the hill every morning with his sisters and his satchel, he watched the houses get larger and the cars get newer. He spotted (and notched or etched) the Jaguar on the red-gravelled drive that belonged to Mandy's father (Laura's father had one too but Laura didn't have long hair) and the Mini that her mother drove (Laura's mother had one too but her mother wasn't called Bunty and wasn't a social yardstick). He clocked and ingrained Clifford's Raleigh Chopper abandoned in front of the door to the garden extension and Simon's Scalextrix visible through the window of the den. He even winced slightly as he noticed that David (whose parents hadn't been that rich last year but then took him by surprise by leapfrogging up the social ladder to a top of the hill house) was no longer walking up the hill to St Monica's, but had a new purple uniform and cap and was walking down the hill towards the tube station. He had gone private. It happened to a lot of the little boys at seven. By the time Hugo was eleven there were only five boys in a class of twenty-four. All the other boys had been taken away to schools where you learnt French, sat exams and had to study on Saturday mornings.

Despite the lowly altitude and therefore lowly stature of 40 Mulberry Drive, Hugo had no problem acquiring the attitude of the rich. A talented liar who, at a safe distance from his house, could invent all the attributes and accoutrements he had winced at (he would in time disown St Monica's and claim a prep school tutelage with coloured cap and Saturday classes), Hugo despised those who languished below the level to which he aspired on behalf of his parents. He just wished his parents could acquire a similar attitude, and then maybe the money it implied would begin to appear. But as families came and went from Mulberry Drive, moving ever onwards and upwards, Hugo's parents remained stolidly unambitious, displaying none of the devotion to up-the-hill mobility that would have allowed Hugo to rest easy.

His parents were not the only problem, however. There was another enigma at the centre of Hugo's world-wealth view. Sarah Devlin. Sarah Devlin was a quiet girl with a frizz of red hair. She was in the same class as Hugo's older sister, who spoke to her sometimes but said she wasn't much fun. Coming from sister senior who, as far as Hugo could see, was no fun at all, this said something very terrible about Sarah Devlin. But if Hugo had been Sarah Devlin he would have never allowed himself to be so boring. In fact, red frizz notwithstanding, Hugo could not imagine anything better than waking up one morning to find that he had become Sarah Devlin, minus her personality (which was a very small loss) and plus his. How he would have swanned into school and stared Mandy straight in the eye. How he would have lolled in the back seat of daddy's car, sneering so very gently at the other poor dears in their lowlife (less than three litre) bangers. How he would have thrilled when the parents rolled up for St Monica's sports day in all their finery and his mother (now Mrs Devlin) set the other mothers hissing into each other's earrings. Because Mrs Devlin had a platinum watch and a daywear diamond necklace, and Mr Devlin drove a brand new Rolls Royce which he changed every year and Sarah Devlin had a horse which she trotted on the green in full riding outfit.

But although Mr Devlin was a millionaire (the first Hugo ever saw) and although the Devlins lived in a very large house with a pool (with special winter cover) and although Sarah was regarded with the sort of awe reserved for visiting royalty and pop stars, she didn't seem to be having any fun, which seemed to Hugo not only a terrible waste, but a terrible mystery. After all, how could being rich not be the best fun in the whole world? Sister senior said Sarah was lonely because she didn't have any brothers and sisters, but Hugo would have gladly traded sister senior (and at a very difficult pinch sister junior) for Sarah's house, family, pool and prospects.

Sarah Devlin bothered Hugo for a while, until she went to the big school with sister senior and disappeared from Hugo's horizons. Money irked him for a lot longer, never really disappearing from the immediate foreground. But something, as he passed seven and eight and nine, was beginning to make Hugo feel guilty. By the time he reached eleven and Class One at St Monica's C. of E. School for the Children of the Comparatively Affluent, Hugo had been feeling guilty for some time. And he was beginning to think that he had always known why.

Although he still didn't really know what the word meant or implied and definitely didn't know what it involved he knew that at the back of all this guilt and uneasiness and his very bad moods that came on at a moment's notice was sex. And he knew that what made it worse, and made his moods so difficult to explain when mother told him to snap out of them, was that he couldn't tell anyone about why he felt guilty about sex. He didn't know what to say, but he knew that what he couldn't say he shouldn't say anyway. So he didn't. And still he felt guilty.

Not all the time, but often. He felt guilty for playing dressing-up with sister junior and her friend Jane and always dressing up as a woman. He felt guiltier when Jane's mother looked round the bedroom door and gave him a long, hard look. He felt guilty for not liking football and getting cross in kiss-chase. He felt guilty because he was upset in a way he didn't quite recognise when the butcher made a fuss of his sisters and not of him. All the women made a fuss of Hugo because he was so polite and so quiet and didn't kick balls through kitchen windows. That made him feel guilty too. When Adrian down the road's mother told him that she wished he was like Hugo and didn't keep coming home covered in mud from swinging against the river bank from the end of a rope, he felt very ashamed. It was hardly surprising that the boys down the road didn't like him and called him names.

It wasn't that he wanted to be one of the boys down the road.

The boys down the road were stupid and failed exams and they weren't going anywhere because their parents still lived in Mulberry Drive and they, unlike Hugo, had not been born to greatness. But when the older boys stripped to the waist to swing on the rope by the brook in the fields at the end of the road, they still gave Hugo that funny feeling in his stomach that mixed up pleasure, just out of reach, and pain, from the pleasure being out of reach, the same feeling he got when he stared at the naked men on the beach on family holidays, and noticed how the tops of their bottoms showed above the tops of their trunks. He still didn't know what the pleasure was, but as he grew older he knew that it had a lot to do with seeing men without their clothes on.

It was the same with the dream. Hugo loved his dream. He wished he could have it every night and that it would go on forever. The saddest moment was always the waking up. Hugo would try and shut out the light leaking through the orange patterns of the curtains; fighting the feelings of loss and desperation, he would try to ignore the trickle of noise coming from his parents' bedroom upstairs. The day must not start. Breakfast and school and life must wait. He had to go back. He never could. And, like everything else, he knew he wasn't really meant to.

The dream was paradise but he knew it was odd. It was too exciting to be right. Hugo was on an iceberg under blue skies. He was naked and small and giggling. He was surrounded by naked men, muscular creatures whose hairless bodies flexed beautifully as, laughing, they threw little Hugo from one to the other. They were tender and loving as they laughed and threw and caught him like big brothers with big caressing hands, like the big brothers Hugo didn't have and Jonathan's father thought he needed (Jonathan's father thought that Hugo should be playing football not skipping, and shouldn't be so bothered about getting his clothes muddy when he played war games with Jonathan and his big brothers at the bottom of Jonathan's garden).

Hugo was a bright kid and he knew that there was something going wrong. He knew that he should have enjoyed the war games and not just the sight of Jonathan's older brother having to take all his clothes off and take a shower. He knew that he wasn't meant to look and that if anyone caught him watching there would be trouble. He knew that his favourite dream shouldn't be his favourite and he shouldn't be in such a bad mood when he woke up and found it wasn't true. He knew that he felt guilty because he was guilty and he knew that sooner or later he would get into trouble and everyone else would know he was guilty. But he still wasn't quite sure what the name for his crime was and how he was going to commit it. In fact the nearest Hugo got to getting into trouble at this stage was on a campsite outside Quimper where the Harveys had parked their caravan. While daddy cursed and sweated, trying to level the caravan so that the fridge would work, and his sisters started playing badminton and his mother went off to order tomorrow's milk and newspapers, Hugo wandered over to the campsite showers.

He didn't really know why the showers exerted this immediate attraction. Maybe it was because he had just seen a man come out of one of the showers wearing only a towel. But as soon as he saw the wooden slatted building with water leaking out from underneath the doors and men dressed only in towels coming and going, he knew he had found his holiday haunt. The showers each had thin partitions which didn't reach the top of the cubicle. Hugo was transfixed by the idea that on the other side of this thin wall with the gap at the top was a naked man. Once inside one of the cubicles, he couldn't leave. He felt possessed. He wanted to go and play and be a good boy, even a normal boy, but his mouth was dry and his heart was racing and he felt as if he had lost direct control over his actions. So he wasn't surprised, just a little alarmed, to find himself aroused beyond caution and clambering onto the loo seat of a cubicle. From here he could see over the wall, and leaning across he peered into an adjacent shower where a hairy Belgian was rubbing himself, the water lining up the hairs of his legs, the water dripping from his penis ... the Belgian turned and saw him and as Hugo darted away he heard the words, 'Ça va pas'. He didn't know what they meant but he knew they didn't mean come and join me. That was all he wanted to do.

Despite his scrabblings onto loo seats and his peerings over shower partitions, Hugo was very ignorant about sex. And he didn't know who or how to ask to solve this problem. Normally, he supposed, he would have asked his parents, but his parents weren't really that normal. Maybe his father was. His father was a nice man who was very easily embarrassed and who embarrassed Hugo with his embarrassment. But his mother wasn't normal. Nowhere near.

Hugo's mother was a sensible, even liberal, woman, but a woman with a temper Hugo later decided bordered on the lunatic. He would later in life jokingly refer to himself as one of the battered children of the middle classes, the wrong side of the welfare tracks to be noticed. He knew that was an exaggeration. There were children who had it much worse. William Hamilton's mother used to beat him with her stiletto until the blood dried in his hair. Hugo's mother hardly ever used things to beat them with, and if she did it was coat hangers not shoes.

Hugo loved his mother. And he hated her. She was the most frightening person in his world and the only real authority he recognised. She was god. He was quite sure that if the god at Sunday school ever met her he would do whatever she told him to. Hugo always did. So did the neighbours, shop assistants, people on the telephone, the milkman and strangers who tried to interfere with how she was bringing up (or beating) her children, because like many gods, Hugo's mother was violent. She had a violent tongue and a tough hand. She told her children what to do and when to do it and if they disobeyed they would count the cost in welts on their legs. Her flying-off-the-handle was legendary. From the smallest interruption in the order of a strictly regulated system, a trickle of annoyance would deepen to irritation, and within minutes widen to a torrent and Hugo and his sisters would be bumping down a rapid stream of abuse crashing and thrashing about as her hands pulled their hair and she threw and kicked and hit them and banned them from bread and jam and sent them to bed and out of her sight, all the time yelling so loud.

So loud.

It wasn't that she didn't care for her children. She loved them fiercely, with determination and ambition, and they loved her unreservedly in return. Except when they hated her, and that was somehow the same. They were caught up in her cult: the cult of no complaining, of not crying until you really had something to cry about, of unquestioning obedience and dedicated hard work. But mother herself was the creature of a cult. Behind this temper and the welts on her children's legs, lay a legacy of her own childhood in occupied Amsterdam, suffering at the hands of a father who beat and bullied his way through life and ended up with a hole in the carpet, no hot water, rats in the kitchen, rock-hard beds, a son dead in the war, another who fled south, a daughter who fled abroad, and a wife who died of a massive thrombosis while sitting on the loo. Running from this man of mints and cigars whose career had been crippled by the war and whose emotions were riddled with jealousy, had sent mother spinning into an engagement with a wild thing in black leather who died under his bike on a hairpin bend and reeling into marriage to a gentle Englishman whom she took on the rebound in mixed doubles on the Unilever tennis courts. Mother was a very bitter woman. The bitter old man was Hugo's grandfather. The wild thing in black leather he had never known. But the gentle Englishman on the Amsterdam tennis court was his father. And the running woman with fear turning to bitterness in her veins was his mother.

Hugo spent his childhood tiptoeing round his mother's temper, tiptoeing round the truth, tiptoeing round himself. And when he wasn't tiptoeing, he was hiding. He hid behind the garden wall when a stray tennis ball hit the milk bottles outside the front door and smashed them all, leaving milk running down the drains. He hid behind sister junior who had to ask all the difficult questions about watching television, about playing outside, about playing upstairs or downstairs, about playing at all. He hid behind his funny faces and funny voices. And he hid behind his lies. All to stay out of the way of the terrifying temper.

So if Hugo was too embarrassed to ask his father, he was definitely too frightened to ask his mother why he got an erection when he stared at hairy Belgian men in the shower and watched the water running down their legs.

He wasn't even sure what an erection was for. At first it had provided a lighthouse for bathtime seascapes and it wasn't until he was eleven and on a school holiday with St Monica's that he discovered erections were somehow naughty too. Jonathan, who was supposed to be his best friend, although he always sat next to Mark at school, asked him, in front of all the boys (there were only five) and some of the gamer girls, the ones who had already dropped their knickers and flashed their privates, if he knew how to make a lighthouse with his willy in the bath. 'Yes,' Hugo answered, cheerful at being able to do something that the boys did. Jonathan laughed, the boys laughed and the girls giggled behind their hands, which was worse. Hugo had been caught out. But what were you meant to do with the lighthouse if it wasn't to wreck boats on?

His willy was an amusing thing that changed shape and size without cause but Hugo enjoyed its unexpected antics, especially the sudden inside glow he got when it got hard in bed and he was lying on his tummy. As he grew up it used to get hard in the most unlikely places. He noticed that travelling on the school coach with his briefcase clutched on his lap would make it rise and push against his underwear, stirring eddies in his belly that were something to do with sunshine and something to do with the workmen the school coach passed every morning and every evening, stripped to the waist and tattooed, their tanned muscles glistening under sweat. But what did you do with it? Where was it supposed to go and what was supposed to happen to it when it got there? And how were you meant to find out?

Hugo's parents were good parents and they did what good parents do. They thought ahead. They bought books about drugs and made their children read them, making Hugo very curious about these multi-coloured sweets. And they bought books titled 'Where Do Babies Come From?', which Hugo read without interest. He'd already seen all the diagrams of vaginas and penises, wombs and testicles, and all the necessary canals through the penis and into the womb on the blackboard in biology lessons with the hirsute and cheery Mr Groat. Hugo was much more interested in what Mr Groat would look like without his shirt on. The diagrams could have been cattle or amoeba or field poppies for all the relevance they had to his errant dong.

The dong was getting its grip. Its random erections left Hugo breathless with anticipation. He felt on the verge of a major experience, a breakthrough. But nothing happened. The turmoil stayed inside and turned to frustration. As he slipped from twelve to thirteen, Hugo's body ceased to be dependable, reliable or just stable. It began instead to grind and creak into puberty. Hitherto unknown glands were beginning their secret excretions, swellings and tremblings. But they were all bottled up, trapped under the lid of Hugo's ignorance, his father's embarrassment and the lewd jargon of schoolboys.

To make matters much worse, his friends were becoming interested in girls. Hugo could have told any one of his friends that having two sisters, one older, one younger, made it perfectly plain to him that there was nothing particularly interesting about girls. He had discovered that for certain in a medical examination performed on sister junior at the age of five (Hugo was seven at the time and called the ritual 'body inspection'). But other boys had sisters, too, and they didn't seem to think that they counted as girls at all. So, however much he might mutter and disagree, girls were definitely appearing on the schedule. Parties were being arranged to which Hugo was only occasionally invited. He had acquired a reputation for being anti-girl, although this had yet to be officially interpreted as being pro anything else. For the moment Hugo and sex were a moot point. His attitude was easily attributed to immaturity, a ghastly slur on his physical development, but a convenient bypassing of his state of mind.

Although the lighting, the music, in fact the entire evening, was designed to encourage a sudden rush of lust in the girls, seduction had no real place at these parties, as everyone had been invited in pairs, pairs discussed exhaustively on the school coach as boys battled for the right to fumble this girl and not that. The entire event was a long and normally frustrating process of extended foreplay, during which the mythical heroine would suddenly open her legs and lie back responding to some extraordinary open sesame performed by a combination of Paul or Tim or Damian's fingers, aftershave, love nibbles and clumsiness.

The girls were only so many names to Hugo. And not even that many names. They all seemed to be called Caroline, Nicole or Jo.

He had never met them. He hadn't been to the other parties where they had been spotted, selected, branded, and mentally stripped. The girls always travelled in groups and left in groups. They stayed at the party long enough to engender enough gossip, reshuffling, rows (over pairings disrupted by rogue males) and then swept off in cars and cabs leaving the boys smoking post-grope cigarettes (the one bit of the act Hugo could manage with aplomb) and pondering their next move at the next party (would they now go for Nicole because John had taken Caroline or should they mount a counter-attack and maybe sweep off Jo at the same time . . . just for a one-nighter?).

That Hugo was also expected to spend the evening fumbling and snogging (or necking as it had become by then), getting his fingers damp in girls' underwear, made our hero cringe and sweat in horrified apprehension. Girls' bodies were sacrosanct. Why? Because they were untouchable – all pale and hairless with curves instead of contours and breasts instead of chests. So Hugo ate wine gums and got drunk and moped from room to room, sometimes interrupting the rising, falling pink buttocks of a particularly daring couple in some forbidden bedroom – Nigel bent sweating over Nicole, Paul red-faced with intent as he tangled with Caroline's tight tank-top – abashed by his complete failure to make any contact with the forlorn female lump (he was always given the lumps) he had abandoned with the wine gums in the over-dark sitting room where they had been winkingly introduced.

Gradually Hugo decided that he wasn't going to find it any easier getting off with the abandoned lumps that nobody else wanted than with the shiny-eyed girls with shapely curves that everyone else was chasing and whom Hugo found so intimidating. He stopped offering himself for the last tickets in the girl pool, and nobody seemed to blame him. Who wouldn't rather fool around with a bottle of wine and the party drugs supplied by Damian who stole sleeping pills from his father and sold them for ten pence each in the house corridors of the big school? It had to be more entertaining than fumbling through the folds of Sally Lewin. So Hugo abandoned the foreplay game and played the fool instead. He would sneak a thimbleful of gin from his parents' drinks cupboard into a poster-paint pot and crack Damian's dad's capsule into the liquor with the knowing hands of a boy who would spend a great deal of his time and money pursuing, indulging in and sometimes vomiting drugs of any description. A boy who had read his anti-drugs pamphlet like a free introductory offer instead of an early warning device.

As Hugo swayed and tumbled into chemical oblivion, slurring his words, rolling his eyes and only very occasionally vomiting (always in the bathroom, always quietly, always out of ear- and eye-shot), sex seemed to be a very distant menace, a problem he couldn't think about right now but would come back to. Paralysed by downers, his libido was on hold. But the hold was only ever temporary. Hugo's penis, or willy, or dong, was getting impatient. As he sat at home, alone at his desk ploughing through algebra and biology, German exercises and French grammar, his penis, or prick, or cock, would poke out from his pyjamas, and lusts, as yet misunderstood and still unsatisfied, would play in his balls. Hugo was fascinated by this straining rod of unruliness and took to writing slogans on it in ballpen. Rude instructions were scribbled on his belly. 'Suck this.' 'Put me in your mouth.' 'Put me in your bottom.' Instructions that came not from experience but instinct. An instinct that he ignored the rest of the day.

And if Hugo wasn't going to go looking for sex (making do with amyl barbitone), then sex was going to come and find Hugo. It started with the soft-core mags on the upper racks of the newsagents, luring him with lurid covers of polished breasts and skimpy underwear. It was the perfect liberation for a shut-down libido. One curious peek and Hugo was an addict, caught up swirling in the sexual whirlpool. It was easy to hold off when the brain was drowning in sedatives, but on Saturday afternoons, Hugo's sap was uncommonly up and, supposedly searching for books and magazines, he would haunt the corners of the longer shelf racks out of view of the till. He started with the girlie mags in W. H. Smith. He would pick some large and harmless periodical from the respectable racks and then with the assured snatch and stash he had learnt so well while shoplifting sweets with his sister from local supermarkets, he would reach up and remove one of the thickly glossed nudies from above, and, placing it between the pages of the other mag, impatiently flick the pages until he found the lushly overlit, underclad pictures of round-bosomed women, sitting amid lacy interiors in a haze of soft-focus luxury. The pictures stirred him, not the women. He imagined himself in their place. Undressed for the camera and the photographer's eye. Admired and desired, preened and posed in an orgy of vanity.

Gradually Hugo discovered the better magazines in the less priggish shops. There were always the *Health and Efficiency* mags of course. The bulky men and women and their underformed children playing on swings or in the sea or on skis on snowy slopes, their willies and bosoms akimbo and flaccid. It was like watching his father in the bath. Exciting but not erotic. In the 'good' newsagents, however, Hugo found magazines that catered for the more developed tastes and even those with pictures of men, although these last were censored with little black triangles over the groin as the models struck muscular poses against heavily coloured backdrops. The best of all were the magazines with stories, uninterrupted by silly, over-glossy photos. They left Hugo's imagination to picture the clusters of highly sexed couplings in dangerous places. Between the small format pages of *Experience* Hugo discovered an Arabian Nights of accidental seductions, casual meetings leading to wildly overheated sex on trains, in classrooms, in parks and behind garages. This was the world of adultery and troilism, orgies and S & M. It left Hugo shaken and stirred. Trembling by the news-stand, Hugo found this brave new world of untrammelled wickedness too much to be digested between the pages of *Train-spotters Monthly* or *Philatelic News* so he would sneak the magazines under his arm inside his blue quilted anorak and sneak off to the public toilets to read alone in the safety of a cubicle.

Toilets already had a strange meaning for Hugo. They were a tiny refuge. A place where he could be alone, hidden, undisturbed.

All that was missing from Hugo's bumpy ride into adolescence was masturbation. He knew it happened and that people did it although he did not know how and he certainly did not know to what end. What he was beginning to realise, however, was that it was intimately related to erections, and probably to the jokes in Swanage about lighthouses all those years ago. There was something you were meant to do with your erection (other than wrecking bath-going boats) and that was called masturbation. Hugo was looking for clues. He knew he could not turn to his father. His father would just become very confused and tell him to ask someone else or to ask another time or just go away and stop asking stupid questions. Whichever, he would not get an answer. He could not ask his mother or his sisters because they were the wrong sex and even if they did know they shouldn't and he didn't want to know if they did. So Hugo hunted among the top rack girlie mags for clues, trying to find a picture or a story that offered full instruction.

He didn't have much luck to begin with. Most of the magazines assumed an adult readership already fully acquainted with technique, purpose and outcome. Indeed, most of the magazines were aimed at the accomplished masturbator. Why would he, this skilled practitioner, need a quick diagrammatical reminder of his all too regular actions? But while Hugo missed the full instructions, he did pick up some useful indicators. In one issue of *Experience* he read a story in which a desperate nymphette, consumed with sexual appetite, pounced on one of the typical porno characters, 'the man with the very small willy'. The point of the story was to show how men with small willies can still be fun. The nymphette, breathlessly randy and finding herself alone on a suburban train with the midget-donged unfortunate, took the little matter into her own hands, bringing it to a less than triumphant but still very excitable erection by raising and lowering the foreskin over the top of the penis, or in this case the nut, the head, and the helmet. Although it was written to sound like putting up and pulling down a tent, Hugo got the gist, and realised that he had just discovered how to give himself an erection, should one not have arrived by any other means (sun, books, men without shirts). He had just learnt his first guilty secret, in a lesson conducted, appropriately enough, in a toilet cubicle, surrounded by desultory graffiti urging adulterous threesomes with wives, sisters, daughters (preferably underage), measurements, ages and talents provided; the farts, wheezes and alcoholic chokes of local tramps and winos seeping over and under the separating walls. What did Hugo do next? He had discovered how to give himself an erection, but having got the erection he still had no idea what should happen to it.

Adventures in pornography opened up his fantasy world with descriptions, but the magazines went no further than the book about where babies came from or his embarrassed father into helping Hugo beyond the brink of the quivering penis, swollen, gorged, pounding and thrusting (the vocabulary was still new to Hugo) but bursting. Something instinctive told Hugo his journey of discovery had to end with an emission, and that that emission was likely to come from the end of the throbbing, bursting, getting-rather-sore penis. But at this point in his life, just arriving at fourteen after a long time at thirteen, the only liquid his penis had emitted so far was piss. So Hugo started playing with his penis and pissing, in the kind of hazy hope, that maybe the pinnacle of sexual excitement would see the water turn to wine . . . or at least in this case, sperm. Hugo knew what sperm was from 'Where Do Babies Come From?'. He even knew the word spunk, as any self-respecting boy of thirteen but very nearly fourteen would. That was what boys' schools were for. Keeping your vocabulary up to date and dirty. He also knew where spunk came from, but not how. How did those testicles whose scrotum heaved and fell, sagged and squeezed as he stared at its wrinkled puckerings, how did those testicles that Jonathan Mendoza had wrung so hard in the swimming lesson when rugby was rained off and they all had to skinny dip in the chlorine and steam of the school swimming pool (knowing they shouldn't look but looking nonetheless), how for Christ's sake did they push their pent-up spermatazoids up into his intent and impatient erection?

On Saturday evenings Hugo's parents would normally go out. Out to dinner or to the ballet or to the cinema. Mrs Harvey was an eager consumer of all things bright and cultural. She had embarked on a programme of education at relentless speed, with insatiable but generally discerning appetite, towing her cowed and muttering husband behind her. Hugo and his sisters were by now beyond babysitters. So they were left at home in each other's volatile company. Hugo's older sister was a dried-up, unappealing and depressive teenager, who had been bullied by her mother (suffering first daughter panics that Hugo as first son was dangerously spared) into an emotional rubble, bitter, twisted, frightened and bold. Hugo loved and loathed her with equal passion. Hugo's younger sister was his sidekick. He bullied her ruthlessly but loved her unequivocally. She unwisely worshipped him and he unscrupulously exploited her, but they were big buddies, living in each other's made-up games in the Hadley backwoods, hunting, shooting, camping and exploring, shoplifting, smoking, taking drugs (sister as terrified witness, only much later as participant prone to vomit) and plotting to escape from home.

This was a Saturday evening and, true to form, Mr and Mrs Harvey were out. It was already late. Sister junior was asleep and sister senior was working or reading or, for all Hugo knew, masturbating. Hugo was downstairs in his striped bedroom reading and working and wrestling with an inability to masturbate. His penis was on overkill. It was proud, outstanding, hot to trot and would not leave him in peace. It stood out from his pyjamas and dressing gown like an insistent barber's pole demanding attention.

Hugo tried everything to calm, feed, cool and assuage his testy dick. He undressed in the hallway, leaving his clothes in a pile at the foot of the stairs, and lay naked in an empty bath pissing over his navel. The erection stayed, swelled. Priapism was settling in. He splashed about in the warm smelling pale yellow liquid but the water didn't metamorphose and he climbed out sticky and ashamed, but still craving. Craving what? He left the bathroom for the kitchen and opened the cupboard he used to raid for jam every evening after school when his mother was still working.

He scooped soft butter out of a pottery dish and slapped it onto his penis, coating the head thickly, extravagantly, with the yellow cream. The penis was unimpressed. This was a battle. He poured sugar over the buttered knob, the glassy crystals falling over the floor and worktop where Hugo had laid his penis on the slab to be worked over. The sugar was a mistake. As he rubbed the covered cock it grated under his foreskin. Still, thus armed, he was about to trip naked out of the back door into the fields beyond the garden gate and attempt a quivering anointment in the brook when he heard his sister (senior) calling him from the top of the stairs. He darted back to the door. Madame Nosy had spotted the pile of clothes at the foot of the staircase. Hugo squeaked terrified answers from the dining room, praying that she wouldn't come downstairs and discover him, shivering, with a half-caramelised prick already going into decline and threatening to leak melted butter onto the carpet.

She didn't descend but she did tell mother and the next day there were unusually subdued suggestions from that quarter, that he might go and speak with his father. That was unthinkable and so Hugo retired, for the moment, into ignorance, waiting for enlightenment and salvation.

Salvation came on a bicycle.

The Harveys were not rich, as we already know, but they did believe in bicycles. They might have believed in them a lot less had they ever known the alleys of debauchery Hugo was to discover on his trusty two-wheeler. For the moment Hugo's relationship with his twenty-six-inch reconstituted pushbike was chaste and energetic, involving long excursions into the untrodden crannies of suburbia. But suburbia was getting boring. Hugo was always expecting some strange and marvellous vista to open up, as if he would turn at the top of Osidge Lane and discover the Scottish Highlands and vast loch-strewn valleys stretching away into the distance. Instead it was always more labyrinthine council estates with oddly named streets commemorating long-gone colonial battles. He would cycle up grey, cramped Mafeking Avenue and back down grey, cramped Khartoum Walk, longing for these exotic names to reveal themselves as not just road signs, but as secret passwords into some wild African souk. They never did and Hugo began to get bored with his local excursions. So he began to hit the arterial roads. The problem with these was that the lorries that thundered past on their way to distant cities caught him in their slipstream, leaving him wet, dirty and screaming with anger. He tired easily and never seemed to manage to make the long, slow haul out of London without having to turn back before he found the perimeter (in any case the perimeter was moving outwards all the time). And then of course there was always the wind, and the rain and often, quite unexpectedly, both. So it was that day. Hugo was once again trying to find the countryside, some sun-splashed rural idyll with leafy lanes and buttered scones, only a short ride from Hadley. He had already got beyond the known world and was sturdily pushing up the A1 when a slight rain began to fall, a gauze of drizzle that was wetter than it looked and had a tiring Hugo demoralised into considering an early return. On the other side of the road stood a wooden public toilet and Hugo decided to shelter there for a bit before turning round for the dull repeat of the home run.

The toilet was crowded and dank. Three cubicles stood side by side and a tinpot urinal ran along the far wall. One of the cubicles was empty, despite several men who seemed to be milling about as Hugo entered, eager to sit, shit and summon resolve for the long journey home.

Inside the cubicle Hugo noticed that the graffiti had an unusually graphic bent. Marker pen pictures of naked men with towering erections dripping tear drops into supplicant faces were drawn among lewd tales of seduction and intrigue involving policemen, boy scouts, and lorry drivers. But there was something much more surprising than all these painstaking drawings. There was a hole in the wall. A large hole carved out of the wood and looking through into the next cubicle. Getting down on his knees on the floor, Hugo looked through the hole very carefully, very quietly, all the time expecting an angry shout from his neighbour, an English 'Ça va pas!'

There was nobody sitting on the toilet but there were two legs standing facing the bowl. Hugo craned a little further, eager for a glimpse of the pissing penis. But the penis wasn't pissing at all. It was standing up rock hard and steaming as a hand rubbed the foreskin backwards and forwards. Who was the owner of this great cock? How long could Hugo feast his eyes on this glory before being dragged out of his cubicle by an irate father of many and at best packed off on his bicycle, at worst delivered to the police for return to his parents with sound lecture and confiscated bicycle? He looked up further and saw the man's face, upside down and looking straight down at his. He darted back and waited for the tirade. Nothing happened. He looked back. The penis was still there and the hand was still working on it and if he looked a little further . . . yes, the man was still looking at him, a pair of eyes through the little hole.

Hugo sat back, dazed, transfixed. The nice schoolboy from the nice home who did his homework on time and got good marks for it, who was polite to adults and expected them to be polite to him, who was terrible at games but enjoyed it when the boys in the upper sixth took their shirts off, who had friends in the fifth form whom he teased and who teased him but whom he didn't really understand, who had a best friend called Sam whom he sat with in every lesson, that boy, that Hugo, was washed under as a new Hugo with lust in his mouth and hunger in his eye squatted on the grimy floor of a roadside toilet and gazed like a child with his nose pressed to the sweetshop window at the mouth-watering delights within. All the caution and fear had gone. Hugo was craving. But since when did a boy's craving make the sweets come through the window? Sweetshop windows, unlike toilet walls, are made of glass, and don't have holes in them and so sweets, unlike the penis in the cubicle next door, don't come through the wall and little boys beside themselves with desire can't squeeze and hold and lick and squeeze again as Hugo did the big fat penis when the big fat penis came through the hole and entered his cubicle.

As soon as Hugo saw the penis he knew he must have it. In his hands. In his mouth. He sat and stared and the penis went away again. Hugo leapt onto his loo seat and while the last traces of caution whispered in the back of his head, he peered over at the man in the cubicle next door. The man looked at him and smiled. Hugo ran out of his cubicle and knocked at the next door. The next door opened. Hugo went in and grabbed the man and the man held him. His fingers strained to feel all they had been stopped from feeling for so long. The man asked him to come for a ride in his car and, to bad Hugo's relief, nice Hugo answered for him and said no thank you and then the man said would you like to see spunk and Hugo said yes and almost immediately white stuff flew out of the man's penis. Hugo looked. It didn't look so strange. But Hugo still didn't know how to make his do the same and his penis was still standing out, hard and hungry when the man started getting dressed. Hugo clung to him, seizing his wilted penis and pulling the hairs on the man's chest beneath his striped T-shirt, but the man just smiled. It was a distant smile. Not friendly.

Not unfriendly. The smile of it's all over. And then the man left and Hugo stood there, his penis big in his pants and everything clinging to memories of his fingers playing over the man's body. The first time. The first time he touched another man's penis with his hands, with his tongue. The first time another man held him against him.

Hugo was halfway home and singing at the top of his voice before he even noticed how far he had already travelled.

Hugo didn't say anything to daddy about his experience in the wooden toilet on the A1. He didn't say anything to sister senior or sister junior about a man putting his erect penis through a hole in the wall in a wooden toilet on the A1. And he certainly wasn't going to tell mummy.

The first thing Hugo did when he got back from the toilet off the A1, after holding the penis of the man with the striped T-shirt and the teardrop sperm and the it's-all-over-now smile, was to plan his next visit. It put him in a frenzy. His tummy somersaulted at every thought. The distance expanded and telescoped. It was too far to be comfortable but close enough to be conceivable. Secrecy was paramount. Lies were inevitable. No-one must know about the toilet, about the men, about the graffiti and the hole in the wall and the penis coming through it. And no-one would know. No-one at home and no-one at school. From now on life itself was almost a secret, and truth was a rare thing that made Hugo feel queasy. Lies were safe, easy, flexible, and dependable. He lived his lies and believed them.

It wasn't, however, that difficult getting back to the toilet on the A1. Not with a bicycle anyway. Hugo's mother loved the idea of physical exercise. 'A healthy body is a healthy mind' was one of her favourite sayings. Another was that the first sign of intelligence is using that intelligence. Lazy people were stupid people. These were strong guidelines. They meant hard work. Self fulfilment. Personal blame. They also meant that long cycle rides were allowed, even in the drizzle and bluster of autumn.

One week later, on Saturday morning, as soon as was respectable after washing up and making the beds, Hugo set off for the A1 and his wooden-walled toilet. His thoughts were in a frenzy of imagined possibilities as his feet pounded the little pedals round all the way down the A1 towards perdition.

The toilet made no scruples about welcoming Hugo to its collection of drifters, drivers, surprised married men and devious older men, a gallery of rogues and leers and penises emerging through holes carved so large legs could push through and people had couplings and grunts through the walls themselves. It was a palace of dark scrawlings. Lust crawled up its walls in tales of seduction and incest. It was Hugo's new theatre, his playpen. He was the star attraction in the skid row music show. The nice boy with the nice parents kicked up his heels with a squeal of delight. But who were his partners in the toilet tango? Old men, lorry drivers, fat sweaty men who gave him ten pence pieces and asked him to come back and a man with a van and a wood nearby. The van and the wood nearby were when the nice boy's warning voice repeating the child's maxim, 'Don't get into cars with strange men,' was drowned by the voices of lust. 'You know what you're doing. You can run fast if things get nasty. This is fun.' And the voice of the groin saying, 'Go for it, go for it, go for it, go for it.'

Hugo was hypnotised and happy. At fourteen years old he climbed into a van with a strange man and drove to a strange wood in the middle of the country.

The man, who was older than Hugo would have liked (but young Hugo liked older men with hair on their chests and bellies and backs), led him with a soft voice and friendly gestures to a clearing of dead leaves and dead twigs. He put down a blanket and they took off some of their clothes. The man started playing and Hugo started touching. The man played with his penis and Hugo's penis and Hugo touched his chest and his back and his balls and his penis. Hugo's penis was the best lighthouse in the ocean and the man told him so. And then the man spat sperm and Hugo's penis had still done nothing.

The man's penis shrank away from Hugo's touch, curling into its foreskin like a frightened snail. But the man didn't leave Hugo lying there unhappy on the blanket in the middle of a strange wood. He didn't stab and strangle him as all the old ladies in life say strange men will. He started rubbing Hugo's lighthouse. He rubbed it up and down. The foreskin tickled the knob and the knob swelled and swelled until Hugo could feel the blood pushing so hard he thought one pin prick would make a fountain of red spurt out into the trees. Then something turned in his stomach. Then his penis began to glow and tickle but not an itch-tickle. It was a tickle as if he needed to piss but couldn't.

He thought he should tell the man to stop but the tickle had him in its grip and Hugo couldn't move. He just twisted inside, twisted and jackknifed and the tickle grew and travelled back down his penis into his balls which rose and tightened and squeezed. He thrashed. His penis lit up and giggled. It was climbing into the sky and he was being pulled after it. It flickered and twitched and he knew he was going to piss and then an unknown hand squeezed his balls and he exploded. He spattered the man with clear liquid but it wasn't piss. It wasn't white either. It was the long-pent-up sperm of no masturbation. It was the long re-strained sperm of a body desperate to release itself but unable to find the catch, to spring the lock, to send the spray flying into the trees.

Hugo writhed. The pleasure was an agony. The agony was unbearable pleasure.

There Hugo lay. He stared up. He looked down at his stretched and still-tense stomach splashed with yellowish drops. He looked at the man in a checked shirt lying next to him and now instead of desire saw age, instead of sex saw fat, instead of pleasure saw disgust. Hugo fell back and the man started talking, irritating but then soothing the disgust that had leaked into his head. 'What's your name?' asked the man and Hugo told him. 'Oh dear,' said the man. 'I wouldn't call yourself that. People will remember that. Call yourself something people won't remember. Something people won't find you out by.' And there, on his back, first spunk sticky-ing his still-hairless belly, David was born, aged fourteen and wise beyond his years.

2

THE TOILET TANGO

Seduced at the age of fourteen in a littered coppice off the A1, Hugo dropped his shorts and danced to the strains of the toilet tango. Well, not Hugo exactly. David. But David was Hugo. David was Hugo's cover, his protection against people who might call, people who might look for him, people who might find him round the tea-table over bread and jam and a slice of cheddar cheese. And gradually David became more than that. He became the other one who wasn't quite Hugo but did what Hugo didn't think he should. He became the naughty one, the one who dared and lied and laughed. The one who played in strange men's bedrooms, cars, offices and kitchens. The one who didn't have a family, who didn't have any sisters senior or junior, who didn't have any school to go to or tea to go back for. David lived to dance and he danced them off the toilet floor.

The toilet tango was not just any dance. There was no music written for it and the steps were unrehearsed. It was a ritual of silence, interrupted by the odd mutter and the occasional, inevitable grunt, but there was no talking and very little smiling. It was a tense, intense, often boring, but always inviting routine for two . . . or more.

You couldn't just tango in any toilet, either. You had to find one with the right mood, the right people, and the right facilities. Cleanliness was a bad sign. Gleaming copper pipes and polished porcelain urinals, lovingly mopped by the man reading the racing form behind the frosted glass, meant polite piss and no dancing. Eyes might flash and teeth flash back, men might fumble as they tucked themselves in, shaking a little too often, lingering a little too long under the notice that said, in polished blue on white, 'No Loitering', but they always went quietly, knowing full well that no loitering meant no dancing. Dead territory. The writing was on the wall and not all of it was polished blue on white: a few football slogans, some furious racism, a half rubbed-off story about a man whose wife wanted three men in a bed and was as horny as hell but that was two years ago according to the date at the bottom.

No dancing there.

The best places were the dark places. The neglected corner of the park, down a little backstreet, at the back of a car park. Dirty, but not too dirty. Crowded, if you were lucky. And though there, too, there were drawings on the wall, they told a different story. Football toughs and smouldering racists gave way to sexual hermits, dreaming up lurid concoctions of age and gender while waiting in silence behind the cubicle door.

David never drew on any wall, but, like Hugo with his stolen porn mags, he read their contents avidly. And if there were enough, if the stories were dated and the dates were recent, if the ink was still unfaded, unscrubbed, then he knew if he showed a little patience and a little self-control someone would come in.

You had to be careful with the stories, careful not to get too turned on, not to finish before anything had started, not to come before anyone had arrived. Some of the stories were very good. Some were very ordinary. Tales of incestuous couplings with teen-age cousins and sons and daughters, with policemen who demanded servicing, with lorry drivers who took sixteen-year-old skinheads on long-distance rides. Tales of men with books and videos, with poppers and rubber sheets, with their own place. Boasts from and demands for men with dicks of mythical dimensions. Confessions of men with no shame who wanted to be beaten, pissed on, shat on, abused like a slave, like a dog.

There were often complaints about age. 'Where are all the young boys?' Angry messages moaning about the old men who loitered unwanted in the corner, staring and winking, spurned without remorse. The old men who, taking their own turn, snuck into the cubicles and scribbled, in old-fashioned handwriting, pencilled stories about lacy underwear and old photos.

David swore at the old men. Hugo felt sorry for them. But the old men had no shame. Why should they have? They'd seen their own flush of youth addle into liver spots. They'd seen every proud little cock-tease reject them when there was action but come on to them when there was nothing around and they were too randy to hold it in.

Some of the messages were for the older men only. Young men who wanted a mature master, an older guy for caring and sharing. But mostly it was the young for the young. 'Hairy twenty-two year old wants big cock fun with butch type/skinhead. 18–22. New in area. Own place. Gen. 7.5.74.

For some time David puzzled over who Gen. was. The ubiquitous tango expert who appeared on every wall, in every suburb, in different handwriting; always making offers and requests, numbers. He'd lived through every combination of every copulation and wanted more. He was available between these hours here and those hours there.

It was a disappointment to realise that Gen. meant genuine. A disappointment not only to find that a man of such prowess did not exist, but that what was left in his place was the pathos of doubt, the fear of rejection, of being ignored, of being one of the old men. But then the walls were full of meetings unmet, of hours wasted and appointments missed.

David never kept his own appointments. The men always wanted a second shot; they never understood that David's time was limited by Hugo's parents. And by Hugo himself. Even as David came, shooting across the eiderdown or counterpane, making his partner nervous and sticky, he began to fade away. The sassy street urchin who knew what he wanted and wanted it now, in the mouth and in the bedroom, dissolved, like a mirage, into an irritable, shy, twitchy Hugo, annoyed because another afternoon had trickled away in wasted hours spent hanging out at the urinal, waiting to stick his dick in a stranger's mouth. It might be his dick but David was looking after it, and what did he have to show for the afternoon? Nothing. At best a couple of pounds that he'd blow at the school tuck-shop the next day. At worst a love bite he had to hide and a stain he had to scrub off.

Hugo might try to blame David, but they both knew they were stuck in the grip of this push-me-pull-you partnership. Hugo handed over to David almost as soon as they were out of the front door. Just as he couldn't walk into a shop without wanting to shoplift, he couldn't walk into the open air without wanting to have sex. No matter what cultural tour of museums and libraries Hugo may have planned, David would not leave him alone until he had been satisfied. Trips to the National Gallery or the British Museum ended up in Leicester Square, staring at mermaids on the sea green toilet tiles as the man at the next urinal worked up an erection or hurried off. Visits to matinée performances of set-text classics were spent earning pound notes being sucked by a bearded foreigner in the disused lift shaft of an underground car park on Panton Street.

Of course, had Hugo been saddled with sex in the wooden loo down the A1 in South Mimms for the rest of his adolescence none of this might have happened. Desire might have succumbed to laziness. The cycle ride fuelled by anticipation was hard enough, but the ride back, energy spent, guilt growing, was hard and the hills were long and slow.

That problem was solved by the local council. They handed Hugo a dance-parlour, a tea-room, a cottage – right on his own doorstep. That was the beginning of David's real career. That was the beginning of everything. South Mimms was wild beyond belief, and soon after burnt to the ground. What might have ended with that fire instead found succour in suburbia.

It started on a Friday night. Hugo was on his way to Woodcraft Folk. He had joined Woodcraft Folk because his older sister had. She had joined Woodcraft Folk because she couldn't stand the twittering bitching of the Girl Guides, whose conversation stretched from lipstick and eye shadow to whom David Rees had snogged last week or the pimple on the end of Suzanne's nose. Hugo's sister didn't wear lipstick or eye shadow (she wasn't allowed to), she didn't know David Rees (she wasn't allowed boyfriends) and she had her own pimples to worry about. She couldn't swap gossip with her friends about last Saturday night's snog or giggle as she planned next week's snog because she didn't have any friends and she wasn't allowed to go to parties. For all Hugo knew or cared then, she had probably never snogged. She was never asked to parties anyway, because she wasn't a laugh. Hugo thought that was her fault. He never realised how unhappy she must be. He just thought that she was bad-tempered.

His sister had left Girl Guides and started looking for adolescent salvation. On her way to God, she tumbled across the Woodcraft Folk and a very different collection of girls . . . and boys. After the endless Union Jacks of guiding and scouting, this was the Red Flag of youth groups, where everyone smoked roll-ups and joints, collected Jimi Hendrix records and had fucked at least once. Hugo knew they had fucked before because they liked talking about it so much. The girls knew of teenage pregnancies that had been aborted. The boys had friends who were fathers before O-Levels were through.

Hugo followed his sister because he, too, was on the run from Baden Powell and badges and church parade. Like his sister, Hugo didn't fit in. Not that the Cubs stood around talking about blue eye-shadow and boys. They didn't even talk about girls. They talked about football and they liked getting muddy.

Hugo left when he was expected to become a real scout. There was nothing he wanted to be less. Cubs had been okay. He knew the boys there from the primary school on the hill. He saw them every day. They knew who he was and they knew what he was like. They didn't expect anything odd from him. They knew he was no good at collecting badges which you were supposed to do, and he wasn't very keen on British Bulldog. But that was fine because nobody minded. At Scouts people minded. They started shouting at you. The teasing was harder and nastier, the boys bigger, stranger and crueller. The leaders were not there to protect you but to throw you in at the deep end. It was all part of being a man. Hugo had no interest in that.

One year his parents had sent him to weekend camp at Well End. He could have told them before he went that it would be dreadful. Even the list of regulation clothing and equipment read like a military order. The camp was littered with retired army people who missed their uniforms and were prepared to wear a woggle and shorts so they could get back into the khaki and shout at a few minions. Hugo had no aptitude for being shouted at. This was clear to him when he got stuck during rock climbing.

It wasn't really rock climbing at all. The rock was a tall wooden wall with little ledges nailed on it. You had to tie yourself up with ropes attached above and below to real Scouts in beige uniforms and long trousers, and then you had to climb.

Hugo could climb rocks easily enough, but not sheer planks of wood while being shouted at. He didn't respond to the shouts, he just stared at the wood in front of him, and didn't move. He was pinned to the spot by panic. He looked down, waiting to jump. The faces below him were divided between the boys who hated him because he was a weed and the boys who hated him because they were weeds too.

That was the whole weekend, the whole point of the weekend – an assault course at which boys like Hugo fell, and other boys laughed at them. Hugo missed his little sister so badly, he would have let her play any game she wanted just to have her with him. They could have run off into the woods and played houses. All the camp games were about making war, about getting wet and muddy, getting your itchy green sweater torn in fights, getting a cut and a couple of bruises and smiling through it all. That was the sign that you knew how to play.

That night he cried with shame and discomfort on his brand new regulation ground sheet in a sweaty little tent with two other cubs and several mosquitoes.

He almost cried with rage the next morning when they announced tent inspection. All the clothes his mother had so neatly folded had to be unpacked, unfolded and laid out in the drizzle to be inspected by a fat man in khaki. Each carefully folded and ironed sock or shirt or handkerchief made him think of his mother, of the two of them, just him and her, sitting in his bedroom packing his bag and talking. All these clothes were his last link with her. She had been the last one to touch them, pushing them down in the rucksack without unfolding or creasing them. Now they had to be exposed to the fat man with the whistle round his neck.

On that day he conceived a cold, speechless loathing for loud men in uniform. He wanted to spit in the eye of the fat man with the whistle and tell him how stupid he looked standing there bollocking little boys in a muddy field on Sunday morning.

When his parents came to collect Hugo from Well End they didn't seem annoyed that he hadn't enjoyed himself, which surprised him because they'd had to pay for the holiday and they were normally very strict about making proper use of money.

After camp it was clear to Hugo that he wasn't going to go into the Scouts, so he told his parents he wanted to go to Woodcraft

Folk with his sister instead. There were no badges at Woodcraft Folk, except the one of the campfire burning you got when you joined. There was country dancing and political debates, and no British Bulldog or tests on knots. There were coffee breaks with biscuits. There was laughter and friendliness. But to begin with, Hugo, still shy and uncertain, lurked, shirking the spotlight that his serious-minded sister drew upon them both.

Besides which Hugo was always late for meetings. Not to begin with, but as the weeks went by he'd arrive sometimes forty minutes after the beginning of the evening. His sister always looked puzzled. Hugo would blame it on his bike or leaving home late or being held up somehow, but he'd never tell her the truth. The truth about why he never had to go to South Mimms again. The truth about the council who had given David his very own place to play in so close to home.

It was all accidental again, really. Although Hugo had his suspicions even as he walked up the chipped path to the open door. He was cycling on his way to Woodcraft Folk when he decided he needed a piss. Whether he saw the loo first and then thought, 'Why not?', or whether he really wanted one and the loo was just there at the right time doesn't matter now, but the truth is that unless he was bursting, which was unlikely because he had only just left home, he could have saved it for the five minutes it would have taken him to get to the meeting. He wasn't giving in to his bladder, but to David. David couldn't walk past a loo without investigating. It was like sweetshops had been for Hugo and his sister. They couldn't walk out without having stolen something. And it was like the drinks cabinet at home when his parents went out. He had to have a go, an inch off one bottle and half an inch off another. If only because it was there.

It was odd that he'd never noticed the loo before. It was tucked away, in a little corner of the high street, wedged between a pub and some derelict houses hidden behind billboards. It was a perfect cottage, semi-secluded but with good parking and a strong flow past of accidental customers; Victorian architecture allowing for the right degree of decay – wooden doors with holes, dim lighting, fifty-odd years of graffiti, no space for an attendant, and within easy reach of the shops, allowing for an endless variety of excuses to cover an endless variety of visits.

Inside it was dark and damp. There was a smell in the air Hugo recognised but had never been able to place. He recognised it from other toilets but not all toilets. It was not a smell of piss or shit. It was a smell of sex, stale sex.

One of the cubicle doors was closed. There were only two and Hugo quietly slipped into the other, leaving his bike parked against the stained tiles opposite the urinals. There was no doubting this place. The stories were frenzied and exciting. The drawings were exaggerated and had been added to by many different pens on many different afternoons.

But there was something extraordinary about this cottage. There was a hole in the wall between the two cubicles. A hole in a metal wall. This hole hadn't been drilled or gouged out. This hole was in the metal and had always been there.

It was at just the right height so, if Hugo sat on the toilet seat in one cubicle, he could see the hands of the man masturbating in the next. He crouched down and looked up until he caught a glimpse of the face staring back at him.

There was a protocol about walls with holes of this size. A protocol everybody knew even though such holes were rare and rarely lasted long, usually being boarded up by diligent toilet maintenance men. Depending on what you saw when you looked up through the hole to the face of the man in the cubicle next to you, you either curtained the hole with a sheet of wetted toilet paper or you put your finger through the hole and wiggled it. The first message couldn't have been clearer. The second message was a formal invitation to the man next door to stick his dick through the hole.

This was not always easy especially if, like Hugo, you were tall. Although the hole was perfect for sightlines, it was at a very inconvenient height for anyone who didn't have very short legs. But with knees bent and belly pressed against the cold bumpy paint of the institution blue wall you managed somehow, for the sake of that first shivering sensation of warm, strange lips and a warm, strange tongue closing over the end of your dick. Standing outside by the stained tiles and the chipped urinals waiting for a cubicle to become empty, David could sometimes hear the first faint gasp of pleasure as one man's mouth reached another man's prick.

Of course there had been a hole at South Mimms. Many holes in fact. But this place was on Hugo's doorstep. It had always been there. He had walked past it a thousand times. It was opposite the bread shop where twice a week on holidays he collected the bread. It was opposite the office block he had watched being built from the windows of his parents' sitting room.

David wanted to hang around, to lure the man from his cubicle. David wanted to take over but Hugo had to get to Woodcraft Folk and his sister, coffee and biscuits and country dancing. He shouldn't be here now, he thought as he bent down and looked through the hole at the hands of the man masturbating in the next cubicle. In the darkness he could see his body lean forward and peer back through the hole at Hugo's blinking eye. Hugo stood up quickly. He was breathless. He opened the cubicle door and went back to his bicycle.

He was halfway down the high road before he looked back. Standing at the end of the little path, staring after him, was a dark-haired man of medium height. He never saw that man again. That was life in and out of cottages. Strangers' faces. Sex for ten minutes with a man whose name you never asked and never saw again. Only a few turned up again and again. Like David.

If Hugo hadn't found this twenty-four-hour tango parlour right on his doorstep, his life might have been different. But now, alerted to the fact that such pleasure palaces lurked on high streets across suburbia, Hugo, David and the bicycle became a three-way conspiracy. They made a great team. Hugo did the lying, the oiling of the domestic waters. He played on his mother's prejudices and snobberies, inventing stories about trips into London that never happened, and when they did were not spent as he said they were. Today it was an art gallery, tomorrow a library. She never asked him what he'd seen. Secretly he wondered how much she guessed, how much she knew, how much she feared but didn't want to find out. He had had some close shaves. Once, driving up the hill in the front seat of a strange man's car he saw his father's car approaching. He ducked in his seat without saying anything to the man next to him, who stared at him in surprise. Afterwards Hugo felt terrible pangs of remorse. His father had been smiling. Probably listening to the radio. The fact that he could have had no idea that Hugo was in the car going in the opposite direction, calling himself David and wearing his pants round his ankles, made him feel sorry. Sorry for his father. Sorry that he had been so bad. Ten minutes later David was spreadeagled on the front seat down a quiet lane, the man next to him chomping at his groin as a smile flickered about David's lips. His brief flirtation with conscience had been quashed by lust.

It wasn't long after that that David, spreadeagled once more in another car with a different man, gazed dreamily through the car window as the sensation of a strange mouth massaging his groin flooded his thighs and belly with pleasure, and looked into the wide, painted eyes of an old lady. Her lips were parted in a grimace of shock and he could see where the lipstick had smudged onto her front teeth. She was out walking her dog and had stopped to peer into the car. Her nosiness had not prepared her for this, however. She was transfixed. David smiled at her. She walked away and he watched her reflection in the wing mirror as he heaved a load of pent-up spunk into the driver's mouth. The driver had had no idea what was happening. The lady was writing down the car's registration number in her address book while her poodle shat on the verge. The driver (David never knew his name – he never knew any of their names) didn't notice. He was probably visited by police later.

That wouldn't have occurred to David. He had no idea how illegal he was. He was always irritated by people's fears. Scared men were so uneasy, so difficult. He didn't understand why they were so scared. He thought that if anyone was taking the risk it was him. If someone had asked him straight off whether what he was doing was illegal and, if so, under what law, he might have known that there was an age limit on sex set at somewhere like sixteen. But he probably wouldn't have known that he couldn't have sex for another seven years, and it certainly never dawned on him that all the men he had lured and cajoled and bullied into sex (and although not all of them needed cajoling, all of them seemed wary) were, potentially at least, the same men in the papers who were locked up after humiliating trials in courtrooms surrounded by hysterical mothers and troublemakers. It was only much later that he realised that the Playland scandals of Leicester Square saw men he knew if not by name at least by smile and address and shape of cock locked up until the end of the next ice age. In the rough and tumble and two-quid-for-chocolates-after of David's sex life, he had been blissfully unaware that his sexual appetite could spell the end of someone's perfectly civilised chintz-and-glass ornamented life. That he was like a black widow capable of administering not death but worse, torture as a nonce in a British jail. And although he was never a blackmailer, and not interested in fear, the danger would have given him an instant hard-on had he known.

The fun was having sex in front of people who couldn't see you or people who could have done but just didn't look. There was the time David was lying in the scraggly brush of local woodland with a bulky merchant seaman whose lorry was parked up the road when a gaggle of mothers and push-chairs went by. They didn't stop. They didn't even look. Neither did the mothers. And there were his trysts in the disused car park lift shaft off Panton Street, which, if anyone had cared to look over the fence at the top where the shaft reached the open air, would have revealed a man and a boy with their trousers round their knees locked in a clinch, the one feeding off the other's hanging fruit. The whole eroticism of thinly veiled seduction and thinly concealed sex led David to bolder and better coups. He collected men. No, he collected incidents. He could trap someone in the street with a look, have him turn around, abandoning any shopping or errands he may have had to do or run, and trawl him back to a lair; a cottage, an alley, a dark corner, even sometimes in the heat and dust of summers, simply a secluded corner of an open park. The cottage was also his refuge. The beehive which the drones were guaranteed to visit. It was his holiday home, his weekend retreat, his refreshment stop on the way to and from home and the shops, home and the library, home and school.

And all the time, Hugo who may have disapproved of David's more unorthodox manoeuvres, protected him, piling the lies on thicker and thicker. The bicycle provided the perfect cover, with its connotations of healthy pursuits. But cycle rides took whole afternoons. For quicker visits Hugo devised snappier alibis and took advantage of every opportunity – the dentist or the doctor or a shopping errand, each of them allowed for quick visits – and if he was late, Hugo blamed it all on errant buses and super-market queues.

Hugo worked hard to keep David happy, although they seemed to have less and less in common. David was terse, sometimes even rude. He preferred to appear tough, even dirty. Hugo was shy where David was brazen and yet talkative where David was sullen. And for all David's street-tough masquerade, it was Hugo who frightened people.

David was always looking for people with a place. People with their own places were the best, because then the fun could go on for longer, could be wilder, could be naked and out of control. He loved trampling naked across the domestic landscape, the siren dragging his victim into the pit. But once sex was over and a spent David dissolved, leaving tense and testy Hugo in his place, David's catches were unnerved to find an intelligent, nicely-spoken local boy in their house. It was as if they felt they had less to fear from the tough little tyke who might blackmail them than from the nice local schoolboy who might tell his parents and remember the ad-dress.

But if Hugo was the wise one, David was the expert. He knew every cottage and all the regulars.

He hated the regulars. Most of them had had him once. He didn't like having people more than once unless there was some-thing special or they had a place. He was always waiting for the glorious stranger – the big, tanned, hairy man. The insipid moths of cottage life who spent their afternoons (like his) wandering from cubicle to cubicle, cottage to cottage, the lip-licking creatures in the too-tight T-shirts, weren't what he wanted. They were just what he got, most of the time.

The Hadley find, between the pub and the billboards, led to others across town, up hills and down streets Hugo had known all his childhood. Within weeks David knew every hole in every doorway; which one looked over the urinal and the row of rising and falling dicks; which one gave the sweep of profiled faces, chins, sagging jaws, running noses, baggy eyes; which one panned the waiting line leaning against the stained tiles for the cubicles to change over. He knew the hours too.

There were peak times for cottages and long, dull, empty times. Early mornings were busy, when men emerged from their households, suited, washed, shaved and horny, looking for a blow-job before the bus ride, before the nine o'clock meeting. Something to take the pressure off.

Lunchtime in the high street was hot but cautious. People were randy but worried about their jobs. Nobody knew who else was about. There was no getting into cars in the daylight. Hugo didn't like that either. His mother and his mother's friends shopped at the supermarket and all the little greengrocers, stationers, butchers, and delis lined up along the high street. They were in and out, eyes sparkling, teeth bared, looking for gossip. It was bad enough that they had seen Hugo and his sister shoplifting at Waitrose. There was no need for them to see him in a strange car with a strange man taking off for a strange house. If he did get into a car he sat on the floor until they were safely through the danger zone.

In between times could be boring. An empty cottage might hold great potential but usually meant long hours standing still, waiting with the flotsam, the old men who could loiter and dribble away their hours with such patience that David would end up wanking in front of them as if they weren't there, or as if they were some distant audience. He felt like a stripper toiling and sweating under cheap strip lighting or broken down lampshades with under-wattage bulbs in front of a gathering of old men, straining for the relief of an orgasm which, when it came, was only a spasm without the shudder, an anti-climax that offered no feeling of relief. Just a small grey wave of depression.

But David liked to have an audience. Even if it was the despised old men he wouldn't let touch him. He was a rarity in the tea-dance tango parlour world. A teenager with a big cock and lascivious mind, who'd play without inhibition, who'd get in your car and come in your house without tears or fears. And Hugo was pretty so David could persuade his playmates, his partners, to do the things they knew they shouldn't so near to the crowded pavement, to the respectable citizenry passing by, to the police station and to long prison sentences.

That summer, that first summer of Woodcraft and sex, David devoted hours of Hugo's life to the toilet tango. Standing by the cracked pane of wire-reinforced glass, peering at the passing traffic, at an outside world framed by the jagged edges of a dirty window, he'd wait for a customer, a bait, a prospect. He'd see them coming up the path and suddenly stiffen into the camouflage of one just finishing or just starting a pee. If it was someone he recognised and loathed he'd put himself away and either hide in the cubicle or lean arrogantly against the wall, neither pissing nor shitting, waiting but obviously not for them. He enjoyed that pose. He felt like a drug dealer with good protection. He felt mean and streetwise. He felt in control.

If it was a new face he'd stand and shake his penis as if finishing a pee while his eyes peered out of their corners, watching for the tell-tale signs, the one stroke too many, the eyes glancing down along the urinal, quick and furtive, the hunch of the shoulders, the wariness.

With most people David could tell very quickly if they were pissing or playing. The ordinary passers-by ignored the tension, ignored the eyes, were too casual. Whistling, they sauntered in and out, preoccupied, sometimes hurrying, worried about the bus down the road or the wife outside or the children waiting in the street with the Saturday shopping – a normal life briefly falling under the watchful eyes of an underworld. The ordinary men even pissed differently. They would stand leaning into the urinal as they peed, the gurgle in the drains warning the bystanders to be wary. With a slight moan, a slight shudder of relief they would shake, zip up and leave; eyes never wandering, mission never diverted.

The presence of such a stranger would cause ripples of imitative behaviour from the waiting, watching cottagemen. All the masturbating penises would stop masturbating and shake vigorously, miming the jerks and brisk movements of the intruder. If the urinal was against the wall, and not in little self-contained bowls, all the erect dicks, swollen with half an hour's toying and tweaking, would be pushed down, until almost parallel with the body as their owners stared at them as if astonished to see that they still weren't peeing.

And these same waiting, watching cottagers, David's partners in the secret dances behind the broken glass windows, among the

soggy bogrolls, would switch back as quickly to their dance positions the minute the intruder was gone. The whole cast list was
so perfectly trained, no matter how little they felt they belonged.
And like all good tangos, like all good carnivals, the cast list was
varied and colourful. Married men on the run from loneliness
who took David to high rise apartments, peachy with the smells
of female laundry and did sex with him on the marital bed before
fleeing, ducking the gaze of fascinated neighbours. Quiet men
living in solitary confinement in suburban backwaters with
untended gardens and unhoovered carpets, whose lives revolved
around the television, the Music For Pleasure record collection
and the fridge. Builders who did it in secret corners on site, local
halfwits whose penises had drained their brains of vital blood,
office workers dying to rip open their waistcoats. Men whose
faces flushed red in blotches when they came, who gasped and
leaked a dribble of sperm after half an hour of sweating and
panting. Men with small, floppy dicks, men with hard cut dicks,
men with dicks that bent to the left or to the right or dribbled too
much before they came, and very occasionally men who begged to
be thrashed with a belt and made to lick his shoes.

The game was easy at first, while Hugo was so young and
David so fearless and hungry. Even when the situations became
bizarre, the car journeys too long or the men too strange and the
danger too close, David smiled through his apprehension, clinging
to the hope of an orgasm at someone else's hand with someone
else's body there to touch.

Sometimes he lost it. He lost it with the man in the woods who
asked him to take his trousers off and hung them on the fence
next to the railway track and then asked him take his underwear
off and did the same with that and then tried to ram (not slide or
work or glide or slip) his dick into David's arse. David was
shocked to hear Hugo scream and vanished leaving Hugo bleating
like a baby, clinging to the man whose name he didn't know.
(David never asked their names, even when they asked his. After
all, he was lying so why shouldn't they and what could he do with
a false name?)

Sometimes he just dumped Hugo in it. He dumped Hugo in it
with the old man down the street and he really dumped him in it

with the sickness in his dick that hurt when he peed and leaked pus into his underpants.

What frightened Hugo about the old man was that people were obviously talking, talking about David but thinking it was him. He was being marked out and David wasn't helping.

Normally he wouldn't have known about the old man. He would never have spoken to him if his mother hadn't been too busy cooking for guests who were coming to dinner and had had time to go out and do her charity collecting and hadn't decided to send Hugo instead, giving him a list of doorbells to ring and names to ask for and a little speech to say, which she had made him rehearse over and over in the kitchen, getting the begging bits in the right place. Hugo never wanted to do his mother's collecting but he was still on his school holidays and didn't seem to be doing much, just fiddling about and once an idea like that was in her head Hugo didn't really have a chance. He just had the option of accepting gracefully and going into credit or being bolshy and getting shouted at. The end result was the same.

So he was out doorstepping, meeting all the old ladies down the street who remembered when he was just so high and stood reminiscing in mumbles and dribbles as he stared past them at their dark hallways with dried flowers and long mirrors, waiting for their stiff old fingers to find the coins in their stiff old purses. He was doing quite well. They all remembered his name from when he was a baby, although they saw him every day and walked right past him, muttering into their beards. They all had the money ready in their purses and didn't want to talk anymore than just to give their regards to his mother who was such a nice lady. He was doing very well. He might even be finished in time to watch some television before his sisters came home from school and it was tea-time.

Then he came to number seven.

He knew that the lady at number seven was the one with the dark hair and the flame-red lipstick smudged across her lips as if she'd been smacked in the mouth and didn't care anymore who saw. She wore a blue headscarf and walked at great speed, talking all the time, sometimes shouting, always alone. She wasn't the only madwoman on the street, but she was the only one who didn't drink, so she was feared more than loathed by the ladies of the Union Church, who twitched their net curtains as she walked past.

The mad lady at number seven lived with her brother. Hugo had seen him in the street in a sombre gabardine and a sombre hat. He had a thin face and watery eyes to match a watery smile. He wasn't someone Hugo had really noticed. Like all old men, his clothes were the grey-green of the houses and the pavements, the colourless patina of suburbia, and he just blended in. It was her brother who answered the door when Hugo rang, and he stood there smiling his watery smile as Hugo delivered his little speech. When Hugo had finished the old man started talking and at first Hugo didn't listen because he was talking so quietly. Besides, Hugo was staring over his shoulder looking for a glimpse of smudged flame lipstick and mad eyes. Then he noticed that the look in the old man's swimming eyes was the wrong look: it wasn't the look of a kindly old sir who wanted to tell Hugo a few stories. The way he was grinning, the way he was staring made Hugo listen to him, and then he realised that the old man was talking about David and the toilet at the top of the hill.

'I hear you're a clever boy,' he smiled. 'You must come and show me how clever you really are.' Hugo stared hard at him, nodded, mumbled and backed off down the drive. He felt squeamish with the look of the man still on his neck. He felt terrified that someone might have seen or heard. Number seven was only a few yards from his parents' house, and if the old man knew all about the top of the hill games, they couldn't be far from knowing themselves.

Hugo hated the old man. He wanted revenge. All the man had done was to invite Hugo to come back another day, for games in the black space behind his front door but Hugo was angry with himself because when the man had invited him, he had smiled. Smiled because he wasn't really listening and couldn't really hear until it was too late. By the time he had understood what the man was saying, he had already smiled at him, the normal polite smile of Mrs Harvey's son from over the road, instead of flashing him something altogether nastier from David. What worried him the most was that the man might think his smile was an acceptance.

No, that wasn't true. What frightened him even more than that was that the man only had to cross the road and ring the doorbell and he could tell Mrs Harvey the whole story about her nice charity collecting son and his dick.

Hugo hated the old man because his eyes ran and his mouth leered. He hated him because he was old. He was one of the men in the corner, watching and waiting, as the younger men came and went. Like insects crawling out from behind the stained tiles, the old men were slimed with the damp stench of the soggy bogroll world. Before, none of them had known anything about Hugo or David. But now one of them lived in Hugo's world. David had let one of them in. And every day he had to pass this man, who knew his dirty secrets. And every day he wanted to spit in his eye.

He wanted to spit in the eye of the young man with the shaved pubes as well. The young man with the black curly hair and the thin white polo-necked sweater, who had let an old man watch, wanking, as he and Hugo had sex in his bed in his apartment. The young man who had made pissing painful.

When it first started to hurt Hugo put it down to an acidic stomach. He didn't really know what an acidic stomach was, or what it entailed, but the first and the second time it hurt, he thought that was what it must be. The third time the pain was so bad he had to bite his hand so one pain cancelled the other. His stomach didn't feel acidic. He felt faint.

Over the next two days the bite marks in his hand got deeper. Then the white stuff started appearing at the end of his dick. By this time Hugo really suspected that he had what at school they called VD, but he couldn't be sure because 'Where Do Babies Come From?' didn't have any illustrations or descriptions and the encyclopaedia didn't give you the symptoms, just the history. But he guessed it must be because of what had happened in the flat of the young man with the shaved pubes.

Hugo met the man with the shaved pubes at the top of the hill cottage and had gone back to his flat in Finchley. It was a bedsit with big windows, a carpet that didn't fit at the edges and an old bedstead. Next to the bedstead there was a mean little basin by Armitage Shanks and a pair of dirty toothmugs. In the middle of the ill-fitting carpet stood an old man with glasses and trousers round his knees.

Hugo couldn't remember when the old man appeared, and he couldn't remember being surprised when he did appear, or was suddenly there. They had done a deal in whispers behind the door while David paced the room and probably the man had sneaked in when David was naked and in the bed. It was a good plan because once David was started, nothing was going to stop him. Except this time it really wasn't much fun because the man in the white pullover wanted David to fuck him and David had never fucked before. One thing he noticed about fucking was that you had to concentrate very hard to keep it interesting. Otherwise your dick went soft and slipped out with an unerotic slurp.

David liked men's chests. He liked pectorals and the line of the hair running from the belly button down into the groin. Backs left him cold. Kneeling behind the bent-over body of a young man, pummelling into him while noticing how many blackheads grew in the pale and sweaty furrows of his back, left his erection up only out of habit, not out of any desire. He was fucking the man just as he might have washed the dishes. He wasn't even sure that the man he was fucking was having a good time. His grunts sounded pedestrian, predictable. They left the sexual temperature of the occasion flickering near freezing. The only person Hugo could tell was having a good time was the old man.

The old man stood in the middle of the carpet, panting, his glasses steamed up. David glanced across at him and frowned, concentrating on the rhythm he had to keep going under the sheets, feeling his thighs tire and the sweat prickle on the back of his neck. Hugo was nagging at him to give up and go. The old man winked and gasped, watched as his dick dribbled white spots onto the carpet and, rubbing them in with his slipper, left the room. David tensed his stomach and bullied the arse of the quietly grunting young man. He felt no tenderness, no desire, no need to touch the body or fondle it. With other men's bodies, real and imagined, rotating in front of his half-closed eyes, David finally managed to sink into orgasm, and that at least was good. Ejaculating into the hidden inner spaces of a man's body felt strange, out of control but contained. He shuddered and withdrew, making that horrible slurping suction sound again. The young man farted. Hugo was furious. He had to leave. He was disgusted at the sight of his dick, soiled with shit. Washing it in the mean basin, standing on tip-toe and pouring hot water over it with one of the dirty tooth mugs he felt sure something wrong had happened. The young man slept. All Hugo wanted was to be back safe in the clutches of his family, reading his book in an armchair before being called for tea. He walked fast the whole way back and muttered the whole time. 'Oh no. No. No. How dare he. No.'

But Hugo couldn't simply sink back into the armchair and forget. Because now every time he peed it took him ten minutes to recover enough to leave the loo. And even then he was whey-faced and dizzy.

What could he do? What did one do? He knew it was dangerous to do nothing. His mother had always made his doctor's appointments for him. Maybe he should try Boots. But how did you explain to the lady in Boots, who sat in a prominent pew in the Union Church on Sunday mornings, that your willy was giving off white stuff and hurt like hot pins every time you pissed? How did you tell her about the split second of hope between the first trickle of piss and the first pain? A tiny second when you thought that maybe it was all over. Now even that second had gone. The pain was there gently but insistently the whole time. How could you tell her all that in a queue of Hadley mothers, each one of them knowing that fourteen-year-old Hugo was in the cubs with Paul and at primary school with Johnny and now at big school with Michael and Simon.

Eventually the story had to come out. The pain became too bad to hide. Hugo's mother found him in his bedroom with his head hung between his knees and his trousers round his ankles clutching his penis and weeping. She sat next to him and put an arm round him and he sobbed his pain out. She rang the doctor straight away and he went that afternoon. It wasn't his normal doctor when he got there. He was on holiday. So Hugo saw an old lady with silver hair who examined him with cellophane gloves. She asked him no questions, gave him no words of warning. She just looked, squeezed, dabbed and smeared. Then she wrote him a prescription. Hugo could still remember those pills fifteen years later. They were red and black and called Penbritin. They were angels in capsules. She must have been a saint, this lady doctor. She never asked to speak to Hugo's parents. She never brought the matter up again. She just wrote, in rather elegant longhand, with a fountain pen, the word 'gonorrhea' on Hugo's card.

Hugo never knew whether his mother tried to find out from the doctor what was wrong with him, but he knew that the family had talked about it among themselves and the verdict from Maidenhead, where Hugo had a grandmother he liked and an aunt he couldn't stand, was that he must have had cystitis.

David was dismayed but not discouraged by this setback, although fucking joined two already forbidden practices on his dance card. David, for all his daring, would not let men put their tongues in his mouth or their penises in his bottom. He had banned penises on all counts but the truth was that the pain was too much. He had banned tongues from the very beginning, and even he was not sure why. There was something about the face to face, mouth to mouth that frightened him. It was just too close. David liked sex to be taut and tense. Kissing was intimate in a way that troubled him.

Blow-jobs were fine. Of course. If they wanted to bend and eat as he looked down on them, he would smile and lean back against the cold bumpy wall, pulling his T-shirt up over his stomach, still tanned and skinny, and smile. If they wanted him to eat and suck and bite them, he would. And willingly. He flew at their nipples, their bellies and all the hairy confusion of their balls. But the mouth to mouth was out. He shrank away as the tongues probed his lips, turning his head so they sucked his ears. He shrank away and the men looked hurt and surprised. Annoyed. What was wrong with the little tart? Did they have bad breath? Did he have something to hide? Weren't they good enough for him? Maybe that was it. Maybe of all the men he had been with, he had always chosen them for their bodies, not for their faces and their mouths and lips, and adventurous tongues were allowed to play across his body but not to touch his virgin mouth. David didn't know. Maybe it was simply a question of virginity. Maybe it was waiting for the right lover.

The right lover came in the end, over the wall between the two cubicles in the cottage at the top of the hill, and lowered himself lithe and hairless (shirtless too) into David's realm. He smiled as he looked David straight in the eyes. And without a word he took David's head between his hands and kissed him. He pushed his tongue between David's lips and past his teeth, and suddenly David's mouth was open wide and full of swirling soft, non-stop tongue. He leaned back against the wall and the man leaned towards him, pushing his way further into David's mouth as he swooned unstruggling in the sweet pleasure. They didn't stop kissing, it seemed, until both had come and the queue of irritated men leaning against the stained tiles reached almost out of the door. The strange hairless man climbed over the wall again and disappeared. David opened his door and, a smile still playing around the corners of his lips, walked past the irritable queue, chin up and eyes forward.

Both David's dance card bans were broken by force.

David's mouth lost its virginity to a man whose name he never knew, but whose muscles and smile were bathed in a romantic afterglow like some chevalier coming to the rescue of a lonely maiden. Hugo summoned him for wank fantasies on long, boring evenings wrestling with the sex lives of amoeba and spirogyra. David watched for him in cottages from Hadley to Barnet. Neither of them ever saw him again.

The first man to squeeze his prick into David's bottom occupied a very different corner of Hugo's mind. The Thin Man was no fantasy. He was the real bogroll species. The toilet regular. What you were left with after a long, lonely wait.

The first man to squeeze his prick into David's bottom did it in the right hand cubicle of the top of the hill cottage on a rainy afternoon when nobody seemed to be about. David knew him by sight, as he knew many in his strange collection of regulars. He knew the Scout Master from Ponders End who would always be waiting there at five p.m. on Sunday afternoons, waiting to drive him off to a little suburban flat for an hour of rolling, slapping, sucking, bouncing sex for which Hugo would be given two pounds. He knew the Fat Man who was so round he had to move slowly in the confined space of the hillside tea room, who took David for rides in a grubby van down secluded lanes, who parked the van in leafy lay-bys and bent over David's groin as David lifted his shirt and stared at the great white corpulence spreading underneath.

He knew the Denim Man with the tattooed earlobes, and the Wet-Lipped Man with the curved prick who hung around the loos at the open-air swimming pool.

He knew the Round-Bellied Man who rubbed his body against David's by a brook as gnats bit their buttocks, and who told David he was pretty.

He knew the Blue Cortina Man who always wanted to come straight away so he could take longer over his second orgasm. Who was worried about coming too soon otherwise, and not getting his fill. Who lived in a room with chintz-covered sofas and little lace cloths on occasional tables, and breathed very heavily just before orgasm. Once he asked David if he was still on the game, which was strange because he had never offered him any money.

He knew the Nervous Man who had an office next to the estate agents in Cockfosters where they could have sex because he had the key. He called David 'tiger' because he was so wild, but he was worried when David came across the sensible grey carpet tiles. He had had a tissue ready. David didn't come into tissues. He liked to see his sperm fly.

And he knew the Thin Man.

It wasn't that the Thin Man was so bad. He wasn't. He didn't mean badly. He wasn't dangerous. But he hurt David. He hurt David so badly, David didn't let anyone near his bottom again for a very long time.

They never said anything to each other when they met, David and the Thin Man. That made David respect him. He was obviously a veteran. He obviously wasn't nervous. He turned David round in the cubicle and put his finger up his bottom. David looked at the world through the dirty window at the back of the cubicle that looked over blocks of army flats. He wasn't in control. The Thin Man wet another finger and pushed David so he had to bend over. It was like an experiment. It was like going to the doctor. It didn't feel sexy. It felt like he was being used. His arse tightened as the man shoved another finger in. He didn't slide it in or feel his way, he just pushed. He was in a hurry and wanted satisfaction. David was just another underage virgin. He wasn't scared of virgins. He knew David wouldn't scream. He'd watched him coming out of this cubicle with too many men too many times. He wasn't angry. He wasn't violent. He was just determined.

He pushed David further over so his face stared into the toilet bowl and he was forced to grip the sides with his hands. The rim was damp with piss spray and stray pubes stuck to the edge like mementos. David clung on, knowing this was a test. The Thin Man took out his erection and pushed it into David's arse without even a lick of saliva. David lurched forward as the pain shot up his body. He squirmed away as the man squirmed further in. He howled in anger and outrage and, pulling away, turned to face the Thin Man. Both their erections had collapsed. David stared at him, swaying slightly with pain and nausea. The Thin Man stared at him without remorse, without rebuke. Then he just turned and walked out of the cubicle, letting the door bang behind him.

Another man tried to push his way in and instead of slamming the door in his face, David just stood there, trousers at his knees, a tear stain on his face, his eyes staring past the newcomer, past the curious queue leaning against the stained tiles, out to the street and the fresh air, where the Thin Man had gone.

David hated the Thin Man for the pain he had given him, for the wet feeling between his legs that felt like blood. David hated himself for having bent over so obediently.

Most of all he hated himself because he wanted to run after the Thin Man and apologise.

July 4th 1979

Dear Mr and Mrs Harvey,

I am writing this letter to accompany your son Hugo's school report for the end of his fourth year. I have sent this letter by separate cover as I do not think that it would be a good idea if Hugo were to see it. Indeed, I would even go so far as to suggest that you do not discuss it with him, although this is, of course, your own decision. It is important that, as Hugo's housemaster, he and I trust each other, and he may feel that this letter, going behind his back as it were, damages that trust.

It is only because I feel that you need to be aware of certain worrying aspects of Hugo's behaviour, that I am writing. I am not suggesting any direct action, but maybe we can find the time in the near future to discuss Hugo and these issues and decide how they can best be tackled.

The problem, as you can see from his report, is not one of achievement. High grades seem to come easily to Hugo. He is an intelligent and conscientious pupil whose homework is always on time and always of the highest standard. He takes his studies very seriously and I know that the headmaster fully expects Hugo to go on to take the Oxford and Cambridge entrance examination in due course.

However, the effort remarks on this report reveal a worrying trait. Many of his masters gave him an effort grade of S– (less than satisfactory) and two masters were only persuaded at the last minute against giving him a U (unsatisfactory), notwithstanding his high grades in the end of the year exams.

This is an alarming but not desperate circumstance. My feeling is that by paying attention to this problem now we can prevent Hugo's apparent incipient anti-sociality from affecting his work. Clearly these grades do not reflect the amount of work Hugo has put into his examinations, where his results once again placed him easily within the top ten of his year. They do reflect, however, his behaviour in class, which has deteriorated from the mischievous (a matter we had cause to discuss in his first year) to the almost eccentric. You may not be aware of the fact that Hugo had to be demoted from his position as house sub-prefect earlier this year when he was discovered having 'water-fights' with friends in the house changing rooms. Water-fights may, on paper, strike you as a harmless enough exploit, but that all depends on the volume of water in use. Several boys, who had left their blazers hanging in the changing rooms, as is perfectly normal, have made claims against Hugo and his colleagues for the replacement of their ruined clothes (in which claim, they and their parents have my full support). A basin in the changing rooms was smashed, two toilets were purposely flooded and a teacher, investigating the source of the considerable rumpus accompanying the fight, slipped on a dangerously wet floor and was forced to take a week off school to nurse a bruised coccyx. Quite apart from a lack of discipline appropriate in a house prefect and the bruising visited upon a schoolmaster, the school had to go to the extra expense of bringing in a replacement teacher for the duration of the wounded party's absence. Thankfully there is no intention of charging this to Hugo as well, otherwise we might find we are driving him to theft to meet his various obligations.

There have, however, been other incidents. The

number of times Hugo and his friends have been discovered wandering out of bounds has led me to suspect that there is more to their lunchtime walks than the love of bluebells. The woods in question are a popular venue for illegal smoking among senior boys, and I would not be surprised to find Hugo appearing on a future rollcall of such miscreants. Smoking during school hours while in school uniform is an offence generally rewarded with suspension. I cannot believe that Hugo smokes with your approval or collaboration so may I take the liberty of suggesting a few swift checks on his bag and clothes for telltale traces. Maybe he can be intimidated into stopping. It is parental clout versus peer group pressure in this one, I fear. There is very little the school can do but enforce rules and advise (as indeed we do repeatedly).

This school has a very high academic reputation, and one that it appears to find easy to sustain. It also has the reputation for being a hotbed of subversives of one kind or another, and this is a reputation we seem to be having much trouble in shaking off. While I would not suggest that Hugo himself is one of our main concerns, he numbers among his friends three or four young men whose careers at this school are unlikely to run their whole length.

We have had for some years now a high incidence of drug offences at this school, and while I am in no way accusing Hugo of being involved in such pursuits – innocence must always be presumed until there is evidence otherwise – I am aware that the degree of trafficking taking place within Hugo's year and in particular among his friends is setting new highs (please forgive the pun). Hugo may have told you himself that two of his friends are already up for one term suspensions and may well be expelled for having rolling papers and rolling tobacco at school. We have reason to believe that they have simply hidden the marijuana with which they intended to make their 'joints'. We are currently closely watching three boys, one a close associate of Hugo's and the school may yet take the decision to call in the police, deciding that the bad publicity will be outweighed by the fact that we are being seen to be dealing with the problem in an appropriately aggressive fashion.

I should add at this stage that by no means all of Hugo's friends – and he appears to have many – are such school outlaws. His closest friend, Sam Judd, is widely tipped as a future school captain, and is also one of the cleverest boys in a clever year. But Hugo has become part of a small cabal of school toughs and there are several incidents in which they, and therefore Hugo, may have had a hand. Again I would stress that he can only be presumed innocent and I would strongly advise against taking these matters up with him, but when I tell you that among others they involve the gratuitous smashing of a valuable cello, the severe scratching of the bonnet of a car belonging to the gym master, Mr Bob Tallpit, and the theft of twelve valuable library books (believed to have been sold to second hand book dealers), I hope you can understand my sense of alarm.

My feeling is that Hugo's problem is not really that he is anti-social or rebellious. He is, rather, looking for an excitement that the average school lunchtime probably does not afford him. It was with some dismay therefore, that I learned from him only recently that his reason for not auditioning for the middle school play was because you had told him it would interfere with his exams and that he therefore must not. Nothing will interfere with Hugo's exams more than his possible suspension or expulsion, and, had I known that this was your view at the time, I would have argued most strenuously that Hugo badly needed the extra activity to channel some of his apparently otherwise destructive energy.

Hugo has finished his fourth school year with flying academic colours and a growing sense of unease among the staff that they are not going to see the fruit of his and their labours if he is not taken in hand quite soon. May I suggest that we meet, either before the summer break, which admittedly leaves us little time, or in the few weeks at the beginning of next term, to discuss how his energies can best be tapped to more constructive and creative purpose. I happen to know, for example, that Hugo is very keen to pursue his art lessons and was dismayed to learn that you felt this again was a waste of his time.

I do hope that we can keep this letter and any further discussions between ourselves. Among other things Hugo appears to thrive on the spurious 'glamour' he gets among his colleagues and junior boys for being repeatedly in trouble. It is almost as if it is a matter of some pride to see who can be asked for a special interview by the deputy headmaster the most times in one term, even though such interviews are generally the sign of some rather serious infringement of school rules.

I look forward to seeing you or speaking to you both soon, and would add that I feel confident that we can find a solution to this problem before it becomes a serious one.

Your sincerely,

Neville Grenville

3

VISITING TIME – MOTHER

'She'll be here in half an hour. She just rang to say she's sorry she's late. It's the buses. Are you all right, dear? You look so grey.'

'It's the sky. I'm reflecting the sky. You know, like the sea. It's all I have to look at, so I take it on, and then immerse myself. It's very restful. I think when I do go,' – he looked sharply at the nurse for the sign of a wince, but she was the Scottish one, with an indestructible breeziness like spring, full of life that rang like a rebuke in his overheated cell – 'when I do go, I'll just float up. All you'll have to do is open the window.' Hugo let his head loll to the left, lounging in his mood of poetic bravery. After all, what good was it dying if you couldn't do it with sparkle? He had always been the one to be flippant at funerals.

He resented her coming and resented her not coming. He wanted visitors to be like his little sister when he was ill in bed at home, a little boy in Hadley without a pubic hair, untouched by old men's hands. She always wanted to climb into bed with him so they could both sit there side by side against the two pillows and wait to be waited on. Nobody wanted to climb into this bed. He knew how they felt because he'd been a visitor here too. If he didn't see the look he suspected it. The look of nervousness, of relief that they hadn't been caught.

It wasn't like that with mother, but with mother the looks ran so deep in her lines, new lines, new grey hairs, that her face ripped great strips out of his heart.

The biggest battle every day was against regrets. He'd conquered regrets for things done. The past was not to be denied. He'd owned up to it all and refused to feel repentant, to wish all that undone, unsucked, unscrewed, undrugged. If he was back out there again, without this grey skin, without these lumps on his arms and the scum in his mouth and the whistle through his lungs as he breathed and the headache that froze his brain like an icepack filled with needles – if he was fit and well again, he'd be back there on the dance floor, doing his toilet tango, rattling off lists of excuses to his twittering head. But it was regrets for what he hadn't had time to do that stuck in his throat and made dark rings of late-night tears round his mother's eyes. She stared at him. Not with the breezy zeal of the Scottish nurse, but with long looks through quivering tears that never quite rolled out of her eyes. At first they had, and he'd told her, quite sharply, that she should get her crying done before she came as he had no use for it, and she looked at him so suddenly he knew he'd burned her. He didn't want to. But he hated being her disappointment. He'd always been her champion, making her laugh with a sloppy-jawed face and fake accents.

It was so strange how she'd changed.

'If you ever want to run away, you can come here, you know, Hugo,' said the mother of a friend once, a friend he had inadvertently fallen in love with, a friend whose family and happy, untidy fun he yearned to join. His mother had that kind of reputation, the sort of mother children run away from. But it was all temper. She was the children's sunshine and their thunderclap.

Sitting next to her on the bus coming back from a summer holiday afternoon at the swimming baths and passing a willow tree, Hugo had said to her, 'I like willow trees.' 'Yes,' said his mother, 'they are beautiful,' and Hugo sat bathed in pleasure. He had been right in her eyes and he had won the smile of approval that filled up his chest with happiness. There were other times when they agreed; about the happiness of Christmas (she always managed to be in a good mood for Christmas Day, although the fights on Christmas Eve would leave the children cowering among last year's toys in the upstairs bedroom watching the drizzle fall over the garden and the fields beyond), about the effect of the sun on your mood and how it made the world a suddenly prettier place. And each one Hugo remembered like a championship trophy: amid all the hatred and violence they were his beacons of love.

They were part of his collection of sunny snapshots of his mother as a beautiful woman. He knew each of her dresses, each of her styles and she would consult him about what she should wear for a certain event as if he were her secret gigolo. His

sunniest snapshot was 'taken' outside Aberdeen. They were all
playing rounders in a field of battered thistles with some cousins,
who were athletic and good-looking, and the oldest of whom
Hugo wanted as his own brother. His mother's hair was still
blonde then. With her hair swept up in the wind and a cotton
dress whose sprays of flowers in blues and reds were like wind
through blossom, with her high-heeled shoes, silly but grand in a
stony field in Scotland, he looked at her and looked at his aunt, a
cheerful dowdy creature in glasses and grey hair, and he loved his
mother's style.

'Why did you never run away?' they asked him later; people
who knew him as cocky and opinionated, not cowed or timid. But
he loved her. He wanted to please her. And even when he hated
her most, he never lost his fear of her. He would tell primary
school friends stories about her being a witch so that even the
Jeffreys twins, the tearaway girls with long black hair, wouldn't
come round to play for fear of her. But she was his heroine and he
was her knight, the boy who would win her the glittering prizes.
Her smile, her laugh, would have him chattering away in trans-
ports and one cruel word would leave him stunned and staring
out of the window.

All this was before the diary episode. They had always been
friends until she read his diary. After that Hugo fell from favour
so far, so fast he was the non-person of the house. He could not
be trusted, he was depraved, he could never be believed again.

She said so over and over. But why was she so surprised at his
lies? All the Harvey children were gifted liars. They had all learned
to withstand an interrogation and they had all learned, in painful,
tearful ways, how lying could bring the roof down on your head.
But so could the truth. And, although you got punished more
heavily for lying, at least with the lie you had the chance of
escape.

'Why do you lie to me?' she would yell, a fist in their hair,
hurling them about the room (so that when they were finally
banished to the sanctuary of their bedrooms they would stand in
front of the mirror and nervously comb their heads, watching the
tufts that came out in the comb's teeth).

'Why can't you tell me the truth?'

'I don't know,' they would wail, cowering from the next blow, wondering which was the fastest way out of the nightmare.

Never did any one of them say, 'Because we're too scared.'

They accepted that the truth, even if it brought great pain, was better than lying, even if it brought no pain.

Then, much later, mummy started lying too, lying her way through an affair that everyone knew about and thought no-one else did. And when mummy started lying, it was as if a plank had fallen in from the roof of the world and hit them all over the head. They were too dazed to believe it for a while.

Hugo knew the most because his bedroom was next to the telephone. He knew from the moment that she started talking that her whisper was the whisper of secrecy. He knew that whisper from his own sneaked calls, just as he knew how a whisper immediately suggested conspiracy and drew attention. But mother was new to this game. She hadn't realised how revealing her attempts to conceal could be. Hugo sat at his homework desk listening to the whispered lies, angry with her for not being better at lying. Every Sunday afternoon when her husband went upstairs for his after-lunch nap he would hear the ping of the telephone receiver going up, hear the slightly slowed dialling of someone keeping their finger in the hole as the dial goes round and then hear her first whisper.

'They're all asleep. It's okay,' she always started off and she was always wrong because Hugo was never asleep. Every Sunday and some Wednesdays and occasionally if Sunday was going to be difficult then Saturday afternoon instead. Hugo listened to every whispered word, transfixed, his work pushed aside, compelled by a sort of horror, a sort of fascination and wounded pride, wounded by the idea that she didn't need his help and hadn't confided in him. That, more than anything else, was what made him lose his temper that day.

And then he found out how cool she could be.

It had started in the normal way. Sunday afternoon. Late lunch torpor sweeping the house. His father upstairs snoring. Sister junior upstairs working. Sister senior away at university in Scotland.

'It's okay,' she started, and Hugo's ears switched to whisper mode. She was better this time. Nothing she said was clear, but when she put the phone down and went into the kitchen, Hugo followed her, his eyes burning with accusation, his mind filled with angry disappointment. He didn't care about the deceit, about her double standards, about the torture she had put him through for the principle of honesty. He cared about being lumped in with the rest of his family as irrelevant, asleep, deaf, gullible.

'Who were you speaking to?' Hugo demanded. His mother turned to look at him from the kitchen stool but he couldn't read her face because he didn't dare look in her eyes.

'I was speaking to Kate,' she replied.

'No, you weren't. You were whispering. You don't whisper to Kate.'

'Who do you think I was talking to then?'

She was clever. There was amused mockery in her voice, incredulity and surprise rather than anger. Hugo was getting flustered. His father walked into the room. Mother played the master stroke.

'I think Hugo thinks I'm having an affair with someone. He keeps asking me who I was speaking to on the phone.'

Hugo rushed from the room. He pushed past his father, muttering something about it all being a stupid mistake. He sat in his room, his heart pounding, and thought back to how cool she had just been. He could never have managed that . . . except he did. He did it all the time. Answering prying questions with bald lies. Blank stares. Deadpan words. He knew what she was doing. Maybe she was only copying him. Part of him wanted to tell her he understood, that they both had secret lives and they could both share their secrets. Part of him knew that that was absurd. Things had grown too far estranged between them. There were occasional flashes of the old friendship. He could still make her laugh. He could still persuade her to let him do things, but the trust had gone. It wasn't for years that she found the confidence to tell him anything and he her, in the quiet safety of a dusty room in Muswell Hill. Years after he had left. Years after the diary.

The diary. Why did he ever have to keep it? Why did he ever have to keep it at home?

'Your mother's on her way up,' popped a nurse-capped head

round the door and Hugo turned away from the blinking nightlights of Fulham. 'Let me straighten you up,' said the brisk Scottish face as she walked through the door with hands ready to prop and prod and pump him up in his bedraggled pyjamas, his bedraggled beard and grey skin. The nurse rearranged him and set his hands until he felt like asking her to stay to answer his mother's questions for him, to shake his mother's hand and kiss her cheek and hold her when she almost cried because she often did, almost. But then his mother walked in and the nurse left and his reverie was wrecked. His mother walked in and looked at him and he looked at her. He watched her eyes to see how much worse he was and they dropped and he knew. She looked aged and Hugo wished it was possible to die in a corner quietly where nobody could get emotionally entangled and then send polite change of address cards round the family and avoid –

'How are you feeling?' she asked. Her voice was quiet. Intimidated by his anger.

'How do I look?' He was always pushing her, as if they both had to be punished.

His mother bit her lip and looked out of the window. She was dressed in a grey suit. Clothes for the antechamber to a funeral. Respectful and grim. From the very first, even in those early days when he was just a gamble, when it might have disappeared and never got its grip, people reacted to the illness with such grim faces. With grim mouths they told him to be optimistic and he smiled at them with his practised fatalism and told jaunty tales of other deaths, sounding grand and sometimes brave. But they nodded grimly, as if his wittering was another symptom.

It was as if they were just waiting for the grief and had to restrain the temptation to weep because the moment was not yet there. Their faces were set hard like gobstoppers on emotion. And Hugo watched them all. Stared at them. He didn't have the energy to talk half the time and loved it when they would just ramble on. But only a few people would do that. The others were so reverent they seemed to venerate the disease. It's my spirit you've got to entertain, not my illness, Hugo would yell inside, receiving their little presents of fruit and chocolate with a distracted smile.

'OK, so I look awful. Did you speak to the nurse? Did they tell you anything? They never tell me anything.'

'They said you'd been easier. Slept better.'

'My dreams are terrible.'

'Nightmares?'

'Worse. They are so boring. They get stuck in one frame and won't budge.'

How could he explain how he hated dreaming now? It had always been such entertainment. An imagination that behaved without logic, telling stories that were childish fantasies full of magic tricks, transformations and untranslatable stories. Now they dwelt on a single image and nagged at it from every angle, making him sweat through the night until the bed was wet through and he lay on his back, an arm across his eyes, trying to lull himself into oblivion.

'They're going to keep you in a little longer.'

'Where else can I go? I can't look after myself.'

'You could come back to Hadley.'

Oh, no. That would be returning to live in his own sarcophagus. The twittering ladies of Hadley would walk past the net curtains and nod to each other about the wages of sin and he would sit, propped up in bed with a book he couldn't concentrate on, waiting for tea he couldn't finish. Here at least he could pretend he was in prison. There he might as well already be dead. Nothing more would happen.

'We'd love to have you at home.'

'I'd get in the way. I'm no fun to be with. Anyway, I like it here. Besides, if I came home, then everyone would know.'

'Oh, Hugo, what does that matter? I want you at home. I want you with me.'

'I don't want to come. I need the quiet here.'

'It's quiet at home. There'd be nothing to disturb you.'

'Mother, I'd die of comfort. I need something to complain about.'

He knew she knew what he was saying and how deeply it stung her. That Hadley was too boring to survive in. That her home, for all its armchairs and tasteful pottery, was a worse cell than his institutional bedroom.

'How are you? You look tired.'

He watched her hands pinching and fingering her gold and

coral ring. Whatever she wore and however she painted up her nails those hands always confused the picture. This smart, upright woman, who used to leave him smiling with affection and admiration at garden parties and school visits, had hands beaten raw by bleach and scouring and the grinding rotation of cleaning chores from bedrooms to kitchen. The nails were hard and yellowed, thick and wide, and the fingers crooked. But these hands, chapped and ruddied, capable of terrifying strength that would send blows stinging across Hugo's face and arms before wrenching at his hair, these same hands made him weep with compassion for this wasted woman, who could have been so much and wanted everything for him and now had followed him meekly to his hospital bedside with no accusation in her voice. No accusation in her eyes even.

Things had changed a lot between them since the confrontation in the kitchen. More confrontations. But more honesty. More trust. He had scared her that day. He knew he had. She had told him later, in the room in Muswell Hill. She was scared that he would talk to his sisters though, not his father. She had never been scared of his father. His love she knew she could rely on. But she was worried about her children. What would they do if she left? Would they abandon her? To Hugo, who had decided never to care about her because otherwise he would chew himself up in trying to break through her bitterness over the diary, it was all a sweet, tearful revelation, that she should even be thinking about what they thought of her. But he didn't find that out straight away. He didn't find that out until they sat in his flat in Muswell Hill and she poured out her heart to him. He didn't find that out until the ballet, when she told him, just after the last bell . . . 'I'm thinking of leaving your father.' That was three years after the scene in the kitchen. Six years after the diary. Two years after he had left home in a cloud of tears.

'What have you been up to? How's father?'

'He's away. It's been very quiet. Just the cat and me. Kay came round to invite me to the ballet last week. I just don't understand that woman. You know her brother used to be with the RSC and then did a tour for some left-wing company up in the North East. Anyway she got the tickets because her husband's company . . .'

She was off. Like her long telephone conversations, all that was needed was the occasional punctuation of the monologue with 'uhuhs'. When she finished or tripped up in her flow she would switch suddenly to questions and ask, 'Any news from you?' He would answer, 'Nothing much,' not mentioning news of recent job changes, or now of new medical opinions. When she was in this wittering mood he didn't want to talk. He didn't mind her talking. These days he had nothing else to do. Time was he would have been on the floor banging his head on the carpet as the monologue dragged on, but here, where there was only the rumble and occasional exasperated squeal of traffic far below, and the emaciated dawn chorus of birds whacked out on pollution, the gentle lulling stream of her unstoppable flow was soothing, reassuring. It reminded him of being alive. It reminded him of the outside world and all its frantic obsession with nothing in particular, all its hair-tearing worry over things that seemed huge until you walked away from them, until you lay in a hospital bed doing battle with battalions of strange and obscure viruses, lying on your back pondering the infinite. He almost missed stress. At least stress was instant and faded again. Here there was no stress. Just fear. Fear didn't fade. It just took occasional rests, and then snuck back up on you and grinned with no teeth right in your eye.

He leaned back against his pillows and listened to the rising and falling wittering of her voice as they both gazed out of the window at the view.

'. . . And what I don't understand, because it's not the first time, well, you know, if you go to the theatre you want a nice seat, don't you? Otherwise why spend the money in the first place? . . .'

He began to feel nauseous again, but he couldn't take his usual refuge in slow dreamings about the past while his mother sat chattering on the edge of his bed. She was unstopping her thoughts probably for the first time this week, for the first time since she'd last visited. Hadley, with its big houses and bigger gardens and brick walls and Beware-of-the-dogs, was hardly the place for street-life. The only people she ever saw were in the supermarket and they all avoided her now. They'd swallowed twenty-odd years of her showing off about her children and they had long since had enough of being irked by the comparisons with their dull, dishwater daughters and cheerless, chartered husbands. They had never cared whether or not their children made it as doctors and teachers and writers. Now maybe they would be happier with the comparisons. But what would his mother say at the checkout – 'Oh, June. I have some wonderful news about Hugo. He's in St Stephen's and they think he might live for another six months'?

She'd never do that, hoped Hugo, but the others were probably still talking to each other, exacting their retribution over sponge fingers at joint coffee mornings. 'What, her? Haven't you heard about her son? You know, the Cambridge one, the tall one, the one who lied all the time and never played football like the rest of the boys and cried too much when he fell over and who was as quiet as a mouse at parties? You know how she always thought he would end up as the next Bernard Levin? Well, how wrong can you be? I hear from Maggie, who spoke to Dick Richards, that he's in one of those clinics, friends and relatives only . . . yes, with THAT. He's got IT.'

'. . . So I went anyway but it really was an awful load of rubbish. I don't know why she ever got the tickets in the first place and I can quite see why her husband didn't want to go and then have to strain your eyes to see it.'

Suddenly she broke off. She looked round at Hugo who, lolling slightly, was struggling to keep his eyes open. 'Am I boring you, darling?'

'I'm very pleased to see you. Have you spoken to the doctors?'

'I shall on the way out. Is there anything you want?'

'Energy. I want to stay awake. I always thought dying in your sleep was the best way but I've changed my mind. It's a major event. I want to be there.'

She still didn't believe he would die. As soon as he made his joke, and it wasn't meant as one, he saw her face tighten and tears rise. She didn't dare blink in case they spilt over, so she sat there trying to widen her eyes and stared out at the grey sky. It wasn't fair to be so casual about everything with her. He was hers and sometimes he felt he didn't even have the right to die without her permission. That permission hadn't been given yet. She was expecting him to fight. But he'd done all the fighting before he came in here. Now, in bed, under the warm supervision of an institution, he had handed over responsibility for his health and concentrated on putting the past in order, setting it out in his head, telling it out loud, walking through the running order of seductions, minor crimes and constant self-abuse. He spent most of his time drifting through the past now. It seemed to make sense. There was nothing happening in the present except more nurses, new doctors, more bed, new medicine and more visitors. And the future. He never thought about the future. It was difficult to focus on a grey cloud of low expectation. Even thinking about tomorrow depressed him. How could one day be so like another? He had really begun to appreciate television lately. It was the only thing that helped him discriminate between the days of the week. The television schedule had become his diary.

She dabbed at her eyes. It was still strange to him, the power he had over her – the power to upset her. It seemed such a very long way from the past. From her as god. From her as the monument of strength, the dictator whose word was law and for whom disobedience was unthinkable. But the change had happened long before.

The first time he made her cry was at the breakfast table.

He was about to go to school. It was after the diary saga. Two, maybe three years after. It was Hugo at his coldest. For those two, maybe three years, it seemed as if he had been shut out from the family as a liar who couldn't be trusted. If anything in the house went missing, he had hidden it. If it was found again, he'd put it back in sight because he'd got bored with hiding it. He had never touched or seen any of the things that went missing, but he took on the role because it excused him from being dutiful. If he was to be cast as a liar, he could play the part and lead his own life, his toilet tango, with no obligation to feel guilty.

That morning she had been asking him about a party the night before. Who was there? What happened? He hated these enquiries. They weren't anybody's business. At these parties he was someone else. He was not their Hugo and he didn't want to share the evening with them.

'Was Fred there?'

'I told you yesterday who was there. Why do I have to say it all again?'

Before, she would have stood up and thrashed him out of the house for such cheek. But this time she stared up at him as he stood by the door, trying to escape from the dining room, from the house, and her face crumpled, her eyes flooded. Hugo stood transfixed. He felt the sickening twinge of regret next to the impulse to hurt again, to drive the nail in, to see what happened next.

'Yes, Fred was there. I went with him in the car.'

'Oh, does Fred have a car?'

Her voice was wavering. The walls of Jericho were cracking.

'No.'

His voice was icy with annoyance. Did he have to tell her everything again? His sister watched him, her mouth full of toast. His father slurped noisily at percolated coffee. 'It's his mother's car.'

Each statement led to another question. The less he said the easier it was for her to continue.

'She lends him her car?'

This was dangling the red cloak in front of his temper. A question that got nobody any further. That slowed the conversation and his progress through the dining room door to a standstill.

'I just said that.'

And with those unremarkable words his mother began to cry. He watched the tears running down her cheek, leaving snail trails behind them, and couldn't at first imagine what they were. When he admitted that she was crying, his first thought was that he would be punished for this. But he wasn't. Suddenly it seemed to him that his mother was frightened of him, frightened of losing him. And he wasn't frightened of her. Wasn't frightened of leaving her.

'. . . I had another letter from your sister, Mary . . .'

She was off again, the momentum up, the motor ticking happily along. He could dip back into reverie, punctuating his silence with gentle grunts. He felt nauseous again. It always upset him that being ill involved so much time spent feeling ill. Whenever he had thought about hospital in the old days it had always seemed like the perfect refuge. Days in bed reading and watching television. But feeling sick ruined all the fun. Everything became too tiring to enjoy and then the boredom sapped him further. Reading was too tiring. Concentration evaporated after two paragraphs. Even his memory rebelled and started inventing as he lay and leafed through the back pages of experience. It lied to him, telescoping events into one long evening. Confusing names and faces.

'. . . I don't really know what's happening over there. One of the boys seems to have got into trouble. But she sounded very cheerful. Joshua, her husband (Yes, mother. I was at the wedding. They have stayed with me. I remember their names), is away so much on his lecture tours that the children don't have a strong father-figure to look to, and of course Mary is devoted to the maladjusted children, so her own boys run riot. One of them is up for shoplifting. I don't know why she doesn't . . .'

So you think we never went shoplifting? You think we were as good as gold, as you made out to all the mothers in the super-market? You don't know the chocolate sprees we went on through the same supermarket, probably watched by the same mothers, who hated us even more. Always stealing more than we could eat and arriving home to face jam sandwiches and a biscuit with chocolate brimming at the back of our throats.

'But they seem to be happy and hardly bothered about Jason. I was going to visit but . . .'

Her voice trailed away as she realised she couldn't say what she was thinking. He knew. She couldn't leave because he might die while she was away and even if he didn't want an audience, she had all the post mortem duties to contend with. He wished she didn't have to be there. All her weeping. Could he rely on death to be final?

At least they'd dispensed with religion in the hospital. There was precious little in the way of unction in the air. They had spent too much effort trying to eradicate the blame. But he could have done with some mellifluous priest calmly depicting after-worlds by his bedside. He wanted to feel that there was at least something to look forward to. In the past it had always been summer holidays and Christmas breaks. Maybe he should ask for some books. He could look at the pictures and choose a religion. Ask for some books? They'd be a bit surprised. It would be the talk of the corridor if Hugo started asking for Bibles. He couldn't bear to be the talk of the corridor. He knew he wasn't popular with the others anyway. He didn't communicate, they said. They all wanted to help each other. That was fine. He had nothing against them helping each other, but why did they want to help him? He didn't want their help. He didn't want to be pestered by the macabre Tupperware party attitude. Coffee mornings with the terminally ill. It made him tired and very angry. Why, just because he was ill, was he expected to bond with a lot of other ill people? And they weren't his type of person. They were all so committed. Committed to their sex. That always made him squirm. Hugo was very bad on solidarity. It made him feel too submerged. As far as he was concerned his sex was secondary to himself. People should be interested in him, not who he slept with. He wished there was somebody to talk to. He wished Chas was still around. He wished Chas was in the same room. But that was all water under the bridge, coffins under the ashes by now. And that was another story –

'. . . It's so awkward getting visas and your father is away such a lot and there's Dawn working so hard for so little, she needs us to be around and . . .'

Her voice trailed away again. He wished she'd just switch subject. Getting bogged down in embarrassment only meant he had to be pulled into the conversation and he didn't want to be. He liked looking at her as she relaxed. Found her tongue. Took her mind off the journey and its destination, a sick son. But her face was falling. He had to think of a question. Something she hadn't covered.

'Have you spoken to Grandma?'

'She won't speak to us. Didn't you hear about that? I told her off on the telephone. It was about you. She said some outrageous things . . .'

'Like what?'

'That you should have been taken in hand years ago and none of this would have happened. You would have settled down with a nice home and family and she'd have a nice great-grandchild in England instead of three in America, and we'd all be on visiting terms. All that. As if it was like teaching a left-handed person to write right-handed. It's the matron in her. She'll always be matron.

So I said some rude things and she never speaks to me anymore. Have you heard from her?'

'Not a word.'

He could see silence coming, wrapping their tongues, and he let it come. He had no need of all this tittle-tattle. He could lie back and speak when there was something to say. Her back seemed to unwind, slumping slightly, and her fingers stroked the bedclothes. It took people so long to touch anything near him. Everybody used to kiss him. One cheek, two cheeks and then three. A room full of women stretching for his cheek. Now he was alone inside his plague aura. An untouchable. The quietness that gave him was exquisite. The loneliness was agony.

Her hand moved towards his and held his fingers and a wave of warmth ran up from his toes, wriggling in the end of the crumpled bed. They said nothing. They stared out at the grey sky above grey towers, and said nothing. It was as if their breathing said it all. Each rhythm of their bodies purred with the rhythms of the other. The wittering was over. Now some quiet. Hugo struggled to keep awake. He used to daydream about sleep as he sat over his typewriter in an ill-lit office. Now sleep was his enemy. It wasted his time. Stopped him reading. Stopped him concentrating.

Mother tugged at his fingers.

'Are you all right, darling?'

'Just falling asleep.'

'I'll leave you to sleep then. It's better I go. It's a long way back because I've lost my green pass, so I have to go through Southgate to get a duplicate. I hate that place. There was a fire – did you read about it? – at this club in Southgate, and they know it's arson but the police didn't even arrive on the scene until after the club was burnt out. Ten people died. No ambulances, nothing. The police arrived after the event. They said it was a mistake. It's awful. But they don't give a damn.'

'I know.'

'Have you been there?'

'Many times.'

'Well, it's gone now.'

'I shan't be going there again then, shall I?'

His mother looked at him and he flashed her his biggest grin and quite suddenly, her eyes filled with tears and she broke down on the bed in front of him. He knew then that she'd be leaving soon. Nobody else cried in his room. With everyone else it was brisk and brittle smiles. Except for Chas, who had had the tact to talk about sex, and in detail, so they could sit squealing with the excitement of a new conquest, an old memory. There were few new conquests these days. There were no toilets left to tango in. They'd all been bulldozed away by Superloo Inc. and replaced with asexual, self-washing, muzaked cylinders that trapped and drowned five-year-old girls, washing them in detergent until dead. He smiled at the ghastliness of a homicidal loo as his mother dabbed at her blood-shot eyes and rummaged in the chaos of a woman's handbag for crumpled tissues smelling of lipstick and cigarettes, tipping out lighters and old theatre tickets, out-of-date bus passes and a photograph. Hugo grabbed it just before his mother's hand darted after it. She stared at him, suddenly furious.

'I'll have that back, please.'

He looked at the photo. It was of a stocky man, balding but handsome, smiling at the camera. He had no clothes on.

'Did you take this picture?'

'Don't be absurd.'

She had taken it. She had taken a new lover. He handed her the photo back magnanimously. Her lips started to move round the beginnings of get-out sentences but no sound came out. The 'Don't tell your father,' or 'It's all over now,' or 'It's nothing serious' . . . they didn't come. He watched her. She watched him. Was she expecting him to be angry? He couldn't be. But it was sad. He thought of his father and felt sad. The nicest man on the block. The kindest man. And he hadn't won his wife's fidelity.

'What's his name?'

'I think I might leave your father.'

'You said that years ago. At the ballet. I remember so well. You waited until the last bell at the interval and just as we were getting up from our coffees you said, "I think I'm going to leave your father."'

'I was going to.'

'I know. Don't you remember? We sat for hours in that room in Muswell Hill, discussing the pros and cons. You never went.'

It had been one of their closest moments.

Hugo brought his mother back to his room after the ballet. He had spent the second half of the ballet trying to watch her out of the corner of his eye wondering what they were going to do, and why it was that so many years after he had invented his parents' divorce (when it had been rare and fashionable to have separated parents) she had now decided to leave her husband (when it was rare and fashionable to still be together). The thought made him smile. He didn't need his parents to be fashionable anymore. But his mother's voice, her silent agitation through the second half, her white knuckles, her filled eyes and teeth gnawing at her lip made him want to hug her and take her home and give her a hot water bottle.

He didn't hug her. They were not good at hugging in the Harvey family. He took her home to the room he rented during university holidays from William and Barry. She wanted so badly to talk. Suddenly he didn't mind her invading. He had asked her and he didn't regret it.

Mrs Harvey had no idea how Hugo knew William and Barry. She didn't really want to know. There were things she didn't really want to know, things she thought it better her son sorted out for himself. As long as he was safe and warm, dry and happy. Of course Hugo had to give her something to go on. He had told her William was the cousin of a friend at Cambridge. This was almost true. William's cousin was at Cambridge and Hugo knew him. Vaguely. She had no idea that Hugo had known William since Hugo was David, but then they weren't here for that reason and anyway William was away and Barry was upstairs and he wasn't about to show her round the house. Not this evening. Instead they just sat in Hugo's room with the high ceiling among the dusty boxes on old chairs with worn covers and talked for hours and hours. Barry brought them dinner in the bedroom. Barry loved mothers. He wasn't so keen on their sons. He brought Hugo and his mother gin and tonics and his mother smiled at Barry the same way she smiled at waiters and nurses. As if she could only half see him through the fog. As if he were a mirage. She was too far away in her own unhappiness to see him clearly.

They sat together into the early hours of the morning, raking over bits of their past, reassuring each other of their love for each other. Hugo could retell stories now that had been deep secrets then and she could laugh at how she had been deceived or how he thought he had succeeded in deceiving her. And she could pick piece by piece over a disastrous affair that had left her wrung dry, unhappy and desperate to do something desperate like leaving his father. It was a conference weekend affair. A fling that had turned into something it never should have or would have were it not for her husband's inattention and her own inactivity. She was bored. Her children had left home. Her life was panning out in a long, grey horizon, echoing the long grey line where the Scarborough sea met the Scarborough sky. And here suddenly was a man who made her feel like a woman. A man who pampered her and flattered her and took her dancing on provincial dance floors under nearly-new chandeliers while her husband was in late evening meetings. He took her to tea dances on the pier and seduced her over iced buns. It could have been the stuff of American movies – heartache and room service in motels across the Midwest, guilty moments in secluded bedrooms. But this was cramped, grey-green England with no skyline, no wide open roads leading to wide open vistas. This was an affair that ran the routes of conference circuit executives. Cold coastal towns, off-season, off-colour, off-limits.

And he, the man with whom she risked her pride, for whom she lied to her family, to whom she had whispered on the telephone, and for whom she had outfaced Hugo in the kitchen. Hugo had never met him, mind you. But he had his picture. He had him figured. Just from what he'd heard. A womaniser. A man with a getaway cottage and a deft step on the nearly-new dance floor. He was a creature of these cold, comfortless coastlines. A lizard of plastic lounges with their red mock leather seats and yellow mock glass lights. A man who blossomed after midnight under artificial candle-light and steered his chosen prey through seven shorts (hers) and three beers (his). Just enough but not too much.

Hugo couldn't believe it had gone on as long as it had. It had started in those days of him sitting at his homework, listening to her whispering. And now, three years later she was staring at the wreckage and deciding to leave his father.

He'd known it had gone on for a while. Even after he left home. His sister told him. She started disappearing for weekends away with a mythical Dutch woman who had suddenly materialised out of her past. But even though each of them on their own had guessed something was wrong, none of them dared say anything to anyone else for fear of being wrong themselves. And Hugo only tried that once to say something to her. But by now he realised that was why she had invited him to the ballet. That was why she had said what she said after the second bell in the interval. That was why she was in his rented room telling him how she had been humiliated by her fancy man. Fancy men are fickle, she found out. The same promises made to her over iced buns on Scarborough pier were repeated to women of a certain age on certain piers all over conference town England. And suddenly Mrs Harvey couldn't rely on her country weekends, and she couldn't rely on her own discretion. She spied on her own betrayal. She watched her own humiliation through camera lenses, through windows and keyholes. She heard herself betrayed on telephone answering machines. She died quietly over and over again, all alone in a silence that she was too terrified, too angry and too hurt to break. Until then. To him.

And Hugo tried to resuscitate her over gin and tonics and hot stew in the room with dusty boxes and tall ceilings as he heard the full account of a dead affair, an affair he had always suspected and sometimes wished for, but which, now that it was revealed to him in all its casual cliché, seemed simply silly, a sorry tale of self-deception, of vulnerability exploited, of flattery swallowed, of too many iced buns and too many secret promises.

Hugo, who had had no successful affairs and only painful partings, felt so wise and so old, he told his mother what to do and she believed that he was right. He told her not to leave his father. He told her to go back and accept the forgiveness being offered, not sit and nurse her wounds until she had nothing more than scabs to pick at and loneliness to watch for. And slowly the tears in her eyes drained away, and slowly her red-painted lips twitched into smiles and her glass, smudged with the same red paint, emptied again and again.

He put her to bed in his room at four o'clock that morning and watched her quietly for a few minutes and thought how strange it was that this woman, whom he had loved and hated all his life and now so loved and so pitied, he still could not hug. Why was that the way with the Harveys?

And now, again, things were going the same way, with another short, stocky man naked in a photograph in her purse. And now, once again, she was denying everything and turning away from his invitation. They were so tense and brittle, the Harveys. Honesty never came easily to any of them except his father and he had nothing to tell.

There was to be no hug now either.

She collected her things back into the tell-tale bag and, with a flick of her wrist, opened a compact, dabbing powder about her face with an expression of artificial concentration. The compact clicked shut, and the air became brisk. She stood up and he suddenly felt like an invalid. He couldn't stand up to see her out. He felt like a child trapped in a bad dream where he is grown too big for everything but no-one realises he is an adult. She bent forward and pecked him on the forehead. This was a bad way to leave but he didn't have the strength to argue, to ask her to stay, to tell him the whole story. So she went. With barely a word. A backward glance and a smile, but the smile was expressionless. She was annoyed and ashamed and annoyed at her shame.

It was always sex that made these messes.

Hugo turned on his side and stared out of the window, waiting for the nurse to come, and thought back, back to the diary scandal, to Sam, to that year at school, to the first big trial of his life. He wondered how he had lived through it all without ever crying. He knew afterwards when people said he was strong, when people said he was a tough personality, that that year had been his hardening. It had cauterised him. But it had wounded him. He never stepped so far out of his shell for anybody again as he did for Sam. He never revealed so much about himself as he did in that diary. Hugo from that time on changed from the liar to the secret.

He wondered what his mother was going through with the bald stocky man with no clothes on. Would this one last a little longer or was he just another joyrider? Did he know what she was? What she wanted? Would he care? Would she give more than a damn about him? He wasn't good enough for her, of course. What did she want with a stocky little man who got photographed in the nude? Or maybe she took the photo. It didn't bear thinking about. He would have to think of his mother naked if he wasn't careful. But would his father get through it? And then just for a minute he tried very hard to remember what his father looked like. And when he couldn't he fell asleep. He dreamed that his mother and he were standing on either side of a glass wall at an airport and neither of them could find the way through the glass to the other side. People kept disappearing from Hugo's side and reappearing on his mother's side but they could find no door. She had his tickets and he had to kiss her good-bye. Instead they just paced up and down the glass wall staring at each other and trying to read each other's lips.

22 September, 1980

Dear Hugo,

Presumably there are still some doubts in your mind as to why I broke off our friendship so completely; I feel now that enough time has elapsed to allow me to explain the circumstances without embarrassment.

Quite simply, I realised – God it took me long enough to catch on! – that you are a homosexual (or bisexual). Please do not now rip up this sheet in a rage. Both you and I know this is true, so please read on. I have absolutely nothing against homosexuality, believe me, but I do not think it should be imposed on other people, as I felt was the case between us. My decision was not impromptu; I had spent many weeks of miserable indecision before that time, trying to summon up enough courage to leave you – a task made all the more difficult by my genuine affection and liking for you. As this belated message indicates, I still have not built up enough courage. I'm sorry. I have also told only one or two people about the reason for our separation, only in moods of spite which I deeply regret now.

I also apologise if this letter (?) seems impersonal; in reality it is highly emotional. I still have a very high respect for you and look back on our friendship with many happy memories; I only wish it did not end with this unpleasantness.

Sam

4

LOVE DID TEAR US APART

Hugo was fifteen. So was Sam. They were best friends.

And then Hugo fell in love with Sam and that was it. And then Mrs Harvey found the diary where Hugo had written that he loved Sam and that was worse. Maybe that was what being fifteen was all about. Trouble . . .

For three years Sam and Hugo had lived in each other's laps. They sat together in every lesson. They had compared and swapped and copied notes. They had told each other each other's stories (or some of them). They had been the sort of schoolfriends you get in Ladybird books and boarding school *Boys' Own* tales. They were in love. Sort of. And then one morning Sam just walked away. One morning he walked into the classroom for the early morning register and without a word, without even looking at Hugo, he crossed the classroom and went and sat next to Perry Rickston.

Perry had been Sam's friend before Hugo had appeared and for three years Perry had hated Hugo but been unable to show it for fear of losing Sam completely. Now Hugo had lost and Perry could gloat. His smile across the classroom even now was reptilian but triumphant. But Hugo didn't care about Perry, who combed his hair too much and had pronounced sibilants. Nobody liked Perry, probably not even Perry himself. He was spiteful and treacherous, the sort of boy who mocked deformities.

Hugo was in shock. He couldn't believe what had happened. Sam had gone and there was now an empty space at the desk next to him, the only empty space in the classroom. Hugo was left alone like a fallen woman. Already, by the second period after first break, the class had taken note and the sarcastic comments started coming. 'Have you got divorced?' asked Pritchard, who had the smile of an intoxicated crocodile. 'These tiffs,' sighed Marker, who would become school captain, his halitosis notwithstanding. But the trouble was, it wasn't a tiff. They hadn't argued. They hadn't fought. Sam had just walked away without any explanation and Hugo had no choice. He had to get up off the ground and come up with an act. He felt like the stooge in a double act whose partner has just walked off stage, and who suddenly has to think of new material under the spotlight.

Of course Hugo had other friends. But not the same type of friends. He ran with the misfits, the boys who courted trouble, the lads and toughs of the school corridors who played with fire and spent every lunchtime smoking in the woods. He ran with them because they were fun, they lived for a thrill, they wore their hair long and their trousers wide (at least until 1976), they had inner city postal codes and longstanding record collections, and best of all they took and bought and sometimes sold drugs. But they weren't friends like Sam was a friend. They were mates. And even though at the end of the year in the last weeks of the summer term, a whole school year after Sam had chucked him, Hugo had secret sex with one of them in the woods every lunchtime, they were never in love and the rest of them never knew.

They couldn't know. It wasn't done. Not at Hugo's school. Everything at Hugo's school was male except sex. And love. Or the wrong sort of love. The sort of love that certainly wouldn't dare speak its name in the fifth form; the sort of love that made Sam run off and several months later provoked him to write a note of explanation of such emotional refrigeration it seemed to Hugo like the fossil of a friendship.

So Hugo ran with the wild bunch in and out of the woods, took drugs to avoid groping girls and, every night before he passed out, picked over the fossil of his friendship with Sam. A friendship that had been so much more than a friendship and a relationship that had been so much less than a relationship. First love and first blood.

When he arrived at the big school outside London for his first day, Hugo Harvey, aged 11, was very worried about finding a friend. Nobody from St Monica's had followed him to the big school and the boys he already knew from Hadley were all much older and taller and nastier than he had remembered. They looked at him in his cap and blazer and new-pressed trousers and they laughed because they always laughed at boys who wore their caps. But what was worrying Hugo, more than the laughs of the older boys who thought his cap was silly, was the fact that the school was full of boys and only boys. Hugo had grown up with sisters and with girls. At lunchtime at St Monica's he had spent more time playing skipping than football, and although officially, for the sake of parents and birthday parties and going for tea, he had a best friend called Jonathan, they didn't sit next to each other in class because Jonathan wanted to sit next to Mark who was best in the class at football and only second best at homework. (Hugo was top, but Mark was close behind.)

Hugo was not the only one who wanted Jonathan for a friend. There was Mandy. Mandy who had long hair and a rich father and always won at kiss-chase, giving Jonathan the longest snog and leaving Hugo strangely bad-tempered on the touchline. Hugo was never sure why he got so cross during kiss-chase. But he knew, as he had known for a long time, that his failure to be kissed in kiss-chase, just like his failure to play football, was part of the problem that wouldn't go away. Part of the problem that kept boy friends away. So what was he going to do in a school that was full of boys? Only boys. What would he do when the only lunchtime game was football? How would he make any friends at all?

But when Hugo went home at the end of the first day at the big school, he realised that he had never really noticed that there were only boys. They were all so different: small and tall and fat and red-haired and black-haired and Jewish and Chinese and tough and stupid. It didn't really make any difference that there were no girls except that nobody played kiss-chase, which seemed like a good thing to Hugo. The other strange thing that Hugo didn't notice straight away was that, to begin with, it seemed easier to find friends among the older boys. The older boys seemed to take a great interest in Hugo. They were in the fourth form already, and had long hair and made strange jokes about boys being with boys that Hugo didn't really understand but which made him laugh, and although they never touched him, they used to keep him around as if he was one of their lot.

But still Hugo needed to find his own friend. The older boys were alright for sweets and strange stories and sudden gifts of books and help with his homework on the school coach, but they couldn't come home for tea. On the other hand, the way Hugo went about recruiting new friends, nobody could come home for tea. By the time Sam and Hugo became friends Hugo's domestic life, as perceived by the school, was an odd mixture of fabulous wealth, reclusive gin-sodden relatives and parental discord.

Sam Judd and Hugo had never spoken to each other before when they both moved up one year and into the same class. Sam had won the English prize in the previous year's end of year exams. Hugo had won the German prize. They were both clever, and although their new class was full of such cleverness, Sam Judd was easily the cleverest and Hugo easily second best.

Even so, Sam and Hugo didn't notice each other immediately. Hugo already had a friend from the previous year. He was a small, tubby Jewish boy called Milman. Darren Milman was simply the latest in the uncertain line-up of Hugo's friends. Nobody in Class One Ten was very certain of Hugo. He had, after all, been caught stealing Ian King's foreign coins and Mr Grenville had asked to see him in the house room. Someone said they had even written to his parents. But then he was the cleverest boy in the class too, by an uncomfortably long way, and he did earn a lot of points in the inter-class housepoint battle which stopped One Ten coming last. One Twelve won it easily because they had loads of clever boys. One Eleven was Sam's form and they came fourth, ahead of One Ten. Despite Hugo's reputation and despite a rather motley list of friends which had included Dinsey until Hugo had discovered how thick he was, and Collins until Hugo had started hanging around his older brother in the fourth form, and even Rawlinson who had been born in Manchester and told the best stories in English lessons about gangs and wastelands which could have been straight out of Stig of the Dump, Darren Milman was considered quite a catch. His father drove a Mercedes. His parents lived in mock-Georgian Stanmore. He went skiing on the school ski trip (Hugo didn't because it was too expensive, although he told schoolfriends it was because his uncle – one of a large and always useful supply – had died in an avalanche). And he had his Barmitzvah at the Piccadilly Hotel, which was the first time Hugo ate poached salmon and the first time he saw one boy receive so many plain white envelopes (two weeks later he saw the same thing happen at Stephen Moyes' Barmitzvah).

But in the rarefied atmosphere of Two Nineteen, Darren Milman's attractions faded. He began to appear smaller and tubbier and altogether less interesting. Where he had seemed clever in One Ten, he now seemed slow and dependent and maybe Hugo wouldn't have minded carrying him for a while, but his interest had been distracted. It had come to his attention that the slightly overweight, flaxen-haired, bespectacled and spotty boy with blackheads clustering in every corner of a wide face was not only very clever but seemed to sweat charisma. Hugo was becoming transfixed by its odour. The seduction was beginning.

The two of them competed in class, first with aggression, then gradually with humour as it became clear that no-one else was in on the battle. Their exchanges of smiles of congratulation and commiseration, depending who had won which battle, grew broader. Darren Milman began to fade from sight. Hugo shed him carelessly, like an unwanted skin. He barely noticed him go. His eyes were on Sam and Sam's eyes were on him. Like two strangers on the floor of a lowlife singles bar, they were caught in a long slow-dance, bringing them inexorably closer and closer until one brisk morning Sam went and sat next to Hugo instead of next to Perry Rickston. Perry seethed. Darren blinked. Hugo rejoiced. He had found his friend.

But even at the beginning there were problems for Hugo. Sam always seemed much more interesting than he did. This was fine at one level – it meant that Hugo never tired of Sam. But it was disastrous at another level – Hugo was always terrified that Sam would tire of him. Falling in love was simply another part of the same problem, as was Sam's failure to fall in love. In Two Nineteen the rack and ruin of puberty still seemed at a comfortable distance. But parents were dangerously close.

Hugo's parents were good parents. His mother had a brutal temper and heavy hand. She believed in discipline, manners, excellence and hard work. She also believed in health, education, vitamins and playing outside. Hugo grew up battered, intimidated, happy and healthy. But he also grew up with a complex about not being exotic. He knew that he was exotic really and that the rest of his family had let him down, but he had nothing to show, nothing concrete to prove he was the strange and wonderful person he supposed he must be. Unfortunately for Hugo, who was still quietly convinced there had been some idiotic post-natal mix-up at the Alexandra Maternity Hospital, and he had ended up in three-bedroomed suburban Grimsville without anybody noticing the error, Sam had parental exotica in dollops. To begin with there was the fact that his father lived in Nigeria with his second wife. Then there was the issue of Sam's mother.

Hugo wasn't meant to know about Sam's mother. In fact in all the three years of sitting side by side every day for every lesson, Sam never told Hugo. But Hugo, desperately trying to pull together the threads of his scattered lies, needed to know what Sam's secret was. He only knew he had a secret because of the incident in English when Anthony Argyll gave him his book back.

Form Two Nineteen was taught English by Mr Argyll, a very tall butterfly-catcher in crumpled cream suit and brogues who told the boys to call him Anthony and then called some of the boys by their Christian names and not others. That was typical of Mr Argyll. A burnished giant of a man, he strode through the school corridors, an odd little smile always tugging at the corners of his lips, as if reminded of some odd little scene at an immoral evening among friends. He strode over the first-years, leaving them scuppered among stickered briefcases, scrambling after scribbled homework, watching the great brogues charging on. By the second year those scuppered first-year boys had developed the school's resilient attitude. They had learned words like cynic and mature and spunk. They were not easily scattered by brogues. But they were still impressed by Anthony Argyll. And they all wanted to be Anthony Argyll's favourites.

While Mr Argyll's pleasure was difficult to predict and his favour sometimes difficult to fathom, having as much to do with a nice face as nice work, there was no greater accolade for a boy in form Two Nineteen than the Argyll approval of an English composition. That Argyll approval normally meant that the essay was read out aloud, by Argyll himself. With one exception: Sam Judd's first essay of the year.

The first essay of the year was an open title. Choose your own subject, said Mr Argyll, smiling round the classroom with a mystifying smirk. Hugo's essay, an open conversation on the problems of trying to think of a subject for an essay, which concluded with the sudden realisation that enough words had already been written, received the terse comment: 'A substitute for an essay'. Sam Judd's received an A. Hugo knew because, although they were not yet friends, they were sitting next to each other. Hugo also heard Argyll pay him a special compliment. But the essay was not read aloud. Sam quickly tucked it away into his briefcase like a piece of shame . . . or a piece of truth. Hugo watched.

Now that Sam and he were friends, he wanted to know the facts. He knew that Sam boarded because his father and family lived and worked in Africa, so he had a built-in exotic holiday for every school break. He knew that Sam had a stepmother and that his real mother was dead. But how, and when?

Hugo was not above snooping. Hugo was not above much. He was not above raids on inside blazer pockets in the changing rooms. He was not above lies. So he certainly was not above searching Sam's briefcase while Sam went to chess club, and, having found it, he was certainly not above reading it. It was worse than he'd expected. A long time ago. Five years maybe. Sam less than ten years old. Driving down the motorway on a family holiday. A lorry veering across the lanes. His mother shouting 'Look out!' And then nothing. And then waking up in hospital to find his father looking down at him in misery and loss written across his eyes. The last words Sam ever heard his mother say were 'Look out!' Then she was crushed to death in the car. Nobody else died.

It was terrible.

Hugo didn't know what to do.

It was bad enough that both Hugo's parents were very much alive in three-bedroomed security, working their standard hours and holidaying abroad only once every two or three years. It was bad enough that Sam spent his school holidays touring distant tribal kingdoms with a geopolitically correct father and a brand new mother while Hugo languished on interminable walking holidays spent charging up and down sundry minor peaks, visiting various ruined abbeys and well-stocked stately homes, trapesing round steam and railway and mining and general engineering museums, as father delivered lectures on Telford, Brunel, Watt and Stephenson, and eating sandwiches in the car. They always had sandwiches in the car wherever they were. It was sandwiches in the car to escape the ladybird epidemic at Rye and sandwiches in the car in the pouring rain at Saundersfoot after the toy museum was closed. So it didn't help that Sam had had a major infant trauma.

Hugo encountered several survivors of major infant traumas as he staggered through life and each time he heard the story, normally told by a friend of the traumatised, he felt intimidated by the depth of their suffering. There was the boy who watched his mother drown as she sank to the sea-bed after falling off the family mooring. There was the boy whose mother had drowned, drunk in the bath, and whose father had blown out his own organs with overeating and overdrinking in a determined consumer suicide. There was the boy whose parents were struck by lightning while camping on a mountainside in Spain, and who was left alone to fetch help and care for his younger brother who was already deaf and now nearly blind. The older boy was nine at the time. Hugo stood speechless in front of these experiences and their victims and envied them. They were different. They had somehow touched the bottom of the barrel and resurfaced. They had an aura. Sorrow had touched their raw nerves and left them transformed, burned, branded.

It was something you couldn't fake. There it stood in Sam's essay. Crisp. Matter of fact. Each line neatly written in a tidy compact hand. No emotion betrayed but every emotion implied. What could Hugo do? He needed a family tragedy. He had to fake it. He needed it for the attention, maybe; for the pity, certainly not; but for his own painstaking recreation of himself, definitely. Hugo was slowly reinventing himself from the inadequate raw material his parents had provided, and he knew that a major trauma was a crucial part of the new Hugo's emotional make-up. A trauma, moreover that people knew of, but wouldn't talk of in front of him. He had long since flirted with daydreams of disaster and the pious face he would wear to school the next day as boys gathered round him whispering their sympathy. Whenever his mother was late back from the shops he'd eagerly jump to the worst conclusions and assume that there had been a major car accident or a sudden supermarket massacre or a freak bolt of lightning. Not, of course, that Hugo had ever felt obliged to wait for the truth before he told his stories. As Hugo and his reinvented Hugo spun out their fantasy web, and later, as David made his first tentative appearances on the streets of North London, Hugo learnt to forget about the irritating gap between what he said and what was real.

As Hugo worked to make himself more interesting to Sam, he created an imaginary life of impressive detail.

What he lacked was strong links with foreign parts and manifestations of obvious wealth. These weren't easy to fake, but that wasn't going to stop Hugo trying. He just invented everything he needed. He started with his own name. It wasn't good enough. Hugo was alright, but anything was better than Harvey. The telephone book was full of Harveys. School was full of Harveys. Harveys came from anywhere and went nowhere in particular and when Harvey was called out in assembly, three people in his year, several in the whole school and one in his own class could have answered, 'Here, sir'. So Hugo began by creating a complex Jewish ancestry and the moniker Schneeberger. He felt the Jews at school had an immediate advantage. They all had European families, went abroad on holidays and had obvious money. Their fathers all drove Jaguars and Mercedes and their mothers had permanent tans before the days of charter travel. From his name, Hugo turned to his home: he expanded it, added another one in the country, added a swimming pool to one and tennis courts to the other and was about to add another one in a southern Mediterranean resort when he decided that a drama was called for.

Fabulous wealth was tiresome and difficult to prove. More to the point, the truth of three-bedroomed homelife on the bottom of the Hadley Richter scale was difficult to conceal. Nobody could come home for parties or teas. Father had to be kept away from the school coach-stop unless Hugo could maintain stories about always using the second or third car and never the Jensen (which was later promoted to a Bentley). Equally galling was the fact that as he grew older and his friends grew wiser, Hugo found he was having to undo much of what he said. While eleven-year-olds were agog at imaginary mansions and super-fast cars, fourteen-year-olds took a perverse inverse view that money was naff and poverty was cool. Suddenly Jaguars, Mercedes, Jensens, and Bentleys, holidays in the Med and Miami, swimming pools, tennis courts and indoor saunas were all a grotesque embarrassment. Hugo watched and listened in disbelief as two-up, two-downs in Hornsey became recherché, family rows in Blackpool all the rage and Saturday jobs to make up the family income de rigueur. Of course he still couldn't win. Either way Hadley, with its cluster of enormous wealth and its slow slide down the hill to dull normality was offensive. Hugo's house was too small for the super-rich and his town was too rich for the trendy poor. So he quietly dropped the super-rich line and waited for the image to fade away before he started any experiments with sudden poverty. And while he was waiting for one image to dissolve and another to congeal, he switched all his attention to his family, channelling all the interest his friends had shown in his unmanifested wealth into his invisible relatives.

Only one person didn't appear to be bothered either way and never talked about having or not having money and that was Sam and yet somehow Hugo never believed that Sam didn't care. He never seemed to notice that Sam never asked any questions and never paid any attention to his lies. He just went on creating more elastic baroque, more flexi-tales of the bizarre and the domestic, and hoping that one day Sam would turn to him and say, My God, your family is weird, and rich, and wild . . . How do you cope? Of course, had Sam ever asked that, Hugo wouldn't have known what to say, because the only thing he had to cope with was orchestrating the lies. Reality had never really intruded, let alone the idea that he was any less weird and rich and wild than they were.

From upgrading their bank balances Hugo turned to meddling with his family's peace and quiet. He had already created a retinue of disastrous ancillaries – in particular a gin-sodden grandmother for whom he invented alcoholic perambulations in an eternal quest for the largest gin and orange in the world, but now his parents had to come into the action. Parental discord had real pathos. Divorce was still very uncommon, at least among affluent parents of nice children, and those who had been through it (their parents') had come out tinged with the colours of Bohemia while receiving long, sorrowful talks from other boys about how miserable, shattered and helpless they'd feel if the same tragedy occurred within their home. So Hugo's parents had an imaginary divorce, at least a year before divorce became compulsory among his contemporaries. His father went to live in New York and Miami on imaginary business while his mother stayed in the imaginary 35-room home with billiard room, reception rooms, morning rooms and all the other rooms he read off the cards in estate agents' windows, but which was now rapidly being scaled down to a flat or somewhere of a more suitable size.

Hugo was not entirely in the dark on this subject as Howard Mallory-Smart, one of Hugo's gang, had had a parental divorce when he was five and now had a maniacal airline pilot as a stepfather. Howard Mallory-Smart lived at the peak of cool. He had older brothers in upper years who were good at art. He was good at art. All three Mallory-Smart boys had long hair, and they all lived in Belsize Park. That was enough to make them deities in Hugo's hierarchy of cool. Hugo's tremendous snobbery – whether up, down, inverse or perverse – was intimately entwined with London's geography and the impact of a postcode. Any postcode with single figures was a serious advantage, working on the basic premise that the nearer to the centre you lived the cooler you were. Money was not everything in this status play. It was no good spending hundreds of thousands of pounds on a house in Stanmore, for example. But when Michael McPadden came to the school from Canada and it emerged that he lived in a flat with his mother in Hyde Park Square, the bells in Hugo's social It's-a-Knockout rang bull'seye and McPadden won thousands of bonus points. (They were eliminated just as rapidly when Simon Moyes gave McPadden a joint and he went white and threw up through his fingers.)

Divorce for Hugo was therefore meshed with visions of white porticoed houses with peeling paint, huge ferns and books and a kind of endless bohemian bickering from which the boys (the brothers Hugo had always wanted) disappeared to the far-up rooms to paint and smoke and drink and grow their hair. The invention of his parents' busted nuptials went swimmingly. Not only did Hugo soon find himself receiving the sympathetic soft-toned speeches of worried and concerned schoolboys, but Sam seemed to be biting.

Hugo, finding himself on a winning streak, played it out with great skill. Each step in the long, painful process of trial separations, attempted reconciliations and sudden betrayals was described in the deprecating tone of the liar who pretends to be having his own stories pulled from him like teeth, but in fact is handing out the cue lines like forceps – go on, pull out another, let me suffer in front of you. These stories always had to be started with minor friends, so that the real audience, Sam, could be pulled in by the smart manoeuvre of having someone else refer to Hugo's tragic domestic circumstances in front of him. But the process worked. Sam would make concerned enquiries about what was happening to his sisters (that always made Hugo impatient as he had hardly had the time to invent a whole emotional landscape for them as well as himself), his mother (Hugo also had a problem remembering which of his parents had initiated the divorce and which was guilty of the adultery so he shared the crimes between them, hoping to confuse the pernickety with the scale of the disaster) and most particularly in Hugo's eyes, the house. The fate of the house was the perfect get-out from all those months of inventing and adding to its dilated proportions. Now, just before it could be seen, it had to be sold and the money from its sale (which would of course be huge) would be frittered away in settlements and fees and alimonies and trust funds, allowing Hugo the effortless passage from an embarrassment of riches to fashionable poverty. Only one thing he couldn't change as long as his parents refused to move, and that still intrigued some – why did the whole family continue to live in Hadley? Even his father – who was supposedly spending most of the year in New York, seemed regularly on hand for lifts home from the teenage parties. Questions like this left Hugo smiling over his exhaustion and rapidly editing the stories to include more sudden, less predictable paternal vanishings to foreign locations. His mother remained rooted in Hadley. This was, after all, 1979. It was men who had transatlantic dalliances, wives had local flings. So to baffle the querulous Hugo devised a schedule for his father (whose work to date had rarely taken him off the North Circular) that would have dropped him into a vast pool of jet lag.

Whenever skepticism began to creep into the voices of his audience, Hugo always found succour in new tales of the domestic fracas ongoing in Hadley. There were catfights and hurled furniture, recriminations, abandoned children cowering over upstairs board games, refusenik grandparents, tipsy aunts – the whole caterwauling paraphernalia of imaginary relatives was wheeled through these intricate stories. And there was no-one to check up on them. To begin with.

To begin with, there was no-one even to rival them. Then, suddenly, divorces became commonplace. Everyone's parents were at it. From having been the kind of domestic tragedy that was only whispered about, like bad breath and ugly sisters, divorce suddenly became the rage and Hugo found his pitch thoroughly queered. Every Adam and Mark and Simon and Paul seemed to have acquired separating and adulterating and departing parents. There were older boyfriends and younger girlfriends, there were family ructions and sibling splits. The furore barely masked the new social desirability of joining the divorce class, and Hugo's stories became unusable from the sympathy and tragedy perspective. Oddly, he felt uneasy with the trendy aspect. He had played the sobbing strings too long, perhaps, to switch tack. He decided to abandon his divorce stories completely, demoralised by overcrowding and exhaustion.

What Hugo needed was a new pitch.

A new pitch to deal with new pressure. He wasn't feeling certain of Sam. There seemed to be a nick of irritation in his voice at times. What made it worse was that Hugo was feeling less certain of himself. Life had moved on from the halcyon days in the spell of Anthony Argyll and the excitement of his newfound friendship with Sam. Hugo thought back to the Hugo of those days and imagined some uncomplicated innocent, who told the truth and never bothered to impress; whose good soul shone through his eyes and won friends (called Sam) across classrooms.

Since then he had watched himself change into a creature for whom reality was simply a raw material and not one he found much use for. The lies were hard work and required constant vigilance against those who had been told one lie but would then talk to those who had been told another. Although Hugo was a gifted liar, able to beat out incredulity or suspicion with another whopper, he was getting tired of building bridges between two different Hugos: the one at home and the one at school. Home was for jam and bread, breakfast and homework, washing up and hiding out. School was where the lies took over and the fun began. Hugo could rise to the image he had created. The problem was that Hugo had grown bored with the image. And he had fallen in love with Sam. Where before he could have been perfectly relaxed if Sam was quiet, or pissed off, or shirty, now he took it personally, as indicative of some mistake he had made, and by apologising too quickly for things he hadn't done, he was pissing Sam off even more. Hugo was getting jumpy. He needed a big number to make him tragic and lovable again. So he killed a large number of his non-immediate family in a motorway massacre.

The logic was simple. Domestic territory was overcrowded with real divorces. But Hugo's lies weren't going to be stopped by local problems like overcrowding. They merely switched country. Not that there was anything premeditated in this. Hugo simply showed a quick skill with bending a situation to his advantage. He merely exploited the death of his grandmother.

When Mr Tattersall, the deputy headmaster, came into the history class and asked for Hugo Harvey a ripple of nods and looks ran through the class. Hugo already had a reputation as a troubleseeker who ran with a bad crowd and they, the nodders and the lookers, would all want to know when he came back what it was he had been done for this time. Sam, however, whose leg Hugo had been very gently leaning his own leg against, didn't seem in the least bit interested and looked out of the window as he went. Hugo himself was a bit mystified as to what he could have done this time, although he had always been mystified when Mr Tattersall came for him and on every previous occasion he had soon remembered the crime of which he was accused. In fact, this time Hugo was right; there was no derring-do this time, no criminal laddishness, no smoking by the assault course pond or wrecking of the fifth-form common room. Mr Tattersall was bringing bad news. Hugo's grandmother had died.

Hugo looked blank. He barely knew his grandmother. They didn't speak the same language and they didn't live in the same country. They had met maybe four or five times in his life, that he remembered, and she had always been very old. Now she had died after a long illness. There wasn't much to say. He didn't feel anything. He hoped that that was only temporary. He was always worried by his lack of response. Emotions seemed to be so far down, so inaccessible that they drained away before he could reach them. He sat there listening and started plotting his return to the classroom as Mr Tattersall explained that his mother would have to go away for a few days and his father would not be back from work when he got home so could he get his sister's tea and all the other dull and irritating messages his mother had left about dull and irritating life at home.

There had been a death, which most people would consider to be a major event. But the death of a grandmother seemed routine. Certainly it could in no way rival the death of a parent, whether from illness or accident, so on his walk back to the history class, young Hugo began to invent a drama, conveniently offshore, that equalled, in fact surpassed, Sam's infant trauma. It wasn't just that his grandmother had died, she had been killed ... on the motorway ... in a car accident which involved her son (Hugo's uncle) and various cousins.

By the time Hugo reentered the classroom the death toll had reached six and the expression on his face was stricken with tragedy.

Hugo knew that his return would be greeted with whispered enquiries, notes, nods, questioning looks, smiles of support, sympathy, glee and he met each with a look of mortification. He hadn't worn a look of mortification very often but he found it sat rather nicely around the mouth. He couldn't quite summon a tear. He found it difficult enough to summon tears at real deaths.

Sam didn't say a word. He disappeared quickly after the class. Hugo wasn't sure straight away what to do, but decided to go for the ripple. He would drop the story like a stone among the rabble and then wait for the waves of its news to reach Sam. By the afternoon he would be sure to have heard and would come back from lunch contrite and even loving.

With the refined art of the long-distance liar, Hugo developed the story gradually, in spurts of revelation, underpinned by understatement, errant flashes of exaggeration adding colour (grotesque in varying shades). By the middle of the lunch break he had a bevy of friends and well-wishers in his lap. He was unchallenged as the object of the afternoon's attention. But then it was a terrible story. The dreadful skid across three lanes into the central reservation of a car loaded with relatives returning to Breda after a wedding party in Kampen. The savage mutilation of familiar bodies, hurled through the windscreen, crushed against the steering wheel and whiplashed into spinal contortions.

While Hugo had succeeded in winning the attention of all the Marks and Pauls and Simons and Timothys with his gothic account of a motorway mishap, the main purpose of his lie was defeated. He wanted Sam to hear. But Sam didn't come back after lunch. The waves and ripples were crashing on brick walls. Sam had gone off to play rugby against Harrow and wouldn't be back until after the end of the day and the day was Friday so Hugo wouldn't see him again until Monday. And as he laboured on throughout the afternoon with his look of mortification, it occurred to Hugo that a great many people had been killed that morning, to very little effect.

It wouldn't have worked anyway. The motorway massacre was only two weeks before Sam left Hugo completely. It wasn't his stories that had killed the friendship. It wasn't that he was getting boring. It was love that destroyed everything, and it was Hugo pushing at Sam for love, pushing at Sam's leg with his, touching him and prodding him and trying to hide his mid-afternoon hard-on that killed it off. It was that little line in the fossil of their friendship. 'I have absolutely nothing against homosexuality, believe me, but I do not think that it should be imposed on other people, as was the case between us.'

Hugo had probably been in love with Sam from the beginning. He had looked on Sam as the object of his entire affection since the early days of that long, slow seduction across the desks of second year geography and second year maths. Hugo had sat next to him throughout three years of lessons glowing with pride, possession, happiness. He had passed the long, dreary summer holidays pining for Sam, dreaming over and over of the first day of school, the first day he would walk back into the classroom and sit next to his spotty, flaxen-haired friend and glow again. But it was only during those last few weeks that he had pushed too far. Touched too often. Maybe Sam had seen the scribbled messages, 'I love Sam, I love Sam, I love Sam', written over and over again across page after page of Hugo's rough books, lines that Sam wasn't supposed to see, but which Hugo dreamt he would stumble across accidentally and then, beaming, turn to Hugo and say 'I love you too.' 'I love Sam, I love Sam, I love Sam', written in long lists in every imagined typeface, in every pen and nib and colour. 'I love Sam.' It was like screaming from behind a glass wall. The silence was straining to its limit. And then it shattered.

Sam abandoned Hugo only three weeks before the diary scandal. And, once again, it wasn't his lies that got Hugo into trouble, but the truth, his love for Sam. In three short weeks his life lay in ribbons, cut to pieces. At school he was abandoned to the sneers of a vengeful Perry Rickston. At home he was the outlaw and vagrant who had stepped beyond the bounds of forgiveness. And all because he had fallen in love with his best friend. And had written it down. In his rough book and in his diary.

It seems absurd that he should ever have kept a diary like that.

The diary was a grand affair. It was a book with a hard, dark-blue cover and gilt decorations. Pretend gilt. Each double page carried a week and each day had enough for three or four paragraphs. He wrote in it every day. He was fourteen when he got it and fifteen when he burnt it. It was only a one year diary but he didn't get to finish it. If Hugo regretted anything, however, he regretted burning it.

The diary started life as a Christmas present from the Oxfam catalogue. Present-buying in the Harvey household was a very organised affair. Mother would cut out reviews of the books she wanted bought for her at least two months before her birthday. Christmas present lists had to be prepared by mid-October.

Although he spent the rest of the year seeing things he longed for, there was something about that day in October that squashed Hugo's imagination. He found himself thinking about prices, sensible gifts at sensible costs, instead of the strange, unexpected surprises he wanted. The charity catalogues were an easy route out. The diary was an easy option.

Both Hugo's sisters kept journals in which they stuck bus tickets, picture postcards and the general accumulated litter of holidays, school outings, birthday parties at the house of this week's best friend. Hugo never did. He'd pry into theirs, and then at sneaky moments mention something secret they'd confessed to the page . . . but he couldn't be bothered with all this hoarding of titbits. He didn't have titbits. If he did, he had to get rid of them. They weren't litter – they were evidence. Hugo didn't stick anything in his diary. But he wrote down everything he did. Everything he did that he couldn't tell anyone else. No further evidence was needed. Everything was there, day by day, week by week. Every evening he'd fill in the day.

The diary was Hugo's way of keeping up with David. He listed David's assignations and described his partners. He didn't write their names. He described them by their bellies and chests and hair and how hot the sex was. They became curt little footnotes to Hugo's complicated schoolday. David's life was so bald and relentless that between the grip, the squeeze, the stroke and the cum there was little to write except for how hairy, how fat, how bellied and how chested the men were. The chests were always the most important. The curve. The shadow. The contour. He would look at his scrawny, flat chest in the mirror, the skin stretched across his ribs and long for one of the tight brown chests of the boys playing basketball in the gym. Or the men that David played with. The men he chose from the daily tango parade in another damp suburban piss-parlour.

David was doing all the dancing but Hugo was jerking the strings. That was the whole point of the diary. Hugo was exerting control. He was in charge. David was doing the deed, but Hugo was keeping the score. David was still his creature and he was charting all his activities. For . . . for whom? Not for his family. For himself? For the record? For posterity? He didn't know. For himself. For no-one else. It was a compulsion. The diary had become his confessor. All crimes were exonerated in the retelling or the rewriting. Once on the page they had been exorcised, absolved. The diary became his valve. It leaked all the pressure out of life and left him relaxed again. He used it to keep tabs on David, and to chart the touch-hungry moves Hugo made on Sam, the touches under the table and the evening tussles.

As he sat next to Sam on long, hot, autumn afternoons in fifth-form English, listening to the droning on and on of Mr Routledge, intoning the depressing cadences of 'The Rime of the Ancient Mariner' like some obscure and unsuccessful hypnosis, Hugo's desire grew like an itch in his groin and a moving of insects in his belly. The sun and the closeness of Sam's body, shabbily clad in the raggle-taggle of battered school navy swelled a lust in him that starved for contact. Slowly, gently his leg would move across the space under the table to touch Sam's leg. Briefly, Hugo would feel, through two layers of regulation issue flannel, the pressure of his leg on Sam's and of Sam's back on his before suddenly, sharply, Sam's leg would move away and his face would bury itself in his book, head down, eyes down, communication off.

The evening tussles were more successful, although they too in the end must have contributed to the rupture. The imposition of sexuality. For the moment, however, they were the high point of Hugo's day. Every evening he would lie in wait round Sparrows, Sam's house where Sam's locker was and where Sam went every evening to collect the books he needed for homework in the male sanctuary of the boarding house. (How Hugo dreamed of boarding, of going to bed in dorms shut off from parental eyes and living at school with Sam twenty-four hours a day.) Every evening Hugo would surprise Sam and provoke and prod him into a fight. Not a real fight but a wrestling, grabbing, grasping, giggling, breathless fight in which they pulled and tugged at each other until clothes came astray from bodies, shirts were pulled up, revealing sudden pink stretches of flesh and Hugo capitulated before his hard-on became too evident.

Every night Hugo would chart these fights and what he saw and what he touched and how it went. There they lay side by side, Hugo and Sam and David and all the other men. The diary covered it all: it derided the disgust of bad encounters, celebrated new discoveries, cherished brief encounters, kept notes of new haunts. But, apart from Sam, it never mentioned any names and it never listed any numbers. So maybe Hugo always knew it would be found. Sooner or later.

Hugo never hid the diary because if he hid it he knew she'd look for it. She'd notice it had gone. He had to rely on it being obvious and presumed innocent. He could have moved it. But he was paralysed by a fear of breaking the spell. The spell of privacy. There was no precedent for such a spell. His mother was ruthless in her investigations and she was worried about Hugo, he knew. But like the police, she had to have proper cause. A diary is a dangerous book. Opening its covers is like unlocking Pandora's box or turning over a heavy stone. Worms and beasts of all descriptions fly at you. Maybe this was what kept the diary safe. Maybe mother wasn't sure she wanted to know, until she felt she had to. Maybe she wanted not to need to know. Maybe she just didn't think twice about it. Whichever way, the spell had worked for ten months. The diary had remained on the windowsill of his bedroom. Untouched. Unread. Until . . . Mary did.

Sister senior broke the spell and started the end. The end of Hugo's peace and quiet. The end of David's free-and-easiness.

Hugo had a birthday party. Not that it amounted to much of a party. He sat in the dining room of his house with some friends. All the chairs were pushed against the wallpaper. The music centre from the front room was playing his latest tapes. There was a bowl of fruit on the sideboard and people kept asking if they could have an orange and Hugo kept having to say no because every apple and orange in the bowl had been planned for a particular meal on a particular day.

Hugo's friends sat on the chairs pushed against the wallpaper and didn't smoke because they knew what that would cost Hugo in family trouble and they liked Hugo. They felt sorry for him. His mother was famous and she was living up to her reputation, sitting in the front room with his father watching television and waiting for too much noise or a breakage. At eleven o'clock she swept in and would have asked them all if it wasn't their going-home time had they not already gone, on to someone else's party, bent double, breathless with laughter, quickly lighting the cigarettes they had been dreaming of. She found only Hugo sitting there listening to his latest tapes and feeling very odd about having had to spend a Saturday evening in his own house and not being able to go on to the party with the rest of them. And all the while Hugo's older sister sat in his bedroom, uninvited to the party, supposedly doing her homework, but really reading, beavering her eager, jealous way through the pages of Hugo's and David's sexual business.

Hugo's older sister. Unglamorous, serious, unpopular, laughed at. While Hugo lied his way into his own world, Mary stood stolidly by the truth. And when it failed her, when she discovered that parents could be cruel, friends could be fickle, her heroes could be foolish and her honesty could be hateful, she tumbled down the steps of depression. She fell a long way. Friendless. Misunderstood. There was no obstacle to her fall. The Harvey family, who were not very good with failures or emotions or embarrassment, looked away. It was just Mary being difficult. It was just Mary not having a sense of humour. It was just Mary letting the side down as she had let the side down when she needed to get glasses because somehow it was letting the side down that her eyes weren't good enough to focus on the gooseberry bushes at the bottom of the garden. The Harvey children had to be bright and beautiful.

Mary told him that she had read his diary and he didn't know what to say. She didn't quite put it like that. She asked him how often he accepted money from men. She asked him while they were doing the washing-up one afternoon after lunch and he just looked at her as if she was out of her mind and then she started to explain. She told him that she had read his diary while he was having his party and she was in his room because her room, which was right above the dining room, would have been too noisy and while she was sitting at his desk she had read his diary.

His first desire was to fly at her throat. But the Harvey children had to be bright and beautiful and he wasn't allowed to murder his sister. His second desire was to kick her very hard but he couldn't do that because she was sitting on top of the worktop and there was nothing low enough to kick. So he said, 'Oh that's all made up and it's none of your business.' And even then he didn't hide his diary. Maybe he wanted it to be found. That is absurd. Nothing could have terrified him more. He was even frightened of his sister now. Frightened of what she knew and frightened of what she was trying to find out as she followed him up the hill when he went for walks. But she wouldn't tell mother. That much she had said.

So why didn't he take good warning? Why didn't he hide it at school, in the garden, in a plastic bag, anywhere? Why did he just leave it there, to be found, read, hurled at him and eventually burnt by him?

His sister was right. She didn't tell mother. Mother found it on her own. But Hugo led her there.

Sam might not have seen the endless scribbled declarations of love in Hugo's rough book, but Mother did. Mother was a prying type. The kindly would say she was concerned for the welfare of her sulkiest child, a son who slipped in and out of terrible moods that left his face riddled with a furious pout and sullen brows. But he knew better. She just wanted to know what was going on. And once her fears were awakened, privacy was not an issue. It never had been. If she posted Hugo's postcards on holiday, she read them and then, unabashed, berated him for describing the familiar up-and-down mountain trudges as boring. She opened letters that arrived for him, read them and then attacked things that had been said in the letters, again completely unashamed. She was looking for clues to her miserable son and principles like privacy were no obstacles to a determined mother.

The first clue she found was his rough book. She found it in his waste paper bin. She flicked through it, past all the doodles and the biology notes and on to the pages of repeated over and over again scrawls: 'I love Sam, I love Sam, I love Sam.' The screaming behind the glass had broken through. Sam had left him and his mother was on the warpath. Somebody had heard him.

At first Hugo had no idea how it all happened. He just knew it had happened. He knew in a flash.

He had spent the last two weeks in solitary shock sitting alone next to an empty space that should have been Sam, staring at the back of Sam's neck and Perry Rickston's over the shoulder leer.

He was dazed. Stunned. Almost completely silent with misery. His only refuge had become work. Now that he needed his other friends more he wanted them less. Before they had been unnecessary and fun. But now that they were his only lifeline, he found them pointless and irritating. And they responded. Sensing his new need for them, they abused it. He had fallen from grace, he had lost his protector, and now, his head hung like a victim, he was fair game. They teased and ridiculed him, chased him through puddles and thumped him for answering back.

For the first time since the age of twelve, Hugo began to hate school, but he knew he had to survive, he knew he had to keep face. He had to find some new friends, some new allies. He had to find something to do to take his mind off Sam. After-school badminton was a start.

Hugo's mother answered the telephone.

'Is it alright if I stay late tonight? I want to play badminton. I'll catch the five-thirty coach.' He knew she wouldn't mind. She'd be pleased he was taking an interest in sport. And in a clean sport that didn't need any extra washing. His tea could wait.

'I think you'd better come home.' Her voice sounded flat, choked. Suppressed.

'Why?' asked Hugo.

'I just think you ought to come home now.' She hung up. Hugo went white. He walked down to the coach stop and all he could feel was that sick sinking in his stomach and his heart beating through his skin. He saw people he knew at the coach stop and he couldn't chat or smile.

His blood ran like trickles of cold water. The journey home was like a step-by-step voyage to perdition. There was the coach journey when home was still far off when he couldn't raise more than a shaky smile. There was the walk from the coach to the train down the steep slope when his knees felt rusted up. There was the two-stop train journey while he watched the scenery go past with the longing eyes of a condemned man prepared to escape to live in the woods. There was the slow walk from the station home, past houses with lights on and families at ease with one another, during which the terror gripped Hugo's windpipe like an icy glove and squeezed.

He should have run away. Maybe that could have turned the tables. 'If you ever want to run away you can always come here, you know.' That's what James's mother had said. The furore there would have been. It would have been a master stroke of tactics, making him the unfairly pursued instead of the schoolboy sinner. Or would it? What would James's mum think of him when Mrs Harvey rang her, and told her about the diary. Because he knew that's what it was. He knew from the very moment his mother spoke on the phone. It had happened. And how long could he stay away? He'd always have to go back. She'd always win in the end. Hugo was too frightened to break his mother's spell, so his feet continued in the same direction and he moved down the street towards the house where she lived.

There have been other walks of terror in Hugo's life – across the headmaster's study to his huge apoplectic face, capillaries exploding in hysteria as he demanded to know why Hugo was trying to get himself thrown out of the school; towards the results pinned in the glass case on the side of the Senate House in Cambridge, to peer over a clamour of heads and see at one glance into which class he'd fallen; onto a stage to deliver a first line lost in a befuddlement of cheap sherry gulped in front of the gas fire to stave off the wet and wintry gloom of an attic room in college. But this walk was the death march.

Hugo approached the corrugated glass of the back door. He walked in. His mother looked at him. Her face was pinched back. She stood in her work clothes, those red-raw hands, capable of such sudden blows, ragged with scrubbing cooker and floor and pots and plates. 'I thought you probably had a lot of homework,' she said. And for a second Hugo thought he had been saved. He went to his room. Nothing was disturbed. His diary lay on the windowsill, for all he knew where it had always lain. He went to tea. But something was up. Sister senior didn't emerge from the kitchen throughout the whole teatime. She was ensconced with mother behind a closed door, whispering, waiting for father to return. Sister junior, infected by the conspiratorial silences and whispers, said nothing but stared at her sandwiches and milk and cheese. Hugo chewed, tasting nothing, and as soon as he had finished, escaped to the silence and solitude of his room, waiting until his father's car pulled up. It was absurd that they waited for his father before they punished him. His father never punished anyone. Occasionally, if he lost his temper, he'd hit them on the bottom in a great wallop of fury, but he couldn't do to them what mother did. He never pulled them by their hair or hit them in the face or stood them in the corner. He never shouted or yelled or burst blood vessels over them. It took Hugo a long time to realise that this wasn't weakness (and shouldn't have been laughed at) but was sweetness. Father was a sweet man.

But they were saving this one up for father because it was about boys and because he was a man; because it was a capital crime and he was the Head of State; because mother was distraught and, as she proved next morning, couldn't have restrained herself from violence.

When he returned from work, father was immediately sucked into the whispering which had, by now, moved upstairs. Hugo perched on the unsqueaky stair two up from the bottom and strained to hear. Nothing had been said to him yet. Nothing to confirm what he knew but wished was just his worried imagination. He went back to his desk and stared at the text books, trying to concentrate on the bonking habits of the amoeba and the fondling tendrils of spirogyra, but the raised hisses and sobs from the room above came through his ceiling in little shudders of danger. And then the footsteps came down the stairs. Heavy carpet slipper footsteps. Daddy's feet. And daddy came through the door of Hugo's room and stood there in confusion. Without turning round to look, Hugo knew he was standing there in confusion, too embarrassed by the nakedness that had happened to be explicit.

'Your mother has been telling me some bad things,' said Mr Harvey and Hugo frowned at the amoeba. He was more embarrassed for his father than ashamed of himself. He wasn't at all ashamed of what he'd done. He was terrified that he'd been caught. He was terrified of the punishment that his mother would think up.

'You've been telling us a lot of lies,' he continued. That was it again. The lying. They always made that the big sin. What did they expect? 'Hi mum, I'm just going up the road to the toilets to meet the scoutmaster I have sex with every Sunday and who gives me two pounds to spend on sweets after we've had forty-five minutes of rough and tumble all over his flat and he's driven me back to the toilets. Hi mum, I've had a great cycle ride but not much cycling. I just parked my bike outside the toilets in the High Street and got into the car with a man from Highgate who took me back to his flat where we had great sex and he showed me some pornographic films from America on his Super-Eight projector and I came all over again and then he gave me a lift back to my bicycle. Hi mummy. I've just escaped an attempted rape in the woods by a man who took my trousers off and hung them on the barbed wire fence and then tried to force himself into me and it was only because I made such a fuss and bleated and pleaded and carried on that he lost his hard-on and drove me back to my bicycle.'

His father was determined to stick to this line of attack. The soft one. 'When you told us that the valves and pump had been stolen on your bicycle, you didn't tell us the truth about where your bicycle was.' It was outside the cottage at the top of the hill. It had been there all afternoon. He was right. He hadn't told them that. He couldn't remember where he had said it was. This was typical of his father. The practical considerations. Cling to the concrete, the machinery he knew and loved. Bicycles, cars, washing machines, central heating systems . . . they were the moral norms on an odd map of life. People could get up to all sorts of weird things but as long as he could bury his face in a motor, he didn't have to notice.

Hugo didn't say a word. He knew his father would dry up soon. He did. He petered out. And Hugo came up with a line he never expected to use. 'I'll turn over a new leaf,' he said. 'It's just a phase,' he said. For a moment, for a few days, maybe a week or so, Hugo actually believed himself.

Hugo's father left his room satisfied. He went back upstairs to tell Hugo's mother. Still nobody had mentioned the diary. Nobody had said how they knew what they knew. Mrs Harvey was no fool when it came to espionage, and the first thing she made sure of was that she didn't reveal her sources.

Mrs Harvey was no fool when it came to confessions either.

She wasn't one to be taken in by such glib off-the-cuff homespun philosophies, the let-out line for a hundred public schoolboys caught fellating, sodomising and kissing beneath the sheets and in the boathouse and behind the cricket scoring boards and in the woods. She wasn't going to accept turning over a new leaf as an adequate response. What about all the lies? What about the money? What about the disease and the degradation? But what could she do? So far she had done nothing. She was still upstairs. And Hugo, who went quietly to bed, couldn't believe his luck.

His luck didn't hold. He'd known it couldn't. It would have been too surreal. A forgiving mother. Hugo had his first encounter with her the following morning, when she walked into his room and drew his curtains, as she did every morning at six so that they were all up and washed and brushed and dressed in time to lay the table for the family breakfast. Too frightened to speak, he watched her let in the grey September morning. He swung gingerly out of bed and was stunned by a blow to the head that knocked him backwards against the wall. 'Don't you say "good morning" any more?' she yelled and left the room. He got dressed and washed, bathing his stung cheeks in cold water, and then went into the kitchen where his mother was frying the eggs and bacon. She turned on him.

'You're nothing more than a filthy prostitute,' she spat, closing the door between the kitchen and the sitting room so that other members of the family wouldn't have to hear the foul story. All the time he stood there, prepared to flinch from any sudden movement, Hugo was waiting for her to explain a little further. Nobody had told him how they knew. Nobody had presented the diary as evidence. How did they know? Had Mary told? That was unlike her. She might lecture him, she might have taken to following him up the lane to try and make sure he didn't go back to the high street toilets she'd read about in the diary, but he knew how to evade her. He wasn't born yesterday. She was. And she wouldn't tell on him. Not to mother, anyway. There was an unwritten law that said you couldn't tell in cold blood. Not that Mary was above casting blame about when she herself was on the spot. But she wouldn't have done this.

Then Mrs Harvey invented her alibi. 'You were followed, you

know. You were seen on several occasions. Coming and going. It's a disgrace. You're nothing more than a filthy prostitute.' Hugo felt quite proud of being described as a prostitute. He'd always thought they had style. He hadn't met any then. He hadn't even really worked at being one yet, then. The two pounds from the scoutmaster in Cockfosters after Sunday afternoon sex was a perk, but he would have had sex with him anyway. The money had never been a condition, and David, for all his self-conscious savvy, took a long time to learn how to ask for cash without looking sheepish.

They sat and ate breakfast in silence. Hugo's disgrace stifled everything. He didn't look up from his cornflakes. He ate his fried egg and bacon, chewing methodically. The silence was too heavy to be broken. Hugo's cheek was still red with the early-morning blow. And then, at last, he finished his meal and went into his room to make his bed before leaving for school.

Throughout the silence, through the stinging cheek, one thought nagged. Who was this friend of the family who had dogged his moves for long enough to know what happened on so many afternoons, so many early-evening walks? How could she (he always thought it was she) have seen, have known? But Hugo was willingly fooled. He wanted to believe his mother's alibi, because if he believed that she had read the diary, all of the diary, she knew so much that was secret between David and Hugo. She knew David, who was Hugo's secret.

The alibi couldn't last. His mother, having discovered the source of all his secrets, couldn't keep away and she enlisted sister senior in her persistent spying. But it was amateur spying. While Hugo and sister junior ate their tea, only a few days after the storm had first broken, Mary was asked out of the room by Mrs Harvey. Hugo knew they were in his bedroom. He knew they were going through his diary. He left his biscuit and milk and went into the hall. From outside his bedroom door he could hear the rustle of pages and whispers. He pushed the door open. There they sat, huddled over the mock leather and the mock gilt. Nobody had followed Hugo or David. They had read about him. They had plundered his diary, gone past all the notices saying FUCK OFF, MARY and IF YOU'RE READING THIS MARY, FUCK OFF AND

DIE and read all his confessions, all David's seductions and Hugo's failures, and now they were simply trying to keep up step. Maybe they thought it was like a serial they could go back to every day. Maybe they were enjoying it. Maybe he should have sent it to a newspaper and asked them if they wanted extracts. Instead Hugo threw the diary on the school incinerator by the bicycle sheds the day after he caught his mother and sister snooping.

Now, cut off from his best friend, cut off from the family, at loggerheads with sister senior, abused by mother, ignored (as always) by father and in love only with sister junior (who never understood what was going on and walked around the house with tears in her eyes) Hugo felt no need to develop a conscience, felt no need to give a fuck. They could all, with the exception of sister junior, whom he would rescue from this purgatory, go rot in hell.

David, unrepentant and reliably devious, got on with the sex as Hugo covered his tracks with more ingenuity. His mother would question him thoroughly, she would impose ludicrous curfews but she could not trap him indoors. Admittedly, when she caught Hugo stealing from Mr Harvey's wallet and threw him down the stairs (the last occasion on which Hugo wet himself), she imprisoned him in the house away from any social life for the next six weeks, including Christmas. But he still had to go to school and he still had to travel home from school and the school coach still went past some of David's favourite haunts. Hugo was his own man now. She might punish him, but he was beyond her reach.

Hugo was alone. He had entered his ice age. Nobody could reach him. And nobody seemed to want to try. He still had friends. He could still make people laugh. They seemed to like him and he was invited to parties where he still took drugs that still made people laugh even more. But if every one of them had died the very next day Hugo would have had to search for a tear. They were just people. They were not close. He was too frozen up to get close to.

Until Charlie.

And Charlie did more damage than good.

5

THE LOVE THAT DARE NOT
SPEAK IN LONG WORDS

The Hoover started upstairs. Hugo crept to the door of the candy-striped bedroom and edged into the hall. Sister senior and sister junior were heads-down over their homework in the dining room. The Hoover stopped suddenly. He stood flat, backed against the door of the front room, breathing heavily with fear and frustration. Why couldn't she just get on with it? This whole game of Hoover-cat and telephone-mouse was wearing him down. He hadn't done any homework since seven o'clock when she'd first gone upstairs. He'd just sat there writing Charlie's name on his book and trying to remember every single touch of his body, from the hair between his pectorals to the . . . then the Hoover started, and stopped, and started. Like an erratic siren, giving the all-clear. After all, even once he'd got on the telephone and dialled the number, anything could go wrong.

The Hoover started again. He could hear its little squeaky wheels. He could hear her feet moving across the floor. He moved briskly across the hall to the phone. This was the danger zone. If she emerged onto the little landing at the top of the stairs, she had a clear view of him in the middle of his illicit call. She would demand to know whom he was ringing and why. The children weren't meant to ring people at this time of the evening. They were doing their homework ready for checking before bed time. There was no time for chatting. If he was ringing someone about a difficult question, she would want to know which it was and why he didn't know the answer without having to ring someone else. How could he get back to the phone after that? She'd be listening. In other homes the telephone was legitimate, like the television. It was seen as a tool, something useful and to be used. In this house it was a drain on resources – it cost money and took time and was meant for calls to grandma on birthdays to say thank you for a book token.

He picked up the receiver with the light fingers of one now used to deception. One lunchtime at school Hugo had seen a boy put a five pound note in his blazer pocket. Not the breast pocket but the low, baggy, misshapen pockets made flabby with conkers and change and sweet wrappers. The boy had then sat down for lunch. Hugo walked over to the table where the boy was eating and dropped to the ground, pretending to do up his shoelace. Without looking to either side, following the golden rule that caution arouses suspicion, he dipped his fingers into the pocket, removed the note and walked away with his booty in his fist and his heart racing. It was a spectacular piece of derring-do. It was an audacious piece of pick-pocketry. It stood him in good stead for lifting telephone receivers.

The two little buttons under the receiver went ping and it seemed that the Hoover stopped at that very moment. He listened, the receiver in his hand, waiting for a sign. The door to the bedroom didn't open. The feet on the floor continued to move. He heard things being lifted and plugs being switched. He stood, not daring to look at his reflection in the hall mirror as if he would catch himself out, tell tales or point an accusing finger.

The Hoover started again and Hugo began dialling the number. Would it be engaged? Would there be no answer at all? Would he be there?

It started ringing. It seemed that his mood, his stomach, his life, was controlled by these little tones. The purr of the dialling tone, welcoming him but promising nothing. The hiatus while he dialled. Then the agonising, incontrovertible peepeepeepee of the engaged tone, or the open sesame of the ringing broobrooo broo-brooo. Codes and signals gaining or denying access to 'Love City', aka the first floor bedsit at number 37 Grosvenor Gardens. It was ringing. Access may be permitted. He was on pause, his heart was on hold. No answer and access was denied.

'Hello,' said a nasal twang at the other end of the phone.

'This is Hugo,' said Hugo to the nasal twang.

'I know,' said the twang back. The twang was Charlie's land-lord.

Hugo hadn't met the landlord, but the man he pictured was not a pretty one. He was the creature who fed on the stilted dialogues between Adonis upstairs and the pleading, bleating boy on the telephone. He was a short-sighted Cerberus who resented his guard duties but would have welcomed Charlie into his ground-floor lair with glistening lips. Hugo was the only one admitted to the rickety bed in the chill bedsit on the first floor where Adonis held court in Love City. So the landlord hated Hugo and played games with Hugo. Spiteful games. He had Charlie under his roof. He could make people wait, and while they waited he could make them cringe with his sigh and the voice that said, 'He's in my house. I'll let him see whom I wish.'

'Is Charlie there?'

The sigh. 'I don't know.'

'Would you mind seeing if he's . . .' Hugo always petered out here.

'Do you want me to give him a call?' The question was acid with contempt.

'Oh, thank you. Yes, please,' gushed Hugo. Hurry up, hurry up. She'll be out in a moment. His heart started playing bongo rhythms in his chest and his stomach shrank to a small ball of knots. If at that moment the landlord had demanded a fee for every second they spoke, Hugo would have promised it.

'Charlie!' The nasal twang shouted up the stairs.

The silence was awful.

'Hello?'

The warm Scottish voice swam down the phone and enveloped Hugo in a mist that blurred his voice and set the bongos popping at a nightmare rate. That was Charlie.

'It's Hugo,' said Hugo.

David was dead. Killed in the front seat of a blue pick-up truck. The truck was Charlie's.

There comes a time in everybody's love life when the words of popular songs on the radio are taken personally. All the saccharine ballads strike sharp chords in a mishmashed heart. The entire playlist of a day-glo jukebox looms out of the pub corner like a blow-by-blow account of heartache and heartburst. Hugo was there. He was brimming over with love. He was up to his neck, up to his eyes in love. He listened avidly to the winsome waxings churned out over the radio waves, each one written from his story

... excluding, of course, the fact that he and his beau had met in a toilet, that they made love under a blue nylon sleeping bag on a bed that creaked, and that he wasn't allowed to smoke, to use long words, to drink gin and tonics, or to be upset when it turned out that there was another man in Charlie's life.

So what if the love songs were soppy slush? The despair came on its heels like a hangover. But at this moment, sneaking loveliness beneath the racket of a Hoovering mother as she ploughed the carpets of his sisters' bedroom, abandoning the round of school grope-parties and all-night downers for hours in the chill of a bedsit, snuggling under the nylon sleeping bag on the mattress in front of the television, Hugo was happy. Happier than he could remember. Happier maybe than the day Sam sat next to him for the first time. He was in Love City with Adonis, the ITV summer special was on the box, a glass of lager stood by the pillow, cigarettes, matches and ashtray were only an arm's length away. It was like camping. It was like last year had never happened.

Last year. He still hadn't spoken to Sam. Or been spoken to by him. He'd left a note in his briefcase. A reply to the note he received. But it was all lies, the same lies he had told his father. I'm turning over a new cliché. It's all just a phrase.

The diary was so much dust in the school incinerator now. The trust his mother might have had in him was now just sour misgiving in her eyes, dry disbelief in her smile. He had no allies, no confessors except sister junior, the one person in the world he would have snatched from a burning house. But even she trod carefully around him, frightened by his stories of running away, sent scurrying to the family encyclopaedia looking for side effects as he emptied barbiturates into poster paint pots filled with gin nicked from the front room drinks cabinet on Saturday mornings.

His friends liked each other more than him. He couldn't run with the pack. He ran alongside. He may have been bad but he wasn't tough. Inside or outside. When they hit him, he answered back and got slapped down again. When they teased him, he snapped back and they hit him again. They could be nice. They were his friends. They asked him to their parties and they worried that he didn't have a girlfriend. He was having sex with one of them secretly in the woods at lunchtime. But they weren't real friends. They would have laughed if he'd fallen under a train. Not cried, anyway. He felt weak, mean, wrong and alone.

And then he met Charlie.

If you had asked Hugo to draw a picture of the man he wanted to lie with, the body he wanted to undress, the voice he wanted to be wooed with, it would have been Charlie.

When Hugo saw him for the first time his mouth went so dry he couldn't speak. He was on his way to meet some friends for a drink in a pub where people were stabbed from time to time and bands played caterwauls to enthusiastic applause while Hugo drank gin and orange (it was the only drink he knew off by heart) and got odd looks from the barman.

He walked up the hill in split-knee jeans with frayed hems that caught his toes, making him stumble. He was on his way to meet Igor and Igor's friend, the beautiful boy with dark, flowing hair and soulful eyes, whose carpet Hugo had thrown up over the week before, lost in a backward hurtling daze of joints, gin and barbiturates. He had been slammed back against the fretwork minibar that curved across the corner of the room as Igor's friend's mother tried to get her hand into his jeans. These were people he barely knew. These were his friends. Hugo knew things were going badly. Igor was tall, dirty, lank-haired and mad – spouting endless new musical theorems and attracting endless fleapacks of belligerents, wanting to push his teeth in. He was an artist, and Hugo lapped up his maverick monologues, but never felt he could match him.

He was on his way to meet Igor and Igor's friend, wearing split-knee jeans with an impossible flare. They were all that was left to wear. His clothes were operated on a strict rota system which was only allowed to be influenced by the weather. Although he had already started spending his paper-round money on second-hand oddities from the new Oxfam shop in the High Street, he still didn't have enough to provide a proper counter-culture wardrobe. So he was off to meet the punk mavericks of the Duke of Lancaster in serious flares. He was unhappy. The evening sun was still warm. He was unhappy and randy.

The toilet tango was an obvious solution. So many meetings on so many evenings had been missed, postponed, blown out by the toilet tango that friends no longer expected Hugo to turn up where or when he said he would and if he did, he was often in a weird mood they couldn't figure out, so they left him to himself, sitting quiet, depressed, feeling sullied by the miserable cockplay, the trickle of an orgasm he had just pulled off in front of some panicky husband. If he didn't show at all it was because he had stumbled on an adventure; someone with a bedroom, a place indoors to tumble in. David was well-known on the high road strip by now, and Friday evenings were good for the hunt, as executives, frustrated with a week's work in a pinstripe strait-jacket with no time for a mid-morning wank, were bursting at their seams with unrelieved sex. They used to cruise by in their pale blue Ford Cortinas and treat him like a sinister seducer, with deference and fascination. He was jailbait. He was the end of their careers, their marriages, their freedom if they were seen or trapped. But he was sex. He was good. And he was very available. They'd known him, some of them, for three years. And he was still good, even at seventeen.

As for David, he was just horny. Unsmiling, uninvolved, un-talkative, and unbearably horny. It didn't seem to matter whether the men were ample or skinny, were under thirty-five or just over forty-five. If David was randy he could turn anything to sex. The chintz and quilts and ornamental mantelpieces of their suburban sitting rooms only made him more randy. It was desecration and blasphemy in the sitting room, and, like stripping off in the hall and pissing in the bath, it was all part of the flouting, flaunting rudeboy act. He could find anything sexy if his mood was right.

As David crossed the road to the tango parlour, he noticed the driver of a truck at the traffic lights look at him with a slight grin. Not a grin of recognition. More like the wolf's grin in Little Red Riding Hood. The grin of an appetite that sees its satisfaction ahead. His buttocks clenched and his stomach hardened. The flirt was on.

He walked into his toilet boudoir, the institution-blue dank with mould, scrawled with graffiti, some of it addressed to David by name. Some of it he knew. Desperate pleas from the scout-master in Cockfosters he'd had to abandon two years ago when his Sunday walks for a romp in the bed and two quid in the pocket were exposed by the diary scandal. He would have kept a bit quieter about David if he'd been the scoutmaster. His parents could easily have pressured for names and addresses. And who knows when Hugo would have cracked? He wasn't terrific under interrogation. Mr Tattersall knew that. The scoutmaster would have lost more than his cubs.

The cubicles were full but the stalls were deserted. He stood watching eyes come and go from the little holes in the cubicle doors, as they tried to see who these new footsteps belonged to. He heard a handbrake and a car door outside. This was good news. Fresh blood with a car. It could be the wolf. Of course, half the time the driver was running into the pub for cigarettes or dropping someone off or walking in the opposite direction or maybe worse, it was a car whose dented wings and stained seats he already knew from trips up the A1 to a deserted field or a shadowy coppice. David wasn't fond of repeats. He made very few exceptions.

David went to the window, and looked out through the cracks in the rusty wire mesh. The wolf was walking up the path. The wolf was gorgeous.

He didn't know which way to move.

Even a natural like Hugo was sometimes nonplussed by the toilet tango. Its steps were intricate. Bad timing or bad luck could leave him stranded.

The wolf walked in. The wolf looked at David and then leant against the wall. David was faking a piss but his bladder had shrunk to a pea and he couldn't wring a drop out of it. He zipped up and leant against the wall. He didn't look up. This was one of his worst problems. With the sly and seductive older men he could play the preening tart. With the panicky married men he could put on an act of bold control. With men like the wolf he went soft in the knee and dry on the tongue. If this man had turned and asked him for a light, he would have croaked soundlessly.

Strategies hurtled by, but Hugo was trapped. The man was making no signs. Hugo thought he was looking at him, but he was too shy, too scared to check. He was worried if someone didn't emerge from a cubicle soon, the man would give up and leave. He had dusty boots. A workman, maybe? He had tanned arms and blond hair. A cistern flushed in a cubicle and a man left. David went in. He was stuck now. Would the wolf look through the holes? He searched for him through each hole but couldn't find him. He'd left with the other man? They'd just seen each other and gone? An eye came up against the door. David unlatched the door. This was dangerous but part of a skilled game. The door remained closed but the wolf would have heard the latch slide across. The next move was his. He started to push the door open.

They stood there looking at each other through the slightly ajar door. David with his trousers round his knees, staring into pale blue eyes and a suntanned smile as if he had just found the spring of life and was catching his breath before drinking. The man spoke in a light Scottish accent. 'I've got a car outside,' he said. David nodded to save croaking. He pulled up his trousers and followed the wolf outside to the blue pick-up truck.

That was how Hugo met Charlie. He told him his name was David and said little else as Charlie drove them back to the bedsit in Finchley. When they got to the bedsit, Charlie went to the loo and told David to take his clothes off. David lay naked on top of the nylon blue sleeping bag quivering with anticipation. Charlie smiled when he came back and said he should get under the covers. Under the sleeping bag there were sheets.

They lay together for two and a half hours and David never came. They lay together for two and a half hours and Hugo didn't care whether he came or not. He just wanted to be in the arms of this man, this wolf. His wolf with a light Scottish accent.

When he left Charlie's bedsit with Charlie, in Charlie's pick-up, his heart was so full he felt giddy. There was a smile tugging at both ends of his mouth that wanted to break into a laugh. An irrepressible bubble of laughter.

Charlie had to go to Devon the next day for a job. He worked in heavy haulage, and had since he left school in Edinburgh at sixteen. He was twenty now. He was going to drive all the way back from Devon the next afternoon to make sure he could meet David for another night. David promised he would be there. He had never yet kept such a promise.

As he walked into the kitchen of his parents' house, Hugo

could not crush David's smile, could not squeeze his happiness into a manageable face, and could not stop talking in a Scottish accent.

His mother laughed when he spoke in a Scottish accent. It was one of her favourites. She always thought he was imitating his doctor. She was always pleased when he saw his doctor. Someone had to take Hugo in hand. Someone had to get behind that glassy look of superiority, those effortless lies and devious circumventions. She didn't know what was going on. She didn't understand how so much could have been going on beneath her nose without her realising. Sunday afternoon walks, school holidays and eager trips to the art galleries, school field days and charitable work at the playgroups. She had believed it all. She could interrogate him about his friends, catch him stealing money from his father's wallet and ground him for six weeks, but she still couldn't get beneath his moods to find out what he thought; what pain, what pleasure, what longings sat there, what memories and what fantasies. She wouldn't ask. He wouldn't tell her. So she appealed to the doctor and the doctor called him in once a fortnight, to look at his spots and to talk to him.

Hugo had never had spots until the fifth form when he woke up with a swipe of zits running from his mouth to his neck that looked as if someone had sprayed him across the face with a red inked pen. The doctor gave him cream to dry them up. The cream came in small tubes and Hugo needed a new tube every two weeks. He could not just ring up and get a repeat prescription. The doctor always wanted to see him before he would give him one.

Hugo didn't mind. He liked the doctor. The doctor was an ally. He gave him whisky and cigars and let him talk about himself.

But Hugo knew he was there for some reason. They were trying to find out about him. He trusted his doctor. He knew that nothing he said would go any further. But he knew too that he had been handed over. He wasn't keeping any secrets but he wasn't telling the whole story until he was ready to.

So when Hugo burst in through the kitchen door and made his mother jump over her sieved flour and his father turn round from the washing up with a dishcloth stuck in his waistband, even the steam and grind of family living could not quell his heartburst and he sang out in the rich Scottish brogue, the lilting melodies of Edinburgh and Aberdeen until the smile on his face hurt with the stretching and his throat felt hoarse. His mother laughed. His father grinned but continued with the washing up. Sister senior looked at him suspiciously. She never trusted his good moods. Half of it was resentment. She herself was never in a good mood. Half of it was doubt. She knew that his good moods meant pleasure and pleasure for Hugo was rarely proper.

He sailed to his room and floated into bed in the candy-striped surround of his orange wallpaper and dreamt over and over again of Charlie. Charlie's voice. Charlie's chest with its downy hair just between the pectorals. His tanned stomach. His smooth, shapely dick. His grin of white teeth. His pale blue swimming pool eyes.

He was in love.

But if this was the first time Hugo was going to keep his promise and turn up, could he be so sure that Charlie was being honest? He might have told every young boy he met that he was going to drive back from Devon for them and then decided to give it a miss. Hugo knew where he lived. But he wasn't the window-breaking sort. He saw himself sitting mournfully against the front garden wall in that suburban street near Tally Ho Corner, just waiting for his bronzed man to walk by.

Hugo spent Saturday waiting for the evening. He had cleared the way for his evening out with little trouble. His mother was always suspicious but he had a flexi-lie that could cover the whole Saturday evening. There was a party and he was invited. He was meeting his friends at East Finchley tube station and going with them. He had to be there for a certain time otherwise he would miss them. He would come back with them and then get a taxi. And it was true. Some of it. He had adopted the same principle in lying as in shoplifting. A little truth can disguise a much larger lie. If you went past the till and paid for one thing they never seemed to guess that all the other things in your hands hadn't been paid for. There was a party tonight and he was invited. He knew where the party was and who was going. He had an invitation and he had even been to the house before so he could describe that.

He had nothing to cover the day though. Nothing to kill the sensation of marbles rolling over and over each other in his stomach. His appetite was numb. He sat at the lunch table spooning food between his teeth, pushing it down his throat without tasting anything. He wasn't living in the present. He was on hold. Half of him bubbled with excitement, the other half fizzed with nerves. Had Charlie been honest? Could he bear to wait another two hours before his bath, before tea, before leaving with a cheery artificial smile concealing a wide inside grin? Could he stop his hand from shaking as he spooned Pavlova into his dry mouth? Would Charlie be there? Was this real?

At half past seven on a Saturday night Hugo stood outside Finchley Central station. He had been there for half an hour already. He had even walked down past Charlie's flat to check that the truck was there. It was. Charlie was back. At seven thirty-five the blue truck rolled up and Charlie sat there grinning a climb-in-and-love-me smile. Hugo clambered in and they rumbled off down the hill, perched high in the sky on the lorry seats like teenagers at a fairground ride.

'I've got something to tell you,' started Hugo.

It sounded so suspicious.

'I told you a lie yesterday.' A cloud scudded past Charlie's brow. 'My name isn't really David. It's Hugo.'

Charlie's face looked dented. As if he had just reversed into him. Maybe he should have said nothing. Hugo tried to explain. But it wasn't easy. It made him sound old and hard-bitten. Too canny and too tawdry. 'The thing is, I didn't want to tell you the same lie.'

'The one you told everyone else?'

'Yes.'

'How many others have there been?'

What was he meant to say? He hated this sort of question. What was reasonable? What was realistic? What did he want to hear?

Charlie looked at him. Hugo was staring out of the window looking confused. He had no idea how to start. Charlie laughed.

'Don't worry about it. I don't fucking care. You're here now. I didn't think you would be. I don't care what you call yourself.

Although you have to admit Hugo's a pretty stupid fucking name.'
And he laughed again. Loudly.

There. David was dead. Hugo's strange and bossy friend was
dead. Dropped. Betrayed. Sold out as soon as the going got good.
Something thudded in Hugo's stomach. Was he cutting himself off
from his only ally? Shouldn't he have said longer good-byes to his
... his ... his what? His evil genius? His mentor? His tutor in
life's heartless, ruthless, grab-what-you-can and take-what-you-
need easy-living, easy-lying sex-carousel? What was happening?
Was this bower of bliss, this cosy leather lorry seat next to the
denim thighs of the man he loved taking away his killer instinct?
David was a survivor. That was how he liked to be seen. But
Hugo had done all the work for him and, now he was gone, Hugo
felt relieved, more relieved than guilty. He had taken one step
towards the truth. His life was so enmeshed in lies. The truth was
like a huge pair of steel scissors. He had just cut his way through
part of the mesh.

That night Hugo had an orgasm. So did Charlie. After sex they
lay front to back, Charlie in front, Hugo behind, watching Saturday night television, the soggy pot pourri of summer specials and
variety shows. Nothing mattered. Nothing could be bad in this
mood. Everything became bewitching. Each person on the programme, each host, each guest, each bimbo on the scoreboard was
touched with the dust of Hugo's happiness.

On Sunday he went to Quaker Meeting and sat for an hour
tracing Charlie's body in his mind, and remembering every word
they said, every smile he provoked. He didn't fall asleep that meeting.

Quaker Meeting was Hugo's safety valve. His lagoon of calm.
Not that this little teen-hooker who wore his morality round his
ankles had discovered God. He had discovered silence and kind
people. He had simply followed sister senior's tracks. Sister senior
was on a pilgrimage. She was looking for a personal salvation, a
way out of self-loathing, a way to self-respect and a vision of a
world not riven with furies and freaks who abused her and
neglected her and mocked her in equal measure.

Hugo and sister junior just trailed behind her, following her as
they had followed her to Woodcraft Folk. Sister, with her sweet

smile and youngster innocence, was first through the door. Hugo followed a few weeks later, itching with resentments he knew he wanted to scratch out. Religion was such an unlikely refuge for Hugo, but it worked. Quakers were just what Hugo wanted. They were not birch-and-brimstone flagellants. They were a rest home for the bruised mind. They were people with a bottomless capacity for forgiveness and none of its usual bland meaninglessness.

As Hugo entered the Meeting House, he felt the air soften with the gentle tones, the half whispers, the full smiles of people too intelligent to be sheep, too full of faith to judge. Their eyes searched out inner goods. Nothing Hugo could wear, no way he combed his hair or wore his trousers, nothing he said about drugs or boredom, no anger he dug up could survive their quelling kindness. He unwound in this quiet corner of suburbia. He watched. He was taken in and accepted.

Every Sunday he would sit with the rest of the Meeting in the square room round a table with a vase of wildflowers in the centre and the light would stream in through the windows that ran from floor to ceiling, leaving great puddles of sun on the floor, splashing about the feet of all the old ladies, some snoring beneath blue raffia hats, others sitting brisk and upright with a smile playing about their lips.

Hugo always hid in a corner. He often had a problem staying awake and hated it when his body jerked into consciousness and eyes, wandering the room, would stare at him. As he sat there, his ankles bathing in the sunshine, he would piece together the week before. Before Charlie this would have been the week at school, the work, the teasing, Sam, homework, trouble. Now with Charlie in every corner of his head he spent the hour in the quiet, weighing up the battle between hope and despair. The interruptions from the elders, their sprightly homilies on the spiritual significance of an exchange with the greengrocer the week before, became tiresome, irritating invasions of his complicated system of penance and remorse.

Hugo blamed himself for everything that had gone wrong. And God was his umpire, clocking up bad points that were punished by Charlie's absence. It was so easy to clock up bad points. Most of the time he only realised he had retrospectively, when Charlie hadn't showed and he had to search back through the week to find out why. He had masturbated on Wednesday, or shoplifted on Thursday. More and more things became forbidden in a regime of such severity it left his confidence and humour flayed with guilt. And all because Charlie hadn't showed. Hugo was negotiating with a primal screaming God of spite and retribution. Meeting was the room where he licked his wounds and bound himself up mentally and physically for another week of waiting for the weekend.

In fact Meeting became the mainstay of his relationship with Charlie. Not because they ever went together (this restless Scottish roughneck, who'd travelled Europe at sixteen in a lorry cabin with a heavy hauler, who hated education, who recoiled from the middle classes and their polite little children, whose suntan came not from the beach but from the heat on his back while shipping generators from truck to truck in a foreman's cap, would never have understood what Hugo was doing there), but as times grew complicated and rough, Hugo used the Meeting as a personal confessional, a cloister protecting him, for one hour, one day a week only, sheltering him from the buffetings of the outside wind. He felt vulnerable outside. He felt the wind blowing through to his bones. He was miserable.

Miserable because he was in love and his lover was not. They had started so well. Every Friday. Every Saturday. In the truck. Back to the bedsit. Sex. Television – lying front to back, warm skin to warm skin under the blue nylon sleeping bag. They didn't say much. They didn't have much to say. They hardly knew each other. But they were in love, or Hugo thought they were. But then as the novelty slid away, Charlie became elusive and when he was not elusive he became irritable.

Hugo was too much in love. He clung as Charlie shook. Rules were laid down and he swallowed each of them. He was to stop using long words; he was to stop wearing certain clothes; if they went to the pub he was only allowed to drink beer; he wasn't allowed to talk about school, or homework or university; he was to stop writing the letters that streamed out of his pen like long moans of passion, incoherent, rambling, giving everything away.

None of the rules worried Hugo. What frightened him was the cool temper behind the eyes. They still had moments of passion.

They still had evenings of laughter, fooling around in the laundrette with half-concealed erections (here too Hugo showed himself up – the boy whose hands hadn't seen a hard day's work lost the money for the soap in the soap machine. It should have been second nature but he pushed the wrong button, read the wrong column and lost the twenty pence. He felt ridiculous, like the princess about to sleep on the pea), but the light was fading fast. Charlie didn't look at him. The smile had gone out of his face. Hugo was frightened of what he would do if they finished. He was frightened of his own depression. He didn't want to be a suicide, but he didn't see how he would be able to avoid it if they ended. Charlie saw to that. They didn't end. They petered out.

That was the car park winter.

This was Hugo's trial by despair. He had always been a happy boy. Up. Unlike sister senior, who struggled to face every day and cried herself to sleep every evening. But the car park winter almost killed his smile for good.

At first it was easy. Charlie had agreed to a rendezvous point at the car park on the corner of the High Street outside the Hand and Flower pub.

The only days they could meet were Friday and Saturday evenings. Every Friday and Saturday evening, after a few secret telephone calls during the week, under cover of the upstairs Hoover, Hugo would wait in the car park. He'd wait for half an hour and then spot those blue eyes, the flashing smile, the come-up-here-and-love-me look, and Hugo, catching his breath, would run to his lover. But then, for eight weeks in a row Charlie didn't arrive. His blue truck never turned the corner and Hugo, shivering beside the telephone box in between humiliating calls to the landlord, watched the traffic come and go.

Every Friday evening he watched the flower seller wrap up his unsold stems and pack up the stand into boxes before leaving in his van. He watched cars parking at the pub and people leaving again to go to parties, in a warm gaggle of noise and friendship. And Hugo just stood there, tapping his feet against the cold. Chin up, best lip forward.

For eight weeks Charlie didn't turn up. But every week he promised to be there. Every week he apologised and sounded as if he meant it. Hugo was young. It was his first time. He wanted to believe, so he did, and for the first few weeks he fought back the tears, the frustration. But he fought it all alone. There was no-one he could tell.

He measured out the wait in five minute episodes, each one one step closer to the awful chime of the hour. And at the end of each hour he crept off in the chill February drizzle to the Marquee, to the pub or to a party he'd said he might turn up to. Each time he bottled back his tears.

He couldn't say anything to anyone at school. He tried stories about a black woman, trying to invent something that people would see had to be secret (it was such an insult to his parents who would never have thought twice about a person's colour). Nobody really believed that story. He dropped it. Dropped the whole subject. Silence at home, silence at school, silence in the car park. And then the silence of the Meeting House. If someone had said to Hugo, 'I feel sorry for you,' he would have drowned in tears, the floodgates washed away, the banks of restraint burst. He swallowed it all, but he could feel the clouds creeping deeper into his heart.

Only once did the screen begin to fall apart, at a party in maybe the sixth, maybe the seventh week of the car park winter.

He knew everybody at the party. They were all friends or friends of friends. They liked him. He made them laugh. He liked them. They laughed with him. They hardly knew each other.

He walked into the living room, the garden, the kitchen. Everywhere was swollen with drinking friends, all happy, all flirting, squeezing, giggling, greeting him with teeth and smiles and he felt this black space open inside his chest into which every smile he'd ever been going to smile, every happy thought he'd ever been going to think, vanished. The black space kept growing. It had uneven edges and it spread like an oil slick through his chest. It hated the smiles around him. It even hated the light.

Hugo stretched his lips and bared his teeth in a fake smile as dry as sawdust. Easing himself past the crowd, he slipped upstairs. He pushed through a quiet door into a dark bedroom. The curtains were open and the thin, grey light of the moon cast a pallor on the frills and trinkets of a teenage girl's bedroom. He sat on the bed, perfectly still in the silvery dark, and listened to his heartbeat. He listened to the voices in the garden. He felt so far away. He couldn't move. He couldn't cry. He couldn't talk. He wanted to merge with the thin, grey light and to feel nothing ever again. He didn't want to die, he wanted to turn to ashes.

He sat and heard girls' voices coming up the stairs and towards the door and through the door and the light came on like a lightning attack. There were two girls he knew well looking at him strangely because he looked so strange. He had dried tears he didn't know he'd cried half way down his cheeks. His hands were clutched in his lap. He sat and stared straight in front of him like a mystic. When they spoke to him through the wincing, harsh light, he asked them to switch the light off. He was surprised when they did. Then they asked him again what was wrong and he started to weep. Not sob. Weep. And through the water that tumbled down his face like a shower, he tried to explain the black space without mentioning Charlie, without mentioning the car park, or the landlord who mocked him, or the wind that bared him to the bone, or the couples that came and went in happy throngs in front of him, or even the flower seller who never spoke to him and always looked so blistered and blue in the wind that it made Hugo still colder to watch him.

The girls were very kind. They sat and listened and talked to him. He persuaded them that it was best that he stayed upstairs in the dark until he felt he could come down, and he persuaded them not to tell anyone. They closed the door quietly behind them and went downstairs. A short while later Hugo slipped away.

Hugo never blamed Charlie for not arriving. He blamed himself. In his strict game of obedience, reward, transgression and punishment, Charlie's own actions were not included. It was all between Hugo and God. Throughout the car park winter, this religious superstition infected every look he gave to men on the street, every visit he made to a cottage, every touch of his dick under his dressing gown while wrestling with his maths homework. Hugo fought hard for Charlie, with God's mean eye prying into the dankest corners of his imaginings. And still Charlie didn't arrive. And still, each time Hugo rang, he said he'd be there the next time. And still he wasn't.

The telephone rang at the other end of the line. The open sesame. His parents were in the kitchen, squabbling, he hoped. That would keep the volume high. It was Saturday night. The eighth Saturday of the car park winter. Hugo hadn't spoken to Charlie the night before. He had waited the whole hour in the cold of the car park until his toes hurt and his nose ran. He had been into the tango parlour and been chewed by a drunk whose teeth hurt his dick. He just stood and watched himself being eaten up by the man's sloppy jaws – the sick-sweet smell of fermented fruit wafting up. He had no morale, no pleasure. He had no smiles, no feeling. Just a long, grey face.

Charlie picked up the phone. Hugo fought for air.

'It's Hugo.'

'I know.'

'I was there last night.'

'Where?'

He could have wept. He didn't. The adrenalin was ebbing away.

'Can we meet tonight?'

'No.'

'Why not?'

What use was pride at this stage? He'd already said so much.

'I think we should call it off for a while.'

'Call what off?'

'You know. Stop seeing each other for a bit.'

The conversation was as brittle as a glass ornament.

'Is there someone else . . . there?'

'Yes.'

'I'd better hang up.'

'Call me again, right. I want to explain.'

'Yep.'

That yep swallowed everything. Full stop. He put the phone down.

He was about to think about what had happened. About to reel from the short sharp shock. He didn't have time.

'Who was that you were speaking to?'

His mother was in the hall. She was half slapped-up for the night's dinner party. Her face was split between varnish and the raw.

'Paul.'

'Paul who?'

'Paul from school.'

'No, it wasn't.'

'Yes, it was.'

'What's his number?'

'Why do you want it?'

'I want to ring him. He'll tell me if he's just spoken to you.'

Occasionally Hugo had flashes of strategic brilliance. He needed one now. It came.

'Okay, ring him. It's 836 9241.'

She looked slightly surprised, on the varnished side of her face. It was only that side he could watch.

'But if you do ring him, everybody at school will know that you did, and I'll be the laughing stock of the whole place.'

She didn't ring.

He never quite knew why that worked so well. Perhaps it echoed a battle she'd had with her own father. There was no doubt she loved her children. She didn't want to make fools of them. And yet she had made an idiot of sister senior, when she had been stupid enough to come home from school and tell her mother about people smoking pot in the school changing rooms. Mrs Harvey, full of the drug literature of door to door pamphlets, took her foolish daughter all the way back to school to the head-mistress and made her hand over the names. And all the time beneath her own roof, Mrs Harvey's only son was mixing amyl barbitone with gin in his bedroom and shuddering like a suicide as it went down.

Hugo emptied two turquoise barbs into the poster paint pot of gin and shook it up. He always had to brace himself for the shock. A train started coming into Hadley station. He threw back the liquid and gulped, swallowing the residue of powder. The train doors opened. He dropped the poster paint pot between the train and the platform and stepped on to the train. He lit a cigarette to kill the taste in his mouth and sat back. He felt dead. The only refuge he could imagine, where he would be safe from other people's looks and laughter, was the Marquee.

Wardour Street was slimy with drizzle. The Marquee crouched

between the buildings like a shack for the homeless. The boom of the bass bins rumbled through the narrow entrance. Seventy-five pence for a night of noise. The band all had dyed blond crewcuts, wore black leather and probably came from Ealing Common. They were called The Depressions. Even that didn't make him smile. By now the barbs were working. He stood in front of the bass bin and felt the barbs dim his senses. He wasn't really thinking about anything. Even on the train going up to the Marquee, he hadn't thought about his conversation with Charlie. He was trapping it in an airlock away from shock. He wasn't shocked. He was surprised at his calmness. He had always been frightened of the end. Now it came it wasn't frightening. It was just another little anticlimax of life. Now it was in the open he realised he'd already known it was all over. He felt scarred not bruised. The scar tissue was already healed. He felt very sad. And the sadness felt like medicine.

He wasn't angry with Charlie. Charlie had already turned into a daydream. He hadn't seen him for so long. He was angry with his mother. He needed to cry on her shoulder and couldn't. He needed her to tell him there were other fish in the sea and that he deserved better. Instead she stared at him with the telephone receiver in her hand and threats in her mouth.

He was ready for a confrontation. If one word was said about the telephone call when he got home, he would leave that evening. He stared at The Depressions, swallowed his beer and went home.

He walked into the sitting room at half past midnight. His parents sat watching Michael Parkinson. His mother had her feet up on the sofa and her glasses on. Her slippers were on the floor. His father sat with a glass of whisky under the standard lamp. They looked up at him with kind smiles and asked him how his evening had been. He said it was fine. He couldn't hear his voice very well. The barbiturates were blurring his eyes.

Dear Cynthia,

First of all I have to let off steam. Whose idea was it
for me to travel Europe with my bloody nagging sister?
This holiday has deteriorated into a series of major-league
slanging matches. Like a parody of the Japanese, we
manage to have a big screaming and shouting row in
front of almost every famous monument. That guarantees
us a crowd, even if the onlookers don't always understand
the idiom. There is barely a word either of us can say
that the other doesn't disagree with. I would like to
scream. And so I shall. Excuse me. (Our hero leaves the
room to scream. Several neighbours in this fleapit hotel
wake up, yell at him, start crying, start beating their
wives: this is Rome after all.)

The irony is she even managed to screw things up
for me after we separated. We had this major humdinger
of a barney outside the youth hostel in Florence. I can't
remember what it was about (I never can). I had had a
sleepless night in a room that recalled pictures of hospital
wards during the Crimean War. A bloke in one of the
beds in my ward spent the whole night dry vomiting,
curled in a corner over a bucket, retching fit for an
exorcism. Normally you would curl up and think, thank
god it's not me, but everyone in the dorm was awake,
transfixed by what sounded like this man's death throes.
So this morning when Mary comes on all heavy about
something irrelevant (she's eternally pissy anyway because
she fell in love with someone in France and he didn't fall

in love with her and now she's in a big lovelorn mope), I snap and she snaps and we both stand there snapping and shouting and just before I move to tear her hair out by its roots she says, 'Well I'm going to Fiesole. I'll meet you in Rome the night after next.'

Brilliant, I think. Freedom. Well, that should have been the case, but what she manages to do then is take my passport, leaving me hers, which effectively means I can't get into a single hotel or youth hostel in Rome. Of course, I don't find out that I've got the wrong passport until five o'clock. That is after an unscheduled six hours on the train, which decided to take a rest in a vineyard in the middle of nowhere, and after a two hour wait to get into the youth hostel. So by now my accommodation prospects are zilch, and the evening air is getting chilly.

I successfully negotiate the purchase of an unripe peach, which after two bites I have to throw away (do these people see me coming, or do they just figure me for a sap as soon as my broken Italian falls out?) and head off to Rome Termini station, where every piece of Europacker driftwood has washed up.

You may or may not know this but Rome Termini is a bastard. My sister may be a cow but this station is a bastard. Outside in the park is one of the most notorious areas in Europe for bag slitting and possession stealing. One much-quoted story tells of the English bloke who went to sleep in the Villa Borghese park with all his possessions stuffed at the bottom of his sleeping bag. When he woke up, everything, including his clothes were gone. He had to make his way, in his underwear, with no money, to the British Embassy. Yuuurgh.

Inside the station the carabinieri play footsie with anyone who lies on the platform (footsie to the stomach, or footsie to the back) and then at about midnight they hose down all the people sleeping in the foyer. So it's well friendly.

Well, it is, actually. Or at least the young men are. I was sitting there, looking and feeling tired and forlorn, clutching my bags and trying not to nod off, when I noticed I was being cruised (more like sailed past . . . is that assailed?) by two young arm-in-arm men. You know the kind. They walk as if they had lockjaw in their hips. They only turn above the waist.

Anyway, I do my bit. A stare, a smile, a sheepish look. And they come over and talk to me. One of them speaks French, the other only Italian, but the Italian speaker is clearly the one who has the hots for me. He's one of these over-tanned queens who wears too much white and is low on male hormones, but that also means he's harmless (he does not, for example, appear to be carrying a switchblade). The French speaker and I immediately get on very well, which leaves Mr Over-tan grinning with over-white teeth, and they offer me a room for the night. I cannot believe my luck.

We stop on the way to pick up Frenchie's lover, Sergio or Claudio or somesuch. He's a hustler on the main drag out of the station, where all the sexual mishmash ply their wares. His wares are very pliable but not in my hands. Despite the fact that we stare at each other all night and are each expected to sit there with our shirts off (why, I can't imagine, unless this was some kind of battle of the sexual status symbols between the other two). He is clearly Frenchie's and I am clearly Mr Melanoma's.

Such is life. In return for closing my eyes and raising my hips so that Mr Freedent can do his business (which he does very well: I pretend I am asleep and only responding instinctively to the sensations of a bloody good blow job), I get a warm bath, dinner and a very comfortable bed and breakfast the next morning (this morning), by which time Frenchie and the hooker have vanished and Mr Melanoma and I have to communicate in broken sign language.

I rather miss Frenchie and his hustler. The hustler especially. He had a sort of impenetrable calm about him, even as he sat there with his shirt off. And a very bold stare. As someone whose eyes normally live on the floor during encounters with any hint of sex (the rest of me is fine . . . just the eyes are wrong), I am very impressed by that frank, unabashed hooker-stare. Pay me or fuck you.

I've never found it attractive before, but I have often found it enviable. I don't want to sleep with it, I want to be it. Mind you, I've often wondered what it would be like to take a hustler home. Would you spend all your time trying to persuade them to persuade you that you are somehow different? Given the men some of them must have to deal with, I think I'd be a pretty good deal. But then they'd take one look at me and think 'no tips,' and there would go any chance of special treatment. What does appeal to me about the idea, though, is that there would be none of this worry about moving too fast, of having got the wrong signal. They would be there for sex. So often (well, no . . . well, yes, but I'm sure I shouldn't say so often) you lure someone into your nest and the air is full of lust and then you sit down (on my hard, uncomfortable chairs) and you offer them a cup of tea and all sex dissolves like a sugar lump in hot water. It takes a long time to get the temperature up again.

I am writing the rest of this at the station, and even as I speak, the first mid-afternoon rent is appearing – like the blonde, big-boobed women who do the lunchtime businessmen in Shepherds Market. But they at least have a certain gutsy charm. Like lowlife Dolly Parton clones. These boys – the ones sitting at the table opposite me at the station cafe – look as if they could do with a week in the sun and a large meal.

My sister should be in on the 12:47, which will not arrive anywhere near 12:47, but which I have to wait for anyway. I have been rehearsing different bollocking speeches all morning. The trouble is she is bound to interrupt before I reach my crescendo, and I don't have any really good threats to frighten her with. I think she is even stronger than me and definitely tougher. But I bet she found a room in Fiesole without any trouble. Girls, don't you hate them. Oh, whoops! Sorry, Cynth!

Anyway. We are both heading for Paris soon and then she has to go down to Nantes to find herself a room. She is doing a year out of university as part of her French degree, and she has selected Nantes (no-one knows why). She has to move there in October. So I will be foot-loose and fancy-free except for the cloud of imminent A-level results. Oh, Ugh.

See you when I get back and you get back from New York.

Lots of love,

Hugo

6

VISITING TIME – CYNTHIA

When he leant forward, he could see through all the wooden holes a long line of men craning forward, beating their arms up and down. In the cubicle next to him sat a black boy. Maybe seventeen, maybe younger. In this light people changed all the time. One moment they were pristine youth, the next a skull peered through the dark and cavities replaced the eyes. He stared at the black boy and, as he stared, the hole in the wall began to close up. It puckered like a tensed arsehole.

His arse tensed and a razor of pain passed up through his bowels. Still it didn't wake him. The pains entered his dreams but the dreams accommodated them. The fever and the sweat were transformed into images, dull and repetitive, never the fantastic hallucinations of delirium, just the boredom of a sick dream.

Once he stood on the corner of the street looking at a building all night. It went on for hours.

He would wake up to drink some water, debate the crawl to the toilet and another feeble bowel movement, a dribble of acid shit searing his skin, already raw with the wiping and washing and burning. And then he'd close his eyes and try to create a dream in fields of flowers, days on a river in the sunshine, dappled light and laughing friends. But each time he'd find himself back in front of the house. And the house didn't change. It only seemed to change. And he couldn't walk away. Whenever he did, he never arrived anywhere new.

He winced with pain and the boy knocked at his cubicle door. Hugo was dirty and needed to clean himself, but if he didn't let the boy in he might miss his chance. He hadn't had a chance like this for such a time. He opened the door. The latch fell off in his hand and the wood turned damp and cold. He couldn't smell anything but he knew that he smelt bad. The black boy entered and stared at him, his licked lips pouting as a tongue flipped in and out, inviting, demanding, luring Hugo's prick to his mouth. Hugo had his trousers round his knees and hadn't wiped himself clean. He had an erection standing between his legs like a pink lolly and the boy was staring at it. The boy knelt in front of him and his head came down over the lolly like a calf suckling at an udder. He sucked so hard the blood suffused the knob in a great upward surge and Hugo groaned.

He looked at the boy and saw the life being sucked out of him. He lay back against the cistern and smiled. The boy's skin was dark but blotched with pale patches like blond bruises. His eyes were slits. They didn't waver in their obsession. They pounced on Hugo's dick and saw nothing else. His hair was tangled and his shirt torn. Hugo pushed the shirt off the boy's shoulders and gripped his nipples. He squeezed them and they swelled too large. He gripped the boy's breast and squeezed it, fearing a dribble of ooze would appear from each teat, but the boy's hand brushed him off and then returned to his prick. All the time he gorged and slurped on Hugo's dick, he wanked his own, which swelled into a fat organ dribbling colourless fluid. Hugo moved his hips up and down, fucking the boy's mouth. He felt the shit drying on his arse and knew that the smell wafting from the pan was death. The holes in the walls had opened again and revealed a line of penises all aimed at him, all swollen, some purple with too much beating, others trapped inside their foreskins. They beat and beat like furious pistons. Hugo turned the other way and saw an old man's head with glasses and a rictus smile licking his lips and he smiled at Hugo, so Hugo smiled back and groaned.

The boy stood up and, pulling Hugo forward by the chin, pushed his dick towards him. Hugo didn't want it. It dribbled and those dribbles were poison. But the boy's slit eyes didn't want to be argued with. Hugo plunged and gagged. He drew back and gasped for breath. His hand reached down to his willy but the lolly had flopped. The boy's dick was speckled with spittle. Hugo turned away and saw through the hole the old man with the rictus smile pulling off his clothes and reaching for his dick. But where the dick should have been there was a hole. Hugo turned away. The line of penises were now by his ear and they were all dribbling and as the dribbles hit the floor, they sizzled like acid. Hugo clenched his arse and a spasm of pain shot through his bowel like a serrated bullet. He felt the prickle of sweat on his head, the trickle as it ran into his hair and then a warm, wet mess moved over his head like a soft slug, but a comforting, wrapping sort of warmth like home and hot baths and bedtime. The dream was suffused with orange and red light and the images, skulls and smiles, the dribbling penises and the blotchy boy all faded in the glow. The glow became so warm Hugo opened his eyes and woke to see Cynthia on his bed, holding a warm, wet flannel in her hand.

She stared at him in a long look as if she hadn't seen his eyes open. The soft sensation of the flannel bathing his brow still swooned over him like a sunset on a distant horizon. It sapped the pain from his bowels and cooled the panic in his blood. He'd known the dream would end badly. He'd been saved only seconds before the horror.

He never dreamed about sex anymore. Only horrid couplings in corners. His first wet dream ever had been the deflowering of a wizened dwarf, a hobbled creature who left Hugo sticky and depressed in bed, next to the muscle boy who had refused him sex the night before. That was in the old days. In a wrecked squat on the Talgarth Road with a blue-eyed bad boy he'd stolen from his friend's bedroom. The boy was playing games. It was the only thing he was good at. The game was to refuse sex to the men he invited back. He allowed Hugo a kiss, a long, luxuriant kiss, and then rolled over to sleep, leaving Hugo quivering with a desire that entered his dream like an incubus, and took the shape of the wizened dwarf as punishment.

'You were dreaming,' said Cynthia and Hugo felt all the shame of the unspeakable stick in his throat.

There she sat on his bed with her long, black hair draping towards his sheets, its sheen like combed silk. Her eyes were full of warmth. He was hers now.

He hadn't seen her here for some time. Things had been bad for a while and they hadn't allowed him visitors. Not even the regular ones. His mother had sat vigil for three nights, paralysed beside a telephone. But the swell of the fever had abated and he was beached in its wake, slipping in and out of dreams.

When he saw Cynthia on his bed, he knew that some of the charm of an old life, his old life, was still there. He seemed to have been locked away from it for so long. So many people didn't come. They knew he didn't want to be seen, all grey, his skin stretched across his bones like old tissue paper. But Cynthia came and with her the aroma of a life he had left.

He had been frightened of the visitors he might have had. The professional carers. They had worried him even before he was ill. Lolling sleepily in a Turkish bath in Bethnal Green, sitting untidily among men whose lank bodies were doused in sweat, Hugo had eavesdropped a conversation between a young black of immaculate limbs and skin and a bony creature whose teeth stood at an angle to his gums and whose voice twanged in the air like chicken wire. Hugo was watching a shaven-headed Negro pulverising the men on the slabs; watching him slap on the oils and run skilful strong hands up legs and down backs into the buttock cleavage and between the thighs in the groin where the glands lie. He watched legs being bent backwards so toes touched shoulders and the faces of men, head down in the towel, rolling and smiling with surprise as their bodies performed acrobatics, turned lithe and supple by the masseur's palms.

Hugo was watching the Negro but his ears were pinned to conversation between the young black and the crone. The crone droned, wheedled, trying to lure the young man back for cups of tea or dinner and wine and the mysterious whatever-happens-next-happens. He was a vulture perched on the still-fleshy bodies in the white-tiled charnel house that stank of lemon soap and sweat in a sickly commingling. And he was a Visitor. He talked of his charity calls on the sick and housebound. Every day he'd go to their houses for an hour or two. They were helpless to stop him. He had claimed them. He was a misfit, a reject. He was ugly with an ugly voice and an ugly manner. Not powerful but insipid. Not intimidating but irritating. And he was a Visitor. A man who visited the helpless, the prostrate, the weakened. He was their nursemaid. They had no choice. They had come to this.

He looked for a while at Cynthia's eyes with their fleck of brown in the white like a smudge from her iris. She wasn't searching for a look the way his mother did, her blue eyes wavering between anger and love and helplessness. She was just looking at him. Waiting for him to say what he could, to do what he could.

With Cynthia he could be silent. There had been that much between them. That much love and misunderstanding. That much help and that much criticism.

She had loved him and, unlike the others, had attacked his sexuality. Unlike the others, she had made love to him. But she took his sexuality as a slur on her womanhood.

'Go off and get your arse greased then,' she said once on a doorstep in Manhattan. Then she looked horrified and said she was sorry. Then he went off and got his arse greased by a hairy New Yorker in a smart apartment. The New Yorker, whose name was Edward, gave him a T-shirt with the name of a fashionable nightclub on it. Then next morning, Hugo gave Cynthia the T-shirt and, as they walked through the perfume halls at Bloomingdales, all the queens and fag hags whispered questions. 'Is it open again yet? I hate it when it closes for the summer. You know they've been running it out on Fire Island.'

Cynthia loved the attention and Hugo was proud. It was his first New York visit and no other city had ever allowed him to be so ambiguous.

Cynthia had invited him. Ross, her father, owned a gallery in a garish, sloping building on Madison. They lived an uptown life from a simple room at the back of his gallery, while Ross stayed upstate with one of his lithe black girlfriends, eating apple slices with peanut butter and doing sex in weird contortions and different rooms.

It was a new world, and Hugo was transfixed.

It was a rite of passage, through the arms, through the love of two entwined people – a father and daughter. It was a crystallised moment of elegance, euphoria and exploration. One year later, that moment became forever irretrievable, when Ross keeled over in his karate class and died.

When Hugo got the news, over the telephone in his tutor's rooms at Cambridge, he couldn't swallow the experience whole. It was impossible to snuff Ross out as easily, as quickly, as death had. He felt as if a mentor had been snatched away after only the first lesson. A lover had been killed minutes after the first mutual declaration of love. He had spent so little time with this man who had told him so much. Not what he should or might do, but what he could, would do. This man, who had peeled back the world and offered it to him like a ripe fruit, the man who had discovered the tree where the ripe fruit fell into your lap, and who hadn't had to sell any bits of his soul to eat there, the man Hugo fell in love with, just as Cynthia herself had, died.

Ross was Cynthia's muse, her faith, her smile, her fantasy world. Her parents had divorced when she was fat-legged and still gurgling, and her father had disappeared across the Atlantic, leaving his baby and his ex-wife in a tiny, over-furnished West London flat.

Some children would never have forgiven him. Some would never have recovered from the lack of a man. The family females gathered about Cynthia in horn-rimmed clusters of wealth and spinsterhood. She was educated. She was given horses to ride and party frocks to play in. She was told to call for tea in Berkeley Square, where some of the formidable spinsters lived, and she did. She visited them in their flower-choked villas in the Algarve and Spain, and they frightened her with their stern looks and serious talk.

She was a child brought up among adults. Her mother dispensed with babysitters as soon as Cynthia could hold her own and hold her water, and took her young daughter on nightclub jaunts with tyros and gamblers, with the charmers and the spenders who courted her. For Cynthia's mother was a beautiful woman.

But the dream behind Cynthia's eyes throughout this long slow passage past restaurant tables and polite glasses of cold water, warm tea and tepid lemonade, was her father. Every year her father descended from the clouds and swept his brown-eyed, black-haired daughter off to breakfast at the Inn On The Park, where he would make her flush inside with the joy of his smile and his laugh, the bounce of his outrageous moustache, the perfection of his manners. They were in love. All their lives apart they were in love, and now Hugo was with them in their bower of bliss and he was watching them with the curiosity of someone who had never seen people so public in their private happiness before. It made him tearful with shame for his own shy-faced inhibitions. It made him quiet. It soothed him and made him smile.

On the night of Ross's birthday, they went out for a black bean dinner at the Cuban Chinaman. The two teenagers and the teacher. The children and the man of the world. Hugo watched him with the intensity of a boy reinventing his own father. He wanted Ross to be his, to be his blood. More than that he wanted to belong to Ross, to be his son. For a man he was pretty cool. For a father he was unheard of. His musketeer moustache and flock of black curls gave him the look of a gypsy fiddler. His body was a ripple of tense muscle from boxing and karate. He was lean and poised. He talked to them as if they were in command, as if any choice were theirs to make or leave, as if the future was stretched out before them like a sheet of spangled paper on which they could dance whichever steps they chose. He told Hugo that the world was his oyster and he asked him, over a birthday dinner in the Cuban Chinaman, why he wouldn't take his daughter. How could he refuse her?

He needed to go to the toilet, and he needed help. Every movement away from the horizontal made him queasy. He could feel fluids in him run thin and sickly, he could sense the trickle of poison in his veins. When he looked down at his feet, yellow, cold and shrivelled on the lino, he felt his legs would snap like twiglets into many pieces and he would lie, dying at the foot of a toilet bowl. A fitting burial urn. A last glimmer of humour in a life dribbling down the waste disposal unit.

He needed to go to the toilet and he needed Cynthia's help. She was there. She knew what needed to be done. He hadn't really greeted her yet. So he said, 'Hello. Can you take me to the toilet?' His voice was so far away when he woke up. An echo in a distant room. He was so far ebbed nothing seemed to be near but the pain. The acid trickle of shit between his legs. The hollow, eating pain in his chest that made him breathless. The pain that rose and fell between his teeth and his head like quick-changing tides.

Cynthia smiled. She put his hands on her shoulders and eased him out of bed. It might have been a smile of victory but it wasn't. After all, she had been spurned for anonymous men and hairy Edward, for strangers in stations and bathhouses and bars. She had demanded to know why and he had only one answer – it's what I want.

Now, this feeble end, this slow and lingering, loitering death could have been her proof, her self-righteous revenge on his rejection, her proof that he should have chosen her. But she wasn't smiling that way. She was smiling like warm tea, like soothing oils, like the past.

How could he have refused her? He had no choice. Cynthia should have been his wife . . . but even when they made love, that once, between the blue and pink appliqué cushions on the bed of a black catwalk model, a girlfriend of her father's, he thought about a photograph of men in their underpants he'd seen only minutes earlier, and came quietly, detachedly, into the vagina of this girl who was trying so hard to persuade him what he was missing.

But why did Cynthia, why did others, always think it was a choice? Who would have chosen this? All the secrecy, all the lies, all the hiding, all the covert watching, all the childlessness, all the expensive presents bought for other people's children. All the euphemisms. Uncle Hugo. It was a future whose past was always more exciting. Times lived. Men loved.

It was a future with loneliness sewn into the seam and death woven into the fabric, unseen until too late, a single sinister thread.

But while Hugo knew and understood and had swallowed and digested this, he was not ashamed. He was not guilty. He knew where the blame lay. It lay between his legs. It rarely just lay. It called itself by fancy names. He liked to know it as his libido. It had an appetite that any other world would not have been able to sate. The gay world, the toilet life, the barfly crawl dished up an endless round of torsos, penises, mouths, incidental conversations and nameswaps and nights in ill-clad council flats, tossing and writhing with another stranger. He couldn't have had it any other way.

Imagine he'd been born a girl and fed the appetite beneath his school skirt in the villages and towns of outer London, in woods and copses and fields. Suppose that he'd hiked up his petticoats and dropped his knickers in so many public places, after dark, in strange car parks, behind pubs, in car seats, by brooks being bitten by mosquitoes. He would have been dead by now. He would have been dead long before. And sick. Abused. Tarred with the name slut, saddled with the mess of abortion, with the disease of pussy pricks fumbling into a youthful snatch.

And if he'd been a boy, all straight and honest and girl-fearing but with a lust beneath his jockstrap fit to swell? If he'd been such a one – a muscular Christian with a rugby blue and his own cricket bat, where could he have let his libido lap? On which young female's juices would he have supped to sate the querulous, obsessive sex that tugged and nagged at him? Nowhere. None of the boys had sex until long after Hugo.

Hugo was a fatalist. Sex had been his making and his undoing. He had drunk too long, too far, too fast from the fountain and caught the germ that hid within the pipe. But he would have died of thirst had he not drunk. Sex was instilled in his blood like an addiction and it led him down the path to rack and ruin, laughing and gurgling all the way . . .

He wasn't laughing right now. He was shivering with pain and weakness. This was a filthy trick. But even in the jaws of the disease, even as the cities he played in were turning to funeral parlours and the cry of the moral echoed throughout the dens, yelling abuse and demanding abstinence, still then he had grinned his gurgling smile and plunged into the arms of sex.

He remembered a Parisian bathhouse in the rue St Anne. He had been driving for three days from Florence with a girl. They were returning from a holiday, a group of friends in a villa in Tuscany, well-bred privileged youths treating themselves with in-dulgence and Hugo played as if to the manner born. They had driven back through the dirty haze of Northern Italy into the ridiculous melodrama of Switzerland, a land cowed by its own scenery into fat-headed banality. They had left Switzerland through the neon concrete of Berne, a city of lights and closed bars, of inviting signs and hostile restaurants. They had driven across the murky plains of eastern France and through the roll and comfort of Troyes.

In Paris, possessed by the sticky summer air, fuelled by the speed they had licked off paper packages as they drove, egged on by the cold beers outside Café Cost, he had tipped into the bath-house after midnight with sex choking his throat and thumping against his chest.

And there, locked in a back-room bathroom with a fat-lipped man of perfect buttocks, he had thrown himself into the clinch of sex with the smile of one preparing his last fix. There, in the stream of sweat and hallucination of amyl that they gulped up nostrils, there, as the man's penis swelled and loomed like some vast fleshly fruit and Hugo's mouth and eyes drooled in one gasping hunger, a quiet voice whispered – this could be the boy that kills you. And a quiet voice answered back – so then, this is the way to die.

He sat on the cold rim of the toilet bowl, his arse shrinking away from the pain it knew had to come. Cynthia waited by the bed, flicking through a glossy magazine, looking down on the streets of Fulham scuttling past in a business of car lights and bicycle baskets.

Where would they be now if they had married? Where would they live? What would their children be like?

In those early days they were the all-night dancers. Ross looked on amused as they dolled themselves in the gallery mirrors, preparing for another nightlife onslaught. A night of drinking free water at expensive bars, of dancing in secondhand shoes and being very London. Being London in those days was still effective. The New Yorkers had not discovered hair dye or pierced ears or black and white clothing. They had heard about punk and were rather impressed and rather intimidated. Cynthia with her jet black, sheer-to-the-shoulder hair and Hugo with his peroxide crop and a two inch fork dangling from his earlobe, took the floors by storm. They danced on slimming pills and water and the occasional joint passed down the line. They stopped to pee or sweat or stand under one of the fans and pretended not to notice the looks of passing New Yorkers.

People always mistook them for English pop stars. It was understandable, thought Hugo. Had he been able to sing, he would, of course, have been a pop star. He knew all the right moves. That look of translucence when a camera appeared, as if he hadn't noticed it. That unflinching poise as the flash went off, as if lost in some daydream of Berlin cellars and expensive cocaine.

They practised their fashionable walk. All the beautiful boys in New York had a walk and Cynthia and Hugo practised in the gallery in front of the tall mirrors. You leaned backwards away from the smoke and air-conditioning, your hands sunk into the wide pockets of your pleat-top trousers, your shoulders rigid beneath their shoulder-pads, and you sloped into the room, sloped to the bar. It was a little awkward when ordering drinks as you were so far away from the barman's ear, but eventually he understood the watch-my-lips mime for water (without bubbles) and you sloped off again, looking for a niche with a dance floor view.

The first trickle hit the pan with a plop. It was a rebuke really. Such a high-pitched noise. So little shit. The acid ate into his rectum. He dug his nails into his hand. It was already punctured with little half-moon nail shapes. Everything took so long to go away – the pain, the bruises, the grazes, itchy spots, even the nail marks. He smiled. His own little stigmata. A pathetic version of a great tragedy. He concentrated on the tiles, counting them, transforming them. One started to breathe and he smiled, a thin smile at the thought of an acid flashback. He loved acid flashbacks.

They had been very well-behaved in New York. They led a wholesome daytime life of major buildings and significant museums, punctuated by iced coffees. You couldn't walk too far in that air without a cool drink. The city clung to your shirt as soon as you left the building. The air dribbled air-conditioning effluent on your head as you passed under skyscrapers. It was like walking through a steam bath.

They walked slowly. They talked beneath the trees in Central Park. They went window shopping on Madison Avenue. It was like love. But there was no sex. Except that once.

He still had the photographs somewhere. In an empty flat full of the abandoned clutter of a healthy life. Black and white photographs of Cynthia, face to the wind on the Staten Island Ferry. Her features were so precise. In the distance the Statue of Liberty was washed in grey mist and the World Trade Centre towers rose like a sky high fortress, lapped by the murk of the Hudson. They were pictures of arrogance and innocence. They were pictures of children playing in the adult theme park. They were pictures of Cynthia before the world fell on her head; of Hugo before the world fell from under his feet.

He called to her and she was there, lifting him up. His joints were so brittle, they ground as he moved.

'What are you up to? How's Christopher?'

Hugo had never liked Christopher. Cynthia knew that. So did Christopher.

'He's busy. A new show. In Aberdeen. He wants me to go and see it.'

'I'm so pleased you still come. It must be awfully miserable for you.'

Why did he say these things? There were tears welling up in her eyes. He wanted to hug her. He wanted to comfort her. He wanted her to weep on his shoulder and cry away all the deaths she'd had to suffer.

Ross had been Hugo's first real death. And Cynthia's too.

A real death is when someone you don't expect to, dies. A real death is when someone who doesn't deserve to, dies. Someone who hasn't lived their life yet. It doesn't include grandparents. Written into the relationship with grandparents is their closeness to the grave. It's part of what makes them precious. Just as the child is nearest the womb, they are nearest the earth. It's the parents who are in limbo, with too long behind them and too far in front of them to feel anchored.

Hugo had lost three of four grandparents before he left school. When his first grandfather died, he couldn't cry. Everybody around him was weeping and wailing. He was ten years old and couldn't cry. He couldn't see the logic. He couldn't feel the shock. His grandfather had been ill in a hospital bed for some time. He was young, they said, but to Hugo he was old. A great, smiling teddy bear of a man who smacked his lips over the apple sauce with the Sunday pork. Grandpa took them on long walks and talked all the time. Hugo never listened to what he said, only to the sound of his voice, a warm low rumble. He built a garage out of wood for Hugo's toy cars – his workshop hummed with tools and the air was rich in the smell of sawdust. He was an inventor who had discovered his vocation at sixty-five and dropped dead of the family heart-attack only a few months later.

It was a bitter story Hugo only understood later, when his sorrow was too postponed, too sad for tears. Tears were spontaneous and angry and selfish. He had none of them. Only a vague feeling, about Grandpa having been released. He watched his grandmother cry as they sat and stood and sat through the dregs of a religion dragged out with the Sunday best for a po-faced rainy day in a Kent chapel. The children were let off the hook after that, and were sent home with a babysitter, who wore a face of sympathetic sweetness that crushed all their games.

When Hugo's grandmother on the other side died, she died abroad where she had always lived. They had never spoken the same language, and had only seen each other once every three or so years. She was a big woman with a loud laugh that shook her chins and made Hugo love her. But he hardly knew her and when her death came, he simply used it as a vehicle for his motorway massacre, the biggest lie he ever told.

That evening, his mother already departed for her mother's deathbed, the family stayed home, sitting round cheese-on-toast dinners, feeling the adrenalin of liberation but unable to show it because they were supposed to be sad and sombre. They pulled faces at each other while father disappeared behind the newspaper.

Mr Harvey didn't have to go either this time. Death was becoming a very low-key business.

He lay back. He hadn't said a word for ten minutes and the air was dank with silence. It weighed in on him. He had nothing to discuss except his disabilities. She was looking at him and looking out of the window. He wanted her to be there, but he wanted her to talk to him. She rested a hand on his brow that made him sweat. He was so weak that even people's gestures exhausted him.

'Will you organise the funeral party?' His voice sounded like someone scratching at a door with broken nails. He wasn't sure whether she could have heard. His breathing was already going out of control.

'But . . .'

He moved his hand in a tiny gesture of impatience. She left that line.

'I know the music I want. "Popcorn". Please make it a party . . .' His chest was rising and falling like a panicked pigeon. He waited for the breath to come back. He couldn't trap the air. He had to wait for it to trickle in. Life was a trickle. '. . . We always gave good parties. Maybe I'll be there. Who . . . knows?'

Cynthia smiled. At last.

'At my father's funeral they danced until the early hours. The food and drink never stopped coming.'

She'll pull it off, he thought. She'll guarantee me a bang. Not this ghastly whimper. She knows about funerals.

Hugo was in Cambridge, in his tutor's room, standing in the bay window, making a telephone call to Cynthia in Oxford. By some stupid trick of fate they had ended up in different places. It was probably for the best. They could be very hard on each other.

He was put through to Cynthia, but a friend of hers answered the telephone. They said she couldn't speak. He pressed. He needed to ask her about selling some tickets for a play he wanted to take to Oxford. They said, haven't you heard. Her father –

A piece of the world fell away.

'Tell her it's Hugo. I'll understand if she doesn't want to come to the phone.'

The sound Cynthia made when she came to the phone was despair. The tears boiled up and she couldn't talk, only breathe and shudder and sob. In her incoherent, shuddering breath, Hugo heard for the first time the inexpressible, uncomprehending pain of a woman whose man has been snatched away without time to prepare, without time to argue and demand a reprieve.

He arrived in Oxford the next morning and she met him at the coach stop with a small group of friends. She was pale. Her lips were bloodless and her eyes battered with tears. She shook slightly.

'Oh, Hugo. I'm mortified,' she whispered as she clung to his arm. The friends fell away silently, sympathetically. They walked slowly, quietly, back to her room.

Hugo kept turning over the last image he had of Ross. They were sitting together on the redwood verandah of the house up-state. The view over the Hudson Valley was absurd. It was tropical Wiltshire. Ferns and trees clustering around a postcard church spire that played canned bell music every hour, like a sugary barrel organ churning out carols. The sun danced on the river in the valley like a Woolworths painting.

They sat drinking hot tea and eating his apple and peanut butter slices, talking the future. Hugo stared out over the slopes running down to the silver-pink river and listened. He was in a trance. He had never expected to be here. But he was. That was the first chapter. Anything is possible.

That evening Hugo scampered back into NYC and down to the illicit bars and boulevards of the West Village. Ross had given him money to buy Cynthia's birthday present. He went straight to the queeny bric-à-brac store halfway down Christopher Street, where a fat man with a bald pate swanned among his feathers and knick-knacks with the smile and the voice of a welcoming aunt. He bought her an old perfume atomiser in glass which ran blue at the base and a bright pink Japanese fan. Both items smelt of the musk- and patchouli-flavoured shop. Both of them carried the fat man's blessing.

As they walked into the little college room, there they were on her dresser. Snatched from the sweet-smelling headiness of that shop, that night, that summer and stuck in the cold comfort of an undergraduate's room (recently modernised).

After buying them he had gone to Kelner's bar and got drunk steadily, relentlessly, on nervous pints as a huge black man with a T-shirt rolled up to his nipples, gyrated towards him. They ended up the two of them, the skinny white boy with the peroxide hair and the earring and the black giant with the oiled muscles, locked in a loo at the back of the porn store next door, with the owner banging on the door and freaking out. Hugo was still in a trance. He couldn't remember the man's name five minutes later, but he smiled all the way back to Madison Avenue.

The Oxford room looked parched. The narrow bed and institution magnolia walls. They didn't have time to think about that. Cynthia had to call her mother and tell her the news. Cynthia's mother was remarried and living in Tobago.

This was a heavy piece of news to deliver, even to a remarried woman.

Cynthia fainted on the telephone.

As Hugo listened to Cynthia's mother, shouting down the pay-phone all the way from the Caribbean that Cynthia had to go to New York and claim her father's body before he was disposed of by the city, as Cynthia swooned in one arm and he locked her in his elbow, Hugo felt a lake of calm spread through his mind. Life had caught up with him. Tragedy, disaster, grief and helplessness were hurtling around like out of control bumpercars, and he was having to dodge and duck and head them off.

The main thing was, he didn't have to lie anymore to make his life seem more real. This was real.

Cynthia had been talking for ten minutes or so, about a wedding party in Northumberland and the size of the marquee and how the guests danced and twirled and the champagne that they gurgled. People could never work out whether to tell him sad and serious stories about other people who were ill, or to catalogue cavortings across the town and country to 'cheer him up'.

Neither worked. The best thing with Hugo was to read him a book. But as Cynthia talked so happily with the sun behind her catching her lashes as she turned, he watched her and didn't listen. She had come through.

She nearly didn't but now she had. This fairy-tale child, with outrageous legs and a father on a white charger, had seen the world she had always been waiting to enter collapse and disappear just as she was able to move towards it. Her faith, her smile, the laugh in her voice, her appetite for late-night life with odd young men dissolved.

Her father's death was the first and most crushing of a little avalanche of catastrophes that followed, until it seemed to Hugo, living in Cynthia's flat in London, that every month brought its own particular death, and that this would carry on until everyone had gone.

They nearly ceased to be friends. Hugo the Frivolous, sporting loud clothes and a drug habit – Cynthia the Serious, going out with dependable young gentlemen and frowning at excess. Hugo was excess. He began to feel disapproved of. They had been so close during the tragedy. He had stood by to be leaned on, talked at, as he steered her through traffic and embassy queues and travel agent line-ups. But then the stern, hard self-defence began and Hugo, who couldn't pretend to be serious, felt awkward and foolish and wayward with her.

She had never approved of his sex. She had rarely approved of his friends. Her voice had taken on an edge that sounded like net curtains and chintz sofas and bone china cups. But she had warmed again. She had rediscovered her smile and the laugh in her voice.

He slipped in and out of consciousness. Cynthia fell quiet and sat in the window. The sun was on his pillow. This was a quiet and perfect moment. Even now he could still have perfect moments. She smiled. The bone china was gone now.

'Remember,' he whispered. '"Popcorn". And good food.'

He fell asleep as a brown man with blotchy skin and a wet mouth walked towards him rubbing his crotch. Hugo's legs were suddenly running with urine.

12 February, 1983

Dear Mrs Harvey,

It is now one year and seven months since you first
asked me to take an interest in Hugo, and for that period,
as you know, I have been seeing him once a fortnight in
my surgery on Thursday evenings, ostensibly to renew his
prescription for acne lotion.

Hugo has proved, throughout that period, more than
willing to talk to me. I did not, of course, immediately
broach the issue of his sexuality. I felt it would be too
sudden and would alienate him. I wanted to wait until I
had won his confidence and then let him introduce the
subject himself, which he did some weeks ago.

Now that Hugo is going away for a few months, to
work on the cruise liner, I feel it appropriate to give you
a sort of status report on our discussions.

Some things are clear to both of us. Hugo is very
bright and very sure of himself, or at least supposes he is.
In fact he is, like any boy of his age, a mixture of the
half-baked and the over-cooked. But one thing is certain,
Hugo is by no means naive about his own sexuality and,
I'm sure you will be relieved to hear, is determined to
keep an open mind about it.

He seems uncertain as to how fully he believes that his
preoccupation, to date, with men will continue. He speaks
very warmly of a close friend called Cynthia, whom I
believe you know, and with whom he plans to spend
some time in New York when his tenure on the ship is
over. All in all, I feel that this nine months between
leaving school and going up to university is going to be

very useful to him, particularly because being away from home for some time will mean that he has to come to terms with some of the realities of life (Hugo, like many boys of his age is more dogmatic than informed and his mind has been rather cluttered with a ragbag of pretensions).

It will also help him to separate some of his own thoughts from his simple reactions to your own. It is, of course, not unusual for boys, or any children of his age, to adopt a fairly hostile attitude to their own background and domestic environment. Hugo is still very loyal to his family in some ways, but I have rarely seen a young man more eager to find his own wings and fly the family nest. He speaks incessantly of escaping, escaping Hadley and the Harvey roost, and to an extent escaping school, England, and, I think, some rather unfortunate alliances in the past. He is still a very amiable lad, but there is no doubt that events in his past have bruised him somewhat. Some of his involvements, about which I really have nothing but insubstantial detail, have clearly made him very unhappy, and I am sure that the bruising has been worse because he has been unable to share any of this with either friends or family.

Hugo appears a very solitary figure. He is determined and self-reliant but also rather lonely. He would, of course, deny this and I know as you do that he has many friends. But he is sceptical, if not cynical, about love.

On the other hand he cherishes a deep-seated idealism with regard to Cambridge, and I know he feels that university life will prove the antidote to all previous disappointments. I hope he is right. He is very lucky to be going to Cambridge (even now at this ripe age I envy him that) but I feel he may be over-certain that the university will give him the answer to all his dreams and the lover he is quite clearly seeking.

I know that eighteen months ago you were extremely worried that Hugo was falling in with a very bad lot. I now think that those fears were exaggerated, forgive me for saying so, although I quite understand their root, and I, too, was alarmed to find on his medical records indication that Hugo had been suffering from an attack of gonorrhea at the age of only fourteen. Clearly, if there is a straight and narrow path, he had wandered a long way from it.

But all that notwithstanding, Hugo is a very upright and rather moral young man. I am certain that his time spent with the Quakers has done a great deal more good than we ever suspected it would, and probably helped him more than it has his older sister.

Both Marjorie and I are very fond of Hugo and have thoroughly enjoyed his company on the few occasions he has come here for dinner. He is very refreshing company and one of the very few dinner guests we have that the children also appreciate.

There is really nothing more that I can say. I hope very much that Hugo stays in touch. I think that, whatever path he chooses sexually, he will refuse to be answerable to anyone. He is an odd combination of the sexual sophisticate and the complete innocent. He has not, as far as I can gather, ever done more than tentatively kiss a girl and a great deal of his inactivity in that realm, I believe, is down to basic shyness. He had the misfortune to fall into a sexual morass at a young age and has never really struggled free of it. Experience of one kind appears to have dulled his desire to experiment with any other.

While I still cherish hopes that Hugo will find himself a girlfriend, and Cynthia by his accounts sounds a very alluring possibility, I should note that Hugo himself entertains very little conviction that his sexuality will actually change. He does not believe that these things are decided between the cup and the lip, as it were, but rather that they are part of each person's own sexual chemistry and that each person is a mix of two impulses – hetero and homo – to different degrees. Some exist at either extremity. Some, presumably the full bisexual, at the mid point, and everyone else at various stages in between. The most we can expect from Hugo at this point, I feel, is an acknowledgement that he is not necessarily at one extremity. However, as I said earlier, he has said to me quite sincerely, that he is keeping an open mind.

You know my feelings on the issue and I am sure that you share them with me. There is no point, absolutely nothing to be gained and a great deal to be lost by both you and Hugo, in attempting some kind of overt sexual character change. Even those who see homosexuality as a disease also see it as an incurable one. I know that your fear was not so much that his sexuality was atypical but that he was being exploited and led astray by unsavoury types. I don't think that Hugo will do anything in particular to avoid meeting people we would both call unsavoury. But I do think that we can trust his better judgment and that he is unlikely to become deeply involved with anyone very unsuitable.

I would add that I think you may have been unduly alarmed about his alienation from his family. As I said earlier he still exhibits a great deal of loyalty towards you. He will not brook criticisms of you from other people, but he will deliver them wholesale himself. However, his criticisms are very much centred on your battles with each other. He has a list of wounds and scars that he likes to pick over. At the end of the day I think he is more proud to have emerged from what he sees as a sort of combat than he is bitter about the marks any of that combat may have left.

And finally, contrary to your fears I have had no indications whatsoever of drug taking or of him still performing sexual favours for small amounts of cash.

I look forward to seeing you both soon.
Yours sincerely and with warm regards.

Dr P. S. Wilkinson

7

GYPSIES, TRAMPS AND THIEVES

The first time Hugo asked for money for sex was in a bathroom at the Regent Palace Hotel.

He had been offered money before by strangers who knew that their looks alone would not work. He had been given money by the scoutmaster with the flat in Cockfosters, but he had never asked for it and in any case it wasn't really money. It was pocket money for the tuck shop. He couldn't buy anything except too much chocolate with two quid. This time he wanted the commercial rate, even though he didn't know what it was. And so, squeezed in behind the door of the communal bathroom on the third floor up the plush blue carpeted stairs of the Regent Palace, a staircase and a bathroom familiar to many of the hanging carcasses on the Piccadilly meat rack, he introduced the subject. But he knew he had blown it when he mumbled.

'I'll need some money,' he muttered as the man started unzipping them both and leaning into his groin.

The man straightened up. He wasn't pleased. In fact he was angry. Hugo hadn't fancied him anyway so he didn't really care when the man zipped up and left in a hurry, talking about rules and agreements and how he had many friends who were rent boys on the Dilly and how dare Hugo think that he could take him for a ride. Hugo knew what he meant. How could he think he was one of them? He didn't look or talk like them. He didn't stare at men like them. He didn't look so bored, so cold, so distracted. He looked too keen. Why should anyone pay him? They didn't have to.

But he wanted them to. He wanted to enter the fraternity of hustlers.

It was the daydream of the schoolboy who read Genet on the school coach to and from breakfast and teatime; of the teenager who wanted to be exotic and knew he was suburban; of the kid who was looking for danger and going home to jam sandwiches.

He wanted to be let into the game, to join in the tawdry spectacle, dressed up with tinsel and a smile, sinister and all-knowing, feigning naivety, feigning experience, battered by fate and by pimps, teetering on the brink of the gutter and drugs, living in a nightlife world of sex, violence and cash in the hand.

And he wanted revenge. He wanted his own back.

Hugo had always thought of himself as a canny operator, a street-smart kid. It was half playacting and half reality. He knew the streets well but he was not of them. He was suburban born and bred but he knew his way round cities. He could smell his way through them and into them. It was like a perverse homing instinct, a legacy of David's days scouring London for sexual partners, quick frissons and useful alleys. In any strange city Hugo prided himself on the speed with which he could find the Red Zone. Like a sniffer dog, scouring the gutters for clues, he would meander and weave his way into the city bowels and enjoy that strange rush of adrenalin as the first waves of sleaze washed around him. Sex shops. Peep shows. Erotic lingerie that gave way to brothels and streetwalkers and triple X arcades. Here, in any city, he felt at home.

In every city he visited, Hugo was uncomfortable, restless, impatient until he had found the Red Zone. On school holiday backpackings round European cities, Hugo rarely visited the museums, the great sarcophagi of culture. They made him feel dizzy and hyperventilated. The vast gloomy canvases of history shoved up side by side in vast gloomy halls; tourists, bowed by the weight of prestige, filing quietly, whispering by, like visitors at the funeral of a local godfather.

But on the back streets where the hookers lounged and the peep shows flashed, where the pimps groomed their nails with toothpicks and every perversion was available shrink-wrapped in colour magazines from Scandinavia, Hugo felt he had discovered the city's core, its life, its beating heart. The magazines were alluring and overexposed. The pimps and their crimson and cream pinstripes were flashy. But it was the hookers he watched. Like a drag show that caricatures divas and showgirls, that powders up and blasts out torch songs, the hookers were a caricature of lovemaking. They were the frank, fat face of lust. They were a mess. They were exorbitant, battered, gorgeous, rancid. They were coarse and they had style. They made Hugo smile. They appalled and amused and attracted him.

And it wasn't just the women he loved, or the men dressed as women, whose big hands and gravelled voices gave away their sex. He watched the boys too. The spiders sitting in the web. It was a power game of catch and be caught, no-one ever sure who was catching whom, who had won, what had been lost. Was the smile mocking or desperate? Was the wink real or professional? Were the blemishes youth or age?

Hugo, like the expert voyeur he was, fancied himself an authority on the Red Zone, on its pimps, clients and above all, its hookers, its gypsies and tramps, thieves and pickpockets. He had yet to be either customer or hustler, but still he thought he knew. The boy who stared drop-jawed at strangers in restaurants and on trains, who had to be told to look away by an embarrassed mother or sisters, had watched so long, absorbed so many foibles and habits, gestures and twitches, he thought he knew it all. But he was also an eager learner.

He had malingered across Europe and back on trains on cheap tickets. He had loitered under the signs that said no loitering. He had played games without ever quite being on the game. He was the amateur trying to look professional. The men didn't know quite what to make of this well-spoken English boy cruising among the lowlife, looking for a thrill, but they followed him nonetheless, and he followed them, watching and waiting.

At seventeen in Paris, on a summer holiday with his sister but alone for a week while she went to find herself an apartment in Nantes, he strolled the length of rue Saint Denis, eating crêpes and listening to the bantering of the tarts in their stretch red lurex and black leatherette pants, jabbing the air with their long cigarettes and their arms with yesterday's needle. They teetered on the boundary between attraction and revulsion. They were like cats hissing in the dark. They were feline and dangerous. Their arms were bruised with smack. Their legs, too wide at the calf from years of standing, were hung round the ankle with thin gold chains like the mark of possession, a branding on a sheep.

They saw Hugo and whistled and called and he smiled, embarrassed, into his crêpe, dribbling chocolate.

On Pigalle in the afternoon, he was less coy. Here the travestie hookers worked the daylight hours, standing heads taller than their lumpen counterparts on Saint Denis, their breasts absurdly round and hard, their hands heavy and wide, big fingernails chipped and bitten, painted garish colours. On the corner of his favourite little street stood the queen of contrasts; a mulatto travestie smothered from head to foot in red leatherette with a blond wig crowning a coffee skin and a voice as deep as John Wayne's.

Pigalle offered a conveyor belt of lusts, a line of spangled sex shops with video booths at the back, clustered in the corner behind silly bamboo curtains. Here Hugo loitered, watching as the men arrived and passed from door to door, looking at the video covers stuck to the booth doors to see which combination of torsos and organs they wanted for the five franc wank. If he saw a man staring at the man-to-man wall, he'd emerge further from the bamboo shadows and they'd go into the booth together.

Minutes later he'd emerge, lust sated, his trousers uncomfortable, the rest of the afternoon somehow empty. Time for a museum. Post-coital culture. Bathed in the satisfaction of having won, having played in the city's sex arcade and scored on the fruit machine, he could gaze at the Géricaults and Delacroix without feeling intimidated. He could stare back at the other tourists and smirk, because he was no longer a tourist. He thought.

Paris was Hugo's first great city-sex discovery. Sex ran in deep seams through its centre, titillating, inviting, provoking, preoccupying. Pigalle in the morning, rue Saint Denis from eight till ten and then off to the Jardins des Tuileries for strange encounters in the crisscrossing shadows of trees grown in diagonal lines. But Paris had an emergency thrill of danger that made the blood flow faster and pulse more heavily. People were always whispering about the Tuileries as a place of knife-happy gigolos out for a new pair of Cuban-heeled suede boots, hunting a new leather jacket. They were young, hard, quiffed and picked their teeth with flick-knives. They made thousands of francs a week and spent it all chasing moth-eaten girls, trying to recover their manhood. Hugo had even read about them in a lip-smacking profile in one of the Sunday supplements – pretending to play to people's moral outrage while feeding their desire for scandal between respectable covers. There were many photographs to look at. Hugo devoured the article.

The gigolos became his heroes. But in Paris Hugo kept out of their way, and had no trouble with them. Except once. Not really trouble but an encounter, outside Monoprix in Anvers where he picked up the professor. He was seen making a pick-up on someone else's patch. The boy whose territory he had violated came down upon his back like the school bully, grinning with all his gold teeth, his eyes flashing with malice as he greeted the professor by name, startling a smile out of him.

The professor was a mistake anyway. A balding man with little round glasses, he was the last resort at the end of a long day wandering between the pissoirs in the centre of Pigalle, dishing eye contact until his eyeballs ached.

Hugo was frightened by the gigolo. He looked as if he could bite, hard. When he greeted him, he hit Hugo so hard on the back Hugo fell into the road. If there had been a knife in his hand, Hugo would have been spitted chicken. Then a uniform, a little gendarme cap, appeared above the heads of the shoppers. The boy slid away in his suede boots without looking back. Hugo blinked on the pavement. The professor grabbed a taxi and they bundled into it. He talked all the while about his teaching at the Sorbonne and his afternoon off and his apartment on the Seine. He never mentioned the gigolo who knew him by name. Hugo had discovered that even in this city, to be English made you more attractive, a curiosity, and so he played the English boy to perfection; quiet, blue-eyed and sensitive, all the while wondering why and how and what he was doing on the back seat of the taxi with a man with little round glasses.

But he was still learning, and by the end of this day his baptism by humiliation would be complete.

They arrived at a block overlooking Pont Neuf and the professor, his glasses twinkling with glee, ushered him upstairs into a spacious split-level apartment. Hugo felt that first rush of comfort, that first ache for the softness of a deep carpet and the sinking of the sofa.

The black man arrived just as they were sipping their first spritzers and Hugo was settling into the luxury of a tall-backed armchair. The black man was the professor's live-in lover and had not been expected back that afternoon. Hugo, who was still young and therefore assumed that sex conquered all and the more the merrier, grinned at the black man, who scowled at him. Hugo couldn't wipe the grin. The spritzer had paralysed him. So, as the professor and his live-in lover launched into a furious row, Hugo smiled and looked at the view.

He had no particular desire to have sex with anyone, but if he must have it, he'd much rather have it with the black man than with the little round glasses. Somehow, he felt that taking his clothes off wouldn't mollify either of them though, so he swilled the spritzer and watched the pleasure boats on the Seine, feeling like a kidnapped tourist, snatched from the pursuit of idle sight-seeing. He smiled at the two men fighting, yelling at each other across the bread board and the selection of Sabatier knives. He smiled at the sofa and the tastefully beige paintings that toned so well with the tasteful grey carpet and the tasteful cream of the Gallimard book spines. He smiled at the river and the bridge and the pleasure boats.

They weren't going to resolve this argument with him still there and he wasn't going to seduce the lover while he was fighting with his host, on top of which he had finished his spritzer and couldn't see another being shaken or stirred while the row still raged. So he left. Or at least he walked to the door, and, still smiling his fixed grin of alcohol and sunshine, fiddled with the door lock. The argument went quiet behind him. The professor came over to see him out. They didn't speak, but as he left the professor fished a piece of card out of a pocket and scribbled on the back of it. They were out of sight of the lover, who was pacing the upper split-level, still hovering round the Sabatier knives. Little round glasses misted with sweat blinked at Hugo as the professor slipped into his hand the address of a nightclub on the left bank called Manhattan. On the back of the piece of card it said, nine o'clock.

'Nine o'clock this evening. I'll see you there.'

'Oui, oui,' gargled Hugo, not sure if the sound had actually emerged from his lips.

'Au revoir.'

'Au revoir.'

A piece of ornamental furniture hit the lintel and broke. The professor covered his head with his arms and kicked the door shut. Hugo swayed slightly as he smiled at the stairs.

It was difficult to find the club. Hugo did at least three full lengths of the street, both sides, before he noticed the little door with the little peep hole and the polished plaque outside. He rang the bell and the peep hole winked at him. The latch buzzed, he pushed the door and walked in.

The word nightclub had always had vague Hollywood connotations for Hugo. It conjured shimmering imaginings of vast floors, ballgowns, string quartets and dry martinis. There were candelabra and chandeliers and staircases that divided and rejoined, onto which people arrived to be announced by a liveried footman. It was a vision that hovered somewhere between Ruritania and Berkeley Square, in a strange time capsule that borrowed (like Hollywood costumiers) from any available period, a chintzy mélange of nineteen-fifties costumes and nineteenth-century architecture, eighteenth-century music and timeless small talk. It was a world of Cary Grant, Audrey Hepburn and the occasional ex-king.

It was strange then to be walking into a cramped, black and red lounge where a man with a checked shirt and a moustache was leaning behind a glossy bar. Just beyond the bar, a steep flight of stairs dropped onto the dance floor where Hugo could see three or four men already cavorting. One of them, a thickset, big-necked man with cropped hair and a bushy pale moustache was spinning round in a kilt. The others kept tipping forward in laughter, hands to their mouths and eyebrows to the ceiling as he swirled and spun to make the kilt rise higher.

It all reminded Hugo of the Black Cap in Camden Town, but he pushed such disrespect from his mind and repeated the word nightclub to himself to recapture some of its thrill.

'Bon soir, m'sieur,' lisped the barman.

'Bon soir,' said Hugo, without lisping.

The professor was nowhere to be seen.

The barman wiped the bar in front of Hugo and put a coaster down, before sweeping an ashtray and some matches across. Had

Hugo been sophisticated and not had trembling hands (hiding in his pockets), he would have lit a cigarette. He knew he was meant to order a drink. He had been surprised the club was free to get in, but now they wanted their money.

'Un dry martini, s'il vous plaît.'

'Oui.'

Hugo had no idea about drinking. He didn't know his drinks. He hated beer. His grandmother drank gin and orange but that made him sweat. His mother drank red Martini with ice and lemon, which he liked, but when he ordered it at the Duke of Lancaster, they looked at him as if at a dog that had farted. Or a pouf. His father drank whisky which he couldn't understand. He mentally ran through the parental drinks cabinet which he so often raided with his empty poster paint pot looking for the gin to mix his barbiturate in. The Martini Extra Dry was where he landed. It never occurred to him that there might be a difference between Martini Extra Dry and a dry martini.

Hugo had seven francs in his pocket. He was running on a very tight budget at the end of a holiday. Most of the day that wasn't spent huddled behind silly beaded curtains at the back of the spangled sex shops was spent calculating how many francs he had left to spend on which crêpe and when he could eat next. It was a strange tension behind him always. Alone in a strange city with a ticket to leave and hardly any money. He had hung around the buskers outside Beaubourg for a day or two, chatting to them (they were mostly Australian) and wishing that they'd just say, 'Come join our band of wandering players. Let's strike out across Europe together.' But they didn't. They had enough mouths to feed already. And Hugo couldn't do cartwheels or eat fire.

The barman placed the conical glass on the bar and the olive bobbed.

'Soixante-dix-sept, m'sieur,' he lisped again.

Hugo always got confused when he heard numbers in a foreign language and would just cling to the last sound that he heard. So he gingerly placed his seven francs on the bar.

'Tu rigoles?' asked the barman, frowning.

Hugo was caught between a stammer and a blush. He opened and shut his mouth and looked at the seven francs. He plunged his hand inside his pocket. He knew there was nothing there. He wanted to say that he was meeting the professor, who was bound to help him out, but he didn't know the professor's name and he was already late. Maybe the black man had put his foot down. In any case Hugo was only here because it was a nightclub, not because he wanted to see the professor again.

The barman smiled beneath his moustache.

'La prochaine fois tu sauras, hein?'

He pushed Hugo's seven francs back across the bar.

Hugo sipped the drink. It tasted revolting. He couldn't understand why his martini tasted of gin and why one drink had supposedly cost six pounds. All the fun had gone out of everything. Instead of feeling like a nightclubber, whose home was propping the late night bar sipping mixed drinks and smoking Black Russians, he felt like a backpacker begging for small change and asking for glasses of water. He finished his drink with a grimace. He hated the taste of neat gin. He knew the barman knew that he didn't have any other money. He couldn't order any more drinks and he couldn't summon the courage to walk down the stairs on to the dance floor where the man in the kilt was still swirling. So he left. He stumbled out of the door into St Germain feeling like a vagabond who had just been ejected from a smart gathering.

For all his street-smart sex games, when it came to the crunch, the cash over the counter, the seven francs in his pocket, the gigolo down on his back in Pigalle, the demands for a fiver in the bathroom of the Regent Palace Hotel, Hugo was a beginner and they could see it. No matter how many streets of tarts he wandered up and down, no matter how many Saturday afternoons he spent in Leicester Square while his mother assumed he was at the National Gallery, dunking himself in culture instead of masturbating at the foot of an NCP ventilation shaft with a bearded stranger for two pounds, Hugo was a tourist on a three-day package to lowlife and back, one rip-off, two shocks and a frisson guaranteed.

All the time in Paris, he was trying to play two games. In game one he'd trip down the street, clicking his heels on the paving stones, throwing around glances that lassoed the eyes of young men. He was playing cocky runt with a hard-on and passable

French. In the second game, he'd look at the world from the top of his nose, seeing nothing in a blear of disdain. He'd walk the length of a boulevard, toe-polished and smile-hardened, looking like someone trying to look like someone smart.

But sometimes Hugo was caught without a convenient act at his disposal. Sometimes he was genuinely vulnerable. His instincts were good, but they couldn't always save him. He would stoop lower than most, dip into gutters where his playmates would have drowned, but from time to time, he was left floundering, looking foolish, and sometimes left feeling in danger. In Paris his trials had been by embarrassment. Now he knew what nightclubs were, he knew what a dry martini could taste like and what it was supposed to cost.

In Alexandria six months later, his trials were by fear. Now he knew not to wander off into a strange city when his instincts were dulled by drink and hypnotised by lust. That was a near-lethal combination. Indeed, as Hugo slid out of the officers' mess into the warm air blowing off the sea, he knew if he didn't turn down the quayside and return to his own ship, something, something odd was going to happen.

If he hadn't been drunk, he probably would have gone back to the SS *Miranda*. But then, if he hadn't been drunk, he wouldn't really have needed to. Now, as the tall lamplights and wide con-courses of the port stretched between him and the city, a few hundred yards of concrete certainty and square angles before the crouched and humming jumble of Alexandria, a buzzing unknown through the port gates, Hugo felt something stirring in his gut. The libido paralysed by convention, by the fear of discovery, by the need to adopt the macho postures of winking and sniggering and leering after skirt, was waking up and crawling, like a silk-worm, out of its cocoon. It could only spell trouble. But the wonderful thing about alcohol was its anaesthetic effect on anxiety. He felt the instinctive urge to search for some satisfaction. He muttered to himself that he didn't actually want actual sex, that he was only going to look, that he would come straight back, and then he started down the gangplank.

Three months earlier, Hugo had been a schoolboy in the outer-London countryside. Now he was working a cruise-liner in the eastern Mediterranean. School was behind him, in all its forty-minute segments and mashed potato lunches, in all its smoking out of bounds and shouting with the headmaster. Hugo had left school with a place at Cambridge to read English and nine months of freedom. Freedom had brought him to Alexandria.

Hugo stumbled on the gangplank and walked down the rest of the way with the over-cautious gait of one trying not to appear drunk. He was very, very drunk. The Royal Navy was obviously made of sterner stuff than he. After weeks of long brandy binges in the round, panelled ballroom, running two week tabs on shorts that cost a tiny fraction of London pub prices, he had now acquired a drinker's constitution, or so he thought. After all, there was little to do between ports other than drink, and the officers seemed to organise most of their spare time around it.

This party wasn't on the SS *Miranda*, however. This party was in the officers' mess of a neighbouring Navy frigate moored along-side them in Alexandria port. Tonight the officers of the *Miranda* had been invited over for a friendly celebratory drink, and Hugo had sauntered in, hands thrust into trouser pockets, trying to dis-guise his shyness with an aura of cool. He stood at the back of the mess, avoiding people's eyes and drinking too fast. The Navy officers were in tiptop whites. They gleamed with charisma and confidence. Defenders of the realm each and every one, they made Hugo feel shabby and disconcerted, so he plunged into the drink-ing to keep his mind occupied.

Whether they drank so much that they had ceased to notice, or whether this was a ploy to intoxicate the womenfolk wasn't clear, but every drink bit Hugo's tongue off. Barely diluted spirits shud-dered through him like a purgative. He felt unmanned. He'd lost his bearings. He couldn't panic and bolt for another drink because he'd be sick. He had to keep a grip on his stomach and a hold on his head. He sipped at another gin sparsely sprinkled with tonic. Nobody came to talk to him. The hosts were preoccupied with the women and the women were happy to be a preoccupation. Time for a snap decision.

Outside he felt he had just escaped from England again. The mess had reeked of the Home Counties, of cricket and golf and the rugby club dinner dance at which aging symbols of male prowess, dressed in cream linen suits and the occasional Rolex, rehearsed ancient mating rituals with each other's wives and ignored Hugo, except to drop the occasional look of contempt into his lap. 'They're frightened of you,' he'd tell himself as he went outside to look at the cricket green, golf course, rugby pitch.

He hit the shore with a false step and swayed on a lightly twisted ankle. The lamp-washed concrete looked like adventure. The ships lined up with lightbulbs festooned along their bows looked like fairground rides. But here Hugo didn't even know his way. He couldn't catch the scent. Propelled by alcohol and the twitch of lust, he strode out into the port, but he had done no daytime recce, no judging of clues and signs, no learning of routes and memorising of landmarks. They had arrived only yesterday afternoon, and that morning at six he had been on a coach with thirty passengers hurtling murderously through the traffic towards Cairo and a whistlestop circuit of mosque and museum surrounded by little urchins begging, '50p jerk-off, 50p jerk-off.' That was not the Red Zone.

He was working in the dark without a map and with his better instincts numbed. He strode off up the hill towards the port gates. As he walked up, on the other side of the road a taxi drove down. The driver seemed to take a long look at him and Hugo felt the first ripple of anticipation. Things were going to happen.

He was not surprised when the same taxi pulled up beside him, on its return journey up the hill and out of the port.

'Do you want to see the town?'

'Pardon?'

'I'll show you the town. I'll show it to you. Get in.'

'I haven't got any money.'

That wasn't true. Hugo had fifty pounds in his wallet. That was stupid.

'It doesn't matter. Get in.'

There is something about getting into another man's car that seals one's fate. As the door locks and the engine starts, you are suddenly vulnerable, whisked off your territory with no means of escape. A car is a dangerous place. But Hugo was calm. Calm and unsurprised as they glided past the guards on the security gate to the port.

Why did they look at him with such contempt as they waved the car through the gates?

He was still calm as the man unzipped his trousers and, producing a little brown erection, proceeded to fumble at Hugo's fly.

Sex lurks in every corner, in every groin, in every city.

Hugo's erection was impressive. Suffused with booze and days of frustration cooped-up at sea, it startled his driver, who swore indecipherably and narrowly missed another taxi. Hugo eased himself back into the seat and allowed the man to toy with him. The driver babbled at him and with sudden jerky movements of the head, indicated that a blow job was in order. Hugo smiled and looked the other way. The man grew adamant and, though many years later Hugo excluded it from the retelling of this story, he did put his head in the Egyptian's lap and take his little brown erection into his mouth. It seemed like good manners if the man was giving him a free sightseeing ride round Alexandria. But so far they hadn't seen anything except dusty, anonymous streets of slightly grubby apartment buildings and battered palm trees.

Hugo moved his jaws, wrapping his teeth behind his lips, listening for the telltale gasps that announced an imminent orgasm. Good manners went only so far and the cum of a taxi driver was not an appetising prospect.

He withdrew his head as the driver's breathing became rapid and watched without any interest as the man shuddered over his steering wheel. It was another little emission, like so many others, but this time at thirty miles an hour through strange streets, so far from home. There was no-one to turn to. Hugo still felt calm, and very distant. It was as if David were back, watching Hugo play his game. He was testing Hugo's nerve. And his judgment.

They pulled over.

The car rolled gently into a lock-up garage where other Egyptians were milling around in the light from dipped headlamps. They were expecting him. No-one flickered. No-one smiled. The car stopped and someone opened the door. Hugo got out. He was so detached by now he couldn't really hear anything. He just looked. But he knew what was going to happen.

The boy was sitting in the back of another car. They took Hugo over to the car and showed him the boy through the car window. He had dark brown eyes and a beautiful skin. He was slim, which was not what Hugo preferred, and he was young, which Hugo had never really experienced. But in this lock-up, Hugo was the white tourist, the Englishman, and Englishmen were always served boys. The older men just wanted two-jerk blow jobs over their steering wheels. They were businessmen. When Hugo had started masturbating in the car, the driver had restrained his hand. Hugo's orgasm was not to be wasted. It was valuable.

Hugo had been aware of the fifty pounds in his wallet ever since he told the taxi driver that he had no money. That line in England meant, I am young and dangerous and I like presents. In Egypt it meant nothing. White men, Englishmen, always had money. Any money was better than Egyptian. All he had done was make it clear that he knew money was involved.

He was very aware of the fifty pounds now as he stared at the young boy. They unlocked the car door and opened it. The boy moved across the back seat to make room for him. All Hugo could think of was that he must not hand them his jacket. They were miming at him, holding out their arms to take it and he knew that to do so would mean the end of the fifty pounds. He took his jacket off and laid it on the roof of the car. Somehow he thought they wouldn't do anything if it was in such a prominent position. He would see them if they did and make an awful row.

He had no idea where he was. He was sitting in a parked car surrounded by men moving in and out of the low lights. But he was convinced that honour would prevail.

Whatever happened with the boy, in the cramped half-clothed discomfort of a plastic car seat, Hugo never really remembered. He must have had an orgasm, he supposed. But he didn't remember his hand being sticky or the boy exhibiting any pleasure. He just sat there staring at Hugo with his dark brown eyes. He was bored. Frightened. Maybe stoned. Hugo felt clumsy and colonial. Like the early hangover that arrives before you've finished cheap wine, he felt the post-coital depression, the sagging of spirit and the yearning for home and bed. Maybe, in that case, he did have an orgasm. Or maybe the fatigue crushed it. Either way, when he got out of the car, his jacket was still on the roof and the wallet was still in the jacket.

Why Hugo took his wallet out of the jacket at that point isn't clear. It's unlikely that he was about to pay anyone. Hugo never offered money. He assumed he could get away with anything for free if he tried. But he did take his wallet out and looked in it and the fifty pounds had gone.

It felt so inevitable.

He looked around. The taxi driver was standing in front of him, but there was something slightly different about him. He was wearing different clothes. Hugo gesticulated at him and said something in English. The man looked at him and shrugged. He didn't understand. Hugo became angry. He waved his wallet and pointed. He raised his voice. He wasn't drunk anymore. He was angry. He lost his temper and shouted. The men milled about and came and went. Some of them stroked their beards and others shook their heads and some talked to each other in Egyptian, but no-one understood what Hugo was shouting about.

Another man came into the garage. This one was the taxi driver. The other one couldn't have been. But he too was wearing different clothes. He beckoned to Hugo with a sympathetic smile. Hugo felt the tears rising. This was the man who was going to put an end to the horrible joke they were all playing on him. And he a white Englishman too.

The driver led Hugo over to his car. It was a different car. It was a different driver. Hugo still believed in him. They both got into the car and the man pulled out his wallet and handed Hugo a large banknote.

Hugo could have thrown his arms around the man's neck and kissed him. He had his fifty pounds back. He waved the note and asked the man how much he wanted. The driver looked at him impassively. His smile was missing some teeth. Hugo looked back at the note. In his hand he held One Egyptian Pound. Hugo looked at the man, who was staring at him out of the gloom in the car. He couldn't really see his face. The temper had been swept out of him and now he was simply tired. He thought of demanding to be taken to the Embassy, but he knew how ridiculous he would look. Something else was beginning to worry him. He had no idea where he was. There was going to come a point when they dumped him and the longer he played the angry Brit game, the more likely it was that they'd lose their patience. For a while he had felt angry enough to shout and throw his weight about. Now he felt chilly and vulnerable. The arrogance of his passport was failing him. What-ifs were beginning to fill his head. What if they lost their temper with him? What if they had knives? The Egyptians milled about. Still they didn't smile.

Hugo nodded at the taxi driver and they moved off. He dumped Hugo just outside the port gates. He wasn't going to risk being betrayed to the guard.

Hugo walked through the gates, turned back and walked into the little guardroom. 'I have been robbed,' he announced.

It was another mistake. Within minutes he was surrounded by great moon-fat faces with silly, small, grey caps, brocaded and crested. They huddled and pushed to see him as if he were a freak at a sideshow. He repeated his story to someone who then revealed he understood no English (he had nodded attentively throughout), and again to a third man (more brocade and a bigger crest) who did, but who asked him everything twice.

'Ah, yes. Well, sir we knew this would happen.'

'What? Why didn't you tell me?'

'Sir?'

'When we drove through the gates. Why didn't you tell me?'

'Why did you get into this man's car? Sir?'

They brought out the pieces of paper. The naked lightbulb in the dark grey room lit their faces like a puppet show of Halloween pumpkins. The whole evening was receding into nightmare. He was English and had got into a strange car with a taxi driver who had offered to show him the town for nothing. He was English and drunk. What did he really expect?

The forms came out and the pens and the rubber stamps and the questions. He began his story again, but each time he left out the lock-up and ignored the little brown erection of the taxi driver. He just said that the man had taken his wallet when he went to pay. The story was pathetic and by now it was four a.m. In the middle of all their questioning and copying and rubber stamping, Hugo got up and, pushing gently through the moon faces and brocade shoulders, walked out of the guardhouse and down the hill to the ship. Nobody ran after him. All the pumpkins in crests and brocades just slumped back into apathy.

The ship lay there in the harbour, white and sparkling like a polished relic of colonial splendour. It was home. It was England. It was terra firma after the shifting quicksands of Alexandria. He climbed the gangway and nodded to the officer on duty, leaning against the wall in a white dress uniform. Hugo suspected that the officer knew where he'd been. He could rely on the great British discretion, but knew that he was already being marked down. Gossip seemed to travel by osmosis here. Hugo had always felt that the club doors were closed on him; that the waiters knew he shouldn't be there and the barman looked with disdain when he walked in. Now he felt he had handed back his key.

He was deeply depressed. The loss of the fifty pounds was a major inconvenience. Hugo was still transfixed by money and the need to store it up in his pocket as a last refuge against disaster. He was defenceless now. He would need to pilfer and extort it back again from the pittance the office brought in every day hiring out deck quoits.

But the stronger depression was caused not by the loss of the money, nor even by the access of self-disgust that followed the temper in a delayed post-coital kick-back. What upset him most was his humiliation. He had been the great white English sucker. He had been bled by leeches faster, smarter than he; leeches who had never stopped to think that this white man might be a match for them. He was there to be bled and that was all they saw. And he was lured with a bait as cheap as an unwilling boy on the back seat of a secondhand Ford. The Egyptians weren't to be fooled. They weren't even bothered with his act. They didn't even understand what he said. He was white and washed and that was enough.

And now he wanted his own back.

He wasn't going to outwit the Alexandrian taxi drivers. He wasn't going to beat the gigolos of Paris on their own Tuileries turf. But in London he was determined to prove that he could make that step and strike a blow below the belt for his lowlife longings. He had to prove he was more than just another great white tourist, the easy prey of the canny hunter. He was the wicked, wayward siren now, luring strangers onto the rocks, onto the leatherette back seat, into the chrome communal bathroom on the third floor of the Regent Palace.

And he was going to make some money. Because now he actually needed it. And more than the two quid he used to get for chocolates.

But the incident in the Regent Palace Hotel was not encouraging. Nor, in fact, was the Dilly itself. Its days as London's teenage hire purchase centre, shopping arcade for male rent, the meat rack of popular legend, were over. Even then the meat had been suspect. Cheap cuts. Scrag end. Offal. Giblets. A line of wan, distant faces and skinny bodies in gaudy jackets, clinging to the railings above the tube station, their knuckles red with cold, staring across Regent Street, waiting for a john in a nice, warm coat to take them away and warm their hands.

That all changed. The police and the developers and the man who invented coin-operated toilet entry machines changed all that. By the time Hugo determined to take his revenge, and by the time he realised he needed the money (revenge always sounded the better motive, money was the more immediate cause), the street-lad scene had gone. They worked from bars now, breakfast bars like Barclay Brothers on Whitehall, wheeling and dealing and pill-popping and snoring between their egg and chips and pale grey tea. They weren't what Hugo remembered either. These weren't the boys in the blond bouffants and the crushed velvet jackets, turning tricks and looking for Mr Right. These were runaways with spider's web tattoos on their cheeks. Run by black pimps with fat bellies and fat gold, they were dumped half-asleep in mini-cabs and sent off to distant suburbs to be brutalised by shy deviants. They were danger kids. Straight. Hungry. Desperate. A little more food and warmth and they'd be ready to mug you in your own home.

This wasn't the fraternity Hugo wanted to enter. By this time Hugo needed money badly, but he couldn't turn tricks over egg and chips. He couldn't stand chips. He needed more money than that. He needed the money to pay the rent on the rooms he had taken in London. He only rented the rooms for a few weeks at a time, while he was on vacation from university. But even that small amount was difficult to raise honestly. Most of his friends at Cambridge simply went back to their families. But Hugo couldn't go home anymore, except for the occasional cup of tea.

Well, he could go home. He just wouldn't. After cruising the eastern Mediterranean getting dark-skinned in a relentless sun, shepherding schoolkids to and from wonders of the ancient world; after lying on his back in a petty officer's bed, after drinking himself silly on vodkatinis in a Neapolitan nightclub where transvestites danced ever so slowly to endless reflections of themselves in split strip mirrors; after Alexandria and the taxi drivers; after New York with Ross and Cynthia and after one term at Cambridge with Dolly and Chas and Rudy, he couldn't settle down to the washing-up and laying-the-table and fetching-the-bread-from-the-bakery world of the house in Hadley.

He didn't have a fight. But he knew his mother was relieved he was going. In a way. She didn't want to worry. She didn't want to fight. It was easier if he wasn't there. It was easier if she only heard what he told her and only saw what she wanted to see. But they were friends when he left. They had crossed that barrier, at least. After years of living with her in fear and loathing, Hugo left her behind in love and tears. She had been very patient during that first holiday at home. She hadn't seen him properly for a year. After the ship he had gone straight to New York, from New York back to Europe, from Europe straight to university (one night at home, enough to pack). Now he was home he was hardly there. She saw him in the morning before she went to work but he was normally gone by the evening when she came home, leaving a note and an estimated time of return. He had a key, no money and an appetite to feed.

He had been stopping out with strange men. Strange men he met in pubs where Mrs Shufflewick droned over a dusty handbag and the Trollettes played nudge budge innuendo twice nightly in pink and green sequins. He went home with these men to suburban sitting rooms and quilted bedspreads from Tottenham to Hampstead, from Chalk Farm to Stroud Green. But he could never stay the night. That would be pushing things too far. Already his mother had muttered about the house being his hotel. He didn't want her to think it had become his left luggage. In fact he didn't want her to think about what he was doing at all. For all that Hugo wanted his revenge on the normal world, wanted to take it for a ride and charge it double, he didn't want to shock his mother. He never told her where he was, where he'd been and certainly not who with.

He'd go home with the strange men and tumble under the quilt after tense cups of tea on the three-piece, and then he'd tell them . . . 'I'm sorry, I have to go. I have to go before the last tube. I have to borrow money for a taxi. I have to be home before my mother gets up. I have to sleep head on my pillow, dreaming under my blankets.'

Sometimes it was easy, because his nameless partner was asleep. He'd take a taxi fare from the table, leave a note and slip out. Other times he had to explain and he couldn't. Explain how he could still be afraid of her. Explain why he couldn't give them a number. Occasionally they'd give him a lift home like Charlie used to do, and then he thought, for a few moments at least, that maybe he loved them. But Hugo hated leaving early. He hated stealing five pound notes from trusting wallets. He hated sneaking into the Hadley house and avoiding every creak under the carpet.

So he lied. Of course. It was second nature.

Hugo wanted to stay the night with the boy he had met last week, the boy who had come up to him on a hot summer night in a crowded pub with his shirt open and his smile on and kissed him between the lips without introduction. The boy who told furious lies about an imaginary family and lived in a thin-walled flat in Chalk Farm with the sorry truth of an electric bar fire and a hang-dog mother he called his aunt. Hugo didn't believe the lies but the boy's blond hairy body dried his mouth with desire and they did sex all night in front of the two-bar fire with Michael Jackson going round and round on the radio cassette. It was bliss and he hated leaving it and for once he wasn't going to.

Hugo couldn't say any of this to his mother. Even if she would have understood, he didn't want her to know about his life as a man, his manly love for manly bodies in front of two-bar fires next to thin walls. So he said he was staying with Cynthia. That was possible. He often did, because Cynthia lived on the far side of town. Unfortunately, he forgot to tell Cynthia that he was staying with her.

The next morning when he walked through the kitchen door all unshowered and unshaven, his mother's eyes stayed on the floor.

'There's a message for you in your bedroom,' she said without looking up. Hugo's stomach turned to a stone. The stone turned over.

On his bed lay a message saying, 'Cynthia phoned last night. Could you call her.' His mother's handwriting, in all its regular curves and neat strokes, told him nothing more. It was a picture of restraint. She was saving her temper for later. For the face to face. She was in the kitchen. He was in the bedroom. The face to face was just about to happen, but one of them had to walk towards the other.

Hugo sat on the bed and felt pale. Somehow he had to walk back into the kitchen and into the showdown. He knew she was waiting for it. The longer he stayed here, the more the steam would build up. He had to go through with this one. He wasn't a great one for climbing out of the window and running away. It wouldn't do any good. This had to be dealt with now.

The important thing was to feel innocent, to feel the victim.

He walked into the kitchen with tears of self-pity already filling his eyes. But the woman he met there, the woman in her work clothes and no make-up, her hard hands working at the kitchen with Vim and scourer, the woman he had been terrified of all his life, the woman he had adored all his life, didn't look at him with anger or violence. She wasn't going to shout and scream. She wasn't going to lunge at his hair and pull him to the ground. She looked at him and her eyes were full of tears. She looked at him and her face was lined with sadness.

'Why did you lie to me?' she said in a quiet mournful voice. The self-righteous temper leaked out of him like air from a punctured tyre. He sagged slowly.

This was the oldest question of all. The question Hugo and his sisters were asked every time they were caught eating bubblegum, caught with things in their pockets that gave their game away, caught out, caught short. They would look at each other and know what they were going to say. The answer was always the same.

'Because I was scared.'

And suddenly Hugo realised that for once in his life he was telling the truth when it mattered. And suddenly Hugo burst into tears. They weren't the tears he'd been building up in his bedroom. They were tears he didn't expect. They washed the fake ones out of his eyes and flooded his face. He crumpled into a chair and his mother was right beside him. She had his hand in her hand. She stroked his hair. She held him as he heaved and sobbed and wet her dress with his tears.

'I still love you,' she said. 'I'll always love you.'

And she cried too, as they sat side by side, in the sitting room, holding hands. He told her only so much. She forgave him everything. They were together again, this strange mother and her favourite child. They hugged and smiled and even laughed through each other's tears. They forgave each other. He didn't tell her about the two-bar fire, or the open shirt or the stupid lies. He just told her where he was and why and she just seemed to know. She had been thinking this one over for the last three years. She had been thinking this one over ever since the diary days.

And like that, with smiles still wet from tears cried days before, they parted. Like that, with everything between them cleared. With the little dams of hatred washed away, Hugo waved good-bye to Hadley and went to live with Cynthia, and while Hadley seemed to close round him as he left like a million net curtains brushing against his face with old women's fingers clasping at his collar, his mother's face as he left scorched a scar in his heart. They should have been so much closer. Somehow there was so much unsaid. Hugo had spent so much of the last six years in silence, behind the smokescreen of his lies, his sulks, behind his wooden door. And she had been fighting her own demons all the while, wrestling with the scars of her own past in a fight whose violence spilled out on terrified children. They had been estranged by fear. But the love between them ached in Hugo's stomach and clouded his eyes with tears that wouldn't roll out of his eyes as he put his face to the wind and strolled to the station. Freedom tasted so sad and so delicious. Suddenly the whole infrastructure of Hugo's lies had become obsolete. He had been handed the candy jar and he had no appetite. He let three trains go through the station before he got on one. He didn't want to leave Hadley until he had stopped to feel his sadness.

When Hugo got on the tube, he had the faraway smile of a man who has lost his mind in sunnier climes.

Hugo never knew what his mother said to his father, but his father never said a word to Hugo. He just remained the same shy, friendly man with lame jokes and a big laugh. He just remained Hugo's father, in the background where he had always been, where he was comfortable.

Hugo lived with Cynthia for a month. Lived among the potted plants and the perfume atomisers, the Art Garfunkel records and the heavy sofas. It was a women's flat – the extended boudoir of Cynthia and her mother. An intense, crammed flat of scented air and female toiletries: face-packs, conditioners, toners and scrubs. But now it was Hugo's too. His pyjamas under the pillow. His toothbrush in the glass in the bathroom. His Boots shampoo next to their elaborate mixtures and individually concocted liquids. Or at least Cynthia's. Cynthia's mother was away, on the other side of the world, so Hugo and Cynthia played odd couple between university terms; reading, squabbling, cooking, eating and laughing with the giggly excitement of being alone.

Cynthia knew more about Hugo than anyone. After Alexandria, after being fleeced in the back of a lock-up while staring into the unblinking eyes of a dispassionate Arab teenager, Hugo had written her confessional letters mired in disgust: disgust with himself, disgust with taxi drivers with little brown dicks. He wrote to her all the time.

Cynthia knew more than anyone about Hugo and his mother. His mother had spoken to Cynthia that evening, while Hugo lay in bed in front of a bar-fire, legs and arms locked round his open-shirted man in an upstairs room in Chalk Farm. His mother had wanted to give Hugo a message from a friend, so she rang him at Cynthia's house, where he was having dinner. Except he wasn't, and Cynthia didn't know where he was.

The two of them had talked for an hour or so. The two women of Hugo's life. The only two women with whom Hugo had ever been naked. And Cynthia told Hugo's mother not to shout at Hugo. She asked her not to. She asked her to forgive him. It's difficult to know what might have happened otherwise.

But for all the reading, cooking, eating and squabbling, for all the atmosphere of sudden new-found sophistication, of adult dinner parties and smoking joints after dessert and getting drunk on the sofa with no-one to say stop, the flat in Chiswick wasn't home for Hugo. Although he hummed with the thrill of life alone in London, free from parents, although it felt as if the narrative of his life was only just starting, there wasn't room for him between the sofas and the knick-knacks, wasn't room for him to hide in the ladies' boudoir. And he was still answerable. He was sharing Cynthia's bed and she wanted to know where he went and where he had been. His forays into the nightlife pained her unless they went together. They went well together in smoked glass and chrome niteries, crashing the door with smart lies, and crashing the dance floor, driving the slow-steppers against the wall, staring in each other's smiles and baring their teeth with the arrogance of self-gilded youth. But Hugo wouldn't take Cynthia to the dives and discos of his bodyhunting missions, seeking out men he still couldn't take home. There was no room for strange men's bodies in the boudoir. Hugo was becoming scented by the atomisers, he was spending too much time in Cynthia's red silk caftans. Too long in front of the mirror. He didn't want to find himself polishing his nails. Cynthia looked disapprovingly when he went out of the door in his catch-a-man ripped denim, but Hugo hadn't left home to take on a new set of rules, a new set of do and don't tells. So when Cynthia's mother returned from the Caribbean and wanted to sell up, he didn't mind that the little ménage was over. Cynthia's mother was suspicious of Hugo anyway. Suspicious of her daughter's love for a fag. He wasn't an asset to her future. He wasn't an asset to the flat. His things got in the way of the estate agent's patter.

Hugo couldn't tell his parents he was becoming homeless because they would demand he came home and he couldn't go back to the net curtain streets and the washing-up. His mother and he had said farewell. He hated repeat good-byes. He always avoided people after he'd said good-bye. He wasn't that good at them anyway. Hugo liked to slip away unnoticed.

'Something will turn up,' he thought. Something always did. It was one of his pecker little sayings. They always made him feel better. They had the reassurance of clichés. If so many people said them so much of the time, something must be true about them.

Something would turn up. Something always did. As long as he kept moving around.

So Hugo moved around. He wandered the streets looking for an opportunity and he met a man with long hair and a Ford Capri, a man he hadn't seen since he was fourteen.

He met the man in the high street in Hadley. He had gone home to see his mother and pick up some books and he was wandering by the top-of-the-hill cottage on a visit to the past, to see if the graffiti was still there asking where David had gone (it wasn't), to see if the men were still there (they were) and had got any younger (they hadn't). And he was just standing, thinking, his nose wrinkling snootily at the old smell that had got older and staler and shittier, when a man walked in with long hair and a Ford Capri outside and said 'Hello, David.'

David had been dead now for two years, but his ghost stirred at the sound of his name and Hugo felt a chill, an uneasiness at the memory of so much he had forgotten, a shiver of guilt that David, who had lain on his back and wanked for this man, who had posed for black and white Polaroids in his Marks and Spencer's string vest in this man's ground floor spare bedroom, was dead. Abandoned in the front of a blue pick-up truck and never spoken to again. Until now. Now, when William, the man with long hair, a Capri and a Polaroid camera, called him back from the grave. Hugo paused. He wanted to walk past the man and pretend not to see him. Instead he stopped to talk.

A week after meeting William in the street, Hugo had moved into his house. He had been right. Something turned up. Something always did. You just had to keep moving around. It always worked.

William remembered everything about David and Hugo remembered everything about William. William had always been different from most of the men David had dealt with. He was clever. He was kind. He was careful. He wanted to take a new set of Polaroids. The same poses in the same bed. Hugo was happy. He had found a new home. He stayed for three years. Three years of university vacations.

William had a large house on Highgate Hill, where the drawers were stuffed with pornographic magazines and the walls were hung with sinister paintings of little girls wrapped in shiny snakes next to drawings of dolls with open vaginas. He had a rambling house with dusty corners and strange hidden discoveries. A rare but blurred photograph of James Dean masturbating perched naked halfway up a tree. Hockney drawings of men lying next to each other in beds, gazing at large erections with surprised faces. Everything was dusty – from the Chinese palms to the Shangri-La records to the coloured glass lamps and the fat Persian cats. Everything seemed to wink with sex.

William had a boyfriend called Barry. They had many friends: men in leather jackets with motorbikes and inviting smiles; men with long hair and Afghan coats; men who looked at David as if he was one of them, but as if they'd like to take his clothes off nonetheless. David used to cycle up to the house on odd Saturday nights and just ring the bell and they were always pleased to see him. Sometimes for sex and sometimes just to feed him with drinks and have him sit by the palm trees between the speakers listening to them all talk and laugh. They were clever people. Art college people. Teachers and artists. They thought they were a racy set, although they didn't touch drugs and liked Cat Stevens records. They were nice people who liked sex. They liked sex and they liked talking about it. William most of all.

David liked sex, but not talking about it. He liked looking at it. He liked looking at himself doing it with other people in mirrors. He liked looking at other people doing it to him as he lay back and pretended that he couldn't touch them. He liked looking at other people doing it to each other when he couldn't touch either of them. Most of all he liked the films. Silent Super Eights sneaked in from America and projected onto a makeshift screen, a drab sheet suspended from clothes pegs over a papered wall. The films touched a part of Hugo's sex like a drug that sent him so high, so fast, he was no longer steering. He was teetering on the brink of an orgasm it took all his clenched teeth and tight fists to hold back. He was full to bursting and writhing. He liked these films. They were painful. The silly mock-dramas, preambles to the act, the bodies of the American actors, tanned to the buttock, muscled, toned, left him dreaming, sad, frustrated and impassioned. He wanted so badly to climb into their world of poolside fivesomes, of sex in the back of a pick-up on a long and dusty road, of sex in a gym, in a shower, in a back garden, on the roof, and in the haybarn.

William went one weirder too. He had films of donkeys being given blow jobs by blonde women with cheesy smiles. He showed films of women shitting on glass tables as men lay underneath. And he had fistfucking black-and-whites, black fisting white movies. David didn't take much notice of the donkeys and the shit. When the films were that odd or that cruel, he watched people's faces, not their bodies: he stared at their eyes, looking for signs of panic, looking for the slurred face of drugs. He looked at the silly flock wallpaper and the chintz sofa covers and wondered where it was, in whose street, whether the neighbours knew what was happening.

But the fisting movies were too frightening for such detached suburban anthropology. In any case they weren't suburban. They were American. Rough, scratchy prints of wiry men, lean muscled and crop haired, shot in haybarns away from watchful, prying police and shockable neighbours, these were men crazy with cravings. Their smiles hovered between sweat, fear and the sharp grimace of pain. Occasionally pleasure leaked onto their faces. But this was manly pursuit. This was sex for the brave-hearted and wide-assed. This was the boundary between agony and ecstasy.

To David, who still remembered the sickening, dizzying pain of the Thin Man's dick shoved up his arse as he stared out at the backlot world through a filthy broken window, this was all incredible. To David the mere touch of a finger on his hole meant muscle spasm. A finger. And yet here was a fist, and then an arm up to the elbow, disappearing deep into the gut of a man strung spread-legged from a rope hammock over the hay while another man sat on his face and pushed cock in his mouth.

And all this for an orgasm.

David was too close to orgasm himself to worry. Erect from his toes to his wide eyes, glued to the shaky image on the wall, he left his body to William's pleasures. His mind, or Hugo's worried voice, was quashed in the bloodrush.

Once the films were on, David didn't mind what William did. He didn't see him. His eyes were crisscrossing the screen, soaking up details, storing pictures. As William buried his head in his groin, David leant back against the pillows and sank into the poolside party where the lissom, tanned blond was wearing denim shorts so tight his balls peeked out. He slipped among the gym-dandies pumping up inflated torsos, and hung back at the door to the haybarn as the smell of sweat and shit mingled with Crisco lubricant lard drifted into his nostrils. The films, with their promise of bodies never seen before and sex-acts never believed before, left David paralysed with lust. His body twitched with the pulse of tickled glands. His brain lay numbed by the ooze of sexual anaesthetic. He quivered from top to toe and William chomped messily at his dick.

By the time Hugo made his own porn magazine debut, he knew the poses and the moves by heart. He knew the pout and the come-on and what angle the camera liked. And, fittingly, it was William who made all the introductions.

The house was different. It was a larger Victorian mansion with a larger garden in Muswell, not Highgate, Hill, but Barry was still there and the pornography was still there, filling the drawers so they wouldn't close properly, and the films were still there, all transferred onto numbered video cassettes and stacked up neatly by the television for ready viewing.

When Hugo's mother spent the evening pouring out her woes in the tall ceilinged room among the dusty boxes in William's house, she could have had no idea with whom her son had hung his hat. She would have screamed and run all the way to the police station had she known. William was the man who took black and white Polaroids of her son when he was only fourteen. He was the man who gave him a refuge from his home on Saturday nights, leaving him to romp like a kid with building blocks among piles of pornographic magazines. William was the man who six years later gave Hugo a roof over his head and a reason not to check back into the Hadley Hotel, and who gave Hugo the problem of raising money to pay the rent. It was William Hugo was trying to pay by making botched attempts to hustle tenners in the cramped heat of the Regent Palace Hotel bathroom. And it was William who came up with the solution. It was William who introduced Hugo to the magazine circuit and it was William who introduced Hugo to Tony, who introduced him to Richard, who put him on the game.

It was William who got Hugo into the fraternity and made his dreams come true.

8

DO THE HUSTLE

William was Hugo's fixer, his link with a lowlife he had never dreamed started so close to home – in Highgate Hill and now in Muswell Hill. In Highgate Hill William introduced Hugo to pornography. In Muswell Hill, six years later, he introduced Hugo to pornographers. Hugo asked for the introduction. William was pleased to oblige. After all, they both needed the money. William needed his rent money, and Hugo needed money to pay William his rent. But he didn't have time to wait at table or serve behind the Selfridges toiletry counter, or deliver Christmas cards or work in Harrods dispatch. With work to finish from last term and reading to start for next term, a day-job wasn't practical. A blow job was so much easier.

They were good to him, William and Barry, even though Barry didn't like Hugo because he drank too much of his gin and didn't say thank you and he was sure Hugo was sleeping with William while he was away at work. They looked after him even though William was disappointed because he thought he could sleep with Hugo while Barry was out at work and Hugo never said yes anymore. They were patient with him even though he never cooked for himself and never bought anything for the house, and never cleaned his room, but filled it with strange boys who left early in the morning. They tolerated him even though he came down every term from Cambridge bubbling over with arrogance and selfishness, and each time it took him two weeks to come down to earth. But bit by bit they took him down, peg by peg.

They were good to him and gave him his own room on the ground floor, full of unpacked books and dusty boxes, with a tall window and a dressing table mirror. It was a room with a ceiling, a ceiling you lay back and watched in the morning, as the light dappled through the window and splashed about the cornices. It was a far-away ceiling that could have carried frescoes. Hugo brought people back to his room: boys, ex-dancers, ex-boyfriends, house guests, smack-dealing window cleaners, acid-dealing students, and his mother. But Mrs Harvey was the only one of Hugo's guests that Barry made dinner for. The others made him bitter. He didn't like them and they didn't like him.

Nobody liked Barry much. In the end Hugo decided that Barry didn't like Hugo at all. He also decided that he didn't care much either way.

Barry had once been a beauty. His legs had been a conversation piece and his bum a much-pinched asset. He still wandered around the house in tight, white, satinette shorts. He was still fishing for compliments and pinches. He didn't see how he'd aged. How the gin had flushed a permanent rouge to his face. How his legs were out of fashion – too smooth and skinny for the latest muscle beach tastes. How his hair had thinned and his eyes had muddied. He hadn't noticed, or hadn't wanted to notice. So he still played the younger man. Hugo ruined that. Ten years younger, arrogant, promiscuous and endlessly chattering. With Hugo around, Barry felt old and drank a lot more gin.

Barry didn't like Hugo coming to stay. So it was Barry who made sure that Hugo had to pay. William agreed. The house was expensive and he needed extra money. Hugo was eating their fridge bare every week. So Hugo had to go to work. So William suggested the magazines.

He may have been a well-born social democrat with a penchant for Persian cats and herbaceous borders, but William was also the man who risked his career and his freedom to take black and white Polaroids of a fourteen-year old boy lolling in front of a fistfucking flick on his eiderdown.

So it was by no means odd that William should have pimped for Hugo. And William had all the right ideas. You had to approach the magazines professionally, he said, with all the pretence and euphemisms of modelling. So Hugo stood in the sitting room one afternoon, stark naked by the Chinese palms, as William took Polaroids (colour, this time) of Hugo with and without an erection, with and without his shorts on, with and without a smile. Hugo put the Polaroids in sets of four, wrote a circular letter on his Olivetti Lettera and packed off the prints in white envelopes to all the magazines he knew.

The first to reply was Q, a gay body mag hidden in an Earls Court mews. The letter was very polite. Quietly spoken. They were interested in taking some pictures. Hugo took the tube. Earls Court was still a foreign zone to him. Land of the late night take-away and home of the clone, it spoke an after-hours language that was more seedy than alluring.

The house was tucked away at the end of a mews off Earls Court Road. A little white house with trellised roses trailing outside the ground floor windows and a brass dolphin. A little man in a leather jacket and a moustache answered the door. He didn't smile. He stared at Hugo briefly, blankly, and then took him inside.

Inside, the house seemed to have vanished. There was just one large, bare room full of lights on heavy metal stands. There was a white screen on wheels and a chair. Hugo thought of hospital wards and torture chambers. The lights prickled sweat on his face. He felt about as sexy as a recently dead fish. Hugo took his clothes off as the man solemnly rolled a joint. He handed Hugo it lit and went to find some clothes.

Hugo was already disappointed. He had always imagined these porn emporia to be seething with young men of every measure-ment, scantily clad, tongues wagging in each other's throats, a perpetual tableau of sexual spree, snapped by artfully concealed photographers. Instead he was barefoot in suburbia in a draughty studio with a mealy-mouthed clone. The atmosphere was sullen. Hugo needed to get a hard-on. Maybe the man had gone to find the extras. But Q was a very tame magazine. Faded and failing. That at least Hugo already knew. It was one of the old school. Boys more young than healthy posed in silly pouts, shot to appeal to the poodle queens of upmarket bedsit land; the men who went to bed in hairnets and wore chainstore silk dressing gowns; the men who smoked Sobranies and voted Conservative; the men whom, before long, Hugo would be charging for sexual favours.

The little leather jacket came back with some clothes. Bits and pieces of uniformia. Boy Scouts of America. Schoolboy. Army cadet. Naval cadet. Gauleiter. It was like doing a shady fashion show. The Boy Scouts of America was the man's favourite. It was too small. It pinched Hugo under the arms and in the crutch. It made him feel hot and clumsy. But the man liked it. So Hugo concentrated on trying to keep an erection. The man kept passing him a bottle of poppers and a porn mag, just before each shot. The heat and glare of the lights as the poppers rushed up through his brain turned him dizzy and slow-witted. The man kept repeating his instructions, but all Hugo's blood had gone to gorge his dick. The words had to get through the fog of amyl, the miasma of bloodshot capillaries in front of his eyes. His eyes were weeping and his head felt swollen.

The little leather-jacket-and-moustache never made a pass at him. Hugo was blearily disappointed. Every sphincter had relaxed. All his hormones were on the alert. He was trouserless in the middle of a naked room clutching a magazine and a bottle of Locker Room love potion. But the little leather jacket just buzzed about, changing films and bulbs and snapping instructions as the camera whirred and wound on, popping flash in Hugo's eyes. Hugo sat on a stool, crossed his legs, uncrossed his legs, leaned back with his legs apart and stared transfixed at his own dick. They barely spoke. Hugo was passed a joint and turned his back on the camera, splaying his buttocks. He wondered what the man thought of his work.

He got thirty pounds cash for the Q assignment and that paid William his rent. For three weeks. But there were three more to go and Hugo had nothing to live off. The little man in the leather jacket hadn't been that friendly. There were no repeats. That was the main problem. Once you'd done one, that was it. The same magazine didn't want you back again. The more you worked the less valuable you became. It wasn't very much like real modelling, Hugo supposed. But then neither was the money.

Hugo did a lot of scouting round. He met a German in Chiswick who dressed him up in roller skates and tight shorts and videoed him in his living room. The German was tall and good-looking and went under two different names. He gave Hugo twenty pounds and said he'd call him back. He never did. He seemed pissed off that Hugo had called him in the first place. He was trying to be respectable.

Hugo answered an advertisement in a gay newspaper and went to an audition in Campden Hill, where a man with curly hair and a fat belly told him his chest wasn't big enough. He gave him no money and said he'd call him if anything cropped up. Nothing did.

Time was getting short. Money couldn't get much tighter. Term was approaching and Hugo had bills to settle. So he answered an advertisement in a straight contact magazine. A man answered the phone. They needed four Polaroids from different angles. They were shooting next week for a German magazine. It wouldn't be sold in England. That relieved him. There was always a nagging worry fidgeting at the back of Hugo's mind, full of unanswerable what-ifs. What if a friend of his parents should pick up such a magazine while passing through some mid-German business airport or browsing the shelves of some West London sex store and suddenly recognise his friends' son behind the bleary eyes and the Boy Scouts of America shirt? Would they say nothing because to say anything would reveal too much about their reading habits? Would they be unable to resist bringing it up in conversation over the pêche brulée at his mother's Saturday night dinner table? Or would they just be malicious, happy to disabuse Mrs Harvey of her belief that her children were the paragon of what children should be? Would they simply shove the magazine through the letter box and scuttle off before they could be seen?

There was another what-if pestering Hugo's sang froid. What if he couldn't get it up? This was, after all, a straight magazine. He would be cavorting with a woman. A naked woman: stark from her fanny to her tits and beyond. What would he do? What would he think about? Women's bodies had always terrified him. But for the one dark night in New York with Cynthia, when she had most assuredly taken him to bed and fucked him, he had not touched, and had barely seen, a naked woman in the flesh. He tried to avoid them. They scared him. He would turn away, suddenly drained of energy, confused, irked.

He didn't seem to know what he was frightened of – the invitation, the challenge, the breasts, his ignorance, his failure. He wasn't frightened of women. He loved women. He loved their looks. He loved their clothes and their smiles. He loved their hold over men and their interest in him. But he was terrified of their bodies.

Hugo stood in front of the mirror in his room with the tall

ceiling and long windows and stared hard at himself and saw very little. He looked hard into his eyes and they didn't flinch. He looked hard at the expression on his face but it was frozen over. It revealed nothing. He was looking for the flicker of fear. He was looking for the chance to cry. The chance to crack. But he just stared at himself. If he was frightened of the what-ifs he wasn't going to give it away. Not even to himself. He tried to smile at himself. It didn't work. It didn't come. Maybe he didn't like himself enough for that.

Hugo sent off the Polaroids from his collection and a couple of days later the woman rang back to say that he had been accepted. He was to be at a house in Swiss Cottage on a Sunday morning two weeks later.

It was Easter Sunday.

The Harveys had never taken Easter particularly seriously. Like bank holidays, like any Sunday, Easter Sunday was a washing day. Hugo's father stayed outside tinkering underneath his car. Hugo's mother laboured over her tubs and her ironing board, humming to Frank Sinatra as she draped wet towels over the radiators, steaming up the windows, filling the air with the smell of washing.

The children were given chocolate eggs – one each – and allowed to eat them bit by bit after each meal. Then they were packed off to church or Quaker meeting in Sunday best while Mr and Mrs Harvey made love on an unmade bed in the upstairs bedroom with the curtains open. Mrs Harvey confessed that to Hugo a long time later, as they sat in the downstairs room in William's house. Mrs Harvey didn't blink as she told the story. She didn't smile either. Hugo looked past her at the dirty windows of the room and stared at his reflection. He was more wrapped up in his story than hers. Afterwards he would smile at the thought of his father, sweating under the car, grime in his eyes and the furrows of his forehead, hearing the rap of a wedding ring on the mullioned glass, looking up to a negligéed wife, ready, grinning down from the upstairs bedroom through the open curtains.

Now Easter wasn't even considered an appropriate day for a phone call. It came a long way down the line after Mother's Day. Mother's Day was taken very seriously. Easter Sunday was just a

Sunday. A beached day on a low tide. A mudflat day. A grey sky and nothing-to-do-till-evening day. Hugo felt sorry for his kid sister, marooned among the domestic laundry, with a cut-price chocolate egg and no sense of occasion. He felt sorry for himself as he travelled on the top deck of a Number 2 bus through a London full of windswept front gardens and bus-stops drowning in drizzle. He felt sorry for the queues of passengers, cowering in huddles against the wet wind, a head and a hand darting out to stop the bus. A little row of weatherbeaten tortoises. Timid people too scared to smile.

The kids on the bus were all clutching and chewing and sticky-ing themselves with chocolate eggs. But none of them was smiling. Their mothers, drained of make-up, devoid of energy, sat stolidly by, watching and occasionally wiping. No smiles for no smiles.

It was a cold, grim April day. The sort of day that makes you hate people, buildings, and animals. The sort of day that makes you wonder why you're alive. Not the sort of day to go and make simulated love to a blonde from Huddersfield, down on an away-day to pick up a few bob in the nude.

Hugo arrived slightly late at a large, semi-detached house with a windswept front garden and was shown upstairs by the wife. He supposed she was the wife. A brisk, knitwear type with grey hair cut to style. A no-messing woman whose eyes he never caught the colour of.

'You're taller than we expected,' she said humourlessly.

'Did you see the photos . . . the Polaroids?'

'Yes, but they don't show how tall you are. You should have put that in the letter.'

She looked him up and down. He had forgotten to comb his hair. He always forgot. It hadn't occurred to him to dress up for the porn people. But he was meant to be looking sexy. He could see their point. He tried to remember if he had any spots. No big ones, he knew, otherwise he would have spent the morning pester-ing them. But little ones, ones that showed up in the white heat glare of a tungsten lamp?

She looked him up and down and the colourless eyes behind her glasses didn't flicker. Her mouth didn't twitch. She was as grey and grim as the world outside. Hugo felt an irrational longing for a seat on the top floor of the Number 2. He wanted to be with a book, lost in someone else's world. He wanted to feel fit and bronzed and desirable. He half-expected her to take out measuring instruments and medical tools. But she took out a clipboard and ticked off some numbers.

Hugo was getting worried. If he had to get a hard-on in front of this gorgon, he was going to have to depend on some pretty strong fantasies. He pined for a joint. Something to unknot the elastic golf ball of tension in his head. After the bus ride the only thing he could think of was chocolate eggs and light rain. How could he convert a chocolate egg into a hard-on?

They went up to the bedroom. His co-star was already there. She was medium height and not unattractive. That's how the police would have described her. Or one of the quality newspapers. The tabloids would have gone further. Busty porn star, tragic blonde beauty, peroxide sex-queen. Hugo was already having her killed off in some suburban sex crime. It was one of those days for morbid thoughts. The tabloids would have rerun a library photo of her boobs. She'd probably done page three when she was a teenager. She was loud and her make-up sat on her skin like greasepaint, thick and lifeless. It had no pores. Just occasional hairline cracks. Hugo couldn't see where the make-up stopped and her skin started but he estimated it was nearer her navel than her chin. She pecked him on the cheek and he caught a whiff of cheap perfume mingled with cheese and onion crisps. Now all he could think of was British Rail.

The husband of the bad-tempered woman at the door was sitting in the bedroom with the camera, trying out the lighting. He had grey hair not cut to style and the look of a man who might have been to a war zone with his camera but stayed at home instead. He had the look of a man who has seen much of the world through his lens and all of it in his own house. He looked comfortable and he had a comfortable voice. He wasn't bothered really. Hugo liked him.

He asked Cindy (did her parents call her Cindy? Did they dream of page three when they christened her?) to stand in different parts of the room. Cindy had no clothes on. Hugo hadn't really noticed. She was one of those girls. When they wear clothes they look uncomfortable – squeezed inside denim with zips stretching or tucked inside lacy bodices with breasts lurching out above the elastic. She glanced back at Hugo and rolled her eyes. He smiled at her. The smile came easily. She came easily. Things were loosening up. Hugo's balls rolled over.

The room was like a photofit set for soft core porn. It had the thick carpet and the flock paper. It had the feeling of suburbia and sexplay. Nothing was necessary. Everything was typical. There was a mirror leaning against the wall. A bed. A chair. Some plants. A television. Wires coiled in rolls. And lights on sticks like heavy-headed storks on one metal leg. Silver umbrellas. Spare cameras. And a clipboard. Another clipboard. This was like school parade. On the clipboard was a piece of paper divided up into many squares. In each square was a biro sketch of two bodies in different positions. Each square was numbered. The bad-tempered wife, who had resolved the problem of Hugo's height by suggesting that they did the shots with him lying down, had a biro behind her ear while her glasses dangled on her knitwear breasts. She ticked off the numbers of the positions in the squares as they did them.

It was very organised. Very clinical. And the room was draughty. Hugo took his clothes off and they started.

It was much easier than he had feared. Much easier for him at least. The magazine was a girly magazine, one of those little black and white jobs you can pick up in the backstreet bookshops round any major European railway station. They carry contact stories written by readers about sexual conquests on railway trains, and pictures of sex games with the eyes and the nipples and the dicks blacked out. They have photos of housewives with rollover bellies and flattened breasts sitting legs-apart in new suspenders, wearing an inviting smile and no eyes. Somehow the black squares were what made them so sordid.

Girly magazines are for men readers and men readers aren't interested in what the man in the picture looks like. He's just there for authenticity; to give the girl a reason to be bending over backwards, splitting her spine to give a high-profile view of her once-private parts. Hugo wasn't expected to get an erection. All he had to do was lie back and smile.

Cindy was a professional. She didn't complain and she smiled knowledgeably when they asked her to do Number 78 or 84. She knew the moves. They didn't make much difference to Hugo. He barely had to move. Occasionally he had to face one way or the other, shift a hip or move an arm, and on one occasion he had to take a nipple (her nipple) between his teeth and pull away. This was awkward as the man with the camera had to rearrange lighting and refocus as Hugo kept the nipple between his teeth, trying not to grip too hard and trying to not let go. The little red lumps around the nipple filled his eyes and her perfume, mixed with greasepaint and a faint smell of cheese, filled his nostrils. His neck hurt and his jaw ached as he tried to grimace invitingly without losing his grip.

This was erotic photography.

They sent Hugo home before Cindy. She grinned and he waited for her to wink but she turned round to do a buttock spread over the chair in front of the mirror before he could smile back. He signed a form which promised him fifty pounds soon. Fifty pounds wasn't bad for a morning's work, although he was back at Cambridge and well into the summer term before the fifty pounds arrived. It went straight to William, of course. Five weeks' rent. Arrears.

That was Hugo's last magazine job. He never saw the magazine. He never met anyone who had seen him in it either. The German with the camcorder never called. The man who ran the model agency and jabbed a finger into Hugo's too-small chest never called. He felt he'd saturated the market after only two appearances.

There had to be a better way of paying the rent. There was the whole summer to think of. Four months of leisure with no cash to enjoy it with.

William quite understood the problem. In fact he seemed to find it quite interesting. Barry looked very disenchanted. Four months of Hugo sounded like too much of not such a good thing, but William was keen. So William introduced Hugo to Tony.

It wasn't because he thought they'd get along. They didn't really. Nobody got on terribly well with Tony. But everybody knew him. And everyone was nice to him. Because of whom they thought they knew he knew. Or might know. And what he probably knew about them.

Hugo didn't get on terribly well with Tony. They were very different. Hugo was hungry and Tony was fat. But they worked well together. Once.

Tony was a fat-faced toy boy with a professional flat in Montagu Square and an on-off affair with a millionaire impresario whose fortune had been made on a string of musical hits. The impresario took Tony on cruises and to sit-down dinners with stand-up place cards and stiff menus.

Tony babbled: about the stars he'd met – all strictly light entertainment – about the money they spent on him, about imagined slights and triumphant snubs, about boys, clothes, and cashflow. Stepping gingerly in socked feet round his low glass and brass coffee tables, a long-stemmed wine glass in his hand, a gold-band mentholated cigarette in his mouth, he turned and twirled and babbled. And Hugo sat. Waiting. Listening. Learning. It was like an apprenticeship. Tony was the Madame. Hugo was the novice.

Although he was 'devoted' to the impresario, Tony turned quick tricks on the side in Montagu Square and held down a salesman's job at a Mayfair gunsmith, selling Barbours to the horsy set. With his smart shop job, his showy connections, his permanent tan and perfect teeth, Tony was the consummate professional; a showpiece salesperson with one hand on, and one hand in, the till. There was a lingering aura of blackmail about him. The impresario would never leave his wife. For what? Tony smelt of sex, danger and insincerity. Tony knew his business and was making money at it. He was a hooker in furs and good red wine.

When William introduced Hugo to Tony it wasn't because he thought they'd get along, but because Tony knew the ropes, pulled strings, played the network. He could introduce Hugo to the right people. Most importantly he could introduce Hugo to Richard. Richard ran the 'agency'. Richard could give him work and work could give him money to give to William. It was simple enough. The difficulty was getting the introduction. They all said you couldn't see Richard without an introduction. Tony could introduce him. He worked for Richard on and off. When he wasn't working for himself. But before he introduced Hugo to Richard, he wanted his cut of the meat. He wanted to try Hugo out. So he organised an initiation. And just to make it seem that he, Tony the Happy Hooker of Marble Arch, wasn't falling for this bony young student with posh suburb written all over him, he made it a trick. He invited a client. A regular.

Never have sex without making money. Life's too short. You never know when you'll be on your uppers and past it, and then you'll be thankful for the rainy day money. Home Sweet Home. Tony and his homilies.

The regular arrived in a smart black coat and a smart black Jaguar. Silver hair and a good profile. Tony flapped him into the house, making him smile, oiling him with witterings, sitting him down and pouring him a drink before anyone had had time to breathe. It was a single pirouette from door to drink to mouth . . . and to bed. Hugo was silent, sucking his vodka through the ice in the glass. It was before one. Lunchtime. He would have preferred a sandwich. He watched them through the fog in his head, whispering about deals and additions and extras and bonuses. Hugo was the extra, the bonus who would cost an additional . . . which had to be split between . . . and he was new but very . . . He felt unexcited and unafraid. All he needed was an erection, good timing and a brisk hand. And maybe another vodka.

But what about the regular? How was he supposed to satisfy him? He still wasn't sure how he was going to persuade his tongue and his hands and his body to wrap around the man's tongue and hands and body. Maybe that would come. Maybe Tony would take care of that. Maybe he could just lie back and be done unto.

The fog thickened. Hugo liked vodka. Sweet and sharp, it froze his anxieties. Tony was standing up and smiling. He stood up. It was a long way. They walked into the bedroom, Tony winking and smiling, beckoning. The ice in Hugo's vodka chinked against the glass. He had taken his shoes off and his socked feet sank into the carpet pile.

The bed was large with a ruched canopy above it. There were no windows, just curtains and candles and a single bedside lamp. Although it was still early afternoon outside, the air was musky with evening smells as Tony squeezed drops from little phials onto the lightbulb of the bedside lamp. A wisp of sweet-smelling smoke floated into the air and Tony and the regular began to undress. Hugo started to take his shirt off. They were both watching him. He was watching both of them. The elderly man's body, once athletic, was now slightly collapsed with age. It was covered in five silver hair and tanned dark by long summers on expensive beaches. It was a growing-old-gracefully body, cocooned by money. Tony's tan was yellow. Sunlamps and awayday weekends. His skin was smooth and round, rolling into puppy fat. They stared at Hugo's lean, bony body as his prick bounced out of his trousers and stood hard, excited by their gaze, excited by the smell of bordello and the ruched silliness of the bed, excited by being wanted, and now by being touched.

The bed sank and slid beneath them. Silk sheets on silk sheets. Bodies between, on top, all over. Hugo watched it all from above, from beyond. Maybe they had slipped him a Valium. His mind seemed woozy with ease and cocooned in far-off smiles. And then it began to feel like work. The first blush of the vodka had passed, the giddiness of the scented air had faded and the breathing and grunting intruded.

As the three of them writhed on the bed, Tony helped himself to Hugo's dick and left Hugo to kiss with the man with the silver hair. The man didn't pause for breath. Hugo's tongue was tired and his neck stiff. In the back of his mind, a thin sarcastic voice was telling him how strange he looked on a ruched bedspread in the early afternoon with two men. If he didn't listen to it, the voice got louder. If he smiled at it, he couldn't kiss the man. The voice was getting angrier, more shrill. He wasn't really having fun. But he was working and today he would be able to pay two weeks' rent after one hour's work.

Today he would feel the protection of money, the weight in his pocket keeping his feet on the pavement, his head in the air. Money was very important to Hugo. Having it. Having it without having to count it. Riding in taxis without being glued to the meter. Buying lunch without calculating how far over or under he was going. All through his life, Hugo had counted the pennies. His parents had taught him how. So much for this, so much for that, and nothing left over.

He heard the silver-haired man's breath quickening. He squeezed the silver-haired man's dick just as he started gasping short, croaking breaths into Hugo's ear. He was twitching and sweating. His hands lay heavy and clammy on Hugo's belly. Hugo smiled as an absurd thought passed slowly across his mind. It was like being a metaphysical poet. Lying embroiled in someone else's sweat in someone else's bed and both of them all over him and he, Hugo, just watching from above, from outside, from nowhere. The absurd thought crossed his mind as his hand squeezed and pulled and his tongue, sore and hurting, lapped at the silver man's ear lobe. Maybe he wasn't having an orgasm at all. Maybe he was having a heart attack.

The man squealed. Tony took Hugo's dick out of his mouth, wet his hand and rolled the silver man's knob in his palm. The man groaned and Hugo pulled his tongue out of his ear as the man's teeth clenched. His head swung backwards and his hips up and he spurted all over the ruched canopy.

They all lay there.

What were they thinking, thought Hugo, whose mind was already racing home, thinking about the exit line, how he could avoid being delayed. He wanted his cash and he wanted fresh air.

The silver man got up and walked to the shower. He already knew where it was. Tony was snoring gently. His mouth was open. Hugo wanted to get away from him. He wanted to go home with his money and to pay William. He wanted to be patted on the head for what he'd done.

The man came back all wet with a towel and Hugo went to shower while the others sorted out the cash. He didn't reappear until the man had gone. He thought it was better that way. Tony came into the bathroom and climbed into the shower. Hugo climbed out. He went and dried himself in the other room. Tony had already taken his share of the £100. He'd left Hugo £20. Folded inside was Richard's number. And a note. 'Ring him tomorrow.'

Tony was still in the shower when Hugo reached the cold air of Montagu Square (the shady side) and turned the corner feeling flush. He went straight into Selfridges and sat at the coffee bar. He smiled at the blue-haired ladies and their blue-haired poodles.

He smiled because they didn't know that the boy they were smiling back at was a hustler. They didn't know that the money passing between Hugo and Selfridges coffee bar was sex money. Hugo felt like a lowlife trespassing on highlife and grinned. And then, feeling like a secret agent making his secret contact, he rang Richard.

'I've heard all about you,' said an Australian voice down the phone. 'We're in Ossington Street, off Notting Hill. Come at three. It's always quiet then. 52A. Top bell. See you then. Be good.'

Richard was one of the thinnest men Hugo had ever met. Thin and tanned. He wore a lot of white. White shorts and a white vest. White socks and sneakers. His face was hidden behind the tan and the smile, which sparkled white teeth across the room. It was his best asset. But men didn't go to Richard for his smile. They didn't ring him up for his sunny disposition. They rang him up for his boys. His escorts. His hotel fly-by-nights. And Hugo was about to be put on the team. On the game.

Hugo walked about the room with his trousers off and his shirt open and Richard was pleased with his long legs. 'We get so many tall ones in here and when they take their pants off, their legs are really disappointing.' He looked and smiled but he didn't touch. Hugo liked him for that and returned his smiles. He felt at home.

'Tony told me a lot about you. I wondered when you were going to come in. Do you know the form?'

Hugo blinked.

'You ring in. There's always someone here. Either me or Alan or Greg. And then when someone rings in and asks for someone like you, we call you. At home. Where do you live?'

'Muswell Hill.'

'That's a bit of a way. Most of the jobs are in the West End. Hotels. We only get a few locals and they're sort of South Kensington. Fulham. A couple in Belgravia. Do you have a car?'

If I had a car, I wouldn't be doing this, thought Hugo.

'Well, I'm sure you'll manage. Our commission is taken off the top. You charge £40 and we take £12. You keep all tips. Some of the boys make sixty, seventy pounds in tips on each job. What name would you like to use?'

Hugo didn't want to use Hugo. What if some friend of his

parents called the agency and he was forced to go and call and ring the doorbell of a man who ... well, who would be more frightened? The man or he? 'David,' said Hugo. Would David come back to life now, this late in life, this long after his death?

'We have too many Davids,' said Richard. 'Hugo's better. We don't have any Hugos. And it suits you. It's a good name for you. You can put your clothes back on again. I've seen what I need to.'

And so Hugo walked out of 52A Ossington Street with an agency and a pimp. Life was good and the sun was shining and he could have stepped into any number of the taxis rolling by. He had the money after all. So what if it was rent? So what if it was William's? There would be more soon. More than enough. But Hugo came from a careful home. So he jumped the buses all the way back to Muswell Hill, staring out of the window or faking sleep every time the conductor came by.

The first job they gave him was in Swiss Cottage in an apartment block. Most of the jobs were in apartment blocks or hotels. There was never any space. It was always a bed-sitting evening. The first job they gave him was a regular. He liked the new boys. He'd give them grades. And the agency was always interested in customer feedback. He was safe. He was their trial tester. He had a black poodle and a checked shirt that was too small, so the buttons were pulled tight across his belly.

Hugo was searching for a sexy angle. The man was charming, or kind rather, but womanish. He should have had a hairy chest but there were only three hairs growing in different directions, like stray pubes. Hugo had to think of something erotic. He had to get an erection.

They talked. They drank tea. Hugo stared at the man's body and tried to find something brutish about it. Something masculine. Something to trigger his dick. It still wasn't clear what the £40 entailed. It seemed a lot until you took the £12 off the top. Did it mean a fuck or a suck or a massage and a wank? Was he their toy or their instructor? How did you get into bed? Did they lead or did you?

'Take your shirt off,' smiled the man with the poodle, lighting a cigarette. Hugo was annoyed. The cigarette was a black Sobranie and the poodle-man was using a cigarette holder. He could never get an erection in this house. Through the window he could see the Saturday afternoon shopping in the Finchley Road. John Barnes. Toys Toys Toys. Lindy's Patisserie. Respectable Jewish mothers parked their two-door Mercedes and ran into Waitrose.

His shirt off, he turned and faced the man. 'Undo your trousers.' Hugo's groin twitched. He was being made to strip. This was good. The man with the three-hair chest was taking control. Hugo could play the call boy, and the poodle-man could play the client. He was the client. Hugo had to please. His body had to please. The man was stripping him to see his body. He was a sex object. He was a toy. Toys Boys Toys.

His trousers fell to his knees and his underwear filled up. He felt his balls swell. The man reached out and squeezed them and Hugo's hard-on slipped out of his briefs. The man with the poodle and the black Sobranie and the three-hair chest and the cluttered apartment closed his lips over Hugo's knob and sucked hard as Hugo leaned back against the wall and, through the corner of his eye, watched another woman dashing into Waitrose with her children trailing after her. He smiled to stop himself giggling.

That afternoon in the Finchley Road, Hugo learned a crucial lesson about working for the agency. You had to turn yourself on. No client was ever going to do that for you. In all his dealings, Hugo only ever had one client whom he actually found physically attractive – a Kuwaiti prince who had been studying in America and was on his way back to his Middle Eastern purgatory with a long face and a gym-supple body. Hugo was so surprised to find a body in the bedroom, a good body, he came too soon, and, unnerved, left too early. It was as if he suddenly had to play a different role.

Most of the time the role was clear. He had to do the work and the other person, the swarthy or mangy or grizzled or lined or fat or bony or drooling man was an anonymous audience. Not a word would be said during sex. They could chat about knick-knacks and bric-à-brac and this and that beforehand and Hugo would say almost nothing, keeping his voice to himself and his cards to his chest. He wasn't there to think or dazzle or amuse. He was there to take his clothes off and bring his customer to a slow, fulfilling and unrepeatable (at least within the next thirty minutes) orgasm. He had to turn them on by being turned on. He had to make them hard by getting hard himself. He had to give them an orgasm by giving himself one. It was almost a mime routine. A strip act. A dance of the seven hotel bedrooms.

To bring himself to this peak of self-love and self-sex he had to look at himself as if he were them looking at him, and he had to marvel and desire what he saw. The good thing about this was that it meant that Hugo could always get an erection.

The bad thing was that it ruined his sex life. His talent in bed atrophied. When he picked people, men, up for his own pleasure (or they him for theirs), he couldn't move. He had lost his libido somewhere in this artificial, glazed, distant routine. And so he just lay there and was done unto. Barely stirring. In love with himself. Unable to share. Only able to be watched and touched, stroked and abandoned. They just got bored and left. Hugo hardly noticed. He was lost to the world, caught up in a huge fantasy in which other people were incidental. Often they would never speak to him again. The boy who had been a tiger in the lock-up office to the man with the hairy chest was now a sloth, slumbering through sex like some drugged concubine.

But he was good with the clients and some of them, those who lived in London, asked for him back. There was the restaurateur with a house in Belgravia who took him down to a Sussex farm to watch him make love to an American actor and then paid them both £100. There was the Lebanese man who travelled the world in crocodile shoes and matching briefcase who always answered the door naked. There was the Saudi prince with the coke habit and the six-inch deep carpets in a flat off Regents Park. And in the middle of all of this, there was Hugo faking it. Faking the fun, faking the turn-on, faking his own image, faking his own past, and, standing in the lift afterwards, faking a smile in the smoked glass mirror. Hugo the Hooker was a fake, but so was Hugo the Lover and Hugo the Suburban Boy. Maybe Hugo the Student was real. Maybe no-one had the measure of him. Maybe no-one ever had. Himself least of all. For all the time Hugo had spent alone with himself, talking to himself, arguing and lecturing himself after another afternoon spent in the wrong place with the wrong man and only a couple of quid and an inconvenient lovebite to show for it, he was not sure he had ever really stopped and quizzed himself. Who the fuck are you, instead of who are you fucking?

Somehow it didn't seem that he had ever been that interested before and now that it might have been interesting it was too dangerous. It was much easier to pretend there just wasn't enough time. No time to stop. No time for questions. Just sex, work, fun, life, in whatever order. They all sounded the same. They all sounded like work and now work was sex. And he always seemed to be late.

When Hugo looked at himself in lift mirrors he cocked an eyebrow. Unshowered, wiped off with hotel towels, money in his pocket, two whiskies and maybe a joint in his head, he cocked an eyebrow as if to greet himself and say, 'Hey, stranger. How's it going?' He challenged himself with his own bonhomie. It brooked no serious question. It dared him to shrug it all off. He shrugged it all off. After all, he was now a hooker. He was now lowlife. Wasn't that what he wanted? To kick up his heels in the gutter and play with the gigolos in their Cuban heels and fringed leather jackets.

But this wasn't the gutter. This was air-conditioning, thick beige carpets and cable television. This was sex on a deluxe conveyor belt against the low background murmur of expensive shopping. It was duty-free transit lounge sex. Comfortable chairs. Air-conditioning. Miniature whiskies. And the bonhomie was tissue-thin. Beneath it Hugo was going numb. He was getting professional. He sat back in the taxi to and from jobs like a professional. He smiled and let his lips bare his teeth like a professional. He shook hands, made small talk and gave head like a professional. And behind the tissue-thin bonhomie, something was dying. He caught the flicker in his own eyes in the mirror in the lift, in the mirror in the bathroom when he got home, in the mirror in his bedroom as he got undressed for bed, feeling suddenly vulnerable in his underwear, like a little boy who badly wanted his mother to come and tuck him up and tell him goodnight stories.

It wasn't that he felt dirty. Or at least, not often. People had to work at it to make him feel dirty. Some of them tried. They forced him, spat on him verbally and took him physically. In underlit, grubby hotel rooms on over-crowded London streets, he sucked toes and crouched under synthetic coverlets enduring the high hands of men who thought they'd bought a white slave. They never hurt him. They just made him feel like muck. They made him feel like long baths. They never called again.

It wasn't that he felt guilty. Hugo had never noticed a conscience. If he had one, it was rarely awake. The flicker in his eye in the mirror in the lift wasn't an accusation. It was a signal. A flash. A half-smile. Tentative. To himself. He couldn't indulge it because then he'd laugh, and the laugh wouldn't come, or cry, and no tears would happen. He just stared back as if he'd never seen himself before. He just stared at himself and, with a slight intake of breath, stepped out of the lift, down the beige carpet corridors and knocked on another painted door with three gilt numbers. Mr Hassan. Mr Manzoni. Mr Kastner. Mr Sakamucho. Good evening, gentlemen. A scotch would be perfect.

But all the time that he sat on the bed with Mr Sakamucho and Mr Kastner, all the time that he admired the view from Mr Manzoni's room and tugged on Mr Hassan's short, thick dick, he missed the camaraderie he'd led himself to expect. Hugo didn't feel he was getting the kicks, the streetlife, the raggedy, raunchy tinsel and chipped heels he'd watched from the shadows on Pigalle, on rue St Denis, outside the Termini Station, even among the hairless boys milling among the cloisters of the Cairo mosque.

David would have had more fun, Hugo sometimes thought, wistfully, as he stared at London through the raindrops on a taxi window, making another soundless, effortless journey back from a quick coupling ten five-star floors into the sky.

He had expected a sugar daddy by now. He had expected a man – tall, broad-chested, not too young, with a round-the-year tan (more South Pacific than South of France) to sweep him away. The prince and the showgirl. But that wasn't the point. Hugo was earning the money to pay William. He had studies to return to. He was not available. He was only paying the rent. And what would he do with a sugar daddy? Lie in bed drinking freshly-squeezed orange juice and black coffee, unwrapping gifts and reading special editions of *GQ* and *Esquire* before slipping silently into the limousine for a drive through the park and lunch – The Caprice. Langan's. The men would look at him and wonder. Is he or is he just? The women would look at him and smile. And he'd order in such impeccable tones that the waiters would stop winking and hold their tongues. And he'd smile.

But that wasn't a sugar daddy. That was a knight on a white charger. And Hugo was much too grown up to believe in them. He was much too grown up to attract one of them. After all, he was a professional now. He knew how to play tunes on the erogenous zones of Arabs, Jews, Chinamen and Japanese. He could surprise Americans and lull Germans. All that with a tongue, two hands and a surprise between his legs. After that it was lie back and let their fingers do the walking, as he took in their burst capillaries, bloodshot eyes, chipped teeth, tobacco-stained fingers and calloused hands. The hard, thick hairs that grew out in odd places – from ears and nostrils, from birthmarks and warts. The flesh that had stretched and fallen wearily into sagging belly folds. The scars and marks of age and abuse.

As they sweated over his body, breathing unevenly, shoving their noses into bottles of poppers, he coaxed and listened, played and encouraged, gums wrapped over his teeth, faking the grunts and groans of pleasure as he went down and up and down on their fat, thin, cut, uncut dicks, luring the orgasm that was his escape cue.

If the breathing quickened, he quickened his pace, gently, firmly, allowing no resistance. If the breathing subsided, he switched technique, darting to another part, another gland, another surprise twitch in their bodies. He'd run his nails gently up the inside of their thighs so their balls turned and rolled in consternation. He'd push his hand firmly down from the navel to the groin so their pricks jerked upright, climbing into the air, seeking succour. He'd flick a tongue in their ear and bite on their nipples and slap their buttocks, all the time counting the number of moves, the number of minutes he had left. He watched himself like an ice-skating judge holding up a score card. If the man pushed Hugo's hand away, eager to prolong the game, determined not to come, Hugo would hold the man down by his arms, pin him to the bed, turning him on further and faster in the erotic game of push me, pull you, you on top, me on bottom, and deftly, quickly, gently, firmly, pull them to a shudder, a spurt, a drip and trickle climax.

Sometimes there were problems. Difficult customers. No-one dangerous. No-one like the man in the woods back in Hadley who hung Hugo's trousers on the fence and tried to fuck him. No-one like the Thin Man in the cubicle with the cracked window who made him retch with pain, leaning over a dirty toilet bowl, staring at his reflection in the leftover piss below. None of that. Hugo was up a scale by now. He was in the land of carpets and silent footfalls, of whiskies in heavy tumblers and videos of heavy sex. But some of the customers played up. Some of them didn't know how the game worked. Some of them knew too well. The latter Hugo could handle. They were mean and twisted about having to pay, about not being young enough, sleek enough, contoured and proportioned enough to stand at a bar and waste three, four hours and thirty, forty pounds waiting for someone to breathe hello in their ear. They were bitter that they had to pay instead of pleased they could. They wanted chance, surprise love, not mail order body beautiful. So, when it came, they pissed on it. When it stripped, they smiled at it, mocked it, rubbed it up the wrong way, poked and prodded and never stroked.

Hugo could handle that. He had a hipflask of scotch and a spare Valium in his pocket. If people wound him up too far, he dropped one into the other and washed them both down in one gulp in the lift on the way down. Then he smiled at himself and tried to catch the flicker in his eyes before they went too blurred and the world dissolved into soft-focus wooze.

But Hugo didn't like the beginners. The ones at home. He liked hotels. They had a fast-food atmosphere. No-one felt at home in a hotel but everyone felt randy. No-one played you their old records, or made you coffee. They didn't have the knick-knack bric-à-brac of domestic life in their bedrooms, the framed photographs, the National Trust table mats, the heavy wardrobes and stray carpet slippers that turned Hugo off by making him think of home and family and all the paraphernalia of everyday lonely life.

In hotels, loneliness was horny. It was a no-man's land of no holds barred. Anything could happen, anything could be ordered, anybody could pretend to be anyone. At home there was no escape from the man you were, or weren't. It was written in the curtain fabric, the washing up, the lilac loo paper, the Panadol in the bathroom cabinet. Everywhere it was written. Loneliness. Loneliness was Wogan on the telly and AA guides to Great Britain on the bookshelves, veteran car ashtrays and glass storks on the windowsill. Coasters under the sofa legs and yesterday's spaghetti at the bottom of the saucepan.

Loneliest of all was the man who had asked for a boy biker.

He was a fat, sad, middle-aged, middle-of-the-road, middle-of-nowhere man, with too much time to dwell on too many fantasies. Hugo wasn't right for the fantasy he'd invented.

He wasn't happy the moment Hugo walked through the door with no leathers and no crash helmet. He could see that Hugo wasn't going to make him happy. Hugo was going to remind him how unhappy he was. Hugo was going to remind him that he wasn't a man on a motorbike and he couldn't pull a real man on a motorbike because real men on motorbikes didn't work for thin, tanned, white-clad Australians in Earls Court.

The man had little model motorbikes on everything – on his ashtrays, his bookends, his windowsills – and, as Hugo stared at these fiddly statuettes of men the man had never met, of men the man would never be, he listened to him lisp abuse for two hours. Two hours was the set time. After two hours they had to pay another £40, with another £12 automatically going to skinny Richard and his colleague.

The man complained that Hugo was too skinny, too unsmiling, that he didn't know how to sit, or to dress, that he didn't know how to ride a motorbike, that he wasn't wearing leathers, that he wasn't the right shape or size or age or look, and all the time Hugo just sat on the green velvet sofa with a faint smile watching the clock tick by. It reminded him of tea with his grandmother. The long, slow progress of the minute hand round the circumference of a badly decorated dial. With his grandmother, at least, it was only one hour.

Hugo fiddled with one of the statuettes, counted the buttons on the green velvet sofa, traced each individual leaf on the flock wallpaper, counted the records stacked in their sleeves on the neat and tidy shelves and longed to escape this perfumed old ninny with a savage tongue.

He watched as the two hands of the clock, ornate and silly in curlicued metal, moved together towards twelve o'clock and then slid one on top of the other. Two hours. Time was up. Two hours of quietly swallowed abuse. It was never normally two hours. Never normally full-time. Once a man paid him a hundred pounds to stay the night and he fell asleep there and then (the man paid), but normally he was out within the hour, sometimes within the half-hour.

But when Hugo got up to leave, the lisping motorbike man leapt from his chair and began to plead. He wanted to take Hugo to bed, he begged. They hadn't touched, he whined. His sad cheeks puckered and pouted. His nasty dressing gown flapped open and his nasty paunch peered out, white, fat and hairless.

Hugo simply stood up and said, 'I'd like my money now.'

'You can't go,' bleated the man.

'I am going. I've been here for two hours and that's forty pounds. I would like my money now, please.'

He spoke in a level, bored voice, so detached it sounded danger-ous. He knew the old man was scared. But he was angry. The abuse had been boring and endless and he was now so bored and so tired, all he could think of was the taxi home. He was forever giving taxis half his earnings. The rides were so long. A taxi there and a taxi back. £10 off the top. £12 to the agency. That left him £18 plus tips. There wasn't going to be a tip tonight.

The man was pleading by now. He started slipping out of his dressing gown and walking towards the bedroom, beckoning and winking as if nothing he had said had been true. None of it was, probably. Hugo didn't care. Hugo was a professional now and professionals didn't care. They worked to the rules and the rules said that the man owed money. Hugo was there to collect.

He tried to look hard and strong. The man was smiling. It made him nervous. They were locked in some strange wrestling match, Hugo and this feebly flabby piece of flesh. They were locked in some strange game of nerves as the time got later and the unreality of night crept in.

Hugo tried to sound stern.

'I am not going to stay any longer,' he said. 'Just give me my money now.'

The man told Hugo he didn't have any cash. He'd have to take a cheque. Cheques were not allowed. Everything had to be cash. A cheque could be stopped, bounced or traced. Hugo wanted to lie down and go to sleep and wake up in his own bed with the sunlight streaming through the tall windows and William making coffee and cornflakes upstairs in the kitchen. Hugo wanted his money.

He asked to use the phone and didn't wait for the permission to come. He picked it up and dialled Richard. He tried to look dangerous instead of tired. He stood with his feet apart and his hands out of his pockets. He stared at the man through his eyebrows. He tried to look mad. His mother had said once he had mad eyes. That had pleased Hugo. Being mad was better than being rich. Everybody was frightened of you if you were mad.

Richard came to the phone.

Hugo played to the fact that the man couldn't hear what Richard was saying.

'Hello, Richard, it's Hugo. There seems to be a problem with Mr . . . I'm there now and he won't pay.'

The man squealed in the background.

'He says he hasn't got the cash.' Pause for effect. The man was looking nervous.

'I've already been here for two hours . . . he says he wants to pay by cheque.'

Richard asked to speak to the man. Hugo handed him the phone and then stood a little way behind him so that the man had to glance over his shoulder. Hugo put a hand in his pocket. He was going through the motions of a boy who might attack at any moment. Another bloody murder in an anonymous flat somewhere in North West London. A motorbike statuette through the skull. Blood on the chintz. A body by the telephone. The telephone off the hook.

'Yes . . . no . . . I thought – well, yes . . . no, of course not. I am sorry . . . I'll put my number on the back.' The man sounded shrill. The clock had already moved on half an hour. Why didn't the time go this fast before? thought Hugo.

The man put the receiver down. He looked drained. Deflated. He wrote Hugo a cheque and Hugo left without a word.

It wasn't always easy, this job.

Sometimes it was so easy it made Hugo giggle.

Sometimes nothing happened at all. Hugo arrived at the Hilton one evening, spruce, cocksure, well-ironed (he had never been stopped – he looked the part of a guest, he told himself, as he went upstairs to see guests who looked nothing like him). He knocked on the door, 701, and a bodyguard answered, his gun still slung over his shoulder. He was very polite. He didn't smile. Hugo was grateful for that. Every smile concealed a laugh. He looked serious and courteous. Hugo was a present for his boss, not to be tampered with, not to be bothered. The bodyguard showed Hugo to a seat. Hugo was in the hallway of a large suite. Through the open door he could see a group of men in full Arab regalia. They were sitting around in their caftans and head-dresses, watching a video. On the television a transexual with breasts and a cock was being brutally raped by two men. The Arabs sat there impassively as a murmured conversation continued out of sight. Hugo had no idea who they were – whether they were royalty or oil sheiks or porn traders. He could barely see their faces.

One of them turned round and looked at him, quite hard. He sat upright and didn't smile. He was being sized up. Weighed in the slave scale by men too rich to care how he felt. He was already hard. Their arrogance attracted him. He felt like a gift that they would unwrap slowly in front of the television, the light of the porn video flickering across his body.

The door closed and the murmured conversation dimmed. Hugo looked at the painting opposite him, on the hallway wall. The picture had been chosen to match the seat covers and the colour of the lampshades. He wondered if there was an artist somewhere who worked on commissions like this. They gave him the colour codes and he just painted to match. He wondered whether he was meant to sleep with all of them. One of them would be bound to fuck him, if he was. You can't fight off four men. And Arabs always had such fat dicks. They came quickly but it still hurt and they didn't like KY or poppers. Hugo's buttocks clenched on the seat cover.

The bodyguard returned.

'Thank you very much for coming. You're not quite what they

wanted.' He said it with such tact and politeness, Hugo wanted to say, 'Well, how about you then? Do you want a go?' Then he realised that he was a hooker. Nobody chose a hooker. No-one chose the rentboy who'd been rejected.

The bodyguard put something in Hugo's hand. In the lift Hugo opened his hand. There was one hundred pounds in new £20 notes. Hugo stared at Hugo in the lift mirror. The two of them really didn't know what to make of each other. So they smiled thin, watery smiles. This was too unreal. They giggled, but the gurgle of laughter didn't really come.

Hugo caught a taxi home that night without watching the meter.

There were others who gave him money for doing nothing. The prince with the deep carpets in Regents Park, who poured whisky down his throat and cocaine up his nose and then sent him home with a big smile, saying how nice it had been to meet him. There was the man who was having a dismal birthday and booked two hookers – a black and a white – to come and sit in his bedroom and watch television. Hugo and his black colleague sat there with the man and his confidant – a ballet dancer with a Nureyev face and a fussy voice. They watched *Twenty-Five Years of American Bandstand*. It was good television, but it was Saturday night. Hugo wanted to get laid and get out. They sat on the bed and watched television, the four of them. Hardly anything was said. And then the host left the room. The fussy-voiced ballet dancer gave each of them fifty pounds. He smiled and they left. That was the first time Hugo was paid to watch television.

Hugo made a lot of money as a whore but no friends. He had hoped for someone. A tycoon. A television personality. Just beneath Hugo's polite and smile-on-cue façade lurked an ambition, which, still unfocused, wanted to be a star. But where, of what, for whom and how, he hadn't ever decided.

Somehow it involved the appreciation of his peers, the admiration of his lessers and the kindly acknowledgement of his betters. Somehow it involved being recognised but not mobbed: getting tables in restaurants and whispers as he walked through hotel foyers. Somehow it ignored the trail of blackmail he had laid like gunpowder to his door, half-helpless in the throes of his own sex (how many boys, how many men would come forward to sell their kiss-and-tell stories?). Somehow it involved appearances on chat shows and slow entrances down illuminated staircases, his every snappy ad lib witticism autocued to follow every probing autocued question. Hugo used to rehearse them to himself as he walked down the street, catching the disconcerted eyes of passers by.

'Well, the first time I remember . . . Yes, Michael, that was extremely . . . No, Russell, you know that's not . . .' He had the patter of inanity down to the teeth and smiles. Winning looks at the audience. Knowing asides to the front row. Never the expected. Always a little off on his own tangent. Always a draw but rarely in town.

Hugo believed that celebrity was one of those keys to the magic door. You stepped through to a world where suddenly everything worked for you instead of you working for everything. You had found the ticket office for the gravy train, the entry onto the fame and fortune conveyor belt and life turned into one long Generation Game of free gifts and special appearances, fuelled by the occasional new bon mot, the new literary gem, the new column, or novella, or perhaps nothing at all.

He thought, quietly, uneasily, that the hustler game would bring him his key. He thought that he would find a man, someone already on the other side of the magic door with a season ticket for the gravy train, who would just slip him through without any questions asked. So how could he resist when Richard rang and told him he had a surprise job with a television personality? How could he miss the chance of a free ride to fame and fortune?

Of course it never occurred to him that a television celebrity ringing a callboy agency was not looking for a protégé but a prostitute. The client was after a dick and a neatly arranged set of muscles, not a brain and a neat line in quips. If he had thought about it he might have won by playing to lose. Instead he lost by suddenly, inadvertently but unacceptably, being himself. Whoever that was. Whoever that was, it was still more at home with jam and bread than head down in egg and chips at Barclay Brothers.

The client was a famous talk show host. He was on Saturday night television. He was part of the world Hugo was aiming for.

He wasn't what Hugo wanted to be when he got there. He was everything he disliked about that world. Smug, gossipy, simpering, desperate, proud, pathetic, flabby, randy.

Hugo was his birthday present.

It was an off night. Hugo didn't normally work Saturdays and he had been about to leave the house to join a group of friends when the call came through. Richard said it was special, but he didn't say who. He said there would be extra money. Maybe he thought there would be career prospects, but for Richard a career was not a life in the media with the neon-names. It was the comfort and perks of a life as the kept boy of a famous pouf. Dinner parties with brittle celebrities, weekends in the country, summers on some Riviera, Christmases in Australia and every day a prisoner, on display for friends to envy.

Hugo arrived at a basement flat in Kensington. West Eight. Like the Hilton, the neighbourhood was familiar territory by now. The Hilton was Arabs. Kensington was English. Hugo generally preferred the Arabs. They were more offhand and more polite. The English were always panicking and often rude. The chat show host was very English and very rude.

The door was opened by a blond man with big shoulders and a pasty face that meant nothing to Hugo. The man's expression didn't change as he smiled. There was something glassy about him. Vaselined.

They walked through into a room that was pretending to be a library. Everything was warm, rosy and burnished from the leather of the sofa to the spines of the books. It felt like a book club advert from a Sunday supplement. Hugo smiled inside and some of it slipped out. The chat show host was a studier of men. He didn't miss a smirk and Hugo's didn't slip him by.

From the moment Hugo entered the room, the man's guard was up. He told Hugo he was his birthday present. Hugo could hear the disappointment in his voice. But that wasn't the problem. The problem was that Hugo couldn't forget Hugo. Normally by now he had anaesthetised himself – he wouldn't say much, wouldn't do much, he'd drop his voice, speak in monosyllables and wait for the time to take off his clothes. He'd start as soon as he could. But tonight Hugo couldn't shut himself off. He felt on guard. He couldn't shut himself up. The atmosphere was sarcastic. Barbed. He had to defend himself.

Mr Chat-Show-Host wasn't pleased because Hugo didn't have the muscles he was looking for. Muscles were in and they were ruining Hugo's business. Pecs, deltoids, thyroids, zomboids – you needed a full quota of abnormal swellings and unrealistic curves before anyone loved you these days. Hugo's slim smooth-skinned top to bottom line was a thing of the past.

The air in the artificial library was already sour and hardly a word had been spoken. Hugo wanted a drink but he didn't know what to ask for. Hugo would have asked for scotch. But what about the hustler? Lager. Lemonade. Mineral water. They all smiled artificial smiles and Mr Television started bitching. He started asking questions. He knew what he was doing. He asked questions for a living. But Hugo was giving him answers that he didn't want to hear. They were making him ask more questions. He asked Hugo where he went to school and, like a fool, Hugo told him. Any sexual tension there might have been evaporated. Public school. Mr Slime hadn't rung Caprice for a well-spoken chaperone with O-levels. Hugo didn't mention Cambridge. He knew he was wrong-footing it, but he had so far lost his bearings this was the only path he knew. Mr Television had wanted meat, gristle, rough trade. He'd wanted a Neanderthal who could be dazzled with fame, could be kept for a few pennies. Hugo wasn't being dazzled. He was showing off.

As if it was their duty, they took their clothes off and lay down. The three of them. The blond man with the big shoulders and the Vaseline face was fatter than he looked. He lay down and tried to look inviting. He was Mr Television's real boyfriend. He probably worked in television too. Hugo took off his clothes and lay next to him. Mr Television pulled off his trousers and socks and shirt and wobbled over.

Hugo knew things were going badly because he didn't have an erection. Normally, just the act of taking his clothes off gave him a hard-on. But now, exposed to the sarcastic glare of Mr Television, fielding his bitchy remarks, feeling skinny, wanting to leave, and wanting to win, he couldn't get it up. Some birthday present he was proving to be.

For twenty minutes the three of them tugged at each other's bodies. The only surge of blood came when the blond man and Hugo played with each other. But this was forbidden. They were the possessions of Mr Television and they were there to keep him happy. He was not a voyeur. He kept pulling Hugo back over and flicking his flaccid willy. He had polished fingernails. Transparent nailpolish.

Hugo knew he should leave but he wanted the money. He needed the money to pay off a debt. There was always a debt to pay off. There was always a reason for working again. He could carry on like this and never stop. Solve every problem by turning a trick. He turned over the argument in his mind as Mr Television flicked his willy. He could willingly have hit him but that would have brought the police. Or his blond boyfriend. Should he just get up and go? How long would it take him to put his clothes on? Could he move fast enough? Of course not. He could hardly go running naked into the streets of Kensington.

Mr Television sat up and rolled on top of Hugo. Hugo's ribs caved in. The breath was pushed out of him. He looked and saw the great rolling rotundity of the fat man lolling on his body, on his bones. He was a fleshy nightmare. Hugo pushed back. The man stared at him in surprise.

'I think I'd better go.'

'Where do you think you're going?'

'I just think I'd better leave.'

Hugo tilted his body so the blubber rolled off and lay on his back looking up at him in consternation. The blond boyfriend wasn't saying a word. He wasn't smiling but he wasn't going to hit Hugo either.

Hugo moved swiftly to his clothes, getting the most strategic items on first.

'I shall have to call the agency.'

'I'm sure they can find a replacement.'

The man was furious and wanted to humiliate him. Hugo was being blankly charming. He must not be rude. He must not be sarcastic. He must be deadpan. He wanted to be with his friends. He wanted to be able to laugh, to get drunk, to dance, to run out of money. So what if now he didn't have a wallet full of ten pound notes? They were hardly his anyway. With what he owed to the agency and what he owed to friends, to gasmen and telephone companies, to the bank, to his father – none of it was ever his and it always had to be replaced with more. He was hooked on the ten pound notes.

'What's their number? I shall ring Richard and complain.'

Hugo knew he would never work for them again. He was pleased that the decision had been made for him. They would ban him. He wouldn't have to leave.

'You'll never work again.'

'Oh, dear. I am sorry.'

It came out so wrong. The television fatso looked up, surprised.

'Why are you doing this job? You're not very good at it.'

'I used to be.'

'How long have you been at it?'

'I can't remember now. I must be going. I know the way out.'

It was the nearest he ever came to being interviewed by a famous television chat-show host. It would have made good television. It just needed to be a little longer.

He was dressed and ready to escape. He could almost smell the freedom of the wet streets outside. He had to escape this rosy burnished mock-up library before he squealed with laughter or lost his breath. He wanted to run up the road, through the rain, to the bus stop and jump from bus to bus until he found his friends and the party and then he would get drunk and not tell a soul about his evening with Mr Television.

The blond man stood up and wrapped a towel around himself.

'I'll have to unlock the door.'

'Have a nice birthday.' Hugo gave the blubber a flat smile.

'It's a bit late for that, isn't it? Oh, this fucking country! This fucking city! Now, if this was New York . . .'

They were in the hallway. The blond man and Hugo. The blonde man produced a key. He held out his hand and Hugo went to shake it. But there was something in his hand. Hugo took it.

'Call me there, in the daytime. I'd love to see you again.' The blond man smiled. Giggles bubbled up in Hugo's chest but he squashed them with another flat smile.

'Okay,' he said.

The blond boyfriend of Mr Fat TV had just slipped him a piece of paper. Inside the piece of paper was a fifty pound note. He could get a taxi to the party now. Life was so ridiculous. He put his hand under the man's towel and squeezed his balls. He didn't really know why. It was the elation of the moment. Having made the money without the work. There was a sharp intake of breath. They turned, and there in the doorway was Mr Television. Blubber akimbo. Eyes burning.

Hugo grabbed the door, pulled it open and slipped out, like an eel out of mud.

He couldn't get rid of his smile for the whole taxi ride. When he saw his friends, he couldn't stop laughing and he couldn't tell any of them why.

STATEMENT MADE BY
DETECTIVE CONSTABLE PAUL HODGSON
TO BOW STREET MAGISTRATES' COURT

AUGUST 19TH 1985

On the afternoon of August 5th 1981, DC Trowell and myself were on special duty at the gentlemen's urinal in Jermyn Street, London W1, a known haunt of male homosexuals. We were not in uniform. I was wearing faded denim jeans and a green, short-sleeved Fred Perry shirt. DC Trowell was wearing similar jeans and a yellow shirt. We had been instructed to dress in an attractive and casual manner.

The accused, Mr Hugo Harvey, entered the urinal at 12:46 p.m. He was wearing a light summer shirt and some baggy, checked trousers with white winklepickers. The urinal was already quite crowded with men waiting, although, as two out of the three stalls at the urinal were empty at the time, it would be difficult to say what they were waiting for.

The accused stood at one of the empty stalls and urinated. All the time that he was doing so, he looked around him, observing the waiting men including DC Trowell and myself. He made no direct signal at this time. After he had finished urinating the accused remained at the stall for a further six minutes. He appeared to be masturbating himself in order to attract my attention. Instead, an elderly gentleman, who had been waiting in the urinal for the past thirty-eight minutes, went and stood at the stall adjacent to the accused.

The accused immediately removed himself from the stall, adjusting his clothing accordingly, and stood leaning against the wall of the urinal near to where I was standing.

He stared very hard at me for a couple of minutes but made no verbal or physical suggestion. DC Trowell at this stage left the urinal, and stood at the entrance to the neighbouring car park. I went outside to join DC Trowell in order to discuss what action he felt we should now take. I had begun to feel uncomfortable at the attention I was receiving from the accused.

Having consulted with DC Trowell, I returned to the urinal and stood at the central stall which was now empty again, the elderly gentleman having returned to his position in the corner of the urinal. DC Trowell also entered and stood in the corner near the elderly gentleman. The accused immediately came and stood at the stall next to me and started masturbating, this time with some more vigour. I made no movement with my hands to encourage his attention but was unable to avoid seeing his erection, which he was clearly keen that I should pay some attention to.

I adjusted my clothing and left the stall and the urinal. I went and stood with DC Trowell outside the urinal. The accused also left the urinal, and after giving me a hard look walked along Jermyn Street to Lower Regent Street and then turned right up to Piccadilly Circus.

I followed him with DC Trowell at some distance. The accused repeatedly turned around and saw me following him, and appeared to be pleased that I was doing so. He took the stairs at the corner of Lower Regent Street and Piccadilly into the subway complex of Piccadilly Circus Station and turned left to walk round the subway corridor. I believed that he was heading for the Gentlemen's Convenience within the station. I approached the accused before he entered the conveniences, stopping him opposite the tourist and travel advice bureau. I tapped him on the arm and he turned to me in a friendly and welcoming manner.

I showed him my badge and as D C Trowell approached I told him that he was under arrest and I proceeded to read him his rights. The accused seemed unperturbed by the situation, remarking that he thought that I was about to ask him whether he had a place to go. He then inquired whether D C Trowell and I spent all our time in public toilets. I answered that we had a duty to protect members of the general public. The accused smiled with apparent sarcasm and asked who had complained about the activities in the toilets in Jermyn Street. I answered that the mothers of some boys had expressed some concern. At this point the accused asked what appeared to be a rhetorical question, inquiring whether the entire country was now run by mothers. And he went on to observe that we had both got our costumes very correct. Observing D C Trowell, the accused said, and I quote, 'I had him down for a real dizzy queen in that lemon yellow shirt.'

I informed the accused that we had to take him to Vine Street police station, and he replied that he had always wondered where Vine Street was, since playing Monopoly as a child.

The accused proceeded with us without incident to Vine Street police station, where he was finger-printed and photographed and charged with gross indecency. Despite appearing surprised at the use of the word gross, the accused denied nothing in the statement we read to him, but stared at me throughout the interrogation in a suggestive and provocative manner. He asked whether it would be advisable for him to ask for nine years of previous offences to be taken into consideration, and I said I did not believe this would be of use to the case. He said that he was sure I was right, and in any case this was the first time he had ever been into a public toilet. Further questioning revealed that the accused is an undergraduate, and has recently completed the second year of his degree course in English literature at Cambridge University. He is in London for the customary summer holiday. The accused has no specific means of support other than the social security payments to which he is entitled during this holiday period. The accused also said he had recently given up part-time freelance work in the entertainment industry.

The accused is currently living in rented accommodation with friends in Muswell Hill.

END OF STATEMENT

9

VISITING TIME – NO SIGN OF CHAS

They walked side by side slowly through air damp with the residue of mist, along grey paths puddle-stained and criss-crossed with muddy bicycle tracks, past poodles pulling women in turned-up-collar coats, between naked winter trees probing the low-hung sky, bark shiny with the threat of wetness. They walked side by side slowly, oblivious to the distant traffic rumbling like some unsettled stomach and the buses passing along the Common perimeter like toy boxes on wheels.

They walked towards the bandstand.

The bandstand stood at the centre of the Common, where all the grey, puddle-stained paths met. A stage without an audience. And around it the whisper of ghosts – Sunday afternoon crowds in deck-chairs, licking ice-creams, listening to Uncle Bob and his tuba blowing up a storm in the back row of the brass band.

But they were just ghosts. The bandstand was empty. The stage was cracked. There was talk of condemning the roof. Talk of wrapping the whole thing up in barbed wire and leaving it there for kids to avoid.

They sat on the edge of the platform, staring up at the white, peeling paint of the roof, kicking heels against the blue, peeling paint of the base, caught in an airy cage of iron fretwork, staring out across the grey-green grass, still boggy with autumn rain. And they talked. Talked and talked. About their hopes and fears and dreams and doubts. Combed through every anxiety, each ambition, through past encounters and planned meetings. And they never disagreed.

That was what Hugo loved in Chas. They saw eye to eye. They had different stories and the same fears, different lovers and the same confusions, different friends and the same loneliness. If Hugo was ever scared, depressed, threatened, worried, he always rang Chas. And for half an hour, for an hour, he'd sit on the phone pouring out his panic and then let Chas' familiar voice iron out the wrinkles in his head.

And now Chas was dead. Gone. And Hugo was alone with his memory of a winter afternoon three years before. Alone in an iron bedstead waiting for a nurse to bring him supper. Alone in an iron bedstead waiting to join Chas wherever people went when they left this ward.

It wasn't such a special afternoon. Not really. It wasn't very nice weather. They hadn't gone anywhere exciting. They had both gone home later, on different buses to different parts of town and different flatmates. They hadn't eaten or gone to the pub. They hadn't smoked, except cigarettes. They hadn't even laughed that much. But it was an afternoon Hugo cherished. It was the memory of a pause. Sitting at the apex of all the grey, criss-crossed paths with everything in life left to play for and no cards dealt.

Hugo had been sent down and wasn't likely to go back up. He was better, in the sense that he had been worse. Chas was the comfort he needed. Neither of them was working. Not properly. Hugo was freelancing. Teaching. Writing a little. A week here on a magazine there. Sometimes even a job for three, maybe four weeks. While someone was on holiday. While someone was off sick. He was making a living. Whoring had made him more. But he had died a little in all those strange beds. Each time another layer of him went hard like dead skin until he was trapped inside like a junkie who hasn't the energy to explain that he's dying. A junkie. That was something else again.

It had been a difficult year. But he was making a living. He always made a living. Somehow. Nothing frightened him more than no money. Even now, so many years after Hadley and its cruel tiers of wealth, nothing hurt Hugo more than no money. So he was making a bit here and a bit there. Enough. Chas was not. Sitting at home, writing songs for a musical, planning another imaginary career. The fizz of university life had evaporated into London's anonymous mist and together Chas and Hugo faced this new fresh, damp air with every belief in their eventual fame and fortune. And now Chas was dead and Hugo was next.

He lay next to death, staring it in the face. It wasn't quite an embrace. Hugo was too fragile to think of anything so physical. It was a patient, quiet, silent co-existence, interrupted by the sting of his bedsores, and by the sympathy of visitors. He couldn't remember when death entered the room. Whether he snuck in behind the nice Scottish nurse who still managed to keep a smile, best teeth forward, as she changed the water in his vases and the saline solutions in his drip. Whether he arrived with one of the welfare visitors, who walked in full of professional bonhomie, full of useless conversation and hopeless clichés.

Or whether it was the first day he had been shocked by someone else's reaction: the look on their face as they came round the door and saw a creature they didn't recognise and, like someone trying to make out shapes in a darkened room, they blinked and frowned until something that reminded them of Hugo came into focus. His eyes, normally. They hadn't changed. They just protruded from his head a lot more, because his head had shrunk back.

When visitors came, and few did now, death seemed to slip across the room and sit among the lilies on the cabinet in the corner, staring at them through the petals like some cynical gargoyle. Hugo's room looked like an overdressed graveyard and smelt like a boutique. Lilies of every denomination flung their scents into the air. He was dying in a miasma of pollen and oxygen from the cylinder by his bed, and he and death were sharing a joke at the expense of his callers: winking as his mother talked about her friends at the other end of her street, sniggering as Cynthia suggested she hire some home helps to get his flat cleaned up and fretted about the unpaid bills piling up on his doorstep.

'What difference does it make?' said Hugo, staring death in the eye through the lilies. 'I'll be dead soon.' And as Cynthia's mind raced, trying to find a reply that was neither pessimistic nor patronising, Hugo gulped down some more oxygen, quelling the sick gurgle of acids in his stomach and the thin rattle of his lungs.

They knew he was going to die.

He knew they knew when he heard them whispering and saw their faces change. It wasn't all at once. But he prompted their panic and watched their faces. Nobody would tell him anything. They thought he thought he was going to live. But Hugo had buried too many friends to delude himself. He looked at these emaciated limbs, sore and shrivelled like some poverty photograph on an Oxfam ad and he saw a corpse waiting to take over. But he was playing a game with the corpse. Hiding in a bubble of oxygen, filling his blood with chemical compounds, the corpse was still outwitted.

Chas had already lost the battle. The corpse had slid over him, a caul of death thrown over his head, a last sputter of thin breath and a choke of life dribbling phlegm on his chin and that was that. And Hugo wasn't there.

He'd been there for the others.

For Philip. For Clive. For Jim. For the friends he'd lost before he lost Chas.

None of them was an easy death. Philip's was the first. And the hardest to watch. Because he refused to go. He lingered bitterly on the brink of life, spitting at anyone who came too close.

Hugo had listened to Philip's caustic banter, listened to his delusions, his insistence that the emaciated legs he uncovered with such bitter flamboyance represented nothing more than a setback.

He had watched him send nurses scurrying to refill his vases, water jugs and cordial glasses; seen him refuse his daily doses, determined to doctor himself. The clinical compounds with their hospital pharmacy labels numbered Patient 120054 and their inappropriate warnings about children were flushed down the waste disposal as Philip spooned down mush from plastic containers labelled with B numbers and herbal diagrams.

Philip's doctors looked tired when they came into his room to face the humiliation of Philip's arrogant nagging. Hugo felt for them. Philip was not an easy patient. As his blood grew weaker and reality faded further, he retreated into his own world of strange bunkum, and madhatter theory. Bad-tempered to the last, autocratic and disdainful, lying like a bug-eyed skeleton, crippled, on soiled sheets, his skin taut and brown like dried leaves turning white where it stretched across knuckles and joints, nobody could please him, but a few lucky visitors could distract him.

The long-serving bedside guests were nuisances whose chilled soups and carefully prepared ratatouilles were flung back in their faces, rejected as cookery experiments on a helpless victim. The official welfare visitors were fools who should have had visitors themselves, the ridiculous product of an intolerable government which sent emotional cripples to tend to physical invalids, they had their ooh-aah sympathy shoved back down their surprised throats. And the doctors were conspirators, hiding their ignorance behind a smokescreen of jargon while researching on living guinea pigs, lined up side by side, room by room in the antechamber to the abattoir.

As Philip's hands grew bonier and the rings refused to stay on his fingers, their shaky skeletal movements commanded a terrified audience of siblings and friends.

Half the terror was Philip's temper. 'You must go now. I am tired and you are boring me,' he would say to one, and the others would look nervously at the floor, pleased to have been spared.

Half the terror was Philip's refusal to face death. 'I shall be at home soon. Louisa has arranged everything. She is getting me an exercise bike so I can build up my muscles. They want me to have two home helps, but the place isn't large enough. I couldn't bear to have two women charging around with mops and Hoovers. One would be quite enough.'

Eyes darted in little panics, trying to catch each other to confirm or deny. Had they been misinformed? They had been told he was going to die. Wasn't he? Nobody could ask. Nobody wanted to say, 'But, Philip, are you sure you are going to live long enough?'

If he wanted to, why couldn't he?

He did want to live. And he did die.

Hugo was there. He had been summoned by friends, telling him that if he wanted to see Philip alive again, he should come quickly. He had had no idea. They hadn't seen each other for six months. Six months ago, they had sat opposite each other in a white-paint, glass-front brasserie eating fashionable health food, drinking fruit juice cocktails, cheerfully swapping T-cell counts and AZT side-effects. Death seemed irrelevant. Philip's counts were down but his confidence was brimming. He was prepared for battle, armed with a freshly-squeezed pink grapefruit juice and a pine kernel salad. Hugo felt strong, young, clearheaded and brave. And now Philip was dead and Hugo was treading in his wake.

When you are well, you can never imagine being ill. When you are ill, you can never remember being well. Being well seemed a distant mirage of childhood, of sunny afternoons playing in the back garden, of overcast quiet afternoons on the Common kicking the paintwork of the bandstand, of conversations that were about life, not death, that were about plans, not medication, of flowers in gardens, not jugs.

Philip's death took it out of Hugo. Took that confident breeze out of his sails. Outside in the sunlight, he had felt well. Walking down the quiet corridors of the hospital with his visiting chocolates, he wanted to run back to the light. His footfall on the squeaky floor, the colour of the lino, the curtains, the paintwork, the tired faces of nurses whose stock of caring, sharing, loving feeling was ebbing away, the closed doors and the wan faces behind them through the little windows, angular men perched on beds in shabby dressing gowns staring at television with the disenchantment of the viewers whom nobody wants, whom no advertiser aims at, whose lifestyle no soap or sitcom imitates, made him feel like a secret convict visiting friends in prison. At any moment someone would stop him. Charge him. And lock him in one of the little rooms with the disenchanting televisions. This was the institution where you lost your living identity and acquired a dead one. You were out of the life race and in the queue for death. The nurses were simply there to bring your refreshments. But like any queue, the bus stop, the dole office, the last orders at the bar, you were in the way, something to be worked through, something to be got rid of.

It was more than that that had Hugo scared. It was that Philip was showing him what it was like in the queue, and he was next in line. When he went to visit, Philip would drop all other conversation to talk to Hugo, to ask him questions about his health. The others would turn and stare, waiting for the moment when their sympathy should be transferred. Hugo avoided their eyes. It was as if he and Philip were both part of the same grim club. And they were. And that was what Hugo hated.

The others round the bed wept for themselves because they were going to lose Philip and Philip was the pivot in their lives. Hugo sat at the bed and felt an iceberg growing inside, because Philip was showing him how he was going to die. Angrily. Painfully. With a seething contempt for everything that seemed to be conspiring to humiliate him. And, above all, with a contempt for having to die of a gay disease when he had stood so firmly outside the gay scene, standing on the touchline with his back turned.

But this was a disease designed for gays. It was a disease designed for Philip: playing confidence tricks before hitting below the belt. It was like being queer-bashed in the park after dark. Each blow came from somewhere new, and eventually, alone and crumpled, bloodied and bowed, you cried. But not for being beaten up. Not for the pain or even the humiliation. A little for the shock. But most of all for the exhaustion of keeping up the front. Keeping the smile on your teeth as another disease, another inconvenience and another discomfort swooped.

Clive lost everything but his smile. His eyesight. In the end his water. His faeces. His ability to stand, focus, smoke, hold, concentrate, think anything. His ability. He only kept his smile. It wavered across his face like an unattached memory. There was no irony in it. Just a blithe expectation of something nice about to happen – a smell, a kind word, a flicker of flashback.

He was senile at thirty-three. The disease had eaten into his brain, munching through grey matter like a chimp on a teacake. His brain was vanishing.

Hugo had never known Clive very well. He wasn't really on the same visiting circuit. But they had moved in similar packs in the past, when Clive was dealing smack from a basement flat on the King's Road. They had been to the same illicit raves in Isle of Dogs tower-blocks, to the same all-night MDA binges in after-hours cinemas. They knew the same crowd from different fringes. And Hugo took one of the crowd to see Clive in hospital. He had to. Jim couldn't have taken himself. He couldn't walk that far without sitting down. He was only three weeks out of hospital himself.

Hugo was feeling conspicuous, dangerously healthy. He hardly dared grin in case it looked complacent.

He needn't have worried. In less than a year he was staring at the visitors searching out the healthy ones himself. He liked to see them. They were a genuine connection with the real world. He didn't like to see them see him. Composing their features into all-purpose pity. Clamping down on the curiosity.

With Jim leaning on his arm and walking like a man with third-degree haemorrhoids, Hugo picked his way to Clive's ward. Mistrustful gazes, harrowed looks, eyes sunk deep in grey sockets under wispy, falling-out hair stared at them and then drifted away again, back to the television, back to the visitor in the room, back to the wall. Despondency lay thick in the air, carpeting fear, blanketing panic, muffling despair. Nurses greeted Jim. They looked right through Hugo. They had enough to do without wasting smiles.

Clive's room was nearly bare. A bottle of lemon barley water. Some Michaelmas daisies in a hospital-issue glass jug. Vinyl-covered seats. He had a smart dressing gown someone had bought him, but he couldn't get it on. He had nothing left. No flat, no possessions, no mind. He had fallen ill in the US. An illegal alien with a track record of drug addiction, a convicted homosexual, semi-homeless and near-penniless, he was not on anyone's welfare lists. He stumbled from bad to worse. His memory was dissolving. The only place that beckoned was the gutter. And then some friends clubbed together to put him on a plane back to England. They telephoned someone in London. A local vicar. A friend of his mother's. And Clive was greeted at Terminal 3 with a wheelchair.

Uurgh. Hugo retched. Clutched at the oxygen mask. He gulped and swooned, lying limp against the pillow, a thin film of sweat gathering on his brow and upper lip. The acids in his stomach had woken up. He hurled them a spoonful of Philip's mush. Philip's bequest. He had to get there quickly. His stomach by now was a shrunken fist; clenched and hostile to food, it would suddenly stretch out and demand to be fed. A minute later it would be clenched again, but the digestive juices would still be swilling around, turning in on themselves, fizzing and eating away at his stomach wall. They greeted the mush with a spasm. Hugo lay still again. Staring at the ceiling. Sweating gently. Did Clive ever know what was going on? Like this. Did he know his mind had been eaten away or did senility carry its own anaesthetic? The worse you were, the less you knew about how bad you were. Until death was simply the next stage in a slow slide to oblivion. Or not so slow. For Clive it was like a water chute. By the time they got to hospital, the doctors only gave him six weeks to live. A week later they halved that. He was dead within days of Hugo and Jim's visit.

His eyes never focused on them. They moved around in their sockets in random directions. Like eyeballs in the sockets of a toy that have got loose. Like the nodding cow in the back of a Sunday driver's Cortina. They drifted over Jim and over Hugo and, as Hugo sat there following them like a dog watching a fly, Jim talked non-stop, making a cocoon of friendly chatter around Clive. He maybe didn't understand the words but he could hear the sounds and they made him smile.

Jim gave Clive a cigarette. It slipped through his fingers. He couldn't move them fast enough. They had no strength. He scrabbled in his lap for the cigarette but even when he found it he couldn't pick it up. His expression changed to a look of distress. Hugo thought he wanted to smoke but the puddle on the floor underneath the vinyl chair meant something else. Jim leapt into action. Hugo hovered. Abashed. Trying to look useful. Uneasy. The nurses mopped up the mess and changed Clive's pyjamas. He leaned this way and that as they moved him between them. A smile back on his lips, vague, wavering as if he had remembered some long-lost joke. They put him in a chair and Jim wheeled him out onto the balcony.

They sat in silence for a few moments, looking at the gardens in the Westminster square, feeling the sun on their faces. Hugo stared at another man, three or four people away. He knew him. He sat, hang-dog, attached to a drip on wheels. His skin had the yellow pallor of a hepatitic. His eyes were worn hollow. He stared little more than one foot in front of him. At the floor, not at the garden.

Jim followed his eyes.

'I didn't know Steve was in here,' Hugo said. His voice was dried and cracked. He hadn't expected to see friends here. Not by chance. This was becoming like a club. A pale, sickly reflection of a club.

'They just moved him here from Croydon,' said Jim.

'Why doesn't he look up? Shouldn't we go and say hello?'

'He won't speak.'

'Why not?'

'They operated on his liver in Croydon and Steve says the anaesthetic didn't work. Nobody believed him there. They're not used to AIDS patients, so they gave him the full rubber glove and leper treatment.'

'Is he all right?'

'Look at him.'

Hugo was looking at him.

Three days later Steve died, surrounded by family and friends. He took his leave. But he never smiled again.

That was a bad year. This was a bad year. The last good year seemed out of sight. The last good year was a scrapbook of memories Hugo turned over in his head and stared at as he lay hovering between wakefulness and sleep, between oxygen and air, on the brink of fading away. He turned over the afternoon in the park, and each time he felt the empty space of the Common and the freedom of nothing to do and then he felt the piercing pain of Chas having gone.

He had to get a grip on this, but there was so much unresolved. They hadn't left things in a tidy way. They hadn't organised their separation with any care. There hadn't been time. And maybe not the inclination. Chas had much to be bitter about in the end.

In the beginning it had been one long laugh. Every time Hugo saw Chas, he smiled. Involuntarily. Mirth bubbled in his bloodstream. Any banality was funny. The most mundane events, like going shopping, became a comic adventure. Who knew what they might see? Who knew whom they might follow? They had seen each other almost every day since they met.

The night they met. Hugo had replayed that scene so many times. Rewinding the past like a home movie, shaky pictures and intermittent sound, interrupted by nurses, doctors, visitors and acid in his belly.

He had replayed it many times, but it was still a favourite. It was one of the few occasions when Hugo had taken the initiative, and it had worked.

He was at a party in Cambridge. Not yet a student, he had been invited up by Dolly. Dolly and Hugo were ideal playmates. They drank too much gin, wore too much eyeliner and never learnt when to dress down, shut up or stop dancing. She died five years later in a fastback, souped-up, silver sports car driven by an Iranian millionaire. They were on the wrong side of the road taking the S-bend at something over ninety. It never occurred to the elegant and extremely stoned young Persian that another car might appear on the road. Nothing had ever been allowed to get in his way before. Dolly was thrown forty yards.

Dolly was already 'up', and was showing Hugo the ropes. In his last term at school, his entrance exams behind him and his results to come, Hugo was a willing novice. Away from home, he wanted to be debauched. Dolly was the perfect partner. Skinny, beautiful, with a head for drink that would have shamed a sailor, she spent most of her teenage years steering towards the fast lane. It seemed so stupid that when she got there, it killed her.

She had taken him to a Christmas party at the architecture faculty, a series of houses interconnected by a labyrinth of passages. They had danced to a Cuban cha cha band for an hour and slunk off to the bar for plastic cups filled with electric-blue vodka cocktails. Slumped in their seats, hand in hand, staring vacantly over table-tops brimming with ashtrays and spilt glasses, they fell silent. Hugo looked around him. Across the room, a loud young man in a very bright red shirt was trying to put his tongue down the throat of another young man. There was something about him that made Hugo want to know him. Something about him that he recognised. Something in his desperation and his sense of humour. Hugo stared as his victim, a pale-faced boy with black hair, leaned forwards and threw up across the table.

Hugo saw his moment.

'I have to speak to that man over there,' he said to Dolly.

Chas was screaming, furiously extricating himself from the sudden clutches of his vomiting victim.

Dolly smiled. 'Get a light from him,' she said. 'We've run out of matches,' and she drained her electric-blue cocktail.

'Excuse me,' said Hugo to the young man in the bright red shirt. 'I know you're awfully busy, but I wondered if you had a light.'

Chas looked at Hugo, standing there, lank-haired with sweat, a bedraggled feather boa setting off the slippage of clumsy face make-up.

'What makes you think I'm busy?'

'You seem to have rather a lot on your plate,' said Hugo, looking at the table.

'Too much. Where are you sitting?'

'Over there. With Dolly.'

'Well, you two look much more interesting than these half-wits. I'm sure you won't mind if I join you.'

Hugo, who was too pleased and too drunk to try and be funny, just grinned.

Chas hardly said a word to Dolly. They had met before and weren't interested in each other. But Hugo and Chas talked all night. One minute they were complete strangers. The next they were immersed in each other's company, tumbling over their words to tell each other stories. It was as if they had to catch up on everything they had ever thought, and knew each other's thoughts before the sentence was through. Hugo had never made a friend so quickly or so deeply. Dolly fell asleep while they were still talking and only woke up when the party was over and they all three had to leave.

Nine months later, when Hugo returned to Cambridge as an undergraduate, his first mission was the Monday night gay disco at a local pub. He was standing there, trying to find the comfortable way to lean, hold a glass of beer, look tough and not tread on any toes, when suddenly, out of the fug of smoke, sweat and traffic light disco lamps, came a familiar voice.

'I know you, don't I?'

Hugo turned to face Chas and the conversation started again. It had never stopped. Until now. Until two months ago. When Chas went into hospital, emaciated by a sudden pneumonia. That was it. They never spoke again.

He hadn't seen Chas die.

He wasn't with him when he went.

He shouldn't have gone first. It didn't make sense. Hugo had been ill for longer. And Chas had been there all the time, visiting every day. But when Chas got ill, he sank like a stone. He panicked. Hugo wasn't there to hold his hand, to talk about his fears. Chas had been scared of the whole thing for so long. He had been stacking up the panic like dirty plates, and then turning his back and hoping nothing would fall over. He was more frightened than Hugo when Hugo first got the news.

They were together at the time. Working in an office. Hugo's job. For the time being. He was working on a magazine. Chas was helping out while someone was sick. A day's pay. Paid natter. Hugo used to love it. It made work seem like one long coffee morning. It reminded him of the games he used to play with sister junior. Sitting at the dining room table surrounded by brochures and leaflets swiped from high street shops, making imaginary telephone calls and scribbling letters to imaginary strangers on floors above and below. The letters were in 'grown-up writing', illegible scribble in word-sized gobbets.

It was just like that, except now Hugo was being paid to read the pieces of paper he pushed from side to side and he had typewriters for the grown-up writing and when he picked the telephone up it was real and there was someone at the other end.

It was a difficult day. Hugo knew he had to know today. He had started a letter to a friend that morning. 'Today I find out how long I am going to live . . .' As he wrote it, he thought the melodrama was unfair. But it protected him. The big, dramatic gesture obliterated the small eddies of panic.

He hadn't gone the right way about it, either. His doctor had been trying to help but it was a mistake. He had sent him to a clinic in Harley Street – for that private touch. But this wasn't a clinic. This was an in–out zone for worried long-distance executives who wanted to check out their viruses before they gave one to the wife that night.

'Did you bring me anything back from Bangkok, darling?'

'Just the normal dose, sweetest. Nothing more serious.'

The man with the needle was not interested at all. He was a petrol pump attendant more than a doctor. This was his filling station.

He asked some desultory questions. Are you a homosexual? Are you a drug addict? Are you going to pay now or should we invoice you? Do you have a major credit card?

The room was shabby; stained carpet and dirty curtains. An old leather sofa. Cracked, torn, slightly dusty. A large desk, empty except for a blotter and a telephone. Nondescript prints on the wall of some nondescript Christian denomination.

The whole place was just a blood-letting bay. Endless little bottles from the end of endless disposable hypodermics. One jab, two bottles, rubber gloves off, shake hands, Millicent will take your details. Send in Mr ... Mr ... er, um ... send in the next gentleman, Millicent, would you?

Less than half an hour after ringing the heavy doorbell of the big, black Harley Street door, Hugo was back on the street, pushed out of the side door, down the corridor with the plastic matting protecting the threadbare carpet and past the poorly spider plant on the sickly side-trolley.

'We'll send the results to your doctor,' said the man with the needle, never quite catching Hugo's eye. Why should he? If he caught everyone's eye, he'd be there all day. He was anyway, but it would take him longer. You don't try and make friends with a petrol pump attendant, after all.

It annoyed Hugo that he couldn't simply get the results directly. It would have been different at the hospital. They would have told him, not his doctor. Everything would have been kept in confidence. Off the record. But they made it so difficult to have the test.

It had taken him a long time to build up to this and he hadn't the energy anymore to be dissuaded. He had got as far as the hospital before. He had sat opposite a doctor inside the hospital, and the doctor had told him that his reasons for wanting to know were not strong enough. He was friendly and reassuring, but he wasn't going to take Hugo's blood. They still wanted you to have good reasons in those days. Too many people were flipping out. They found out they were HIV positive and wrote off the rest of their lives. Sometimes they did it publicly. Sometimes they just quietly finished themselves off. It was as if, once a definite end had been confirmed, there was no point waiting any longer. But a definite end was confirmed for everyone. And you still didn't know exactly when. Or how.

People were afraid. Everyone prayed to be negative. They went into the test a normal human being and came out a leper or a lover. Some were still talking in terms of segregation. Camps for the polluted. A dustbin of sexual rejects and social casualties. Hugo had had these fears before. Fears of being the untouchable. Fears of cruising young men in the street and not being able to follow through.

Three years earlier he had contracted syphilis from a local labourer. It hadn't got very far. A perfectly-formed, painless sore on the tip of his dick. He had showed it to the ladies at St Stephen's clinic and suddenly he was on a bed having his groin photographed and admired by a succession of students called in to witness this rare and perfect manifestation of primary syphilis. Somewhere, in some new full-colour medical textbook, is a picture of Hugo's diseased dick. At the time he started to feel rather proud, until a spiteful little voice reminded him that this was syphilis, not some prized tattoo. They rolled him over and injected a treacle of penicillin into his buttock muscle with a fat syringe and a plunger that moved so slowly Hugo could feel every millilitre squeezing in. The pain was breathtaking. After they had finished, when the syringe was empty, he stood up. The nurse asked him if he wanted to sit down for a couple of minutes. Hugo shook his head and fell over.

But it was afterwards that he felt upset.

He didn't mind the social worker, who was so worried he would be worried that Hugo thought she must have done her training among mad religious housewives who thought syphilis an ineradicable curse. What was all the fuss about? Hugo had it, it had a name, and it was curable. That was all he cared about. That they could treat it and remove it. But the social worker gazed at him in wide-eyed sympathy as she tried to soothe away the traumas she imagined he must be going through and Hugo nodded politely.

It was when he got out onto the street and saw one of those young men running for the bus, one of those young men who made him cry out loud with a groan of despair because he was out at loose on the street and not at home, skin to skin, head on his pillow, body in his arms, that Hugo minded, felt upset. He dropped his eyes. He had to. He couldn't play the game. He couldn't begin the game if he couldn't finish it. However unlikely it was that the game ever went beyond a flash of eyes and a look of confusion, he couldn't flash his eyes with the same confidence and confidence was the key. A sudden alarming stare that said, get off the bus and drop your trousers in my house, didn't work if the stare just said, get off the bus and give me your number . . . I'll call you when I'm better.

With a buttock thick with penicillin, Hugo limped towards the bus stop, a sexual cripple.

That was what he had been avoiding. That was why he skipped out of the hospital when the doctor told him his reasons for wanting a test weren't good enough. That was his argument to wary and worried friends. Don't cripple yourself with facts. Confidence is all. Ignorance is bliss.

But the bliss could not fight off the fear. The dread crept in under the confident smile. Suddenly Hugo had to know.

Hugo had to know because of Jim. Jim was always the fun stop. The drug shop. Anything could happen in his flat. People were always turning up, with drugs, with friends, with music and invites and parties. Hugo would turn up. He would turn up with a friend. Rudy. That was how he knew Jim. Through Rudy. He knew Rudy through Cambridge and Rudy knew Jim through sex. That was it. Those were the connections now. The network.

He would turn up with Rudy and they'd just join the craze, fall in with the flow, follow the stream, two students with very little money and a lot of time, down for a weekend of London kicks. It always started at Jim's. He was their father figure, their dealer, their driver, their landlord, their host. And he never complained. He never complained when they arrived without warning and left without a thank you, when they bought on credit and took for granted. He always smiled when he opened the door and rolled his eyes. He always seemed to know it would be them. And he always seemed to have new acid, fresh in just that day.

That was in the old days. Before Chas and Rudy came down. Before Hugo was sent down. Before the world cracked.

Jim rang. He rang Hugo in New York. Hugo was staying with Rudy. He wanted to stay with Jim when he got back. He couldn't go back to William and Barry's. Not anymore. They wouldn't have him. He had gone too far. You could never go too far with Jim.

And then Jim said it was off.

The plan had seemed so perfect. Hugo didn't want to go back to William and Barry's anyway. They were right. Things had gone too far. He didn't want to remember. Jim was going to look after him. He loved Jim like an older brother. An older brother who soothes you, gives you a biscuit, makes you a cup of tea and then spikes it. He thought he had it figured. It all seemed so smooth. This was his convalescence. Rudy was his shrink and Jim was his nurse. Both of them had the key to the medicine chest. But then Hugo's nurse got sick.

Hugo was sitting in the flat when the phone rang. The apartment. Spanish Harlem, Manhattan. A little too upper Upper East Side. The others were asleep. Rudy. Raul. Lin. Outside the air in the Upper Nineties was in the lower eighties. It was thick. Thick with effluent and emissions and sweat and swearing. But the flat slept. And the phone rang. And Hugo, who hadn't slept that well in a while, picked it up before everyone else woke. He was ready. Ready for one of Raul's brothers, one of Lin's loan sharks, one of Rudy's sidewinders. It was none of them. It was for Hugo. It was Jim.

'Hello.'

'Hi, Hugo, Jim speaking. I'm really sorry to trouble you on holiday.'

'Don't worry. This is no holiday. It feels like work when you have to sweat so much. How are you? What's happening?'

'Well, that's why I rang. It's about the flat. I don't think it's going to work out.'

'Why not? What's happened? Has someone else moved in?' Hugo was pissed off. 'Don't tell me. You're in love again. Don't worry, Jim. It'll be over by the time I get back.'

'I'm not there myself anymore.'

'Why? What do you mean?'

'I mean I've got to go to hospital. I'm calling you from hospital.'

'Why?'

That was a stupid question.

There was a pause.

'They think I've got an attack of meningitis and I'm covered in boils. I get these incredible headaches all the time.'

'Where are you?'

'I'm in St Stephen's. Call me when you get back. I'm going to be here for three weeks.'

'Yup. Do you need anything?'

Hugo really couldn't think of anything to say.

In the whole conversation, neither of them had mentioned the word that was sitting on the edge of their tongues. It was like a curse. You said it. You had it.

Hugo held the phone off the hook for a long time. He didn't want any other calls for a while. One was enough. He stared across the apartment. When he was a kid, he had always assumed that telephone calls were good news. Later on they had become his lifeline. An escape rope from his mother's tower.

He let the receiver fall slowly onto the phone. He stood up and went to the bathroom and looked again at the forty red pimples on his chest. He had looked at them before. Each time he hoped they would have gone away.

A few minutes ago he had been on top of his world. Leaning back in the dentist's chair in the middle of the small room in the middle of Raul's small flat, ignoring Lin's snores as he had ignored them for the last four weeks. He was leaning back in the dentist's chair, staring across the room out of the window, past the thumping humming air conditioning jammed like a huge ugly cockroach in the middle of the glass, staring at the dirt smothering the faded gold letters on the windows of the building opposite. J. M. Saperstein. Furs of Excellence.

Now the world seemed at one remove. The romance had gone out of the faded Sapersteins. They just seemed sad.

Now Jim was sick. Obviously really sick. Now sickness, which had been in newspapers and New York, was in his life. In his close closed circle. From near enough, it had come too near. It was sitting next to him. Maybe on him. Maybe in him. And Jim? Was this it? Hugo lit a cigarette, which he didn't normally do before lunch. Spitting the smoke out as if it was sickening him further, he thought again about having the test.

It was what Jim said that persuaded him. When he went to see him, when he got back, he found him sitting up in his bed screaming at the nurses, pleading with them to solve his pain, demanding that they feed him more painkillers. When the nurse had gone, Jim flashed a smile and showed Hugo his stash. Twenty-five top degree painkillers. But he was sick and his head did hurt. And he knew how sick he was.

Ignorance was no longer a sanctuary. Said Jim. And Hugo listened. Ignorance was a limbo of random panics. Like the panic he had had in New York looking at the forty red pimples on his chest. He needed to know what was worth worrying about. He needed to be able to have a cold or a cough, to feel tired, to get the runs, to not feel hungry, without each time going to ice inside and thinking, that's it. Here we go.

It wasn't the dying that worried him. He had nearly died before. In too-fast cars driven by too-stoned, too-young men. That was big-bang-death in which the worst prospect was survival in a wheelchair. But this was a slow slide through an assault course of piggy-backing bugs, opportunistic viruses, mealy-mouthed germs and curious strains of unusual diseases. It was the wasting away and the pain. It was what Jim said as he sat upright in his room screaming at the nurse for extra painkillers, his head being savaged by an internal chainsaw.

'If you leave it too late, you tie their hands behind their backs.'

That was what the doctors had told him. The sooner they knew, the more they could do. The sooner they knew, the longer they could watch. The faster they could act. If you kept it a secret from yourself, you kept it a secret from them and the only time anyone noticed anything was wrong was when it had bubbled out onto the surface, erupting from inner corruption too far festered to be dissolved by a small grey capsule.

That was why Hugo went into the fast-in, fast-out syringe surgery off Harley Street for £35 cash down. That was why the next morning he and Chas were sitting opposite each other in an overheated office and Hugo's fingers were twitching, waiting to phone his doctor.

Chas looked more tense than Hugo. The whole issue wound him up to near tears. His fear for others was mingled with terror for himself. Hugo was the opposite. In crises he went icy. News of another death left him standing at the telephone, waiting for a wave of something to hit as he dribbled the expected words – I'm so sorry, it's so dreadful. But the wave never did hit. The shore remained parched. And then, later, suddenly, unexpectedly, Hugo would feel the loss. Not as a flood of tears, a sudden crashing of the pent-up wave. But as a vacuum. An empty space. A loss.

Something that baffled him. A name would appear on a page in his address book and be dead. Gone. Uncontactable. Off the circuit and not coming back. And the empty space would yawn slowly and then close over again.

This morning Hugo had an empty space in his stomach. It wasn't loss. It was the space he had cleared to stop all reactions. It was emotions on hold. He had to be entirely passive. It was as if he had committed psychological hara kiri. He had disembowelled his fear. Fear always sat in his bowels anyway.

He went upstairs to make the phone call.

Upstairs there was a smaller, empty office.

He rang the surgery briskly.

It was like waiting for exam results. Except the exam results were not a matter of life and death. He knew that because his father had told him so when he was eleven and sent him up the path to take the exam for the big school in the country.

'It isn't a matter of life and death,' he had said as Hugo closed the car door, white-faced.

This was.

He picked up the telephone and, as if watching himself from a distance, saw his hand dial the number of his doctor's surgery. The space in his stomach shifted. Air swirled. It was the feeling you get on the back seat of a car as it goes over an unexpected hump-backed bridge. The earth and all things solid were falling away.

'Surgery.' It was one of the horn-rimmed women on the front-desk. They were the gate-keepers of the doctor's surgery. To get past them required shock tactics or a carefully prepared stratagem. Hugo always went for the battering ram.

'I need to speak to Dr Wilkinson urgently.'

'Dr Wilkinson is on holiday.'

He should have said good morning but he had panicked. Now she was enjoying it. She had the perfect stonewall.

'Who is handling his patients? I have to find out the results of a blood test.'

He knew that would alarm her. Blood test. It was non-specific, but a young man with an arrogant voice obviously not in hospital . . . yet. What could this mean? She didn't answer. A doctor came to the phone.

'This is Dr Hilliard.'

The voice was young. Too fresh. Eager to please. It was a turn-over-a-new-leaf, make-a-fresh-start, every-day-is-another-day type of voice. A boy scout's type of voice.

'This is Hugo Harvey.'

'Ah . . . Mr Harvey . . . yes –'

The doctor's voice was definitely nervous. Hugo felt their conversation swing his way. He was now in control. He had got past the gate-keepers and he had a doctor dangling. Now for the kill. The information. The matter of life and death. At the back of his mind, Hugo realised that this wasn't the normal game. This time he could be the loser either way. And the signs weren't good. Why should the doctor be so nervous?

'I'm ringing about the results of my blood test. They should have come through from the clinic, but they will have been sent to –'

'Yes. I have them here.'

'Good. What was the result?'

He had to approach this head-on. He couldn't lose momentum.

'Well, I don't think I should give you the results over the telephone . . .'

'Why not?'

Hugo felt an edge come into his voice. Why should he have to haggle? It was his health. He was not going to take a train all the way to Hadley.

'I think we should meet to discuss them.'

'I'm at work. I can't just leave here for the afternoon.'

'Well, I think it would be better. I'm not happy about doing this over the phone.'

Why shouldn't he be happy? He was giving the game away. He wouldn't have been so worried if the results had been negative.

'All I want is an answer, yes or no. I know what the tests were for. I just need to know, am I positive or am I negative?'

'They want you to go back for some more tests.'

'Why? Were these only partial tests?'

'Yes.'

'So I'm positive –'

'Well.'

'Otherwise there wouldn't be any need for me to have more tests.'

'Well, it is important that they clarify –'

'Am I likely to be negative if one of their tests has come up positive?'

'No.'

The doctor was not having a good time. He was new on duty. This was his first week. Hugo found that out later. He also found out that the doctor had spent the rest of the day feeling dreadful because of the way that he had handled this conversation. But Hugo hadn't given him any option. He wasn't going to travel on a train for an hour and a half to have some fresh-faced student doctor stumble over his community care manual trying to find instructions for breaking news of serious illness to perfect strangers. Hugo didn't want his counselling and didn't care for his sympathy. The sympathy of strangers is the most depressing of all.

Hugo was not having a good time either. The results were not what he wanted.

'And their tests have shown up positive.'

'Well . . . Yes.'

'Thank you very much.'

Hugo put the phone down and stared at the pinboard on the office wall directly ahead of his face. He looked at some postcards. There was a sunset in Jamaica, heavily touched up. There was a rather dim-looking hotel in Oban. There was one of Piccadilly Circus where the colourist had used the same red for two buses, a lady's coat and three pairs of ladies' shoes.

He stared at the pinboard and wondered what he was supposed to do. How he was supposed to feel. He felt extremely calm. But he felt as if there ought to have been a message in a glass phial round his neck which he could crack open. Inside he would find instructions. They would be simple and terse and written in the style of an old uppercrust RAF pilot. Never fear, old chap. Worse things happen at sea.

Hugo took a deep breath and stood up. He was always disappointed that tears would never flow at the moments when he expected them to. It wasn't so much the drama of tears he wanted as the catharsis. But no. Everything was sitting airtight and compressed.

He went downstairs and sat opposite Chas. Chas stared at him quizzically. Before he could say a word, the phone rang. Work. The jollity in his voice sounded like an echo. He drew a plus sign on a piece of paper and slipped it across the table to Chas.

As Hugo chatted on the telephone, Chas stared at him, and Hugo, the tension inside him bubbling up again, began to grin uncontrollably. When Chas's eyes began to pop, he began to giggle. By the time Hugo put the phone down, Chas had his head in his hands.

'You are?'

Hugo stopped laughing and said in a rather plain voice:

'Yes.'

Hugo enjoyed appearing brave. Cool. Detached from the drama of his own life. Leaning back and whistling through his teeth, he passed off the news as so much inconvenience. Inside, however, the terror was creeping closer.

When he went to the hospital they were snappy with him for having gone privately, and insisted on repeating everything again: every question and every test.

'How many men have you slept with in the past three years?'

'I don't know . . .'

'Five, ten, fifteen . . .?'

'Hundred.'

'One hundred?'

'Fifteen hundred.' Hugo grinned. The man cocked a nasty eyebrow.

'What is the average? . . . I don't know . . . I never stopped to count. Quite a few. A hundred. Easily.'

'Have you ever used recreational narcotics?'

'Yes.'

'Have you ever used drugs intravenously?'

'Yes.'

Hugo wanted him to be impressed. Another cocked eyebrow, perhaps. He didn't bat an eyelid. He just left Hugo sitting there on a hard chair in an empty room. But this wasn't the police. They were there to help. They said so as they gave him a number. That would protect his name. That would stop people trying to trace his medical records.

Hugo had entered the secret world of tainted people.

He signed forms and watched scribblings and saw rubber stamps saying CONTAMINATED come down on the scribbles and the signature. They took his arm and drew out eight little bottles of dark red blood, each one stamped again, CONTAMINATED. He was beginning to get the message. Then they passed him downstairs to the social worker. Hugo wrestled with his nonchalance. Half of him wanted to make a scene. The other half, the stronger half, demanded he remain as always – blasé, cool, detached.

'I shall probably go away for three years and then die,' he said to the social worker, with a pomposity he thought passed for insouciance. 'I don't see any point sitting here waiting for things to happen.'

He had made no plans and wouldn't have known where to start but he wanted the redheaded Scottish girl to understand that he didn't need to be patronised.

'And what if you don't die after three years?' she said pertly. 'What if you don't die after ten years? Will you come back or just sit out there waiting to die?'

She was taking the drama out of his catastrophe. He had liked the idea of a voyage of purgation, the travelling mendicant leper, scribbling notes on his way to the grave.

But he didn't go anywhere. That was the strange thing about being positive. It justified no real action. You were sitting in the anteroom to illness, waiting for your name to be called, but you had better bring something to do while you were waiting because otherwise the boredom would kill you.

Hugo left the hospital with a secret code number and a list of future appointments. He didn't really know how he felt. His stomach was giving him no clues. It felt blank. His mind felt blank. He tried telling some people. Chas knew. He told three others, maybe four. Close friends. Each time he regretted having told them anything. He tried explaining how blank he felt, and they all looked at him long and hard, as if learning the features of his face. Tears welled up out of their eyes, or their arms opened for an embrace. But he didn't want that. He liked the love and the loyalty but not the implication of their sorrow. They thought he was already ill, and he wasn't. Was he?

He tried talking to others he knew who were infected and they just depressed him with their depression. They had been cowed by the news. They believed that they were invalids. If someone had ordered them all into a concentration camp for the untouchables, they would have gone, meekly, heads bowed. And Hugo would have watched, transfixed, on the other side of the barbed wire, having told nobody, making no protest, lying to save his own skin.

There were exceptions: Jim, with his terrier hold on life, and clinical knowledge of everything that could happen, refused to be bowed by his adversity and thrust pamphlets and propaganda about new drugs and vaccines and test into Hugo's hand. Philip, with his arrogant belief that he knew more than the doctors and that all he needed was the right combination of B-numbered powders and organic drinks, insisted he take note of his own T-cell count, that he read his blood results after every hospital visit, that he tell the doctors when to act and when to hold back. Even Chas, once he had finished his shudder of shock, told Hugo he was still allowed to catch cold, cough, and throw up without assuming each shiver was the harbinger of death.

Slowly, however, the news took its toll: quietly, secretly in the back of Hugo's mind. He lost his memory. Not his serious memory: he knew who he was and what he did and where he did it and even sometimes why. But he lost everything everywhere. He lost notebooks, a wallet, his keys. He lost carrier bags with shopping in. His watch. He missed appointments and turned up at the wrong time for others. He began to lose his patience. And then, as suddenly as it had started, it stopped. That was his reaction. In a distant backroom of his mind, business, the business of remembering to pick up carrier bags, wear his watch, collect his notebooks, carry his wallet, had closed down for a holiday. The pressure had all been too much. And now, the pressure had passed, the shockwaves were over, business was back as usual. And Hugo went on, as usual. For a time. For the time being. For the moment.

There was a knock at the door. Hugo closed his eyes and pretended to be asleep. He didn't know who it was, who came in. They had brought something in Cellophane. He heard its sharp rustle as they laid it down. There was only one of them. No

whispered words. He had played this trick before and eavesdropped horrible conversations as a pair of friends he didn't know
stared at his body and talked about death. He knew secretly all
these people wanted to say to him, 'Don't you know you're about
to die? How does it feel? Doesn't it feel strange?' He wasn't going
to give them the pleasure of an answer. He knew because he had
felt the same way. When Jim lost his sight to retinitis, it happened
so fast, one day he could see, the next day he was blind. Hugo
went to see him in hospital. Suddenly, after all the daily battles he
had won against spiteful viruses and freeloading germs, Jim had
been hit an unexpected whammy and didn't know how to field it.
He was gobsmacked at his own bad luck. Hugo sat by his bed
clutching a box of Terry's York Fruits, wondering what to say
and all the time wanting to ask: 'Is it really bad? How much can
you see? How do you deal with it? What do you tell yourself? Is
this the last straw?'

The unknown visitor had sat down. This could be a long one.
A pious devotee of the deathbed. Sometimes Hugo actually fell
asleep while pretending. Sometimes he sneaked a look. But as
soon as his eyes opened a little, the light prized them open still
further and impatience to see who it could be got the better of
him.

He heard a felt pen scratching on paper. Perfect. She – that
much he knew from the smell – was leaving a message. That way
he would know who it had been.

It wasn't that he didn't like visitors. Or perhaps it was. But that
was only since Chas had gone. While Chas was still alive, he had
been the perfect visitor and when others came Hugo would tell
them stories Chas had told him. Gossip. Intrigue. Chas presented
his life to Hugo like daily instalments of a radio soap and Hugo
tuned in eagerly to the politicking and backstabbing of a cast he
had long since lost touch with. Primed with that week's tattle he
could retell, editing for each audience, Chas's tales of disastrous
marriages, furious adulteries, and career collapses. It became
Hugo's only way of staying entertaining. People still expected him
to be entertaining. Or he still expected them to expect it. Chas
could still make him laugh and he could still make them laugh
with Chas's stories. The others came for an audience. Sometimes

they would just sit there staring. Sympathy dripped from their eyes like tears. But since Chas had gone, Hugo had lost interest in his own visitors.

Chas had gone. Gone to his grave and his maker. Much faster than anyone expected. Except Hugo. Hugo knew why he went so quickly. The will went out of him like air out of a balloon. He didn't want to fight. He didn't want to stay. He didn't want to see Hugo. And it wasn't just because they were both in the same miserable boat. They could have had a good time, alone, dying together, warm in each other's good humour.

Chas had gone to his maker alone and lonely, bitter and resentful, hating Hugo maybe more than anyone else in the world, because the man of Chas's dreams, the man Chas had lived with for years, the man who had made him happy and confident, had cheated on him with Hugo. And Hugo, his best friend, his confidant, his first and last refuge, had cheated on him with Mick. It had been Hugo's guiltiest secret. For over a year it had sat festering in the back of his conscience. Until Mick, with all the selfishness of the sinner wanting to be forgiven, told Chas as he lay in his hospital bed.

He didn't want Chas to die without having confessed to him. It was the most selfish reason of them all. Chas could die miserable as long as he didn't have to live on feeling dishonest.

And then Mick had come to see Hugo and told Hugo that he had told Chas. Hugo just stared at him. Without a word.

Mick sat for five minutes staring at the floor. Hugo stared at the window. And then Mick left and never came back.

Why had Hugo ever done it? Chas never asked him that. He never spoke to him to ask him. Hugo never asked himself either. He knew the answer. Wasn't it the same reason he fucked a man in the backroom of a Parisian bathhouse and released jets of poisoned spunk into his bowels? Wasn't it the same reason he knelt on the dirty floor of a service station loo on the M1 and sucked the dick of a lorry driver until . . . Wasn't it? Except he told himself he had no regrets. The man in the bathhouse knew what risk he was taking. Hugo knew what risk he was taking. If that was the way to die, then so be it.

This was different. He regretted it all. But it was the same. He was helpless. Pinioned by lust.

It had happened before. It had happened before between him and Chas. Chas hadn't introduced him to Mick for a year after they had started going out because of Hugo's reputation. He liked stealing other people's boyfriends. It was all part of the competition. It made them more attractive and it made Hugo feel more important. It never lasted. Just for the moment, it was fun. And before Chas hadn't minded because they hadn't been serious lovers. His ego had been bashed but not his emotions. They always made it up and neither of them ever saw the boy in question again. Or, if they did, they both laughed and talked about his dick.

But Mick was different. Mick was the love of Chas's life. Hugo knew Mick was different. Chas had told him of a dream once, a nightmare he had woken up from inconsolable, in floods of tears. He had come home one day from work and found Hugo and Mick in the bedroom. They were lying on the bed, fully clothed, poring over old photos and laughing, contentedly, like lovers. Chas stood in the doorway and watched them. Hugo saw him first and smiled. Chas said the smile was like a reptile. It was a smile of spite, not of welcome. But what frightened Chas still more was the happiness in Mick's face. He looked up at Chas and Chas saw only indifference. As if even the row to come could not disrupt his good mood.

And then Hugo said to Mick, 'Why don't you tell Chas?'

And Mick giggled gently and said, 'Why don't you?'

And Hugo said to Chas, with the reptile smile still on his lips, 'Mick and I are lovers. We have been for a year. I thought you might have guessed.'

And Chas woke up screaming.

That was the dream.

The reality was worse, maybe. Maybe not. It was a secret. It happened when neither of them were looking. Both of them were drunk. But it had been on its way, moving towards them like a slow-moving train, for months. It had started with touches and kisses. It was all playful. Flirtatious. Safe in front of Chas. Chas didn't mind. He had no need to care. Mick was his. But Hugo was getting turned on. He kept having to turn away. He couldn't avoid responding, but then had to hide his discomfiture in smiles.

He had always lusted after Mick but had never made a move. He couldn't. He was his best friend's boyfriend.

He couldn't. But he did.

Chas wasn't there that night. They had had a fight. He and Mick often fought. Stomping off in different directions with curses on their breath. Hugo was out. At a club round the corner from his flat. He hadn't known Mick would be there. He was drunk. He was trying to move around the club but he kept walking into people, wrong-footing himself, toppling off balance. He came to rest against a wall by the stage. A drag act was performing. The audience were being abused and they were abusing back and the atmosphere was rising. It was hot and dark and the drag act was getting crude. Hugo was bored and looked around.

Standing in the corner, leaning against the same wall, was Mick, rolling a cigarette, smiling out of the side of his mouth at the drag act's bad jokes.

Hugo's mouth went dry. Mick looked edible. Just leaning with that half-smile, he looked like an American postcard, all casual manliness and sexual aplomb. No effort. Just hormones. Hugo wanted to leave. He was gripped. He wanted to turn away. He knew that if he could turn and walk out, out of the door, up the street to his house and lie down and have a wank, then everything would be alright in the morning. Nobody would know that he wanted Mick. Nobody would need to know.

He turned and walked up to Mick and said hello.

Mick grabbed him by the waist and held him close. It could have been a friendly hug. It probably was meant to be a friendly hug and just a kiss, a smacker on the lips. But Hugo moved his head back. So Mick's head had to move forward. And Hugo parted his lips slightly. So Mick's tongue slipped between his lips. And Hugo moved his hips gently so their jeans rubbed. And he felt the size of Mick's crotch grow as he leant forwards again, pushing Mick back against the wall.

They didn't speak as they left the club. They both knew where Hugo's flat was. They both knew where his bedroom was. They walked in. They were quivering. Their hands were close to each other's bodies even while they undressed themselves. Still they didn't say a word. They had furious, angry, bitter, passionate, passionless sex. It was passionate with pent-up lust and passionless with obliterated tenderness. They couldn't risk pausing, because pillow talk would lead to guilt and guilt would ruin the moment. They bit and chewed and clawed at each other's bodies. The delay had made them desperate. They both knew they were breaking the rules. They didn't want their eyes to meet because then real life would intrude into their fantasy. They didn't want it to end, because once it was over, the guilt would rise to replace the lust.

And then Hugo came. And then Mick came. And then for a second came relief and a smile. And then their smiles froze over. They just lay there. Each one wrapped up in his own betrayal, already adding up what it was costing him.

Mick got up and went to the bathroom and Hugo didn't move. Mick came back and started to get dressed and Hugo went to the bathroom.

Hugo came out of the bathroom and Mick was standing by the door, ready to go. They both looked gleaming, sleek with sex. They had both bitten deep and eaten well.

'This never happened, right?' Hugo's voice wasn't clear.

'No.'

'It mustn't happen again.'

'I know.'

They smiled. Nervously. And never met again. Until the day Mick came to see Hugo in hospital and told him that he had told Chas.

And now Chas was dead.

Hugo opened his eyes and tried to focus on the present his anonymous caller had left.

Chas was gone.

He had heard that Mick too was ill now. In another hospital. He had lost the use of his legs. Hugo didn't want to go near him. It was as if the air between them was poisoned. The two of them had killed off Chas and killed off a bit of themselves that Chas had loved.

The caller had left some Terry's York Fruits. It was all they had downstairs. She had left a note but Hugo couldn't make it out before his stomach squeezed so hard he gasped and coughed on his own phlegm. He rolled wheezing onto his side. Was Chas watching him now, he wondered. Looking down on him, waiting for him to die. Would he speak to him on the other side? Hugo smiled at himself through the pain. What fucking other side, he muttered. The acid was etching a hole in his stomach. His hips were so sore he couldn't lie like that. He grabbed the oxygen and gulped a throatful. As his head spun slightly, he rolled onto his back again, taking the weight off his sore buttocks with his feet, and breathed more evenly from the oxygen cylinder.

He closed his eyes and, through the dull, orange explosions and the swirl of the dark, he tried to find the image he knew would rest him.

Slowly, it came into focus.

Chas and Hugo. Walking side by side. Through air damp with the residue of mist. Along grey paths puddle-stained and criss-crossed with bicycle tracks.

January 4, 1986

Dear Chas,

I know you will be a little surprised to get this letter. I wish my first letter to you had something more lighthearted to say, but I am very worried about Hugo and I wanted to air this with you.

I hadn't seen Hugo for some months, which is maybe why it struck me so heavily when I did see him, but on Boxing Day I went to his party. You know how Hugo always has these 'escape' evenings on Boxing Day. Well, on this occasion he was really strange.

He answered the door and was halfway through greeting us when he seemed to lose interest and wandered back indoors leaving us to close the door and see to our own coats. We went upstairs where people were sitting – Dolly was there and a few others, most of whom I knew – but, although everybody seemed quite animated, they all seemed nonplussed by Hugo. Whenever he went out of the room people would exchange glances, but were unable to really say anything about it to each other because of the presence in the room of somebody called Larry. I cannot quite believe that Larry is Hugo's current lover. He is unkempt and surly and pasty-faced. He didn't say a word to me or anyone all evening, but sat and stared at the television, even when it wasn't on. He seems to have had a ghastly influence over Hugo, who was equally grim company.

You know what Hugo is normally like at his own parties – quite frenetic until he is drunk, and then just beamish. But on this occasion the most appropriate word to describe him would be absent. He just wasn't there. And from the way in which he every so often disappeared from the room without a word, leaving us with the surly man in the leather jacket, I supposed it must be something to do with drugs.

Have you seen him recently? You two are so close, I am sure you are the only one who could say something to him. Even Dolly hasn't really dared broach the subject with him. You know how savage Hugo can be if you ask him the wrong question at the wrong time. But Dolly thinks it's smack, which I can't believe. Not Hugo. He was always so smart about his drugs.

You'll probably think I'm panicking over nothing, but I know that Hugo confides in you and I just hope you can put my mind at rest.

Much love and I hope things are going well. Please get in touch. I would be so grateful to hear from you.

Cynthia

10

PINS AND NEEDLES

The vein seemed to be breathing gently underneath the skin in the shallow of his elbow. A grey shadow swollen by his clenched fist.

He picked up the needle, keeping the tourniquet clenched between his teeth. He laid the needle against the skin and slipped it in. The pain as it pierced the skin didn't bother him. What made him swoon was the resistance of the vein wall. It pushed back against the point of the hypodermic and then suddenly gave way like a sigh. Hugo flinched.

He pushed the plunger slowly down. The swoon rose in his bloodstream like water filling a milk bottle. He let go of the tourniquet and let go of the needle. It hung off his arm like some poisoned dart. Wounded, his arm fell aside, slipping off the table as he leant his head on his other hand. He had to move. He was either very high or about to die. Either way, he had to be near cold water.

He moved down the corridor to the bathroom and sat on the loo so that the basin was at eye level. He turned the cold tap on and watched the water flow. In the distance the telephone rang. He would answer it later. Lately he couldn't tell whether it was ringing all the time or stopped and rang again. Who could it be, anyway? He hadn't arranged to see anyone. Yesterday he had picked the phone up but couldn't remember what to say and had put it down again before the person on the other end had finished talking. He did remember who that was. Gavin Hill. A schoolfriend he had borrowed fifty pounds from. They weren't friends anymore. He hadn't paid the fifty pounds back. He couldn't remember what he had done with it anyway.

The water ran clear from the tap into the basin. The light from the window behind him gave the basin a soap commercial gleam. He felt better now. He didn't feel sick. Just drained. Ready to lie down and stare at the ceiling. They did this for hours, occasionally groaning, playing with each other, neither able to sustain an erection but both turned on. It killed time. Larry had all the time in the world. He had quit his job, although his employers didn't know that yet. Smack was enough for one person to be dealing with, without having to go to work as well. And since Hugo had appeared on the scene, smack had been in easy supply.

Hugo wasn't stopping. This was just a visit. He was down from Cambridge for Christmas, working nights at a Bond Street night-club, selling over-priced drinks to second-rate socialites. And the days when he wasn't sleeping or working for finals, he was sharing needles with Larry.

It was an odd sort of affair. An itinerant window cleaner from Newcastle who dipped in and out of vagrancy and crime, Larry had been washed up on the doorstep of the large house in Muswell Hill, and taken in. When Hugo came down from Cambridge, Larry was sitting on the brown velvet sofa in the upstairs sitting-room, watching television with William and Barry. They didn't speak much then. Larry had lank hair worn long and a leather jacket. He had lips like an overripe flower. Two nights later, they were in bed together. The next afternoon, they were in an attic flat in Abbey Road, buying smack.

Hugo wasn't really on the smack set scene. Coke, acid, spliff, pills, uppers, downers, roundabouters in all and every combination but not smack. He argued against it. Claimed he didn't feel the need. Said it was boring and pointless and too expensive. Ridiculed it as soporific and negative. Of course he had never had it. Had never been offered. And, like everything else, secretly Hugo wanted a go. If there was a ride going, he wanted a ticket. For one.

At school, it had started with the barbiturates Damian stole from his father. Turquoise capsules broken into a poster paint pot of neat gin and downed in one swallow on the top deck of the 134. That was where he got the habit of doing it alone. Staring at the world through the mist of a downer. Making no contact with anyone. Sitting, watching people and events flash by like a five-year-old child watching the televisions in a shop window. No sound. No meaning. Just pictures. He'd stop to drink some more and arrive at parties with a look in his eyes that kept people away. They drifted apart as he moved through a room. He loved the feeling. Maybe they thought he had a gun in his pocket. The important thing was that people should know. Know he wasn't simply drunk and about to spray his stomach on the toilet floor. They should know he had pills in his pocket, enough to kill if he felt like it. He was dipping out of the sane world, getting lost in barbiturate fog, but all the time he was playing to an imaginary gallery of the impressed and the naive: the others for whom drugs were an untouchable taboo, that somehow they still wished they could reach. It never occurred to him that these people didn't really exist. Or that they were simply images of Hugo.

'God, Hugo, you're wild,' he whispered to himself in imaginary voices.

Meanwhile, the rest of the party turned its back. Pretending not to notice.

Sometimes his little sister watched and worried, but she wasn't the audience he wanted. He wanted a crowd who knew what he was doing and, although they didn't dare themselves, wished they could. He wanted a crowd who thought him brave and weird for living so near the edge.

And the real edge was smack.

He abandoned downers when Damian left school and they stopped fucking in the woods at lunchtime. No more amyl barbitone. No more Librium and Valium. Punk had crashed in at the door and the only pills to take in town were blues: Saturday nights chucking down blues and lager at the back of the Marquee, playing pinball, chewing stale gum, smoking cigarettes down to the filter and drinking too much Diet Coke, while all the time his chest was ticking over like an alarm clock and his heart was beaming at the world through his eyes, like some burning coal sending out goodwill-heat.

He'd swallow two or three sitting in the second smokers' carriage on the Northern Line. At Leicester Square, he'd swing out of the sliding doors, bomb down the tunnels and run up the stone steps between the escalators. As he hit the top step, he'd pause, take a breath on one foot and feel the blood rush the speed into his brain. The whoosh of euphoria swept him past the ticket collector with an ear-to-ear smile. One step beyond the ticket collector and he was in his own private movie show; his heart thumping, his brain muttering, go for it, go for it, go for it, a hundred times a minute and his hands shaking like a wino's as they lit the first of forty fags.

He loved to speed. He was too young to start second-guessing the happiness that burst in his bloodstream like fireworks. He believed its every ripple of adrenalin. Staring at another band thrashing at another tuneless guitar, he'd stand and grin, cigarette in one hand, beer in the other, adrenalin in his veins like the elixir of life.

Now the elixir was sick. Spit quick vomit. Hugo leant over the basin to try and get the water on his head. His brow was speckled with sweat drops. Lined up just under his hair. He had the face of a fevered man. Pale and wan. He looked moth-eaten, limp against the gleaming, white porcelain basin. Even the water running from the tap looked healthy. He reached a hand out and let his fingers be bullied by the stream. A lame trickle of blood ran down the inside of his arm where the needle had been hanging. He couldn't remember whether it had fallen out or he had taken it out. He couldn't remember whether Larry had had the needle first or he had. He couldn't remember whether he had told Larry where he was going. But then, Larry hadn't asked.

They didn't say much.

They barely knew each other. But now they were lovers. Within two days of meeting. An evening side-by-side on the brown velvet sofa, in front of the telly, thighs brushing, small talk, probing eyes. Stupid questions with strong stares. Larry knew everything about Hugo. He knew he was at Cambridge. He knew he was in his last year. He knew he had spent the last summer working as a hooker to pay the rent. He didn't know that by the end of the summer that was all Hugo had, the rent money, and the feeling under his eyes and somewhere at the back of his head that he'd died a small death in those beds. What Larry knew Barry had told him. Barry was trying to poison the water. Barry was like that. He didn't want to see Hugo win. Again.

Hugo knew nothing about Larry, except that he could and had and would again with men. That was all he needed to know. Whatever Barry planned, Hugo knew he would win. All he needed was the opportunity.

He was given the opportunity.

It fell out of the sky overnight and lay on the ground like icing sugar smothering a rock cake. They took a walk the next day in the woods to catch the beauty of the surprise snowfall. London was on holiday. The snow had buried the train lines and brought the buses to a standstill. The Bond Street club was staying closed. Larry was staying home. Hugo suggested they went for a walk. They knew what was going to happen. They just weren't sure how.

They walked to the woods, saying little. Hugo had no idea what to say to this boy with the lips like flowers. He wanted to bite his tongue and plunge a hand into his trousers way below the belt. But instead they walked quietly along the road through the woods where the snow lay thick and unspoilt. The woods looked like a Hansel and Gretel illustration. A giggle grew in Hugo's belly. He felt like the kid he'd been when he and sister junior ran amok on a snow-clad golf course, ducking as the angry shouts of interrupted golfers rang out down the links. He laughed so much in those days, the cold air catching his breath and filling his chest like peppermints. Now the giggle rose at the sight of the snow, untrodden, like a thick white duvet on a huge bed. He wanted to lie in it and hug it and feel it turn to feathers instead of water.

He picked up a handful and, rapidly packing it into a ball, dropped it down Larry's neck. That was the pass. Larry grinned and scooped snow up from the ground. The pass had been accepted. They ran through the woods, further from the tracks of dogprints and the local ladies with their poodles leaving neat poodle turds to burn holes in the snow's crust. The trees, stiff and black like sticks of charcoal, grew thicker as they ran. Hugo ran behind, grabbing snow all the time from branches and sudden low scoops from the ground, pelting Larry with wet balls, laughing as his hard-on made running more difficult. Larry turned and threw a flurry of snow into the air. Hugo crashed through it, spluttering and swiping. He collided with Larry, bringing him to the ground, shaking with laughter. He landed hard on top of him, his mouth to his mouth, his eyes to his eyes. They stared at each other from eyeball to eyeball and Larry licked his lips. It was all the invitation Hugo needed.

He didn't know then about Larry and smack. He didn't know

about Larry and the law, or the violence that was to come. He
didn't know that he was dealing with an unhinged boy. A runaway
teenager. A disturbed man. He just knew that he and Larry were
going to lie together in the big bed in the room at the back with
the step-through windows onto the garden while their clothes
hung on the radiator, drying out. He knew that their skin would
be pink and burning with the change in the temperature and the
clothes would dry stiff, but he didn't know why.

They smoked a joint. Sex had been strange. For all his tough-
guy attitude, his leather bomber jacket and dirty jeans, Larry had
the body of a child. Smooth-skinned, hairless and unformed. Even
his dick seemed somehow vestigial. He was quiet, naive, wary of
sex but wanting it. They lay together and smoked the joint.

And then Larry asked Hugo if he could get any smack and
Hugo said yes.

He could, after all. He just never had.

He said yes to impress.

He always wanted people to think he was connected up and
down with the highlife and the lowlife. So he said yes.

Something might have said, somewhere in the back of Hugo's
head, that this was where he was supposed to say no; that all his
life he had been warned that slipping into heroin meant slipping
into the abyss; that he would end up stuck on a needle, lying on a
trash heap of bony bodies, scrabbling for pennies in the bowels of
Piccadilly Circus station, squirting unwanted blood down the
doors of the cubicles where David had played for two pounds a
time. He may have heard some little peep from a past of parental
pamphlets. After 'Where Do Babies Come From?' came 'Where Do
Drug Addicts End Up?'. But Hugo was already there. He was
already living in a twilight zone of after-dark people, living out of
synchronisation with the bright-eyed, brisk-stepping commuter
world that rushed past his early morning window, still wiping
breakfast from its chin and wifely worries from its mind. Hugo
would watch them through eyes half-crossed with tiredness and
dazzled by the bright grey light of a winter morning.

Hugo had already seen the morning once by then. While these
scurrying men were still sleeping next to their wives in the room
down the corridor from the kids, Hugo was sipping at a cup of

tea in Barclay Brothers (Whitehall) Ltd, staring through its steam
at Maureen the transvestite and queen of the tea urn as she flicked
the taps with chipped fingernails and smiled through green teeth,
looking over a grubby mug rim at the teenage runaways slumped
face-down in the breakfast, spider's web tattoos meeting congealed
egg.

They slumped there, dull-eyed, smileless, waiting for the call
from their pimp, the heavy black man outside, gleaming with gold
teeth, rings, bracelets and one fat medallion, ferrying his runaway
charges in and out of taxis, sending them off to destination
feather-bed, an unknown suburb on the city perimeter. They knew
what to expect. Two hours of sexual investigation at the fingertips
of a stranger with no sleepy wife and no kids down the corridor.
They knew how far they were prepared to go. The stranger had
better not make a mistake. Boys with spider's web tattoos had
short tempers.

That was Hugo's end-of-day morning. From the battered plush
of the Bond Street club where eyes flashed from gloomy corners,
to the unforgiving light of a strip-lit caff, where eyes were down,
averted, blank, lit only by the sudden flare of a Swan Vesta or the
dry twinkle of Maureen's wit.

This was limboland. In that, at least, there was no difference
between Bond Street and Whitehall. Between the red plush and
the grey-green formica, everyone was adrift. Bond Street was
warmer, darker, pudgier, richer but the inhabitants were untethered. And occasionally unhinged. The once-weres, the might-have-
beens and the giddy hopefuls clustering around the recently-arrived,
watching him or him–her splashing about in newfound cash, suddenly generous, suddenly mean. Sons and daughters of the rich
and famous lurked in corners clutching at straws. Smiling at the
brand new pop star like the membership secretary of a rarefied
tennis club welcoming a new recruit. They were always low on
new members. None of them seemed to last very long.

The formerly famous and still rich clung to the bar, staring
hard at their glass, trying to remember what they had to order
next. A man who had sold millions of records promising to die
before he got old swayed in premature dotage, at sea in gin and
tonic. Another held out a hand for him to shake but was left

wobbling alone in the middle of the carpet as the undead pop star loped towards the loos to powder his nose.

It was all in the eyes. The red-rimmed blur of the pop star. The hopeful gaze of the rich kid out for a binge and expecting free cocaine. The twitchy blinks of the queen in streaked hair and beige leather trousers, hoping his tan would smother his age, and the blank, unapologetic stare of his companion, a blond body from some far-flung surf city with the sea still shifting in his eyes, focused far beyond this basement room. Hugo watched them all, watched them as they watched each other. Eyes followed eyes. Waiting for signals. Hoping for a catch. Sinking into the drink. Wandering, restless, watering, blinking, flickering, shallow, dead. The surfer gazed through the men filing past, friends of the desperate leatherette, each one ready to snatch the prize if one signal were given. They raised their lids, flashing an eye-white hello that was seldom returned. Occasionally they'd break into conversation which would die on their lips as the surfer, looking over their shoulder, gave nothing away but a yes or a no.

Hugo moved among them, invisible in a scarlet sweatshirt and baseball cap. They tipped him absentmindedly, hoping their friends noticed.

No one noticed anything at the club. No one noticed the men sneaking into the ladies' loo after furtive exchanges of little white packets. No one noticed the awkward sniffing, the chain smoking, the talking too fast and the last trace of white dust on a moustache. Why should they notice? Who was looking? The manager was in the back with the owner and the coatcheck snorting up the petty cash. The head waiter was stashing crates of champagne in the back of his car, and the barmen stood impassively by, watching nothing through tiny pinprick pupils, heroin slipping silently through their blood like the long, slow slug of lethargy. Quietly and slowly, the time slipped by. Time in limboland went so slowly. Doing nothing and noticing nothing.

It didn't seem so unusual to be lying on his back, staring at the cornice, waiting for the next groan to roll up out of his mouth. It didn't seem so unusual to have nothing to think about and less to do. He could drift from a day lying side-by-side with Larry's vestigial body, to a night sidling between the prick-eyed barmen and the desperate leatherettes without ever emerging from his heroin cocoon.

Only vaguely did one thought nag at his placid mind. Staring at his face in the mirror for fifteen minutes without flinching, and almost without thinking, it occurred to Hugo that tomorrow he might wake up looking like Michael.

Nobody wanted to look like Michael. Michael was smacked out. The vanishing man. The junkie cliché. But he was one better and one worse than the junkie cliché. He wasn't dying, just getting thinner. He wasn't criminal. He was insane. He wasn't a leech. He was rich. He didn't steal to pay for his habit. He sold off pieces of his inheritance, cashing in his family for a hit.

When Larry rolled over after the joint, after sex, after the fight in the snow as the clothes stiffened on the radiators, as they lay looking out at the garden under its frozen white duvet, and asked Hugo to buy him some smack, Hugo said yes because he knew that Michael would love another convert. He knew that Michael was lonely, alone with his habit. That he had buried too many of his friends, that he would welcome Hugo to his door like the evangelist welcoming the self-confessed sinner. But Hugo also thought of Michael because Michael was synonymous with smack. He had the appearance of a needle. Bony, sallow, his hair lank to his collar and greasy, his voice a whine grating the air like a tiny buzz saw. His movements were fragile but mean, his fingers were like darts, jabbing the air as he tried to explain to Hugo and Larry about the milk float at the end of the road, which was really a cover vehicle for the SPG.

'They've been in here and moved everything around. They've put it all back again, but they've been through everything. I know. They think I can't tell. Why don't they just take something? That's what I can't bear.' His whine buzzed irritably. Hugo leaned out of the window of the Abbey Road attic to look at the milk float standing quietly at the kerbside. It was empty and dark. It was a milk float. The milkman probably lived in one of the bedsits in one of the cavernous houses across the road.

'Jamie knew it was the SPG. Nobody else seems to notice, but he knew.'

That was the fourth, maybe the fifth time Michael had said

that. Twitching and scratching, all alone all day with only his fear and loathing for company, now he wanted to talk. He wanted friends he could talk to about other friends. But Michael was always losing his friends. Jamie was the last friend he'd had. Jamie was dead. Jamie was the philosopher-biker from Rotherham who would sit quietly toying with his beads in the corner talking about elephant tranquillisers. Jamie, who had a desire to snuff out all thought from his head and then snuffed himself out with a shotgun in the mouth at his brother's birthday party. He did it in the garden. So it didn't make a mess on the carpets. There may be messier ways to go. Hugo didn't know of any.

Jamie had known what he was doing. He had taken on an adversary he couldn't beat. The elephant tranquillisers had never been a problem. The smack was. The life was leaking out of him. The colour already had.

'I was there when he died, you know,' said Michael. Michael wasn't often anywhere when anything happened. He was normally here. In the overheated bedsit on the top of a house in Abbey Road. 'I wasn't in the garden though.'

Michael was in the bathroom heating up a spoon when the gun went off. He was so jolted by the noise he dropped the spoon. Furious at the loss of one good hit, he came down the stairs looking for a culprit and found the death of his best friend. What he couldn't understand was why Jamie was in the garden at all. He was meant to be on his way up for a hit.

Michael would sell smack to his best friend even if it killed him. It killed Jamie in nine months and a split second. A long whimper and a final bang. Michael showed no remorse; just annoyance that his latest recruit had already gone. Now he had to find another best friend to sit with in his overheated flat. Hugo and Larry were new recruits.

Larry didn't say a word. He just watched as Michael measured out a gram of brown dust on tiny scales. He just watched as Hugo handed over fresh banknotes. He didn't say a word as Michael rolled a joint, sprinkling smack the length of the tobacco. But he inhaled eagerly when the smoke came round to him.

The room was too small, too full and too hot. Michael looked like a long-term patient from a hospital with thick carpets. He should have been sitting there in a dressing gown, reading back issues of the *Tatler*. His eyes were hooded, his skin yellow and, as the smack began to take its toll, his voice just faded away. The three of them slumped into silence, staring at the bars of the gas fire.

Hugo stood in the bathroom, staring at the mirror, registering nothing but the memory of Michael's withered face. The telephone was ringing and he couldn't be bothered to answer it yet. Larry was upstairs watching *Being There* for the fourth time. Every time the video was finished, he punched the rewind and played it back again. It was the perfect smack movie. Peter Sellers spoke like a man with a needle hanging out of his arm. Hugo looked at his arm, at the soft skin inside his elbow where the veins beat gently against the skin. It was bruised yellow. Tiny punctures speckled the surface.

He hadn't used the needle straight away. After they sneaked out of Michael's flat onto the street, leaving Michael staring down the road at the milk float, waiting for the SPG to appear, they ducked into someone's garden and quietly, on a small mirror, on top of the wall, snorted up two lines. Hugo was just following, pretending to know what he was doing. But the world had become a slow-witted place and he and Larry were just drifting through it. Another line was all they needed to stay adrift.

They walked round the corner onto the high street. It was wet in the air and dark. The traffic was bumper to bumper, cars full of discontented men and worried wives getting tense before a night on the town. Larry and Hugo didn't hurry. They just moved through the drizzle. They had the whole night ahead of them.

They moved through the drizzle up Kilburn High Road to Shoot-Up Hill. They swayed through the doors of Bliss the Chemist, the joke, the old junkie joke, playing around Hugo's lips like a smile. Larry turned back and hissed as he went. 'You do it. They know me.'

The girl behind the counter looked up and saw Larry's back and Hugo's face. Hugo stood paralysed among multi-coloured packs of condoms, toothbrushes and face creams. Chemists always made him feel so unlooked-after. All these ointments he didn't use, these creams with their strange organic ingredients he had never dipped a finger into.

'I'd like two hypodermics, please,' he said to the girl behind the counter. She looked well-washed and neatly pressed in her blue nylon overall. He had put on his best respectable voice. He tried to hold her eyes but couldn't keep his concentration. If she asked him for his diabetic's card, he was meant to say something. Larry had told him what to say but he had forgotten it. She didn't ask. She looked at him without a flicker, calmly selling him the means of his destruction in cardboard and cellophane wrappers. She had already written him off. She didn't care whether he died now or later. He was offal. It made Hugo feel proud. A wave of adrenalin crashed in his chest. He was beginning to feel like Jean Genet. He had come in from the rain, fleeing the dirty swish of cars, their headlamps bouncing off puddles rippling under traffic lights, and taken brief refuge in this bright white world of multi-coloured toiletries gleaming under spotlights on polished glass shelves. He had completed another induction: he had bought needles at Bliss the Chemist on Shoot-Up Hill, he had joined the secret world. He was an outlaw, a late-night cowboy running amok on the urban steppe, trailing across the fluorescent desert, jumping buses and swaggering down sidewalks, with only a needle between him and death. Or vomit.

They rode the top deck of a red bus down the Edgware Road into town.

They didn't say a word.

It was dark outside, and wet.

Two skinheads got on the bus and rode behind them down the Edgware Road. Hugo could feel their eyes on his neck. He felt capsized. Vulnerable. Weak. He felt like throwing up. It wasn't a bad feeling, but it was growing more urgent. He didn't want to throw up in front of the two skinheads. It was too much like asking for attention. Attention led to trouble. You had to duck people's eyes in this town. Avoid their line of vision.

He stood up and strolled down the deck without a word to Larry. He swung down the stairs and left the bus at the traffic lights. He walked into the recessed doorway of a closed shop and, bending over, calmly emptied his belly on the chipped mosaic that had once read Colliers. Men's Tailors. The mosaic stood out in relief. Stones were missing like lost teeth. In the corner an old lady in a cardboard coat watched him without a word. He had just thrown up on her doorstep but he couldn't find the energy to begin explaining. He wiped his mouth on the back of his hand, spat on the pavement and took off after the bus. He had never been sick before with so little effort.

The bus had disappeared into the distance, way down the Edgware Road, splashing past traffic lights towards more traffic lights. The wet pavement was dancing with lamplight. Larry was leaning against the first lamppost, staring at the headlamps of oncoming cars. A smile hung on his lips like the memory of a nicer day. There couldn't have been a nicer day. Everything was going so smoothly. The deal. The chemist. The vomit. Larry.

Larry had a bottle in his pocket. A half-bottle of Armagnac. Hugo had no idea where it had appeared from. Maybe it had always been there. Maybe he had just fished it out of a bin. They both took a toke, and then a bus rolled up next to them and clambering on, they continued their way into the distance, measured out in traffic lights, working their way through the strange crowds of the West End, to the Marquee Club.

They were working their way to a dark corner. A place where the warmth of the sweat and the loudness of the music would replace any need for conversation or thought. Hugo hadn't been back to the Marquee for five years. Not since the night of The Depressions, the night when Charlie told him not to call anymore.

The Marquee was a mistake.

Larry didn't think so, but Hugo did.

He was back in his old speed retreat, without speed. From behind a cloud, sitting in front of his head like smog, he watched, dazed, remembering: remembering evenings spent standing next to the speakers, his spine tingling with noise and sweat and the blues he'd swallowed on the Tube, watching the feet of the fast-movers, watching them gob on favourite bands, watching them tear the heart out of each other's T-shirts, as he stood quietly by, dancing inside.

He couldn't dance a step now. Inside or out.

He could lurch. He could topple. He needed to sit down.

Everyone was so young. So mean. So unrelenting.

A band were playing, bashing through 90 mph modrock. The lead singer beat his sides and Hugo watched his white socks fly.

Everything about him – his words, his music, his movements – seemed dangerous. Calculated to threaten. And he looked so neat. Which had to make him more dangerous. The meanest bastards wore tidy clothes. He was egging the kids on, taunting them with the things they knew best: a chip on the shoulder, a smack in the mouth, a bun in the oven, a place in the dole queue. They were eating it raw. They were taking it and loving it and hating what it hated. They were getting steamed up. And Hugo was in the way. They stood around him, erect, eager, hair bristling under gel, smaller than they should have been, paler than they should have been, tough with small tattoos and bare arms.

Hugo capsized. Tottered. Stumbled to a chair and slumped.

'That seat's taken, mate,' said a boy without a hint of matey-ness. Hugo blinked. The boy was sitting next to him. He couldn't form a reply, so he lurched off again. He wanted to tell the boy that he had been here before, that he was a veteran, that he had been pushed away from the bar by Sid Vicious, that he had played pinball with Gaye Advert and TV Smith, that he had smack in his head and was so out of it . . . it . . . it should have been great.

But none of it happened.

He just lurched off, looking for Larry.

Larry didn't care what was going on or what they looked like. He was leaning against the back wall in his black leather jacket and his long hair, staring into the smoke. He wasn't smiling. He didn't smile when Hugo drifted across his vision. He just stared.

'I'm going home,' said Hugo, not expecting his voice to make any impression.

'OK,' said Larry without moving.

The first time with the needle, Larry had done it for him. And the second time. And several times.

Hugo watched as he heated up the lemon Jif and the brown dust in the spoon until the dust dissolved. Hugo watched as he dropped the inside of a cigarette filter in the spoon and then laid the needle against the filter, pulling the liquid through its mesh. The filter always came out stained brown with the shit Michael had cut into the smack.

It was always an OK deal with Michael. Never generous. Never poisonous.

Hugo watched as Larry wrapped the tourniquet round his upper arm as Hugo clenched and unclenched his fist, pumping his veins, and then he watched as the needle slid in, pushing through the skin, pausing a moment at the vein wall and then sinking in, sinking him in a sea of smack, his mouth gasping at the surface for breath.

But Larry was losing patience. He was losing patience with having no work, with having nothing to do. He was losing patience with time. He had to kill it with smack. He was losing patience with smack, so he had to take more. He was losing patience with Hugo, so Hugo had to do his own shooting.

So Hugo had to slide the needle in himself, had to clench the tourniquet in his own teeth as he found a part of his arm, behind the elbow, where the skin was yellow and dotted with holes. And then, under Larry's irritable eye, his hands and head hanging limp, he would groan and limp across the room to the bed.

And so they sat or lay side by side on the sofa or the bed, watching *Being There*, listening to the phone ring, staring at the cornices, groaning and saying nothing and doing nothing and knowing nothing. It was like sitting in an airport departure lounge waiting for a long-haul flight, or sitting on a station platform waiting for a train. Life came to a pause. Outside and beyond, it continued at full tilt, but inside the big house in Muswell Hill, everything slowed to a standstill. They sat or lay side by side, watching the smoke from their cigarettes unfurl in the bedroom air, listening as a late fly died slowly on the windowsill, buzzing a death-rattle that filled the room.

And every hour Larry would start burning candles under a spoon and Hugo would stare at the yellow bruises on his arm and wonder how long it was since they had had sex.

They had a party. A Boxing Day party. Or at least Hugo had a party. Larry was there. Sort of. They were both sort of there. Hugo always had a party on Boxing Day in the big house while the landlords were away. He invited friends to escape from their families. He gave them their excuse. 'I'm sorry, mummy, I don't want to leave this early, but Hugo never goes home for Christmas because they don't want him there, and he'd be awfully ... Oh, and daddy, can you give me a lift to the station, please?'

He hadn't gone home this Christmas. There wasn't much point. They wanted him to and although he'd said no, he sort of missed the day. Missed the heavy turkey and the cranberry sauce. Missed his kid sister being all impressed and loving the presents that he'd got her. Missed his mother who smiled so much on Christmas Day and always said what a happy day it was. Missed standing in the bathroom after everybody else had gone to bed, staring in the mirror crying his eyes red for no particular reason. Just that something was over.

Instead Christmas just drifted by. Larry. Hugo. Two syringes. And the VCR. They watched comedies and didn't laugh because laughing was too tiring. They just smiled vaguely, inside, some-where.

And the next day the guests came. And went. They came early and stayed long and left late and Hugo might have spoken to some of them, he wasn't sure, but he knew that Larry hadn't spoken to anyone. Nobody really tried to talk to him either. He didn't look very welcoming. He sat there in his leather jacket upstairs, quiet, staring at the switched-off television. Or he sat downstairs in his T-shirt, quiet, staring at the needle sliding into his arm. Hugo sometimes passed him on the stairs. They moved past each other silently. They shared a needle, a bed and a bad habit. They didn't have room for anything else. They didn't share friends. They hardly shared conversation by now. Or smiles.

Hugo's friends didn't seem to notice anything. They were excited to see one another, uncoiling like released springs after days cooped up in the kissing hell of Christmas. Hugo was just being laid back, they thought. And had a strange new friend, they noticed. It wouldn't last, they supposed.

They were right, of course.

Larry didn't speak to Hugo's friends but he didn't like them. They were loud and over-confident. They looked through him. They were good-looking. He wanted to sleep with two of the girls, but he didn't tell them that. He just stared at them for a while until they noticed, and then went downstairs for another armful. They hadn't been alarmed to find him staring at them. They had behaved as if it was quite normal.

He was angry. When it was over he was very angry. Hugo had

been smiling and leaning back and laughing on the sofas under the palm trees, talking about a world he didn't know. He didn't know this crowd at all. And this crowd didn't even seem interested in him. They talked across him, walked past him, looked through him, and still passed him nibbles after he'd said no, still asked him his name after he'd given three different answers, still wondered what he was doing here even though he had lived here all autumn and Hugo had only turned up for the Christmas vac like Lord Muck.

Something was going on. Something was dying between them, and something else was filling up the space. They had never been in love but they had been lovers. Now there was hatred in Larry's face when Hugo caught his eye. Just for flashes. Bitter flashes. Larry was beginning to hate Hugo because he knew he was going away. He was beginning to hate Hugo because Hugo was beginning to ignore him. Hugo was beginning to get bored with Larry. He was beginning to get bored with Being There, with staring at the ceiling, with the vestigial hairless body and its vestigial penis.

And that night Larry wet the bed.

The vestigial penis that hadn't had a hard-on for two weeks had peed through two sheets and a mattress.

Hugo woke up in it in the middle of the night while Larry was still asleep in it and he just got up. He woke Larry and said in a quiet voice, 'You've pissed the bed.' And then he went back to his own bedroom. That was the first time they hadn't shared the bed in four weeks.

Maybe Larry wouldn't have minded so much if Hugo had lost his temper. But he didn't. He just said it like that. Quietly. As if it was almost to be expected. Pissed the bed. And he walked out without helping. As if he didn't want to touch. He didn't want to get involved.

That was a bad sign.

Things always started to go wrong for Larry when he pissed the bed.

Things were starting to go wrong, Hugo realised. He had two weeks left before he was out of London again and back up to Cambridge. The landlords were coming back. William was due tomorrow evening. He wanted them back soon. Life with Larry was getting too silent. They had become too introverted. Food was going off in the fridge. Life had gone stale. Somebody needed to open a few windows. Right now, Hugo couldn't be bothered. After the smack had faded off a little, maybe, if he woke up and it was light.

He had lost his job at the club for refusing to take a demotion. They had offered him a demotion because he was late every night and on two nights he forgot to turn up at all. He didn't want to work anyway because he felt sick. So he said no to the demotion. He was asked to clean the loos and refused. He just left. Took a last ride to Barclay Bros and the spider boys, took one last long look at Maureen, belle of the early hours, in her pale blue house-coat and pale green teeth, and then left on the night bus home, hunched against the cold, still feeling sick, quietly.

He was getting worried about Larry. The first romp in the snow seemed so distant. That was another person. One who laughed, at least. One who smiled and flirted and knew he was there. Now Larry seemed sunk in gloom. Nothing ever happened. The washing-up was festering. Hugo stared at it and got angry. But he didn't do it. Larry stared at Hugo and got angry. He couldn't have him. Not since the bed wetting. The chemistry had gone.

Hugo sensed that this was dangerous. Things could only get worse now. Nobody likes to be humiliated. Nobody likes to go to pieces. So Hugo stayed in his room and when Larry asked if they could sleep together, he said no. No. And, as Larry walked away, he thought again that he might have made a mistake. He just wasn't quite sure when.

He wasn't quite sure why he had said no. Perhaps he was just trying the word out in the air. Perhaps he just couldn't be bothered to say yes. Or perhaps he wanted things to reach a peak. He wanted something to happen. Even if it was bad. Even if it was very bad.

Larry hadn't shaved when he came into Hugo's room the next morning. He hadn't shaved for two days. He had a beard that looked accidental. Like a badly sown lawn. It cropped up in strange places with large bald patches in between. He hadn't washed recently either. He had his jeans on and the flies open. He had no shoes on and no shirt. He had no light in his eyes. He wasn't smiling.

Hugo was half-asleep, but even half-asleep he realised that that wasn't going to help. Larry climbed into bed with him without removing his jeans. He started to fondle Hugo. Hugo pushed away. Larry pulled him back. There was no affection in his actions. Just need. No desire. Just hunger. His breath smelt and there was something in his hair. It was matted. He smelt of piss. This was the third night they hadn't slept together. They hadn't spoken all the previous day. Hugo had got up and an hour later shot up. Shot up. That sounded so energetic. He had slipped back into the smack-sea to loll the day away on the pillows, smoking the occasional joint, drifting in and out of sleep. He had only seen Larry once, when he went to the loo to be sick, quite quietly, to spit in the bowl and Larry was asleep on the floor, curled up round the bidet which didn't work. Larry hadn't stirred as Hugo vomited and flushed and wiped. He just lay there, breathing gently. He looked quite sweet. Quite harmless.

The house was turning into a mausoleum. They never turned the lights on. The phone had fallen off the hook. And Hugo wasn't sure whether he had remembered to eat. And in the room next door, the room where he had spent every night of the past four weeks except the last three, a monster was festering. And the monster had just climbed into bed with him.

He pushed him away a little harder. Larry grabbed his wrists and suddenly wrenched them back so his hands were flat against the pillows and then stretched himself at full length on top of Hugo's body. Hugo squirmed and Larry squirmed. Larry pushed his tongue hard against Hugo's teeth and pushed his hips hard against Hugo's. Hugo tried to turn his head, but a hand moved from his wrists to his jaw and yanked it back again. A knee came up into his groin. The tongue was flicking at his teeth and now forcing between them and the hand that had moved his head was back at his wrist and had caught it before he could claw at the matted hair and pull back and, as he opened his mouth slightly to complain, the tongue plunged in and Hugo bit it. And that was the mistake.

It wasn't at all clear afterwards what happened next, but what was clear was the mess. And the mess Hugo was in. The mess everything was in.

He knew that Larry had punched him in the face at that point and he knew that he had tried to fight back but that Larry was stronger, angrier and madder. And he realised that after he passed out, Larry had carried on. Not just on him, but on the room. Not just on the room but on the house. And as Hugo lay there staring at the sleet through the hole where the window had been and wondering what had gone through it, Larry or some piece of furniture, as he lay there looking at the papers and books that were strewn about in torn sheets, muddy and wet with the wind from outside and his blood and Larry's piss, it occurred to him, through the meat cleaver scything through his head and the long, dull ache in his balls where the knee and maybe later a foot had been, that this was as good a moment as any to stop taking smack.

And then he passed out.

And if William hadn't come home an hour later, one doctor said that he could have died of hypothermia.

Larry, on the other hand, was already dead.

They were both blue when William found them. Hugo with the cold. Larry with the syringe still in his arm.

II

INTO THE VOID

Death seemed to be in the air.

Fleeing to New York to escape Larry's accidental suicide had become more of a pilgrimage than a refuge, a voyage of penance to the charnel house of the Western World. The death rattle was almost audible. Hugo half expected to see tumbrels rolling down the street like grand old hearses. Without the flowers. Just one standard issue bereavement bouquet supplied by the florist on the corner of the block.

Hugo had always thought of florists as wedding and greeting and how-to-say-I-love-you places. Now they had become like the ante-chamber to the undertaker. Order your blooms and a coffin to match. They were sending out deathly decorations every day. The little man with the round glasses in the florist, the fussy one whose displays were always a little cramped, could talk about nothing else.

Hugo hated him. He hated his dusty little dried flower bouquets and his too-tasteful collections of pressed field pansies. He hated the way he took his glasses off when he spoke of the sick (as if they would mist-up otherwise. As if he had any tears in him). And most of all he hated the undercurrent of glee beneath his sadness.

Hugo, who had always hated teams, hated the camaraderie of the healthy as much as he dreaded the fraternity of the sick. But every morning, as he left to pick up a dime deal from the bogus chemist on Park and 87th, the man waved at him, and every morning he came out of the shop to wish him a good morning and somehow one thing led to another and Hugo was trapped.

'A friend of mine was just admitted to hospital. He couldn't hold his own water any longer.'

'I just have to go to the chemist.'

'It's the most awful thing. Can you imagine what his apartment was like when they found it? And, you know, I haven't seen that man, oh, what was his name, I always called him Derrick but that wasn't it . . .'

'I don't think I know him. I must just –'

'I called him Derrick, anyway I haven't seen him for maybe two weeks. He looked so wan last time I saw him.'

'I'm sure he's alright.'

'How can you be so sure? There's a plague going on here and don't you forget it. You English think you're immune, I suppose.'

Hugo stumbled off. The florist had a habit of losing his temper if you didn't join in. Secretly, Hugo thought, he wanted everyone to die. It would be his revenge on the tall and the unbespectacled. It would serve them right, all of them, for having ignored him before. And, of course, business was always better when death was in the air. So many funeral parties. Especially round here. People took funerals very seriously in Spanish Harlem. Hugo had already been invited to two.

The florist always moaned. They didn't want his dried flowers for funerals. They wanted big, bursting, fresh flowers in big colours. But he always did them proud. He liked to stay in with the local families.

Of course, the florist was wrong. The English weren't immune. They were just scared in a different way. Quietly, at home. Hidden. They were still too ashamed. There was no shame in Spanish Harlem. Hugo knew the English weren't immune. Yesterday morning, while Raul and Rudy and Lin were still asleep, Jim had rung. Jim was in hospital. He had boils. He had headaches. He was in for three weeks. The slow slide had started. And so close to home. In three weeks' time Jim's flat was to have been Hugo's home. Now, with nowhere to live, he felt like going back.

Hugo slipped into the bogus chemist and walked purposefully to the back of the store.

Nobody in the shop paid any attention to him as he slipped behind the shelf rack at the back of the shop. They knew him by now.

From the entrance to the shop, the rack of shelves at the back of the store seemed to be fixed to the wall or at least leaning against it. But set in the wall behind the shelves was a security glass window and a rotating metal tray. Behind the window stood a brother, a big brother with big gold. He was front of house today. Hugo was on his breakfast mission. He leaned into the hole-in-the-wall window. He put down a ten-dollar bill on the rotating tray. It whisked round and goldfinger slid it out. He barely moved. He never blinked. It was like buying a ticket on British Rail, except they didn't take credit cards here. Which was good. Otherwise a queue might have started. A dime deal of sensemelia came back under the glass partition. Bullet proof glass. The entire transaction was wordless. The minimum eye-contact. No smiles, no recognition. The perfect early morning shopping.

Or it would have been perfect were it not for the florist and his macabre witterings. His litany of premature obituaries had kept Hugo frowning all the way to the chemist and back and now he was almost upon him again. But this time, the florist was tied up. He had a customer. And although he waved, ribbon between his teeth and scissors in one hand, and although Hugo waved back, they both knew that they both hated each other.

Everyone was still asleep in the apartment. Raul and Rudy were curled up in the little room at the back, under a festoon of yesterday's washing, on a single mattress, wrapped round each other, the duvet lost in a confusion of brown arms and white legs. And Lin, boring Lin, who should have been cute but made the mistake of talking, was snoring on the sofa.

Hugo rolled up his mattress and stashed it under the sofa. Lin rolled over onto his side, and the vast back that should have been cute but was spotty, flexed slightly in some dream spasm. That was all Lin ever had. Dream spasms. He never stayed out. He hardly ever went out, except to the gym to build up his back and front. He had long-distance crushes on unavailable delivery boys who were cute for six months in the pause before puberty. He never made a pass. He wasn't that stupid. Make a pass at the wrong delivery boy in Spanish Harlem and you could lose whatever it was you had to pass with. They looked so angelic. A black down on the upper lip, skin still smooth with youth, not yet ruptured and cratered with acne, smiles still white, no silver and gold, no gaps. But the knives in their boots could cut to the bone before you'd seen the blade, and the older brothers at home carried guns.

You didn't make passes at the delivery boys in Spanish Harlem. You smiled at them. They flirted with you. They liked gays. Some of them had brothers who were gay. They liked showing off in front of you: scratching and preening and wearing no shirts. But touch without being asked and you were diced steak. Even if you were asked to touch, you would probably find one of the brothers on your doorstep the next day.

Lin didn't like violence. He didn't like much. He was nervous about everything. He preferred the safety of a crush, the melancholy, distant gaze. He couldn't even dredge up a smile for the boys when they passed him on the street. He was too tortured inside. Rudy used to wind him up about it. Rudy never stopped grinning at them: joshing them and admiring their tattoos. They never knew where they were with Rudy but they liked him.

They liked Raul because with Raul they knew exactly where they were. They knew his Mum, and his brother was big in local business – big in weed, coke and special K. But Lin they steered clear of. He was too much like hard work. Lin moaned about it, about his hopeless life, and the moaning kept him alive, the moaning and his row of hi-grade vitamin pills and his fortified orange juice.

He moaned about the boys. How could they be so beautiful and why did they have to take their shirts off and why did the weather have to be hot today when his zits were popping and he couldn't take his shirt off and show them that he had a fortified chest too even if he didn't have their colour, even if he was somehow always an off-white like a tired shirt?

That wasn't all Lin moaned about. He moaned about Raul and Rudy to Hugo and he probably moaned about Hugo to them. The only thing he didn't seem to moan about was the space. There wasn't any and he didn't seem to mind. Four people to a two-room flat, his only bed a sofa with an Englishman on the floor next to him and still he didn't seem to mind. Nobody seemed to mind too much about space in Spanish Harlem. Nobody had any and nobody knew what it was like to have any.

Instead Lin moaned about Raul and Rudy and the lifestyle they led, and he moaned the most about Raul because of Raul's cough. And though it made Hugo mad to hear him moan, he knew why he did. Raul's cough wasn't one of those quiet, unassuming, one-week coughs, or one of those noisy, strung-out, phlegm-filled coughs. It was dry, it reverberated in his chest and never seemed to go away. Slowly, but noticeably, it was draining the colour out of Raul's cheeks. It was scoring lines in Raul's forehead, and it was making his back curve and his chest cave in. And though nobody said anything about it except Lin, Hugo knew that Rudy knew and Raul probably guessed that this wasn't a cough that was going to go away.

And what made Lin mad and nervous and made him moan was that Raul took no notice and just kept right on hitting the drugs and never looking back.

Hugo sat at the kitchen table in the little kitchen which was really only a fridge, a cooker and a table at the end of the sitting room, next to the bathroom which was really only a cupboard with a loo and a basin and no shower. The coffee was on, heating in the pan, and he started his early morning ritual of rolling up breakfast joints. Everyone got their own joint for breakfast. Only then, with the world gone soft and bendy and the sun bouncing off the ledges straight into his head, could the day begin. That was the rule in the house. The first rule he had been told as Rudy heaved his bag up the four flights of shit-brown staircase to the two-room, four-man apartment.

That was the only rule, apart from the coffee. Other than that, it was just hit it hard and hit it good and sleep it off afterwards, because tomorrow is another binge.

And the funny thing was that Rudy had asked him here to help him escape from smack.

He hadn't really had a problem with smack. He stopped as soon as he had to and never noticed the difference. But Larry had had a problem with smack and Hugo ended up having a problem with Larry. Larry was dead. And Larry was dead on the smack that Hugo had bought him from Michael. And when Larry was found dead, Hugo was found blue in the next room with yellow bruises all over his arm and blue bruises all over his face. And the police seemed much more interested in the yellow bruises than the blue ones.

He hadn't really had time to work out what Larry being dead meant. He knew what it meant to everyone else – that there were questions to be answered and names to be found and people to be blamed. He knew that William, who had been scared and worried, was now angry and wouldn't speak to Hugo. He knew that his parents, who had been scared (by William) and worried, were too shocked to know what to do and were rereading the pamphlets about never touching drugs to see where they had gone wrong. He knew that they thought all their worst fears had been realised, that having a gay son meant having a son who slept with un-employed junkies from the north of England, and quite possibly that having a gay son meant having to deal with death quite unexpectedly. He knew that his college took a dim view and felt it would be better if he took the rest of the year off to clean up, clean up his bruises, his blood, the mess in the room, the mess in Larry's bed, the mess that Larry had left when he squeezed the last hit into his arm and the last breath out of his chest. So he took time off, time out, to think and to recover.

But he didn't know what he felt.

He was worried that maybe he didn't feel enough. He had been so numb. He hadn't really known what he was feeling even as he was being hit around the face and kneed hard in the groin. And when he woke up with William bending over him, he knew that he felt cold and sick and guilty but nothing else seemed to connect. The connections all seemed to be broken. The space in his head which should have been reserved for remorse and sorrow seemed to have closed down. He couldn't wire into it. He couldn't find the triggers to ignite it again. It was just a space. So when he thought about Larry, he felt an empty space and he felt a low quease somewhere down in his belly and then he changed the subject.

Larry and he had never really had time to know each other. Smack had stalled all their emotions, cut off all their conversation, dampened all their lust. Sex had deteriorated into lazy fumblings and languid wanks. Talk had deteriorated into silence. Life had deteriorated into a remote control in front of the video with a half-eaten plate of peanut butter on toast.

And now that it was all over Hugo wasn't sure what he was meant to miss. But everybody looked at him expecting him to miss something. They were waiting for him to break down. They kept asking how he felt and he thought he had to come up with an answer and after a while he got sick of saying tired, so he just said sick, and so they assumed that he was sick of smack or the lack of it and that made them feel better because it was what they had always believed. It would have been inconvenient if Hugo hadn't been sick. He would have punctured too many of their myths. So he was sick for their sake and dead in the head, all the while, quietly, still, deteriorating. He rang Rudy to ask what he suggested and when Rudy picked up the phone, he couldn't say anything. And then he just said, 'It's Hugo.' And only then, finally, did he cry. And even then, he still wasn't sure why he was crying. So Rudy just said, 'Come straight to New York.'

And Hugo went the next day promising everyone that he would be well looked after.

His parents, at least, believed him because they had met Rudy over lunch in Cambridge, and they knew that he was a nice boy who had been a head boy and played water polo for the university team and had his head screwed on. But then Rudy was good at giving good impressions. Hugo had sat choking on his lunch as Rudy plied his mother with compliments and his father with male to male joshing. He had made Hugo look bad. Whenever his parents came to visit, which they liked to do because Cambridge was full of guide books to look at while they wandered round the colleges, Hugo went very quiet. His mother said he was sullen, and although he knew she was right, that just made it worse and he got more so. So while Hugo sat there, sullen, wincing at every question as if it were a cattle prod, Rudy put on the charm and made their visit worth while. And now Hugo was pleased that Rudy had put on such a good act, and that his parents never even suspected.

They never suspected that Rudy was the nearest thing to Hugo Hugo knew. They never suspected that Rudy was Hugo's bad angel.

When they first met, Hugo and Rudy took an instant dislike to each other, as instant as the like Hugo and Chas had taken to each other. When Chas and Rudy met, they slept together. Hugo never slept with either Chas or Rudy. In the end, he was the only one who stayed friendly with both. Almost to the end.

When they first met, Hugo's parents took an instant dislike to

Chas and an instant like to Rudy. So they smiled with relief when he said he was going to New York. They had no idea what staying with Rudy involved. They had no idea that it was through Rudy that Hugo knew Jim. That it was because of Rudy Hugo spent half his weekends in London. They would never have imagined that when Hugo hit the town with Rudy, he ended up in backroom bars, dancing on acid, having many-handed sex in the dark with bottles of amyl and no idea whose hand was whose. Or that when Hugo ran with Rudy, he never knew whether he was going to reach the finishing tape, even though so far he always had. Almost always.

There was only one night when things had gone a little wrong.

It started out like any other weekend escape from Cambridge, like any other desperate run for the big city noise and the big noise clubs. They hit town in a borrowed car, brought up sharp in London's snarl after a burn through the rain down the M11, rolling joints all the way, Hamilton Bohannon booming on all four speakers, not a police car in sight, the needle on the clock bouncing around at 110 mph. By eight thirty they were in West 14. By eight forty-five they were at Jim's. Jim's was always first call. It was the depressurisation chamber. It was also where the circus started.

It started that night with tea. And cakes. More tea. And joints. Then the doorbell. More men and more joints. Then the first drinks. A tab. The quick exchange of notes. Five here. Ten there. Another tab and a Seconal for later. The telly was on. People were talking loudly. Somebody put a record on and turned it up to beat the telly. Nobody bothered to switch the telly off. Hugo dropped his first tab. You had to get them in early. Sometimes they took half an hour to get working. By now it was eleven thirty.

By twelve thirty, Hugo was getting the crazies. So was Rudy. So were Jim, and Bob and Colin and Alfredo and the other men. The chemicals were playing with his muscles. He was clinging to the seat. And still Jim never stopped. More joints. More tea. No cakes. Two taxis. Time to move. Time to move on.

Hugo was fine. He grinned at Rudy, who bared his teeth. It might have been a smile. It might not. Rudy was chewing his cheek. Hugo felt himself laughing soundlessly. He had no idea why he was laughing, but the ripples ran through his body like bubbles through water. His saliva had turned to chewing gum, his cigarettes tasted like chemical waste and everything was fine. Everything was funny. Outside, walking towards the cab, the lamplight bounced off the street in shards that made the paving stones dance like cut glass. That was funny too. Things were going well.

Things were still going well when they arrived at the club and reached the big noise. This time it wasn't the backroom bar with the many-handed sex in darkened rooms. This time it was Heaven and it was big. The men were big, the dance floor was big, the noise was huge, the drugs kept coming and the only thing to do was dance. Hugo and Rudy could dance all night. They'd done it before. They'd do it tonight. You couldn't talk with sticky saliva. You couldn't smoke with cigarettes that tasted like chemical dumps. You couldn't drink anything except water. But the drugs kept coming. The joints. The amyl. And the ethyl.

Everything was going swimmingly. Rudy was dancing with his shirt off, which you could do if you played water polo for the university team and you knew how to go up to strangers in clubs and say, 'Do you want to fuck?' Even if then they mostly said no. Jim was rolling a joint and the others were hanging around, looking serious, moving to the music, waiting to dance or waiting for the joint. Hugo wandered off. He needed a bit of space. There was no space in Heaven. Even the air was crowded, with smoke and sweat and fumes from a few hundred bottles of amyl, a few hundred test-tube sprays of ethyl. So Hugo went and sat on the stage and looked over the dance floor.

Everyone was at it. Dancing, sweating, smoking, steaming. Handkerchiefs soaked in ethyl chloride were crammed in people's mouths, or hung from head to head like laundry lines across the dance floor, each mouth taking a corner. And as Hugo watched the dizzy heads above the naked torsos, big from pumping iron, ready for the big night in the big noise club, a thought passed quietly through his head. That maybe this was the end. The last dance on the *Titanic*. The last squelch of a Roman debauchery. The last rites of a demented sect. The end. And then he sprayed some ethyl on his hankie and sucked hard and something strange happened. He wasn't at the club anymore.

Everything went dark and quiet. His eyes whistled through a tunnel inside his head, past the faces of everyone he knew. As he passed them, he wanted to turn to them to ask them to help him, to stop him, but none of them was the right person to ask and when the right person appeared at the end of the tunnel, he realised it was his mother and he couldn't ask her because she wouldn't understand about the drugs. Then there was nobody left. Black. A big neon sign in the back of his head came on and flashed like a motel advert on a desert road, flashed in big red letters, DON'T PANIC. It flashed twice red and yellow. Hugo knew that if he panicked, he would lose his head. So he waited. In the black. His heart was racing. His mind was frozen. And it seemed like he was blind and deaf. It seemed like forever.

He waited with his head in his hands outside on the steps of the club and listened to a dog barking faintly in the background. The dog started getting closer, or the bark just started getting louder. Slowly, very slowly, louder and somehow strange for the bark of a dog. But then maybe it wasn't a dog barking but the beat of a drum very loud and hard and close to his head. Maybe he wasn't sitting on the steps with his head in his hands at all but was in a room indoors somewhere. There were no people around. Just the noise of the drum. Maybe he had been left there alone until he felt better and didn't feel like panicking anymore. But he was forgetting about the panic anyway. The neon sign was way behind him. He was listening to the drum beat because the drum beat, like a flower suddenly blooming from a single stem, was blossoming into many sounds all at once. It was as if someone had started playing a record at the wrong speed and was slowly winding it up to tempo. The sounds came together and turned slowly into the big noise of the vast dance floor. He wasn't alone in a room at all. As his eyes opened and Hugo saw the men with the hankies in their mouths and the shirts off their backs still dancing, he was very surprised not to find himself lying on the floor with people peering down at him and calling for a stretcher. He was standing just where he had been when he took the hit of ethyl, at the edge of the stage at the end of the dance floor, and nobody around him had noticed anything. Not even Rudy.

Rudy met him at the airport. JFK. Hugo was wan. He felt loose in the world, untethered, and pale. He had one bag in his hand and nothing in his head. He had tried reading on the plane. He had tried watching the inflight movie, and he had tried ignoring the turbulence. But all the time, he just felt too tired.

Rudy looked at him hard.

'Come on. I've got something for you,' he said, and pushed him towards the loo. In the cubicle they did two lines of coke each and then Rudy pushed him out again. It was only as they were leaving the loo that Hugo noticed the sign said Women. Rudy wasn't very good on details. He was much better at effects. He was way in front with Hugo's bag, striding past the taxis, the bag swung over his shoulder as if there was nothing in it. Hugo wanted to ask where they were going, but the coke had caught his tongue and sent his gums numb, so he just followed, breathing in the thick fumes of chequer cabs.

An elephant grey limo was parked, waiting just beyond the taxis. As Rudy approached, the driver got out and took the bag and put it in the boot. They both turned to Hugo. 'This is Raul,' said Rudy and Raul held out his hand and as Hugo held out his hand to shake Raul's, he began to fall, slowly, silently, it seemed, until he smacked his head on the fender of the limo and passed out.

He missed the drive into Manhattan over Brooklyn Bridge into the world of the glittering skyscrapers, their windows shining out like decorations on giant Christmas trees. He missed the two stops Raul made, one to drop off, the other to pick up. He missed the fun of being in a car so big you could do push-ups on the floor. But he came to in time to climb the shit-brown staircase to the two-room apartment and to drink the hot tea and smoke the long sensemelia joint they gave him to take the pain out of his fender-smacked head. And slowly, as he lay there nursing his head, he began to piece things together.

This wasn't the first time he had visited Rudy. The previous summer he had stopped off on his way back from sister senior's wedding in the neat front-lawn America beyond Boston. It had been a polite wedding at a little Quaker meeting house in a little white clapperboard town full of quiet white people. The wedding was dry. The Quakers served lemonade at the reception while Hugo and the best man smoked joints behind the meeting house. He wasn't used to this type of America. He arrived in Manhattan, desperate for fun. He had parked his bags at the best man's uptown Park Avenue flat and gone to meet Rudy at his work, the Gaiety Burlesque on 43rd and Broadway.

Twice an afternoon and sometimes three times an evening, depending on who was in that night and who was conscious, Rudy danced naked with six other boys (if six had showed) while fat old men stared at them from the dark. They didn't just dance; they writhed and grimaced on a stage that extended like a catwalk into the murk of the auditorium. And they caressed and oiled themselves as the old men's flabby arms pleaded up to them for a touch they never got. And to fuel this laborious prick tease, the old men could drink as much punch as they liked from the large bowl in the corner. So they did. And passed out. Punch drunk in front of the naked boys, snoring as the boys writhed and twirled and more old men came and went.

Hugo went up to the ticket office window and spoke to the surly woman with the five o'clock shadow. He already knew who she was from Rudy's postcards: Dykey Denise, who ran the joint to keep her and her young lady in fake furs and take-away dinners.

Hugo said he was a friend of Rudy's.

'Oh, you must be Hugo,' she replied, without showing a smile and let him through the turnstile. 'Now, don't keep Rudy off the stage, I want him out there. I'm two boys under this evening and he's good, your friend, but don't tell him I said that. He's cocky, too.' And then she yelled into her mike: 'Rudy. You have a caller.'

Rudy emerged from a door at the side of the stage, wearing a red lycra posing pouch and some black lace-up dancing shoes. He pulled Hugo through the door and stood him, blinking, in the middle of a tiny dressing room full of naked boys in posing pouches and dancing shoes.

'This is my friend, Hugo, from England, everybody,' said Rudy, as Hugo blinked at the muscles and bulges coming towards him to shake his hand. 'Treat him with respect. They don't have naked men in England.'

Apart from feeling strange wearing so many clothes, Hugo felt at home there. He hung out there for whole afternoons that summer, making the third hand in card games, reminiscing with Rudy and staring at Joe, whom Rudy loved and who loved Rudy but who was married with a wife and kids in Long Island who thought he worked in a midtown diner. He stared at Joe longest, because Joe had the smile and the South American tan and Joe cut the longest lines of coke, and every time Joe touched him Hugo wanted to take off all his clothes. But Joe touched him and gave him coke and played cards with him because he was a friend of Rudy's and Rudy was something special. Rudy was something special. For them. A college boy from an English public school in among the lowlife Puerto Ricans who fed their children and their bloodstream by wiggling on a catwalk and treading on the flailing hands of old men one-hand-wanking in the front row, trying to cop a feel.

Some of the boys liked Rudy but didn't like the fact he was there. If he, the boy with the degree from Cambridge, had to flaunt himself on the stage and turn quick blow job tricks with johns in the curtained-off corner of the dressing room afterwards, what hope was there for them? They were conservative too, at heart. They didn't like to see the world order contravened. This wasn't the right place for him.

Some of the boys just didn't like Rudy. He had too much hope and they couldn't see any. And they were right. A year later, Chris, whose donkey dick had them out of their seats at the back of the murk, and who ignored all the 'official guidelines' by getting a hard-on because he took so much MDA backstage, was dead from a syringe full of poison, sold him by the dealer he owed a thousand dollars. He was written off as a bad debt. A dead loss.

A year later beautiful Joe had lost his big-tooth smile. His wife and kids ran off to live with her mother in San Juan when someone rang her and told her that her husband was working in a gay dance hall where they gave free punch to old men and got them steamed up with dirty dancing before stealing their wallets over a backstage blow job. Instead of playing cards, he was shooting coke and he and Rudy hardly spoke unless he was in bigger trouble than usual and needed help from Raul. Gennaro, the slim Italian, who never looked anything other than mean to Hugo but who Rudy claimed was just a little tense and was only seventeen, which was why he never turned backstage tricks (he was saving himself for something), was shot in the head by a wino in the lobby of his building who thought he was his brother come to turn him in. (The wino had found the gun in the trash can behind the building. The gun was now helping the police with their enquiries. The wino had died in his sleep three nights later.) And Marco, who looked about twelve, but was born with a sad head and a tongue so fast the other boys paid him for blow jobs, was dead from the disease.

That was still early days then. By the following year, when Hugo arrived and fainted at the airport limo stand, the disease was bowling them down backstage like skittles, and Denise, the unshaven lady behind the bullet-proof window, was offering Rudy anything to come back and dance. But Raul wouldn't hear of it.

Raul had rescued Rudy. He was Joe's cousin. They had met at the diner in the mid-afternoon break. Joe needed to score. Raul was a dealer. It wasn't clear in what yet, as Hugo lay on the floor with a split head, putting the pieces together, but as people came and went and left dollars and took packets, Hugo knew Raul was selling. Trust Rudy, thought Hugo. Trust Rudy to guarantee supplies by living with the man himself. But that wasn't fair. Rudy loved Raul and Raul loved him back. They protected each other. And Raul wasn't the man. He was one of the man's men. Even the man probably wasn't the man. But Raul turned a profit and he had good customers and the men above him, working for the man above them, liked the way they could rely on Raul to deliver. So Raul survived and turned a living. Lin moaned but stayed for the free drugs, and Rudy took a job in a midtown bar, leaving the punch drunk men in the lurch. When Denise made a fuss to Raul and told him he'd stolen Rudy from her and she'd sack Joe as revenge, he offered to screw her and she went slightly green and dropped the subject. For a woman who traded in penises, she had a strange loathing of them.

Hugo sat at the little kitchen table in the little kitchen and smoked the first joint of the day. He had done his early morning shopping. He had rung the airport and changed his ticket. He hadn't told Rudy he was going yet. He hadn't told him about the call. With Raul already sicker every day, what was the point?

The others wouldn't be up for hours. Except Lin. And when Lin got up, Hugo would go and sleep in the armchair in front of the telly until Raul and Rudy surfaced. Right now he wasn't tired, but he knew he should be. He was worried instead. On his chest, just below his collar, he had a rash of hard, red spots. Small, dark red pimples. Forty of them.

They could have been anything, but Hugo was ready to fear the worst. Especially now. Especially after last night. Last night had been a Raul special.

Raul had taken pity on Hugo right away. He was soft about the English anyway, either because they had that funny accent or because he, like the florist, now thought that Americans were everything dirty in the world and the English were everything clean. Either way, Hugo had an effect on Raul. Nothing he could do for Hugo was enough. It pissed Rudy off. Rudy knew Hugo for what he was. A sometime hooker, sometime lowgrade porn star, sometime teenage cottage queen with a smart head and a nice suburban home waiting for him anytime if things got too strange. Rudy knew what Hugo was because Rudy was the same. Rudy's nice suburban home was even nicer than Hugo's. On the social barometer of Hadley's hill, Rudy would have been at least half a mile up. But they had both fallen out of the carpeted niche of owner-occupier family housing into low-man's land.

While Hugo was scoring tricks on cab runs in and out of the smart hotels on Park Lane, Rudy was dropping his pants in the face of drunkards and making sure they beat their meat as they sucked. He didn't want anyone taking longer than they should. Unless it was Raul. And he didn't want Raul taking any time over Hugo. But Hugo didn't want Raul and wasn't even sure that Raul wanted him. He just wanted to please his nice new houseguest. So everything skated along cool enough without a row and, when Raul planned a night out, it was to please them both.

Last night had started at Miguel's. Miguel was one of Raul's men. He did better coke than Raul and Raul went there to score while he sold his own stuff to the calling clients who rang the doorbell anytime after eleven. But Miguel was a bitch. He liked to play his friends along. He liked to make them pay. He didn't need their money. He had a nice little trade in hairdressing, which gave him the cash front to launder all the other incomings and enough money on the side to paper his apartment in black and gold leaf flock. But he liked to make his callers pay in time. They had to sit there and listen to Miguel's problems. The tantrums he'd had to put up with from staff and customers. The nightmare boys who pestered him for love (as if) and the heavenly boys who wouldn't. The problems he was having with his plumber, his decorator, his nails, his nerves, his nose.

Raul and Rudy just sat there drinking cold beer and waiting patiently, almost silently, and Hugo followed their lead. Rudy especially had to keep quiet. Miguel had him down as one of the heavenly boys and didn't trust him. Anyone who made his heart flutter was not to be trusted. He was always watching them, waiting for a sign, waiting to see them exchange a smile, a roll of the eye, an arch of the eyebrow, and if he did, he'd make them pay with another half an hour.

Hugo didn't understand why they couldn't just have gone to fat Louie's and skinny Raymond's. So what if their apartment had dirt brown walls and their fish tank was polluted? So what if skinny Raymond was a weasel who moaned all night and fat Louie was a spoilt brat from upstate who never moved a buttock except to squash Raymond or lumber through to the loo to vomit? So what? They were easy. They didn't mess around. They had known Raul since he was a young man and he had always looked after them. The two fat ladies, they called themselves.

'Raul always looks after the two fat ladies,' Louie would say.

And Raymond would hiss, 'I'm not fat.'

'No, Raymond. But you wish you were,' Louie would retort and then hit him, playfully, but too hard.

They always passed the mirror round straight away and kept the mill grinding until the cocaine sat in a little white slag-heap and Hugo and Rudy's jaws ached with the chattering and their throats ached with smoking and their legs ached with something, Hugo never knew what.

It had to be better than sitting here watching this wound-up hairdresser moving his gewgaws from shelf to shelf, stroking his possessions, massaging his frazzled ego, playing for time. It had to be better than sitting next to the three or four other tense little creatures gathered round his smoked-glass coffee table, staring at his onyx ash tray and marble candlesticks, wondering how they wandered into this window dresser's hallucination. It had to be better than listening to the whinges of the failed opera singer whose throat was riddled with drugs, who told stories about his friend whose gut had been punctured by a fist fucker who'd kept his wedding ring on. It had to be better surely. At least the others stayed quiet. All evening. Shadows from another world haunting the coke table like gambling addicts staring at the spin of the roulette wheel.

'Raul, darleeng,' whined Miguel from the bathroom after an hour. 'Do you want to look in the drawer?' Raul winked at Rudy, Rudy nudged Hugo. The party was starting. 'It's on top of the silk shirts. Do you mind starting it going? I am having all this trouble with my hair. That silly fuck Tony, I just ask him to frizz it. You know frizz. Well, what he do? I don't want to look like this. I look like Bette Midler with a hangover. Fat, I look too.'

'No, you don't, honey. You look fine,' Raul purred, the drawer already open, the silk shirts stroked once just for the feel, the coke in his hand, the smile on his lips, the cream for the cat.

'You look lovely, Miguel,' said Rudy. Deadpan.

Hugo stared at him. Rudy stared back. Hard.

'You think so, darleeng?' Miguel was in the doorway, a towel round his fat midriff, his hair fallen flat over his face, hair dye streaming down his back in rivers of black. 'You're not just saying that?'

Rudy looked up at him, straight at him and smiled. 'Come and sit down. You look fine.'

'I've got no clothes on, you wicked boy.'

'That's how I prefer you,' smiled Rudy.

Hugo had to admit, Rudy was good. Hooker deluxe. He was showing off to Hugo and it was working. Hugo had never been able to get beyond the please and thank you. He was a lousy flatterer. Rudy was daring him to laugh and ruin it all. All Hugo had to do was keep a straight face.

'Doesn't he look good, Hugo?'

The bastard. Raul avoided looking at either of them. Head down, he was already working the mill, watching the coke pour onto the smoked-glass table top. The others were oblivious to Hugo's problem. They were concentrating on Raul.

'You look great,' said Hugo. Not a tremor in his voice.

'He's nice, your friend,' Miguel cooed to Rudy. 'He's from England, too?'

'Ask him.'

'Later, honey. Later I'll ask him everything.' And blowing Hugo a kiss that somehow hit him smack in the face, he giggled and returned to his dressing room to tease the flat hair back into frizz.

Rudy turned to Hugo and winked. Hugo grinned and then suddenly thinking of Miguel watching in the mirrors, stopped and lit a cigarette.

'I don't know how you can smoke,' said the opera queen with the ruptured friend. 'It's so bad for you.'

'Is it?' said Rudy, all wide-eyed. 'How so?'

'Girls,' muttered Raul.

'I don't believe we've met,' said the opera queen, leaning across Rudy to shake Hugo's hand. Hugo put his out, Rudy leant forward. 'How's your throat?' he asked.

'Have some coke,' said Raul, passing the straw. He stared at Rudy through eyes like ice. Rudy went quiet. Snorted hard, one nostril after the other, and then called to Miguel. 'Miguel, darling, are you having some?'

'Pass it to Hugo,' hissed Raul.

The opera queen was leaning forward, watching every speck of powder. Rudy had some on his lip. The opera queen would have licked it off.

'Don't wait for me, darleengs. I hardly touch it now, you know. Do I, Raul?' And before Raul could say a word, he appeared in the doorway. Hugo gulped. He nearly, very nearly, choked and coughed over the little white slag-heap Rudy had passed him. Instead he swallowed hard. The coke was soaring up his nostril, freezing his sinuses, shrinking his scalp and Miguel was standing in the doorway in an apricot silk shirt and red trousers, his hair standing out sideways.

'How do I look?'

'Gorgeous, darling,' said the opera queen, who was giggly with anticipation and barely glanced at him.

'Not you, stupid,' snapped Miguel. 'You always say that. What do you think . . . what's his name?'

'Hugo,' said Rudy.

Hugo looked again. Swallowed. The coke had drifted to the top of his head. His brain was rolling in it. 'You look lovely,' he said in a voice so drenched in drug it sounded far away.

'I love the way he talks,' squealed a delighted Miguel. 'He's got the voice much better than you, Rupert.'

'Rudy,' said Raul quietly.

'Oh, whatever. Have some more, darleeng.' Miguel snatched the straw from the opera queen and gave it back to Hugo. Tonight was certainly going to be wild, thought Hugo. There were only two things he had to do. Kick Rudy very hard in the shins and shake off this apricot queen who was snuggling up to him.

He never did kick Rudy. By the time he could, they were laughing too much. And it took him a while to shake off Miguel. All the time in his apartment Miguel sat patting Hugo like a new pet. And then, when they left, finally, their heads lost in some chemical cloud, Miguel was at his heels, yapping like a fat puppy. 'Hugo, darleeng. Come in my car.' Rudy saved him.

'I'm sorry, Miguel. He has to come with us.' He didn't explain why. 'We'll see you there, honey.'

Cocaine didn't buy you anything.

Even when they got to the club, Miguel followed Hugo around, offering him his little bottle. Hugo took his spoonful and moved on. He just kept flashing Miguel a smile. That had to be enough. Besides, by now he was tripping and had to dance and fat Miguel couldn't dance.

They had dropped the acid in the back of the car before arriving at The Saint. It was already starting to work as they stood in the queue. By the time they were inside, Hugo had lost track of time and place. Everything was aglow.

The barmen were aglow in their perma-tan, easy-wipe skintones and white vests. The fruit bowls on the bar were aglow. Even the blue glass and steel loos where Hugo went with Miguel for another spoonful were aglow. The pools on the floor and the spilt toilet paper and the cracked tiles all shone as if new, as if zapped by some television cleaner with fresh mint sparkle. The only one who didn't glow was Miguel. In this light Hugo could see every erupted pore and hollow shadow. He could see the goo of make-up clogged on the end of a shiny nose and the lacquer like a sticky spider's web of candy floss in his hair. He had to shake him off.

They climbed the little black spiral staircase and came out on to a vast circular dancefloor. Overhead a gauzy dome threaded with glitter stars mocked the night sky. Hundreds of men in easy-tan perma-wipe skinvests jigged nonchalantly under the simulated night. The nonchalance was fake. Their heads stayed still but their eyes, dilated and restless, darted after every body. Body to body, they bobbed on the floor. Not really dancing. Just moving up and down. Bobbing, jigging, jogging on the spot. Itchy-footed, his chest tight, adrenalin spilling into his bloodstream, Hugo sailed blindly into the throng, leaving Miguel flailing uncomfortably at the edge. At last. Space. He started to move. Started to warm. The cocaine had seized up in his muscles. He had to start breathing again.

'Where's your sweetheart?' grinned Rudy, appearing out of nowhere, out of the night. 'Don't tell me you've lost lovin' spoonful.'

'He's waiting for you. It's you he wants, Rudy. He's just using me.'

'Honey, he's so hot for you, he's turning into one big damp patch.' Rudy was enjoying this. Hugo didn't have time to dance with Raul while Miguel was pursuing him. And Rudy loved to see Miguel suffer. Cocaine friends. They all hated each other really.

'Don't forget to take him upstairs. That's where things really happen.'

'Where?'

Rudy knew what Hugo wanted. After drugs, after so many drugs, Hugo only ever thought of one pleasure. Dancing could wait. Sex came first. He left a scarcely decent pause, and then, before Miguel could struggle across the dance floor to where they were, he moved off again. To where another black spiral staircase went up to another kingdom. Hugo didn't take a breath. He disappeared up into the circle.

The world went black.

The Saint was an old theatre. The Fillmore East in another life.

And the circle had been left intact, with its passages and seats and booths. But the lights were left off. From the circle you could look down through the gauze of the dome onto the dance floor below and watch the men jigging and bobbing. You could look down, but that wasn't the point. The point was to wait for the action to start.

Hugo leant against the back wall waiting until he could see again. The world was swimming in black. He had to wait for the shadows to emerge, for the clusters of people, the stray whiff of amyl, the stifled groan. He had to find the active core where hands came out of nowhere and wordlessly undressed you. They could have been the hands of ogres or of beauties. It didn't make any difference. In the centre of the hand and body forest, eyes were of no use. Hands and mouths were all that mattered. And dicks. He edged along the back passage. Dark shapes moved in the darkness. Quietly. He brushed past something. Denim. Leather. Flesh. Down below, the gauzy world skipped. Up in the dark, everything moved as if through treacle. Feeling its way slowly. A hand landed on his fly and squeezed. Hugo moved towards it. Another hand was on his buttock. He was finding the forest, but was this the centre? He kept his hands to himself. One stray movement and his hand would hit flesh and then be stuck. It was treacherous, this path. A touch in the wrong place, a stroke of the wrong body, any panicked movement and the illusion would be broken. The silent suspense of the orgy would evaporate into decrepit creatures scrabbling after blind sex with men who would never look twice in the light. Hugo knew he was a sapling in this forest. Old hands would devour him. He wanted to be devoured. In the dark, the acid, deprived of light, turned all its attention to his dick. The hand on his fly fumbled and clung, fingers feeling at buttons. Hugo moved slowly on. He must not trip. To trip was to break the spell too. Hugo stood still. By the brush of leather and grey light of white T-shirts in the dark, he knew he had come to a thicket. The body behind him moved closer. Hugo leaned gently back into it, inviting, submitting. The hand slipped inside his trousers, pushing past buttons with deft twists, like ivy seeking its way into crevices. A small bottle was pressed into his hand. He gasped as the lid came off, hot amyl evaporating into the air caught his nostrils. He drew hard, and the world sank into a bog of flesh. The hands around, that were until now biding their time, moved in on him as the first fingers flipped out his dick. He was down among the roots of the forest now, amid the writhing tendrils that lived in and fed off slime. They pulled at his buckle and tugged at his shirt. It was slow-motion rape in which he played willing hussy. A wet hand turned on his knob and he sagged in helplessness. One hand pushed the other away. A thumb was creeping into his mouth and a hand stroked his spine and, as a mouth closed with hot breath over his dick, he sighed and started to shake. The head that was a hand now moved up and down on his cock. A gap in the forest gave him a view down to the night sky below. Silhouetted against the gauze, a young man was being fucked between the seats. The two bodies, one upright, the other bending, moved in time to the music, rhythmically, heavily, pounding with the beat. Hugo's hips picked up the sway and pushed against the still-eating head. As the boy fucked the boy, so Hugo fucked the mouth, in the dark, in the back passage, the music wafting into his head and the drugs spilling into his brain. He saw the boy's flat stomach hit the boy's rounded buttocks as the mouth ate down to his balls and gagged and retreated and another hand swept up underneath his legs. He wanted to be with the two boys and with the forest of hands. He wanted to be one of the boys, both of the boys and part of the forest of hands and mouths. This was better than the bathhouse. The dark was never dark enough in the bathhouse. Light played tricks, switching the pretty boy of one minute into a skeleton the next, the lissom youth suddenly chomping toothlessly on his dick, a body muscled and rippling in the spotlight that sagged and collapsed in the harsher light of the showers. Darkness was better. The truth was never revealed. Imagination ruled. In the bathhouse reality never quite disappeared. The smell of shit mingled with the amyl and the sweat to leave a sickly perfume lingering among the pvc cushions, the screams of men being banged up too hard punctured the air. But here in the dark, watching the boys, feeling the acid coursing through his veins like an electric elixir, gripping onto random arms and swaying among probing penises, the world was rotating around him for his pleasure, or so it seemed, until the man with the amyl wedged the bottle under Hugo's nose so hard he had to catch his breath, and then just as he did, the man rammed something up his arse, he couldn't say what, and before he could scream, he clamped a cloth soaked in something, maybe chloroform, over his face and pushed again and somewhere, in the dark recesses of a mind now so blind it was underneath the forest in the slime, somewhere down there, the mind knew it was being raped. The mouth on his dick was chewing. His dick had gone limp. He didn't know if he had come or not. The pumping in his back hurt somewhere far off in the distance. Arms were gripping his shoulders. He knew he was leaning forward. There was a penis in his eye. He opened his eye and saw its tip gleam with pre-cum or maybe post-cum or just the normal effluent, just the normal leak and as the fumes from the cloth wore off, he felt the man still pumping and someone's hand or fingers climbing up there too and he would have turned and straightened up but the cloth came back and he swooned back into the slime, his body now little more than a toy, a greased-up sex doll. He didn't know anymore whether he was standing or lying, whether this was sex or death. His mind had left the sex behind and was scrabbling for sense, to make sense of the distant pain, the dribble down his face, the gnarled, dripping root in front of his face pushing its way into his mouth. Another dick was pushing to get in. Another dick so large it was bulldozing its way through. But the pain cut past the drugs like a siren through the fog. Something wouldn't give anymore. The reflexes were back in action. Hugo seized up, stiffened, gave a muted scream which to anyone else was a groan. He was coming to, but the men were through with him. The pumping stopped, and with a thlump something long and sticky slurped out of his butt and he felt as if his innards trailed to the ground behind it and the men let go of his arms and the dick went out of his eye and he slumped forward onto a carpet sticky with cum and effluent. And passed out.

Hugo smoked his joint at the kitchen table. He was pleased they weren't awake yet. He had time to think of a lie. He wanted to tell them the truth and he didn't want anyone to know it. He wanted them to wash and bathe and cuddle him but he didn't want them to know why. He didn't want them to know that when he came to, he had been dragged into the corner with his trousers round his ankles and was bleeding from his arse. That his shirt was covered and daubed in shit and stank of amyl and smoke and his hair was matted and he smelt like someone had maybe just pissed on him, and he felt like Tra La La, banged nearly to death and needing some salvation.

The cleaning lady had found him and screamed. She thought he was a burglar until she saw the state he was in and then she wanted to call the police because she thought he was a murderer with the victim still on him in the mess. She didn't speak any English but Hugo knew from the way she gestured what she meant and he just stood there looking at her until she stopped screaming and then he walked away.

The daylight hit his head like a chainsaw. His coat was locked in the coat check so the world could see his split and battered body spattered with shit and his bruised face. He had no money, so he just walked with his head down block after block, not looking at the faces that stared at him, not looking at the windows he could catch his reflection in, just raising his eyes through his eyebrows every other block to check the number and then head back down against the wind through the chainsaw light to the shit-brown staircase in Spanish Harlem. He was stumbling slightly but had to keep going. The pain in his back went down to his ass. The pain in his ass went up to his spine. The taste in his mouth was like his tongue had died and rotted and his teeth jangled in their gums as if a smile would loose them all. He felt very bad.

Lin stirred slightly when Hugo opened the door. He crept into the bathroom that wasn't a bathroom next to the kitchen that wasn't a kitchen. The mirror wasn't the right height. For once that was good news. He couldn't see his face. Just his shirt. He took his shirt off and threw it in the bin. And then, as he looked back in the mirror, he saw the forty or so little red pimples, hard and shiny, just below his collarbone and he knew somehow then, inside, that the pimples were bad news. He looked himself in the eyes, hard. But as long as he looked there was nothing to see. He barely blinked. He couldn't cry. He wasn't sure whether to hug or hate himself. That was it. He never had been. Most of the time it didn't matter. It was enough to be smart. A step ahead. To know what was what.

So what was what? What had happened? What was he to make of himself now? He felt bad. He went and sat in the dentist's chair in the middle of the room and as the sun hit him on the head and the sign of the Saperstein fur shop written in dusty gold letters on the window opposite winked at him past the ugly bulk of the air conditioner jammed in the window, he felt better. He didn't care. He did know what was what. He just wasn't sure what had happened. Anyway, now he was home. He would have to explain to the others. Tell them some story. But he was home and well. Safe.

And then the telephone rang.

It was Jim.

Hugo drew hard on the joint. The world had capsized a little since Jim had called. The anonymity of the disease had gone. It was on his turf. Maybe it was on his chest.

He knew now that that had been his last weekend. That this was his last day. That when he had been out to score some weed from the dime-a-deal chemist round the corner past the florist, once he had made the coffee and woken Raul and Rudy, who must have gone home thinking he had struck lucky, once he had had his orange juice and maybe one boiled egg and finished smoking his joint, he was saying good-bye to this world and he was taking himself, his forty red pimples, his little travel bag and the books he still hadn't read and he was going home.

He was going home to see Jim. To help him. And to lick his own wounds. To wash and shave. To see Chas. To see Cynthia. To live a little on the straight and narrow. To try again.

That, at least, made him smile. He stood in the bathroom and stared at himself again. Not with anger or accusation. But with sympathy. And irony. He wanted to giggle. Live a little on the straight and narrow? He leaned towards the window and breathed on it. In the mist he wrote with a finger, like a lipstick message to an absent lover, 'Too Late'. And then he stared once again at the forty red pimples and his face fell.

They were still there.

They had been there for two days.

Hugo was scared.

Dear Rudy,

Today I find out how long I have left to live. Well, that is not quite true. If I am positive, they can't be certain and if I am negative it doesn't mean I won't either become positive (and uncertain) later, or die (quite positively) another way. So today, I find out whether I am likely to live less long than I thought I might; but given that I had never given much thought to the matter in the first place, today I am not sure what I find out, other than the quality of my blood, or quite simply whether it is or isn't HIV positive. Anyway, I thought I'd write to you before my life gets the lid put on it, and while I can still live in the blissful misapprehension that I am, at least potentially, immortal. After today everything is melodrama.

You are probably asking yourself a lot of questions right now. Why? Why did he have a test? Why did he disappear at a moment's notice without saying good-bye? Why did he never say thank you for having me? Why did he leave without repaying the forty bucks (enclosed)? Why does he think he can buy me off with forty bucks (please take it . . . it is enclosed, isn't it?)? Why does he think that if he writes semi-coherent, rambling letters I will suddenly decide to forgive him? Why am I reading this?

I can answer some of them. I am having a test because of Jim. I left at a moment's notice because of Jim. I didn't say good-bye because I didn't want to have to tell you about Jim. Skip the next question. The answer to the next question is enclosed. Skip the next question (or just say, Because I know you, and I know you know me). Because I know you and I know you know I know you. Why not? What else are you doing this morning?

How is Raul? How is the cough? I do think about you two a lot. You did me a lot of good. Of course you also ruined my health, gave me a skin rash which I immediately misinterpreted as symptoms of a deep and innerly-festering illness but which turned out to be a skin rash. You frightened my mother by ringing her up and telling her you thought I had gone mad, although why should she always be so frightened of the truth? (By the way, you have lost so many nice-boy points with her that I am having to do your penance for you. She now doesn't believe that I went to NYC to recover.) And worst of all, you saddled me with the dangerous impression that a much better time (even now) is being had by all in NYC than here.

Here things have gone very grey. It is of course the grey season. Chas and I spent a grey day on the grey common the other day looking forward to mythical days when life would be one long Ron Bacardi ad and we would be looking back to the grey old days with nostalgia. That's how lively London is right now. Looking forward to the days when you will look back fondly on the days you spent looking forwards. The here and now is pretty worrying.

Jim is ill. He is out of hospital and is quite well, for an ill person. He might stay quite well for quite a long time, say the nurses, but they do admit that they don't quite know. Jim gets very pissed off until you roll him a joint, bring him a cake, pour him a scotch and load his favourite video (*Blackattack* – well-hung brothers on an American tape out of Amsterdam). He's too tired to work and too lively not to bitch. He is hard work but he is still Jim and you can gossip for hours about not a lot other than the people up and down Bedford Gardens.

The whole atmosphere around the illness is so different here. In New York it felt like an epidemic; a wave of death followed by waves of rumour, conjecture, gossip and hysteria. The whole community was washed by the same tides of death and debilitation. Here the suffering is solitary. Individuals, in individual rooms in quiet, carpeted wards, being visited by their particular family, and nobody talking to each other very much. The suffering is privatised. The English are so afraid. But not of death. They are afraid of embarrassment; of appearing to suffer too much from the wrong thing, of looking too ill, being too weak and certainly of being too dependent. This is after all the country whose leader confidently declared, 'There is no such thing as society.' There is no momentum here, just the feeling that the trickle of death will weave its inexorable way through all our lives again and again in slow and unpredictable twists and bends.

I have done a bit, but not enough, since I got back. My family look at me in astonishment when I speak to them. I can hear it down the telephone when I call. 'It's Hugo,' I can see my mother nodding meaningfully to my father, rolling her eyes round the cornicing that might have been but never was. Astonishment I can deal with. Others are harsher. William will have nothing to do with me, which is probably just as well. He thinks I have destroyed his life. Maybe he thinks I filled his drawers with porn, but he is right in that I filled his house with policemen (although even that is pretty smart, seeing as I was passed out at the time). The University does not return my calls, so I think I will return the favour and not return. I have found some work on a tiny film magazine and the other day they asked me if I knew any good freelancers, so I lied a little and said yes, and twenty-five minutes later Chas was in the office and he and I were having a heart to heart over press releases about unpopular Yugoslavian films.

With a bit of luck one thing will lead to another and I will inveigle my way into journalism without a degree, with no formal training, but with a wide vocabulary and a marginally narrower collection of received opinions. I have been doing some theatre reviews for a magazine in Battersea and *Time Out* have offered me one this week so maybe . . . who knows . . . perhaps . . . one day . . . I could . . . be famous enough to cut the tape at shopping centre openings.

I don't really know what to think about this test. Chas is rather agog, especially as he is going to have to deal with me immediately after the telephone call that will give me the news. You're probably wondering how Jim could be my reason, but it was just something the doctors said to him – about how the more they know and the sooner they know it, the better they can help. I'm certainly not going for anything stoic here. If there is anything wrong with me I want the entire pharmaceutical department of all the North London hospitals at my disposal. Just think of the fun you could have. You would never need to remember you were ill again. Life on the other side of the DF118. A spoonful of morphine sulphate helps more medicine go down.

I'm not going to tell Mumsy and Popsy. For a start it's none of their business (is it?) and more importantly, all they'll do is panic. They haven't quite emerged from the shellshock of the Larry business. I think I have; the

whole experience dwells in some distant cocoon of
drugged stupor. But for them the sky just fell on their
heads. My mother winces whenever anyone mentions the
word Cambridge. I really spoiled it for her with that one.
I think she still tells herself that I was the victim.

Now of course she is trying to get me jobs. She did
this in my year off between school and Cambridge. She'll
probably start suggesting the same sales jobs at W.H.
Smith that she did then. At one point it was the foreign
office but I think even she has realised that that just isn't
going to happen now.

Anyway, I wanted to say thank you and sorry.
Thank you for a great convalescence and I'm sorry for
running off like that. I had had a pretty freaky evening
that night. In fact I still haven't told you or anyone else
everything that happened. I know you still think that I
went off with someone, but I didn't. I was there all along.
But not a pretty sight. I'll tell you all about it. One day.
In the much too distant future. But that was partly what
made me run. I felt that I needed to get home, get washed
and get on with life. And then when Jim rang, it was like
a warning and a summons. I felt as if things had really
started to slip away. I was worried that if I didn't start to
take control again my life would just crumble into dust in
my hands and I wouldn't be able to do anything about it.
So I went.

I had a very strange flight. I took four sleeping pills
and slumped against the window. I missed all the movies,
missed all the food and came to at the other end feeling
tired, cold, cramped and sick. I didn't feel as if I had been
asleep at all.

But things are okay here. And, who knows? After
today, things may be even better. I may get a clean bill of
health and permission to play in any city I care to. I think

if I'm negative, Chas will go straight off and have the test himself. He thinks of me as a definitive example of high risk. I'm not sure that he's not right.

Anyway, if you don't hear from me for a week or so do not assume the worst but send me some gifts anyway.

I'll write again soon and I'm sorry for being such a bad guest.

Lots of love and wish me luck, although it will be too late by the time you get this.

Hugo

Epilogue

THE LIFE AND SOUL

Hugo didn't understand why he felt scared. The room, almost a church, almost a railway waiting hall, was large and airy. The windows, ecclesiastical without stained glass, let the sun stream in between the leading, hitting the floor at an angle sharp enough to make the stone twinkle. It all looked well-scrubbed. The wood of the pews, the white of the walls. Even the lilies in the vase on the starched tablecloth at the front looked ironed. And somehow lifeless. It was like a room taken out of mothballs. A picture on the television set with the colour button turned down low.

Hugo stood at the back in the shadow of the heavy wooden doors. Outside it was raining, despite the sun, and people were talking about a rainbow. They were talking about the fact that there was no rainbow.

'It can't get through the smog,' said one old lady in a blue raffia hat, leaning on her white cane as she walked slowly up the nave. That was Mavis from Number 12. Three doors down from his parents. And the larger lady with her, with the heavy calves and the sensible brogues, was Meg. Lifelong companions. Mavis was a music teacher. Meg had a private income. They were gentlewomen spinsters. Mavis always reminded Hugo of a budgerigar. Brightly coloured in a small suburban sitting room.

They turned to look for Hugo and, seeing him lurking in the shadow, smiled and waved. He waved back but they had turned away. He heard Meg say what a tidy boy he was. 'Never seems to get into scrapes. Not like some of those other scamps. Like the Baker boy at Number 36. Comes home top to toe in mud and goodness knows what. No, Hugo's very good. His mother should be proud.'

His mother sat by the bed, staring at him. He could feel her eyes upon him, staring, burrowing into him, absorbing him, this emaciated, racked skeleton, all that was left of her son. His eyes were gummy now, the retina so deteriorated he could see through one pupil in black and white, and through the other, nothing. Less than nothing. And still he could feel her eyes upon him. Hugo was scared. She was scaring him. He wanted to be alone. He had always hated saying good-bye. How much better to just leave a note and slip away. Slip away into the night. But they wouldn't let him go. They were too worried about losing him. It was ridiculous. They all knew he was going to go, and yet they wouldn't let him leave. He was tired of this now. So tired. He spent less and less time awake. But all the time he dreamed his own death. The night before he had finished telling his stories to the man in the next door room. It seemed to him so strange how suddenly everything stopped. Life had been bowling along. Well, not exactly bowling. There had been the hiccoughs. But it had been moving. And somehow, after Larry, everything went on hold. Larry, Jim, Chas and all the others. From the moment of Larry's death, his friends had made stepping stones to his own. And now it was happening. He had completed the path. He was pretty sure he would die tonight. It was just one of those things. You knew when it was going to happen.

His mother walked into the chapel on somebody's arm. A man. In a well-cut suit and black hair. It could have been his father. It could have been Mr Smithy from Number 16. They both had black hair, shiny in the sun. The sun bounced off the man's shoulders and into his mother's hair. It was blonde. Honey blonde. She was wearing the dress Hugo loved the best; a cotton frock covered in bursts of brightly coloured flowers. It moved in the breeze from the door, wafting round her. She was laughing as she clutched the man's arm. Throwing her head back to laugh and then looking round. She saw Hugo and, smiling, called him over. He felt warmth flowing from her smile and her eyes and the sun in her hair and he wanted to run to her but he didn't move. She turned away without seeming to notice. Hugo looked down at his hands. They were clenched. Something was wrong. He was feeling uneasy. Chill. He felt the heavy door. The varnish had been painted on thick over years of chips and graffiti. The wood was dark and shiny. It felt cold to the touch.

'Hello there, young man.' A tap on his shoulder. He spun round. His doctor was smiling at him. 'Big day for you, huh? Well, good luck.'

'Thanks,' said Hugo. 'I'll be glad when it's over.' He wanted to ask when what was over, but he didn't think he should. He was obviously meant to know. He thought maybe it would all work itself out. Maybe he had just forgotten.

'How is everything going? Busy? We never see you.'

Hugo had the strange impression that his doctor had gone blind. His eyes, still blue, seemed to stop before they reached him. They were looking at him, or at least in his direction. But there was no connection.

'Is your mother here?'

'Yes. She's sitting in the front. With Mr –,' he didn't know who. It didn't matter. His doctor was already off. Pleased to see his mother again. Everybody seemed to be pleased to see his mother. She was standing up in her pew. Greeting, smiling, laughing, occasionally glancing at Hugo and flashing him her eyes. But her look seemed to have become a little puzzled. As the doctor walked towards her, she looked at her son and Hugo thought he saw her frown. A cloud scudding across her face.

The sunlight through the windows faded gently but quickly. The frown hung there for a moment and then the doctor was upon her and the smiles were back.

His mother was talking to him. About his father. Apologising. She didn't seem to notice whether he was awake or asleep. The ceiling had shut out the sky again. The Anglepoise by his bed had replaced the sun. It burnt black holes in his sight. That was all his left eye was. A black hole concealed by fog. The fog they kept trying to dab away, but which formed again and stuck eyelid to eyeball.

'He was going to come and then there's been such trouble at the office, and you know the distance it is. Do you know it still takes him an hour and a half to drive there? But it is a lovely drive. In the daylight. All the trees . . . careful, darling.' She snatched back his hand just as he felt the pain of his fingers on the Anglepoise bulb. He tried to remind himself who she was. He had to follow the pattern again. There were little things that reminded him. The note in her voice when she said darling. Nobody else said darling to him quite like that. Quite like her. His mother. He remembered now. Darling was the clue. Sometimes he hadn't got there at all. She didn't seem to notice.

Darling. The way she said it, the picture it made. A little boy in the back garden, playing on the grass, gurgling in the sun. Blond-haired. His father, tall, gaunt, painting the garage. His sister, the older one, filling up the paddling pool. The younger one sitting in the pushchair in the yard, getting hot in the sun. And the way she said darling. Everything seemed to belong to everything else. He to her, she to him, the man painting the garage to his sister to him to his younger sister . . . a web. He seemed like a golden child then. He had always been her golden child. With the occasional hiccough of course. But now he was withered and old; he had aged to a hundred and fifty while everyone else around him had stayed the same. And, in the end, he hadn't done any of the things she had hoped he would. He hadn't had time. He had started but never finished. After New York, after the test, after the first collapse there was always meant to be time for the big plan to start. But he never even got round to deciding what the big plan would be. He had talked about so many, but they were all just shortcuts to fame. He knew where he wanted to get to but he just hadn't worked out how. And now it was too late. And yet somehow he was relieved, because they couldn't really say he had failed. He hadn't really had time to try. It was out of his hands now.

He had started to get there. He had had his reviews published. A couple of lunches. Some nice attention here and, of course, the corresponding level of bullshit. Bullshit offers, bullshit promises, bullshit proposals. He knew he was getting somewhere. But he had no idea of the schedule. Was this a fast or a slow or an often-stopping train? He was prepared to wait and see and suddenly, quite unexpectedly, it had stopped completely. It made a couple of small manoeuvres, but only to get off the track and into a siding, and that was where he had stayed. Marooned in unwellness for the last six months.

Maybe he had done something wrong. Maybe that was why he felt so uneasy. But Hugo couldn't think what it could have been. That worried him more. Had he forgotten the breakfast washing-up? Don't be stupid. There was no chance of that. He couldn't remember doing it, though. Maybe he didn't live there anymore, anyway. He couldn't be certain just now where he lived. He thought maybe he should go over to her. He moved away from the door into the light. His mother was at the front of the church, suddenly much further away than he had expected.

'Where have you been hiding?' The voice was bright and crisp, as cheerful as morning. His younger sister. In a hat. With a boyfriend, taller than he felt comfortable with, spotty but not unattractive. Where had he been hiding?

'I was there behind the –' She wasn't listening.

'I see mother has brought her fancy man.'

'Fancy man? Who is he?'

'Oh, Hugo. What's wrong with you? You don't seem quite all there. Are you alright? This is your big day. Come on, Hugo.' She turned to her boyfriend. 'My brother is always the life and soul of the party.'

'Am I?'

He wanted to take her away into a corner and have her explain it all to him. He felt she was the only one he could really trust, who wouldn't laugh if he told her he had no idea what was going on or why all these people were here, why he was here, what he was supposed to do. But she was playing with her boyfriend's hand behind her back and she was staring at their mother. He suddenly felt like crying. Maybe that would get her attention. But not in front of her boyfriend.

'Oh, my God, there's grandma,' she said, and ducked away, hissing as she went, 'Good luck.' He turned. She was right. As he saw his grandmother coming up the aisle in a dark crimson wool suit and without the aid of any sticks, he thought how young she looked. Especially for someone who had been dead for four years. And it was only then that he remembered that Mavis from Number 12 had been dead for even longer.

He opened his eyes. He felt as if he had been swinging over an abyss on a thinning rope. Every so often a strand of the rope would snap and he'd sink a little further. She squeezed his arm. The woman in the room. She had been there for a while. As long as he could remember. She was holding his arm so tightly there would be bruises in the morning. Blue bruises. She was holding him tight but his arm slipped through her hands and he started to fall.

'He loves you, darling. We both love you, my darling.'

She was right. They did. Once they had found out, they had been alright. They had been very practical. It hadn't happened that quickly and then suddenly it just picked up speed and bowled him over. He blamed it on feeling so well. After the test he was fine. He was fine for the whole year. Everything stayed the same. His blood count, his weight, his glands, his pulse. And his drug intake. And then something just gave. He sagged. His appetite faded away. His food refused to stay down. And he spent the night bathed in his own sweat. Chas took him in. And Chas called his parents. That was the last big favour he did Hugo. And Mrs Harvey. Hugo would never have called. But Hugo would somehow have been waiting for them to find out, angry at the lack of attention. Chas didn't even tell him that he had done it.

'And here he is, Master Harvey himself.' People always turned when his grandmother spoke. She had a voice that reminded them of times past. Of high street shopping and strong-minded women talking in the greengrocer's queue. Of trams and sixpenny bits and proper British values. It was a good voice. It always made Hugo think of antimacassars.

'Hello, grandma.'

But she walked right past him. 'We'll have plenty of time to talk, Hugo. Later,' she called out as she sailed by. Hugo was about to turn and follow her and ask what she meant by later, and how come she was here anyway, although he wasn't sure quite how to put the question, when he caught sight of Chas. What was happening? What was everyone expecting of him that they were coming back just to see it? Hugo walked straight towards him. He wasn't so surprised to see Chas, as to see him with Rob. Rob and he were history, surely? Mick had long since replaced him. But then Mick wouldn't show his face here, and Mick was still alive.

Chas was in full flow. 'And her up at the front, that's Hugo's Mum with her piece. Hugo's dead wary of her. He won't tell you much. She's a nice enough lady, but she's tough. I've only met her the once.'

'And where's Hugo?' asked Rob, as Hugo stood right in front of them.

'*He's probably out the back in the vestry doing a quick line. Oh, fuck, it's Rudy.*' *And as Rudy came through the door behind Cynthia, Chas sat down.*

'*Chas,*' *said Hugo.*

'*Yes,*' *said Chas, looking up.* '*Oh, there you are, Hugo. Where did you just appear from? Somebody's looking for you. You know Rob, don't you? This real matron in a wool suit. Over there.*' *Chas pointed at Hugo's grandmother.* '*Why did you invite Rudy? I bet he's stoned. And I thought he and Cynthia hated one another.*' *And Hugo was just about to answer, was just about to explain that he didn't remember inviting anybody, when Chas simply turned away.*

'*You will introduce me to Hugo when you see him,*' *said Rob.*

'*But he was just here,*' *said Chas.* '*I thought you'd met him. Well, when he comes back.*'

Hugo hadn't moved. But for some reason, he decided not to say anything. He watched Rudy and Cynthia approach.

Rudy was speaking to Cynthia. That was enough to make Hugo watch. They had never been close. Rudy was speaking about New York. About how he hadn't seen Hugo for so long. Hugo just walked behind them as they spoke. They didn't seem to have noticed him move alongside them and then fall into step with them. People moved out of his way without glancing at him. Even though this was his big day. Rudy was sounding very serious. He was telling Cynthia how he and Hugo had drifted apart. He was good at these serious events. He had a good voice for them. Even though he was really just gossiping. And getting one up on Cynthia. And one up on Hugo.

He said how Chas and Hugo had become much closer. How far London was from New York. How grey it seemed in London. How grey everywhere. How cold it had been in New York this winter. How nice the daffodils were outside in the cemetery, and how he had thought of pinching some for his hotel room but how his chambermaid at Blakes was so particular. Cynthia's smile showed she was listening but not believing. And then Rudy started talking about Hugo's last night in New York, or at least about the forty red pimples.

And Cynthia said, '*So you didn't see him then. In the end.*'

And before Rudy could say anything and before Hugo could interrupt and ask Rudy if he could keep his voice down, because, after all, his mother was here, before Chas and Rudy could exchange glances, and before Hugo could say hello to Dolly, who was standing at the back in a hat with a very large brim and greet Sam, who was sitting in the corner looking shabby in glasses and holding a bottle in a brown paper bag, the organ started and everybody sat down and Hugo, more in alarm than anything else, stood up.

And, as he stood there with everyone sitting round him and no-one looking at him, not even his mother, whose hands were playing games with the hands of the fancy man, it occurred to Hugo that he was feeling very vague. Almost as if he shouldn't really be here. Almost as if they were just waiting for him to go. And then, turning to the church that may just have been a railway waiting hall, and moving past the people in the pews, none of whom stood to let him pass, Hugo realised that really, to all intents and purposes, he had already gone.

He walked to the front of the room. To the table with the starched white tablecloth and the lilies that looked as if they had been ironed. He stood still on the steps leading to the table and turned to face the church. But this time, as he looked back, the only person he saw was his mother, in a grey cardigan, her hair dark brown as it had been for some years, her eyes puffy with tears, sitting alone. He smiled at her and she smiled at him and then he closed his eyes.

His mother called the nurse. She had watched him for ten minutes, letting the fact sink in. But then she was worried he would get too cold, so she rang the bell.

'He's gone, I think,' she said.

The nurse took his pulse. Turned off the oxygen. Closed his eyes.

'Can I get you anything? A cup of tea? An aspirin?' she asked.

'No,' said Hugo's mother. 'I think I had better ring my husband. He has a carphone, you see. He was on his way here. There's no need now. I'll get the bus.' And then she sat down very quickly and stared very hard at Hugo's face, trying to remember every expression it had ever had.

They buried Hugo in Hendon. In the cemetery. He would have hated that. He was always such a stickler for good postal codes. The service was very quiet. The chapel was very clean but sterile, like a railway waiting room. Some of the old friends sent flowers. Cynthia came, in a full-length wolfskin coat. Rudy sent a telegram that nobody understood. The vicar made comments that nobody understood either. But afterwards they thought he may have got his timetable wrong. Hugo would have liked that.

INDEXED IN

stacks Fiction